Praise for Ann Granger's
MEREDITH and MARKBY Mysteries

FLOWERS FOR HIS FUNERAL
"Sure to please."
Denver Post

"The village mystery plot should be ingenious,
the style witty, the setting picturesque and the
characters amusingly idiosyncratic . . .
Ann Granger knows the drill so well
she could write a manual."
The New York Times Book Review

A FINE PLACE FOR DEATH
"Deft plotting and elegant descriptive prose."
Publishers Weekly

WHERE OLD BONES LIE
"Well drawn characters, clever plotting,
and excellent misdirection."
Los Angeles Daily News

"If you appreciate murder most British,
have a look at this one."
Washington Times

MURDER AMONG US
"Wonderful . . . A tightly plotted
and intensely visual feast."
Mystery Lovers' Bookshop News

CANDLE
FOR A
CORPSE

The New Meredith and Markby Mystery

DISCARD

ANN GRANGER

AVON BOOKS ◆ NEW YORK

AVON BOOKS
A division of
The Hearst Corporation
1350 Avenue of the Americas
New York, New York 10019

Copyright © 1995 by Ann Granger
Published by arrangement with St. Martin's Press, Inc.
Visit our website at **http://AvonBooks.com**
Library of Congress Catalog Card Number: 96-2264
ISBN: 0-380-73012-X

First Avon Books Printing: August 1997

AVON TRADEMARK REG. U.S. PAT. OFF. AND IN OTHER COUNTRIES, MARCA
REGISTRADA, HECHO EN U.S.A.

Printed in the U.S.A.

WCD   10 9 8 7 6 5 4 3 2 1

To John, who is always my first reader, and supports me through the travails of each new book. This book is also dedicated to the memory of my parents. Remembering, too, the four-legged members of their household: Rex I, Mandy and Rex II, dachshunds.

Christe, meoum [sic] *commorare,*
Vesper cadens obumbrare,
Diem coepit Tenebris.

(Oh Christ, remember me,
as evening falls
and shadows darken the day.)

Inscription in a country churchyard

One

====

Death had been greatly in Maurice Appleton's thoughts for the last six months. As a priest, he could hardly avoid reflecting on man's mortality. But this time the mortality was his own. He knew himself to be dying.

The imminence of death had not concentrated Maurice's mind wonderfully but impaired its ability to concentrate at all. Any attempt at logical reasoning bounced away from him like an unravelling ball of wool. He was not afraid. Instead he felt like a man waiting for a bus. It might be a little delayed, and he sometimes felt mildly irritated at being kept hanging about like this, but he knew it had left the garage and was on its way. It'd be along shortly. He'd jump aboard.

In the meantime he spent much of his time dozing, that pleasant state between awake and asleep which so perfectly mirrored his situation. He was dropping off nicely now toward the conclusion of the monthly meeting of the parochial church council.

The proceedings, held in the drawing room of his Bamford vicarage, had been, as always, tedious. He'd taken a glass of wine with his dinner (steak and kidney pie, his favorite, and his housekeeper made it very well). Lately his appetite had been poor but tonight he'd felt quite peckish and really enjoyed the meal. Voices droned on interminably. Words floated past his ears and lost themselves in the dusty corners of the room. Maurice's head nodded, spectacles slipping down his nose, eyelids heavy.

"What's more," a voice more vigorous than most declared, forcing itself into his semi-consciousness, "it's a waste!"

The speaker was a bony woman with iron-gray hair in regimented waves, and a suspicion of a mustache. The other members of the council shifted on the assortment of uncomfortable chairs gathered from all over the house for the evening. One or two looked openly at their wristwatches.

Although the question "Any other business?" had been asked as it always was at the end of the meeting, it was almost unknown for anyone to raise any. The question had become a formality, like the one posed at weddings as to whether there were any objections to the union. To jump up and say so was thoroughly bad form.

Maurice jerked upright and, to prove he'd been awake all along, asked pettishly, "What is wasteful, Mrs. Etheridge?"

She returned him a withering look which said clearly, "The old boy is past it. Thank goodness he's retiring at the end of the summer. Let's hope the new chap has got his wits about him!"

Aloud she said in the jarring, raw-edged voice which matched her appearance, "Candles left burning on the altar after a service! What does it cost? Needless expense, whatever it is."

The others were beginning to look concerned. They feared she was about to make a speech and bring up an entirely new and complicated topic which would keep them here for at least another half an hour.

"What's more, it's a fire hazard!" She bit off the last word and, to everyone's manifest relief, sat down, flushed but triumphant.

Maurice blinked his watery blue eyes. "But I don't understand, dear lady. The server always extinguishes the candles at the end of a service. It's part of his job."

"I've seen them with my own eyes!" she retorted.

Their florid-faced treasurer, Derek Archibald, intervened. Since the vicar had taken to snoozing though most of their meetings, Derek had constituted himself *de facto* chairman. "Perhaps Mrs. Etheridge could give us chapter and verse?"

A titter of laughter greeted his mild witticism. Mrs. Etheridge bridled.

"When's this supposed to have happened?" Derek went on. A butcher with a family business, he had little time for Mrs. Etheridge, not least because she was a proselytising vegetarian. Now here they all were, dying to be off home and catch the last of the evening's television, and the woman was wittering about candles.

"They're burning now!" she returned.

This caused some consternation. Maurice's mind decided to put itself on "hold" again and refuse to puzzle out this candle business. He said, "Oh no, it's nearly, um, half past nine. Goodness, so late."

The others seized on the word "late" and began to gather up their belongings.

Mrs. Etheridge wasn't to be put off. "I went into the church this evening on my way to the vicarage. I'd taken along my silver foil collection to put in the sack by the door. To my surprise there was a light in the chancel. So I took a look and was horrified to see at least one candle burning merrily away on the high altar. A brand new one because it was quite tall. And not a soul in there!"

A ripple of unease ran around the room.

"I said evensong at four-thirty," Maurice said, bewildered. "No candles were lit. I was quite alone."

"It's not the only matter I'd like to raise!" She ignored the audible groan which rippled around the company. "Bullen, the grave-digger, is a disgrace to the church! He's a drunkard and very insolent, not to say foul-mouthed, even early in the day. Only the other morning . . ."

Derek Archibald took charge. "Time's getting on. I know some of us have to get home," he rumbled. "Perhaps we'd better call it a day. Nat Bullen digs a tidy grave and, if you had his job, Mrs. Etheridge, you'd very likely take a drop or two! So I'll thank everyone for coming along tonight. The vicar and I—if you agree, Reverend!—will walk over to the church and check Mrs. Etheridge's story."

"It's not a story!" she snapped. "I don't tell untruths, Derek Archibald. I saw—"

"Well, we'll go and have a look then!" He cut short her outraged protest. "If you'd like to say a closing prayer, Vicar?"

The rest of the committee had already begun a shuffle toward the door. Now they all sat down again hurriedly in different chairs as when the music stops in a parlor game, clasped their hands, and shut their eyes tightly. Maurice began his closing blessing.

It was late summer and the evenings shortening. By the time the three of them had walked the short distance from the vicarage to the church, it was already dark. The street light by the vicarage gate glimmered fitfully and emitted a faint buzzing noise.

The two men walked side by side in silence. Mrs. Etheridge, eager to be proved right, hurried ahead, the heels of her sensible shoes tapping on the paving stones. As they passed beyond the humming streetlamp Maurice saw that, in her brushed-felt helmet and voluminous raincoat, she cast a blunt cone of a shadow which was rather sinister.

He sighed. Perhaps he should have retired a year or two ago. The parish had grown considerably in that time and he hadn't been able to cope. He'd failed his flock. The woman was probably right in the criticism which her eyes and manner had so eloquently expressed. He hoped she was wrong about the candle. It didn't make any sense and he couldn't be bothered.

But she hadn't got it wrong. Someone must have found the candle store in the vestry and fixed one of the bigger ones in a pottery holder in the middle of the altar. Wound in clumsy fashion around the neck of the candlestick was a piece of black cloth and, strewn higgledy-piggledy across the altar, a bunch of flowers with frond-like leaves and large single petals colored mauve or white.

"Cosmos!" murmured Maurice. He'd always been interested in his garden until this last year. Cosmos made a nice show, he recalled, even though they were untidy and, of course, once you'd planted them in your garden, you never got them out! Came up everywhere year after year just like weeds, between paving stones, in the vegetable bed . . .

The candle had burned down to just a pool of wax in the middle of which the wick flickered defiantly. He stepped forward and pinched it out. Smoke curled into the air and the smell of hot wax was overpowering. Archibald had switched on the chancel lights as they entered the church, at the box of switches by the north door. The rest of the place was in gloom but up here the electric lighting made the brass altar cross and candlesticks gleam.

The pottery one with its black shroud smoldered sullenly. It wasn't a piece of ribbon, just a strip of black cloth with loose threads at the edges, torn from something. Apart from that, there was no other sign of any desecration. Maurice felt a spurt of relief.

"Here, Vicar!" Derek Archibald whispered hoarsely. "This isn't right. Someone's been fooling about! What d'you reckon? Kids? Or, er, jiggery-pokery?"

Mrs. Etheridge gave a squeak and looked fearfully about her into the shadows. "Black Mass? Oh my—to think I was in here, all alone!"

"No, no!" Maurice summoned up his once accustomed firmness. "Only someone playing a silly practical joke. Extremely dangerous, too! As you rightly said, a definite fire risk!"

Being told she'd been right cheered up Mrs. Etheridge. "I told you so. You'll have to inform the police, Vicar, and the bishop!"

"We'll have to start locking up the church a bit earlier," Derek Archibald muttered. "We can't have this!" He stood before the altar, his heavy round head lowered less in respect than in puzzled defiance, the scent of alarm on him like a beast arriving at the abattoir.

Maurice's wayward mind advised its owner that it was too late for him to turn vegetarian. But perhaps Mrs. Etheridge was right about that, too. It was so annoying when such highly unsympathetic people were proved right. He clung to the matter in hand. "These summer evenings people walking by often come in to say a prayer or just look around," he pointed out.

"Or mess about!" Archibald said sternly. He pointed a finger like one of his own pork sausages at the smoldering candlestick with its sinister black vest. "Them brass things ought to have been locked away, Vicar. People don't respect a church like they did once. There's your proof. Next thing is, the brass will be nicked—I mean, stolen!"

Maurice's depression deepened. He had forgotten to lock away the altar furniture, despite having assured the verger he would see to it. But a rare flicker of annoyance was roused in him at being told off in that fashion by a man who, for goodness sake, was not only a purveyor of dead flesh but was known to go straight from Evensong to the pub of a Sunday. This was still Maurice's church. He was still in charge here. He moved forward authoritatively and gripped the pottery stick.

"I'll put this and all the other things away in the vestry safe, Derek, don't worry. We'll take a good look around before locking up. You can go on home, Mrs. Etheridge. Thank you for calling our attention to the matter!"

"Walk home alone?" she squawked. "After this? Derek, you'll have to drive me. You've got your car, haven't you?"

"Yes, all right, Janet! Sit down over there." He pointed at the first pew.

"Not likely!" she retorted. "I'm staying close by you."

Blundering behind one another like the three blind mice, they toured the building, opening cupboards, disturbing dusty hangings, peering under pews.

They didn't find anything except a fountain-pen Maurice remembered losing a month before and a collection of toffee papers in the choir stalls. He was glad to get the pen back. He'd had it for years and since its loss had been reduced to using a ball-point pen which he disliked. The pen had been a gift from Nancy. Perhaps they'd meet again soon, he and Nancy. He hoped so. It would be nice if Heaven turned out to match up to traditional ideas of it.

Perhaps Nancy would be standing there, waiting for him, with her hands held out in welcome.

They locked up and went home.

As he rose stiffly from his knees and climbed into bed later that night, the vicar reflected that it was really not so serious. Nothing had been stolen or damaged. Someone merely had a misplaced sense of humor. The altar hadn't actually been desecrated. He didn't want to trail over to Bamford police station the next day and fill out a tiresome report. Still less did he want to involve the bishop, an energetic man who would want to hold an investigation for sure. Then there was the local press. They might get hold of the story and make it out to be something it wasn't and that, as he well knew, often put ideas into people's minds.

As Archibald suggested, they'd lock the doors a little earlier and he'd make a real effort to check the cross and brass candlesticks were put away after every service. Archibald was right. People didn't respect a church as they'd once done. He had been fortunate to have carried out his ministry, for the most part, at a time when his cloth was still respected as a symbol of authority. Few respected it now. But young priests, some of them, were very odd. He had heard that his replacement rode a motorcycle.

Maurice had expressed his unwillingness to report the matter to the other two and asked them both to say nothing of the mystery of the candle and cosmos flowers. They'd agreed.

"That kind of thing," Derek had rumbled, nodding vigorously in the lamplight at the vicarage gate, "gets a place a bad name. Not just the church but the whole town. I'm a local businessman. I don't want tales of ritual goings-on. It tends to affect the meat trade, that sort of thing does."

He didn't explain just how it affected the butchery business. It might have been expected to do it a bit of good, Maurice had thought wryly, if only on the poulterer's side, by increasing demand for white chickens. But Derek was, as usual, right. They were both of them right in every way. How very irritating it was.

"We're agreed, then, Mrs. Etheridge?" he'd asked the woman.

"Oh, yes! I shan't say a word! One never knows, I mean, speaking of—of things! It makes them happen." She'd rolled the whites of her eyes at them like a frightened horse.

The silly woman probably feared some ghastly specter, a huge horned goat perhaps, doubly confusing for someone given to such strong anti-meat, animal-welfare activities. But superstition had its uses and Maurice felt he could count on her silence.

"Naturally," he'd said as they parted, "if anything like this should happen again . . ."

But it didn't happen again. At the end of the summer, Maurice Appleton retired and by Christmas that celestial bus had come along and he'd climbed aboard for his final destination.

The new vicar, or to give him his proper title "rector"— for he also had care of several smaller out-lying parishes which in days gone by had rendered tithes, was James Holland. He was a very different kettle of fish. He did, indeed, ride a motorbike. He didn't know anything about the mystery of the candle and flowers because, true to their promise as the years went by, neither Derek Archibald nor Janet Etheridge spoke of it.

Whether, in the long run, it would have made any difference was another matter, because Kimberley Oates was already dead.

Two

==

"What d'you reckon, then, Vicar?"

Father Holland avoided eye contact. But he was only too aware of the speaker, rather as though he'd been a dog of uncertain temper.

There was indeed something feral about the questioner, who was a tall, sinewy man with a receding chin and pointed nose. He had small, close-set eyes beneath a thatch of mottled tawny-gray hair, at present confined under a knitted hat. As if sensing the vicar's discomfort, he allowed a malicious smile to flit across his leathery brown features.

To the right of the shallow pit, by the pile of fresh soil, stood a third man, a little stockier and younger than the first speaker but otherwise having a startling resemblance to him. Father Holland hunched his shoulders miserably in drizzling rain at the foot of the newly begun excavation. He wished, not for the first time, that the Lowe brothers didn't remind him so forcibly of a couple of stoats.

The younger Lowe was hunting feverishly in the pocket of his thick jacket. He produced a squashed packet of cigarettes and lit up. His fingers, stained with earth and nicotine, trembled.

Expelling smoke from his nostrils, he mumbled, "The spade just turned it up, Vic!"

"I understand," murmured Father Holland. "Take it easy, Gordon!"

9

"I see 'em before! We dug 'em up many a time, me and Denny. But not just under the surface like that 'un!"

Denny, leaning on his spade and apparently as unmoved as his brother was distressed, repeated, "What d'we do?"

Father Holland cast a desperate glance around the churchyard as if some inspiration might spring from his surroundings. What did strike him was how familiar, how normal, it looked. The old graves, some sunken; half-illegible headstones, mossy or lichen-covered; the ramshackle remains of once splendid tombs; dripping trees and wet turf, all just as it had been yesterday.

The grass had been cut between the plots at the beginning of the month and was beginning to grow again. On some of the long-unvisited hummocks it had formed a thick green carpet and, being untrimmed in those spots, cosmos flowers had successfully seeded themselves in amongst it and bloomed. They waved in a brave and graceful display of color from pure white through pale pink, darker pink and mauve to a rich, dark magenta. Beneath today's overcast sky they seemed to glow, almost fluorescent, brashly beautiful. Long ago someone must have put a bunch on a grave and thus bequeathed a recurring summer explosion to delight and slightly shock the eye.

He forced his gaze back from this peaceful if untidy scene to the present and the raw wound in the earth at his feet.

The skull lay in a nest of mud, tufts of reddish hair still clinging to its scalp. It had small, square even teeth with a distinct gap between the upper incisors. A few vertebrae were visible below the jaw before the sticky clay took over again. Puddles were forming rapidly in the churned soil. The skull grinned up through a frame of water and a large earthworm, seeking to escape the flood, was struggling up through one empty eye-socket.

Gordon had a pertinent question. " 'Oo is it?" He pointed with the cigarette wedged between his index and middle fingers.

Father Holland repressed the impulse to retort, "How the dickens should I know?" Instead he glanced at the headstone, even though he knew he was unlikely to find the answer to this mystery there.

Excavation had loosened the stone, which tilted backward although the Lowes had propped it up with a couple of lengths of wood before beginning work. The vicar reached out and scratched gently at the inscription, clearing it of moss and lichen. He murmured the two names on it to himself, in the form they appeared there.

"Walter Gresham and Marie his wife."

Walter had died in 1947 and Marie in 1962. Between the latter date and this damp summer morning when the brothers Lowe had arrived to open it up, their resting place ought not to have been disturbed.

Denny said hoarsely, "Well, it ain't either of them! Too shallow, like Gordon says. Only a foot beneath the surface. Bones is nice and white. Wonder some of 'em hadn't worked through. Wouldn't be the first time I see toes sticking up—"

"Yes, all right, Denny!" Father Holland interrupted sharply.

Undeterred, Denny struck the tip of his spade into the soil. "No rotted wood, no brass handles, never no coffin!"

Father Holland rubbed a hand over his bearded face.

Denny, the expert, stooped and peered at the disturbed earth. "That might be a bit of cloth. Yes, that's what that is, right enough. Bit of that synthetic stuff what hasn't rotted."

"Synthetic?" Father Holland stared at him and then peered in turn at the scrap of muddy fabric. "Yes, I do believe you're right, Denny! That settles it! Stop work at once and get this covered over!"

"Fair enough," said the phlegmatic Denny. "Got a couple of tarpaulins in the hut."

"And neither of you is to say one word about this or the churchyard will be full of sightseers! Keep quiet about it till the police get here!" He hesitated. "I'll go and phone them now."

Glancing back as he hastened toward the gate, he saw the Lowes efficiently manhandling a waterproof sheet over the grave. Thankfully, neither of them was a gossip, if only

because few people ever spoke to them. Their occupation—
and perhaps their unprepossessing appearance—inspired a
superstitious awe mixed with repugnance. They lived an
isolated life in a cottage which lacked all but the most basic
amenities but they didn't appear to mind their spartan and
friendless existence. The vicar wondered briefly what had
drawn them to their melancholy but necessary work. Then
he cleared his mind of the jumble of unanswered questions
and began to compose mentally his report to the police.

Meredith Mitchell turned the bicycle into the lane leading
to the vicarage and the church. Unwisely she attempted at
the same time to wipe her face of the film of spray spewed
over her from a passing car. She wobbled.

It was some time since she'd ridden a bicycle, not, in
fact, since childhood. This bike had been borrowed from a
friend, Ursula, who lived in Oxford, that city of many bi-
cycles. It had been lent to Meredith because of the proposed
narrowboat holiday.

"All you have to do," Ursula had said confidently, "is
strap the bikes on the roof of the cabin. Then, when you
tie up for the evening, you can get them down and pedal
off to the nearest pub."

It had all sounded very simple and pleasurable, just like
the holiday on the canals itself. She and Alan Markby had
been talking about holidays, whilst sitting at a table in the
garden of The Trout Inn at Wolvercote, sometime earlier
in the year. Going back to the car park, they'd stopped to
admire the boats moored nearby. Without actually discussing the details, it had seemed suddenly such a good idea.

She had never handled a narrowboat before. But Alan
had chugged peacefully up and down that very stretch a
few times twenty years ago with various pretty and athletic
girls sunbathing on the cabin roof, ready to leap ashore and
deal with the locks. He had reminisced about this at some
length, memory fuelled by a good lunch and a few pints.

"Never mind the details of your misspent youth, can you
remember how to handle the boat?" she'd demanded.

He was sure he could. It wasn't difficult. There was a
strict speed limit on the canal. Moreover, the man they'd

hired their boat from had promised to show them how to deal with any little wrinkles. There would not, he had assured them, be any problem.

The boat itself was currently moored at Thrupp. They'd gone to view it. Very pretty it looked, painted red and green with crocheted curtains at its little portholes or windows, or whatever one called them on a canal boat. It even had a little waterborne garden on the roof in the shape of a pair of wooden boxes containing geraniums.

Then Ursula had suggested taking along the bikes. By now the whole thing was signed and sealed and still without any conscious decision having been taken by either of them.

It had been at that point that Meredith began to suspect it would prove a hideous mistake. She remembered the multitude of mishaps of *Three Men in a Boat*. Worse, the weather had grown progressively gloomier and it seemed they were in for one of those summers when it just rained all the time. Activity holidays of any kind presupposed sunshine.

Meredith put her foot to the ground with some relief at the vicarage gate. After so long the exercise gave one stiff legs, she had discovered, to say nothing of a numb bum. Moreover, on drizzling days like today, one got very wet. If the rain persisted into next week, on the canal, it would be a real case of "water, water, everywhere."

Her annual leave from her Foreign Office desk began today. She'd been moved, a few months earlier, to a post in Administration. Her consular experience abroad was supposed to have equipped her in some way for this, although it was difficult to see how. She'd recently begun to suspect that somewhere along the line in her career she'd blundered. She wondered in what way. Consular duties had been carried out with dogged determination. She'd made none of the obvious errors. Never fallen over drunk at an official reception or thrown up in an ambassadorial loo. Never slept with the wrong person. Never spoken unwisely to the press. She could, had she been so disposed, have worried about it. But not for the next three weeks, anyway, when pleasure at being freed from other people's problems was tempered by the looming prospect of the holiday.

A step into the Unknown, she thought wryly, as she turned the bicycle into the gate and began to wheel it up the drive to the front door. It was that prospect, and the hope of learning a little more before venturing forth afloat, which had brought her to the vicarage this morning.

Father Holland, learning of their proposed holiday, had burst into unexpected enthusiasm for the project. He'd been when younger, so it turned out, one of those people who spent their free time knee-deep in mud, weeds and old pushchairs, "reclaiming" lengths of canal. He owned a small library of books concerning inland waterways. He had once spent a summer negotiating the waterways of northern France and Belgium. He spread charts before them. He produced dusty photograph albums. He'd said he wished he could come with them, a notion not without interest of its own. The keener he'd become on their behalf, the more doubt had grown in Meredith's heart.

But she couldn't express it. It was too late and Alan had seemed so keen on the idea, following the vicar's progress as it was traced across the map, with every sign of being totally absorbed. It wouldn't be fair to cry off when Alan was so set on the trip. Alan deserved his holiday, too. She thrust her misgivings to the back of her mind.

Suddenly, breaking into her reverie, there came a clatter of feet behind her and a sound of labored breathing. She stopped and turned her head, startled, to see the vicar himself hastening along the wet flagged path toward her and his own front door.

He wore a disreputable green cagoule with the hood pulled over his thick black hair against the persistent drizzle. His massive fists grasped the skirts of his cassock clear of the puddles in the manner of a Victorian spinster, revealing the strong boots which were his preferred footwear. He brought to mind the lead role in some amateur production of *Charley's Aunt*. The boots, Meredith noticed automatically, were caked in mud. He must have come from the churchyard. The door of the garage was open and she could see his motorcycle, on which he made rural visits, inside.

"Oh, Meredith!" He drew level with her, gasping. He pushed back the hood of the cagoule and gazed at her, more than usually disheveled and quite unusually distressed.

"Is something wrong?" His alarm had communicated itself to her.

"Yes—I have to phone the police!" He hurried past her and threw the words over his shoulder. "I won't be long. Leave the bike in the porch and go on in. Make yourself some coffee . . ."

He vanished inside and his voice was lost. Following instructions, she chained the bicycle to a wooden porch support, just in case. As she passed down the hall toward the kitchen at the back of the vicarage, she could hear the vicar, shouting into the phone. The one-sided conversation seemed to consist of answers. She'd missed the first part so she couldn't guess at the questions.

"Absolutely sure I haven't! They've covered it up. With a tarpaulin. No, nobody else knows. Who's there? They are, the Lowes. They know that! Yes, all right."

The kitchen was in predictable disorder. A daily woman came in to take care of the vicar's domestic arrangements but she was an indifferent worker and today, for some reason, there was no sign of her at all. She was supposed to cook his lunch before leaving around two in the afternoon, but it seemed the vicar was destined not to have lunch or, at least, not unless he got it himself. A tin of Baxter's Royal Game soup stood all by itself in the middle of the table.

Meredith decided tea might be more suitable than coffee. In England any emergency called for tea. She switched on the electric kettle and took down the dented Swan teapot. She'd made tea in this kitchen before. She knew the lid of the teapot didn't fit and fell off as you poured out if you weren't careful. She knew the milk would be in the fridge in a bottle, never in a jug, and that Father Holland had a weakness for chocolate digestive biscuits which were kept in a tin with a picture of two children feeding a drayhorse on it. She was aware, in short, of all the signs which showed the vicar lived alone. As she did herself, and Alan, and probably thousands of others.

There was a rattle of the receiver being heavy-handedly

returned to its rest. The vicar appeared in the doorway as she forced the lid onto the pot, burning her wrist on the hot metal. She looked at him. His forehead was speckled with pearls of moisture. She was sure they were perspiration, not droplets of rain.

"I'm sorry about that," he said. He sat down at the table and put his hands on the surface. There was grime beneath the fingernails, not earth, but some kind of gritty gray-green substance.

"Something wrong?" She poured out the tea for them both and opened the biscuit tin.

Father Holland automatically reached for the solace of a chocolate digestive then paused, stared at his grimy fingernails, got up and rinsed his hands under the tap. "Lichen!" he said over his shoulder. "I was scratching out the incisions on a tombstone." He returned to his seat. "Denny and Gordon—they're the grave-diggers—they've dug up a body."

Taken aback, Meredith stared at him, not knowing how to reply. Unbidden, the term "Resurrection men" came into her head with all its gruesome connotations. At the very least, it seemed the grave-diggers had got things badly wrong. She stammered, "An exhumation? Don't they take place at first light? Or do you mean, by mistake?"

"By mistake? Yes, you could say that." He glanced at his wristwatch. "The police are sending someone over. He'll call here and I'll take him down to the churchyard. Denny and Gordon are standing guard. I just hope no one else comes into the churchyard. Thank goodness it's raining. The last thing we need is someone coming to put flowers and seeing—It would be all over Bamford! It *will* be all over Bamford soon enough! I just can't understand how it got there!"

Meredith sat for a moment turning over this information in her mind. "James, are you saying it's some sort of unauthorized burial?"

"Has to be." He munched gloomily on his biscuit, crumbs scattering and lodging in his beard.

"But how? I mean, someone couldn't just go into the

churchyard and bury their granny in a convenient spot! Are you sure?"

"Sure as can be. You won't mention this?" He saw her nod and added, "Though, as I said, everyone will know before long. But I simply can't see *how* it could have happened! I mean, as you said, no one could just come in and—and bury someone."

"It has to be a mix-up in the records, James, don't get in a state about it!" she urged.

He was showing more signs of distress, fiddling with the various items on the table. Now he grabbed the tin of Royal Game soup and glared at the picture of the stag before pushing it away.

"Where's Mrs. Harmer?" she asked.

"Gone to see her sick sister. Good thing. I'm glad she's not here today, now this has happened. She'd be flapping around the place."

The old-fashioned doorbell, a legacy from the days when the vicarage had a small staff of servants, jangled above the kitchen lintel. They both started. The vicar's front door was seldom fastened during the day and callers generally stuck their heads around it and shouted. The formality of the doorbell announced a stranger.

"Coppers already! Well, better go and show 'em." Father Holland got up and went out. After a moment she heard his voice again, out in the hall, sounding surprised.

"Margaret? I thought you'd be the—I mean, I was expecting someone else. Come into the kitchen. We're just having a cup of tea."

"I've got Oscar in the car. Will it be all right if he comes in? He gets bored and starts barking at people."

"Yes, of course bring him in!"

There was an interval during which the slam of a car door was heard and the woman's voice ordering, "Just wait a moment, Oscar!"

A deep and full-throated bellow responded. Meredith imagined, with some apprehension, a large and fierce hound of the Baskerville breed. She was wary of strange dogs.

The door re-opened. Father Holland and a woman entered in something of a rush, propelled forward by an unseen force. A scrabbling of claws on the tiled floor suggested the invisible Oscar, as did a hearty panting somewhere near ground level.

When she saw who it was, Meredith relaxed. Her mind still reeling from the vicar's news, she wouldn't have wanted to cope with a complete stranger. But she immediately recognized Margaret Holden, whom she'd met briefly on several previous occasions, all of them semiformal. As the mother of their young bachelor member of parliament, Margaret was a familiar figure in the constituency.

She was in her late fifties. Though probably never a beauty—her mouth and nose were both too large for convention—her features were striking. A high, smooth brow above strongly marked eyebrows and ash-blond hair swept back into a neat pleat suggested the adjective "handsome." Meredith's eye was drawn to a rather grisly brooch formed of a bird of prey's claw in a silver clasp, pinned to the visitor's coat.

"You know Meredith, don't you?" Father Holland was saying.

Mrs. Holden's voice was unexpectedly deep but warm. "Of course. Give me a moment to let Oscar off his lead."

She stooped briefly, then stood up, folding the lead neatly. She held out her hand with formality. "How nice to see you again, Meredith, and how convenient! I was going to phone you today."

Meredith rose to take the proffered hand but before she could, a solid body collided with her ankles and sent her staggering forward over the table.

"Oscar!" reproved his owner.

Meredith looked down. The owner of the large bark was possessed of a long body and very short legs, a barrel chest, long ears, the edges of which were balding, and, either side of a pointed nose, piercing brown eyes which were fixed balefully on her. Oscar was a full-sized standard, black-and-tan dachshund.

"Hullo!" Meredith greeted him and stooped.

Oscar scurried backward with alacrity and burst into his Baskerville boom. As he barked, he bounced up and down on his stubby legs, alternately rushing toward Meredith and darting back.

"Ignore him!" advised his owner.

Meredith sat down again. Oscar edged forward, sniffed her shoes, evidently decided she was harmless and lost interest. He set off at speed toward the door into the hall, his nose to the ground and his tail erect and waving like the whip aerial on a car.

"He's a hound," explained Mrs. Holden. "His instinct is to track. He doesn't do any harm but, in any new place, he wants to run around examining it. Some people object so I always ask before I bring him into anyone's home."

"You know Oscar and I are old friends!" Father Holland said from the kitchen sink. He was filling a bowl with water. He set it on the floor. "For when he gets back from exploring!"

From the direction of the front door came a stamp of feet. A male voice called out, "Anyone home?" The bell jangled again.

This was grist to the mill of Oscar's favorite occupation. He responded with a full-throated yell of aggression, hurling himself at the door panels and bawling defiance like a dog demented.

"There they are!" Father Holland muttered. "Meredith, can I ask you to do the honors for me? I won't be long, Margaret. At least, I don't think so."

He went out and could be heard shouting, "Shut up, Oscar!"

"Perhaps I ought to fetch him!" Margaret Holden half turned. As she spoke, Oscar was summarily returned to the kitchen by a clerical hand on his collar, and the door shut in his face. He took badly to this cavalier treatment and was clearly torn between a desire to listen intently to the noises in the hall from which he'd been ejected and a conflicting urge to raise merry hell.

Outside there was a murmur of men's voices and then silence. Oscar cocked his head. "Wuff?" he inquired experimentally.

But the quarry had gone.

Margaret Holden let him out into the hall again. He shot

out like a rocket and loosed a flurry of defiant barks by way of having the last word and then pattered off to see if he could raise other more promising game. Margaret turned a questioning gaze on Meredith. Mrs. Holden's eyelashes were pale, like her hair, and made her deepset, bluish-gray eyes appear oddly naked. Meredith wondered why she hadn't used mascara, or even had the eyelashes dyed, as was popular nowadays.

"Has something happened? James seems quite distraught. No one's had an accident, I hope?" As she spoke she placed her leather handbag on the table beside Oscar's lead. There was something in the careful enunciation of the words that indicated English wasn't her first language.

"I'm not sure," Meredith told her. "I only just got here and he's been on the phone most of the time. Let me get you a cup."

Margaret pulled off her gloves, smoothing each out and placing them, one on top of the other, over the handbag. She seemed to be thinking. "I wonder if he's going to be a long time. You don't happen to know whether the Gresham funeral will be family only, I suppose?"

"Gresham?" Meredith returned with a cup. "Sorry, I'm afraid I don't know anything about that."

Oscar reappeared in the kitchen, made for the water bowl the vicar had set for him, slurped water around all over the floor and set off again. There was a rattle of treads from the staircase.

"Bother, he's gone upstairs!" murmured his owner. "Still, he can probably get down again. Of course, you wouldn't have known Miss Gresham! You haven't lived here long enough. She died recently. Her family was long-established and very active in local politics. When I first came here to live she was both a parish and a district councillor herself. She followed Lars's career keenly. I visited her shortly before she died and on the last occasion she gave me this." Margaret touched the claw brooch. "Such a kind thought."

That explained the wearing of an adornment very much in Edwardian taste and inappropriate in today's preservation-conscious times.

"It was kind of her to think of me and I would like, you know, to attend the service if it isn't private," Margaret was saying.

Despite the flow of information she seemed to have her mind elsewhere. A faint frown puckered her smooth brow and the words came out in a rapid, jerky sequence. Then the frown vanished.

In a more lively way she went on, "I was meaning to call you, Meredith, and ask whether you and Alan could come to dinner next Saturday. Perhaps a little short notice. I apologize for that. My son will be there and whenever I want to include Lars in anything I have to take his rather crowded diary into account. Things are always cropping up at the last moment to detain him in London." A shadow crossed her face. She looked momentarily older. As before, her brisk manner returned almost at once. "However, he's promised to come this weekend. I intend to ask James Holland too. I don't think you've met my son?"

It was both statement and question. If Meredith had met Lars Holden, his mother would expect to have been informed. If they'd met without her knowledge, Meredith felt Margaret Holden would want to know why.

With some relief, she was able to reply, "Not *met*. I saw him once at a fête, only from a distance."

"Then you must come and meet him. Lars is very interested in overseas affairs."

It occurred to Meredith that giving one's children foreign first names was a risky business. On the one hand it certainly made the name memorable. On the other, it must be a bit of bind for Lars Holden, having to explain his first name all the time.

"I'd love to come. I can't speak for Alan's being free, but as far as I know, he is. The following week, mind you, we'll both be away—on the canal, a narrowboat holiday." Despite herself, a note of apprehension sounded in Meredith's voice.

A picture rose unbidden in her mind, one which had been present often of late. In it, she and Alan huddled together for comfort in a tiny cramped narrowboat cabin, drinking packet soup out of mugs, while rain beat relentlessly on the wooden roof, the canal waters outside a gray-green ooze.

Above their heads Oscar's feet thudded across some uncarpeted area of the vicarage, his claws rattling on bare boards, enhancing the image. Meredith forced it from her mind.

"Really? That sounds nice," Mrs. Holden murmured politely. She'd taken out a pocket notebook and ticked off, presumably, Meredith's name on a list. "I'll phone Alan." She put the notebook away and smiled. "I am my son's hostess and his social secretary in the constituency."

"Is Lars a family name?" Meredith's curiosity got the better of her.

"Yes, my father's name. I am Swedish, you know." She glanced at her watch, a pretty little gold one. Meredith wondered again about the grisly brooch. "I don't think I'll wait for James to come back. He might be a long time and I've got so much to do. Shall we say seven for seven-thirty on Saturday?"

She rose to her feet, gathered handbag, gloves and dog-lead and moved to the door, where she paused. Turning, she asked suddenly, "You really don't know what has happened?"

"To take the vicar away? No, I don't."

Meredith was conscious of uttering a white lie. But the vicar had asked her not to speak of the discovery and, as he'd said, everyone would know, soon enough. Although their member of parliament's mother probably didn't consider herself just anyone.

"I see."

Meredith had the feeling Margaret Holden didn't believe her. For a moment a further question hovered on the woman's lips. But she only said, "Thank you for the tea. Till Saturday."

She went out to the hall. Oscar could be heard noisily descending the staircase. "Stand still!" ordered his owner. Meredith could just glimpse her as she bent to clip on his lead. The front door clicked. A car engine started up and moved away.

Alone, Meredith sipped cooling tea and wondered how the vicar was getting along in the churchyard. Then she began to wonder about the forthcoming Saturday. "I'm my son's hostess." A strong-minded mother to have, Margaret Holden. Had her son's political career been his own idea or hers?

Unbidden, there came into Meredith's head a fragment of Gilbert and Sullivan.

"And I always voted at my party's call, And I never thought of thinking for myself at all."

She washed up the tea-things, tipped out what remained of the water in Oscar's bowl, and mopped up the puddle where it had stood. It didn't look as if the vicar would be back soon. She could call in again for the book sometime.

Meredith went outside and unchained the bike. She pushed it down to the gate and paused there with one foot on a pedal and one on the ground. A police van cruised past headed for the churchyard. As if drawn by a magnet, she cycled slowly after it.

The rain had more or less stopped. Police vehicles were parked nose to tail in the confined area available. She propped herself, still balanced uncomfortably on the bicycle seat, against a portion of the churchyard wall. Its gray, roughly chiselled stone blocks bulged outward. The passing of centuries had led to a four to five foot difference in level between the churchyard and the pavement running alongside it but now considerably lower.

On the other side of this wall, directly beside her, elbow to elbow with her, lay the dead. Perhaps one day, under pressure from the ancient earth, this old wall would finally burst and all the morass of decay would spill out.

Meredith corrected herself. That was pure horror-film stuff. Even if the wall gave way, on the other side now would be little but soil. The graves in that area were amongst the oldest. Whatever they'd once held had long since moldered away. Ashes to ashes, dust to dust. Or in this case, mud to mud. She noticed that in amongst the rough-cut blocks of which the wall was built crept a plant with pale green fleshy leaves sticking out along trailing stems. It looked like a green millipede making its way along the pathways of crumbling mortar. Here and there it was sprinkled with tiny star-like yellow flowers.

She knew its name. Stonecrop. Alan had told her once that it was poisonous, as so many common plants were. That it should be growing here seemed ominous, as though it sprouted directly from that which lay on the other side. An outward and visible sign of an inward and invisible rottenness.

Water dropped from a tree overhanging the wall and hit the top of her head. Meredith drew back further. The police personnel were all busy and no one had noticed her yet. She caught a glimpse of Father Holland amongst the trees. He was talking to a workman in a woolly hat, perhaps one of the grave-diggers who'd made the grisly discovery. Police officers in waterproof jackets were decanting poles and canvas sheets from the van. They were going to put up screens and probably a tent over the site of the horror.

She felt intrusive and knew she oughtn't to be standing by like this, watching every move. "You know what you are, don't you?" she reproached herself. "Just another ghoulish sightseer in search of thrills." But of course she wasn't! So why was she here? What was it about death?

The Victorians and Georgians who were buried on the further side of that bulging wall had lived with daily evidence of their own mortality. People, thought Meredith, dropping in their tracks from extraordinary afflictions like Purples and Gripes. All those poor little children carried off by scarlet fever and diphtheria and goodness knows what. Nowadays we were spared such things. But, oh my, she reflected ruefully, how we love a lurid murder! How we snap up copies of newspapers with all the details! And why *am* I waiting here?

Another car drew up and a man in a crumpled suit got out. He was middle-aged and balding and carried a doctor's case. He looked disgruntled at being called out. No life was to be saved now, but a death was a death and had to be formally established, whatever the circumstances. Perhaps he'd just been sitting down to his lunch when summoned.

A young police constable had noticed her at last and approached her, unseen. Meredith gave a jump as he spoke. "I'm afraid you can't wait there, miss. As you can see, there's a lot of traffic coming through. I'll have to move you on.''

He sounded apologetic. She met his gaze and he smiled. It was a conspiratorial sort of smile. He knew why she was waiting there. She blushed, embarrassed and angry at herself.

''I was at the vicarage.'' She felt impelled to offer some justification for lurking about, to let him know she wasn't just another ghoul. ''I'd come to see Father Holland about something when he was called away.''

''Oh, he'll be busy for quite a while, I should think!'' the young man told her. He had a fresh, round face. He looked, she thought, hardly more than twenty. ''You'd best go on home and try later.'' There was firmness in his gentle chiding.

When policemen start looking young to you, you know you're in trouble, that's what they all said. Age creepeth up. ''Heck!'' she thought crossly. ''I'm thirty-six!''

''So, you're thirty-six!'' retorted a mean little voice in her head. ''In Tudor times average life expectancy was around twenty-one. There are places in the world where it still is around that.''

''Infant mortality rates,'' she argued silently, ''account for much of that!''

''Miss?'' He was looking at her, slightly concerned. ''Did you understand me? You're not a foreign visitor, are you?''

''In a way,'' she said. ''But not the way you mean. Sorry to get under your feet. I'm going now.''

She cycled slowly away. He probably thought she was crackers. She didn't look back to see if he was watching her. But as she turned the corner into the main road it suddenly occurred to her to wonder whether Alan would become involved in what was going on back there.

In her mind's eye, the narrowboat, holed below the waterline, sank swiftly and silently beneath the canal's surface, leaving only a trail of bubbles.

Three

Superintendent Alan Markby sat in his bright new office in the spacious regional crime squad building and knew it would be churlish to complain about the way things had fallen out. He had, after all, been very lucky.

Leaving Bamford on his promotion, he'd spent only six months away in the vastly different surrounds of the North-East, before being offered the opportunity to return to this area. Coincidentally, it included his old haunts. Even better, it had returned him to his old house, which in the currently depressed property market had been languishing unsold. He had simply taken down the sign and moved back in, even though it meant a tidy drive to and from work every day. Best of all, it had returned him to the proximity of Meredith Mitchell. He had reason to believe she was pleased, too.

Unease touched him. She was very enthusiastic about the narrowboat holiday. He'd been pretty keen on the idea himself at first. The gruesome discovery in All Saints' churchyard had changed all that.

Although as yet the case was classified as an unauthorized burial and ''suspicious,'' the local force at Bamford hadn't doubted they'd been presented with a murder victim. As a result, they were treating it as such from the outset and had appealed to the regional squad for help. With an unidentified set of bones and the possibility of expensive forensic research leading to inquiries ranging across area boundaries, they simply couldn't cope at Bamford. Their resources were limited and they hadn't the manpower or the time for such an open-ended inquiry. They'd handed it over to the regional squad and it had landed on Markby's desk.

It made it difficult for him to consider leaving that desk now. He wasn't so arrogant as to suppose himself indispensable! But he hadn't been in the new job long and this was potentially the most important case to come his way since his arrival. It was an opportunity to set his stamp on the way things would be done from now on. Perhaps it would also give him a chance to get away from office-bound police work and out there where it was all happening.

Once upon a time, or so it seemed in memory, he'd always been out there where the action was. Possibly memory, always unreliable, played him false. It was like that other trick it had of making you believe the sun shone all through your childhood and youth. Unlike today! Markby glanced at the window. Or this present summer. What a season. What a time to pick to go narrowboat cruising!

Above all, if he were to be honest, he had a purely personal desire to oversee this investigation taking place on his old patch about which he still nursed proprietorial feelings.

As if to reinforce this sense of it being "his" preserve, here was an old acquaintance, Father Holland, incumbent of the parish in which the remains had been discovered, come to discuss the grisly turn of events.

He had, of course, already encountered the vicar in connection with this business, when he'd gone to inspect the scene in the churchyard. There had been numerous other people present busy about their several grim tasks and he'd had little chance to do more than exchange a brief word with James Holland. The image left in his mind was of the vicar, flanked by the grave-diggers concerned, standing in the drizzling rain and looking utterly bewildered.

Today his visitor looked no happier, slumped before him, nursing a mug of tea in his hamlike fists.

"A pity, James!" Markby said impetuously. "I mean, that our talk has to be all business!"

Father Holland shifted his bulk on the rather narrow chair which had been provided. "Foul business!" he growled. He twitched massive shoulders and glanced around him. "Interesting to see this new place of yours, Alan."

"I'm getting used to it," said Markby.

"Nice countryside."

Thus prompted, the superintendent allowed his gaze to slide again to the window, through which he could see the nodding branches of the trees. It was just starting to rain again. If he did go on this canal boat trip, it was unlikely either he or Meredith would be doing any sunbathing.

Father Holland said absently, "I rode over on my bike," meaning the powerful motorcycle with which he'd alarmed the good citizens of his new parish when he'd first arrived some years before.

He needn't have told Markby. His shiny black helmet rested on a nearby desk and he wore his heavy leather jacket and boots. All this, together with his bushy beard, had caused mild concern when Father Holland had arrived earlier. Sergeant Prescott had assumed that he was about to be subjected to serious verbal assault, if not worse, relative to some dispute between rival gangs of bikers.

The sight of a dog-collar, when the hirsute figure unzipped his leather jacket, had quite unnerved Prescott, who was a young man and still apt to have preconceived ideas about people. He was telling colleagues about it, even now, in the canteen.

"You've talked to Inspector Bryce, of course!" Markby reached for the folder on his desk.

"She's talked to me!" mumbled Father Holland pedantically. "She thinks you stand a fair chance of identifying the—the remains."

"We do have a complete skeleton," Markby agreed. "Which is always a start. Odd bones are always tricky and when heads are missing—"

He caught the vicar's anguished expression and continued more briskly, "The Lowes turned it up, I see! I remember them. Once seen, never forgotten, Denzil and

Gordon! Why were they opening the grave?''

"That bit's easily explained.'' Father Holland leaned forward and clasped his hands. "Miss Eunice Gresham died ten days ago.''

Markby looked surprised. "That's not the same Miss Gresham who used to live at Warren House? She must have been almost ninety! Even before I left Bamford, I hadn't seen her around for years.''

"Eighty-eight. You hadn't seen her around because for the last six years she'd been in a nursing home and for the last four months in St. Winifred's Hospice. It was at the hospice that I visited her. The very last time I saw her she told me she wanted to be buried with her parents. She was quite certain that a three-decker plot had been purchased by her late father in the 1930s. He'd intended himself, his wife and eventually his son to be buried in it. I don't know why Eunice was left out. Anyhow, the son was killed in the last war. So, Miss Gresham reasoned that there was a spare place going begging in her parents' grave and she would like to be interred there. I don't think it was filial devotion so much as the fact that old man Gresham had paid for it, do you see?''

Father Holland raised a weak grin. "She was very sure about that. She was a frail old lady in many ways but her mind was clear enough on that point! She treated me to a lengthy harangue about it.'' He grimaced again. "Anyhow, I checked and found there was a grave, but it was—is—in the old churchyard where burials ceased quite some years ago. However, in the circumstances and as it was a case of opening up an old plot and not creating a new one, I was able to arrange it.''

Father Holland paused and took breath. Markby reflected that an older generation had set much store by being buried in a fit and proper way with appropriate outward show of mourning and, incidentally, at considerable expense.

"Miss Gresham's solicitor contacted me after she died. Truelove, do you know him? He replaced old Macpherson. I can't help feeling Eunice wouldn't have approved of Truelove handling her affairs. She was so very precise and old-fashioned in her ways. Truelove is one of the new breed of young bright lads. Plenty to say for himself and about as subtle or sensitive as a brick! I wish Mrs. Danby were handling this.''

Markby acknowledged the tribute to his sister, Laura, one of the town's more decorative as well as competent legal brains.

"She's on sabbatical.''

"Another baby?'' inquired Father Holland.

"No, just a much-needed rest. They've got four,'' Markby added in reference to his sister's brood.

"She'd probably get more rest in her office, then!'' said Father Holland. "Anyway, to return to Eunice Gresham. She'd also set out instructions for her funeral in her will. The date of the interment had been fixed for tomorrow. I told Denny and his brother to open up the Gresham plot. They'd barely started when they unearthed the skeleton. They saw at once it wasn't likely to be one of the Greshams. The Lowes are by way of experts on bones! They knew it shouldn't be there and contacted me at once. Denny also pointed out some scraps of what looked like man-made fiber of some sort which hadn't decayed. That told me it was not a regular, recent burial.''

He looked up and met Markby's inquiring expression. "Modern regulations,'' he explained. "It's all changed from the old days when you could be buried in your best suit! Now we aren't allowed to bury any man-made fibers or anything which won't rot down or would pollute surrounding soil. The same goes for cremations. Can't burn off anything which might contribute to noxious gases in the atmosphere. We all have to be decked out in officially approved grave-clothes these days.''

It was as well that Eunice Gresham most likely hadn't known that. She certainly wouldn't have approved! Markby touched the folder on his desk.

"Yes, the body had probably been wrapped in a large piece of cheap material. Forensics have made what they can of the surviving scraps. It was quite heavy-duty, perhaps intended for household use as curtains or duvet covers rather than for dresses. They think it was probably of foreign manufacture, the type imported for quick sale on market stalls, that sort of place. It wouldn't be used commercially, at least not in recent years, because it'd have been highly flammable. But in the past regulations were not so strict and people generally less conscious of the hazard.''

''That brisk red-haired girl, Inspector Bryce, said the bones were identified as those of a young woman.'' Father Holland leaned forward to put his empty mug on Markby's desk. ''She seemed a no-nonsense sort, didn't let the task in hand get her down. Admirable, really.''

Markby hid a smile. ''Yes, the deceased was probably between sixteen and twenty years old. We're still not quite sure how she died.'' Markby grew sober, hesitated and glanced at the priest. ''The deceased was pregnant at the time of death. There are bones of a four- to five-month old fetus in the area of the womb.''

Father Holland bowed his head and rested it briefly in his hands as Markby waited. After a moment he sat up. ''I didn't see the whole thing unearthed. I confess I'm glad I didn't. The head was enough. Inspector Bryce didn't say, she didn't mention a baby. When was she buried?'' His voice became more agitated. ''And how? Without anyone noticing? All I know is, I didn't bury her!''

''We've had a word with Denny and Gordon. We know the last time the plot was opened officially was in 1962, so the unofficial burial took place after that. The Lowes insist the grave wasn't disturbed during their time as gravediggers, they'd have noticed. They've been working there ten years. So let's say she was buried eleven or twelve years ago but possibly as long ago as thirty years. Forensics, after much havering, think it likely to be the more recent of those dates.''

Father Holland's solid torso jerked and the spindly chair rocked. ''Of course! When I first took over the parish, burials were still taking place in the old churchyard, land the church owned. A real old soak called Bullen had the job of grave-digger. He was well past retirement age. He'd been an embarrassment for years but getting rid of him hadn't proved easy. He had his defenders, despite his bad habits, and he was determined to stay. It was one of my early tussles in the parish. Change in circumstances solved it. The churchyard was full and had to be closed. The district council opened the new cemetery alongside on land it owned and took on its own grave-diggers, the Lowes. Bullen went muttering into overdue retirement.''

Markby smiled. ''I remember Nat Bullen from my early days at Bamford. He was taken in for abusive behavior in public a record number of times! Eventually there was hardly a pub in town which would let him through the doors. Perhaps his job drove him to drink.''

''He was always falling head-first into whatever grave he was digging,'' Father Holland said tartly and then frowned. ''I came to Bamford just over eleven years ago. So she could have been buried shortly before Appleton retired.''

He heaved an unmistakable sigh of relief then looked apologetically in Markby's direction. ''I have to be honest. If someone could creep into my churchyard and carry out an unauthorized burial it would hardly reflect well on my powers of observation or general efficiency! But poor old Maurice Appleton was a very sick man in his last year or two. He let everything just slide. General parish business got into a terrible muddle. It'd have been worse if they hadn't had a competent parochial church council at the time.''

The priest hesitated. ''As I indicated, I had a few confrontations with the PCC when I came. They'd got used to running things their own way and wanted no changes. A woman called Etheridge accused me of popery and quit the church!''

The vicar shook his bushy head, dismissing the memory of old squabbles. ''How will you find out who she is? Missing persons' register?''

It was Markby's turn to look apologetic. ''Years ago missing persons' registers weren't as efficiently kept as now. The late Father Appleton wasn't the only one to let matters slide. Our best hope is that someone will come forward to suggest a name. We do have records of some missing parties. But we are having to go back thirty years, remember, just in case she was buried as long ago as that. Naturally we'll check all extant files on reported missing persons for the period but it's going to take time. When we've exhausted inquiries here, we'll try neighboring areas. The girl could, in theory, have come from anywhere. Having said that, it's quite possible she'll turn out to be local.''

Father Holland nodded miserably. ''Needle in a haystack is what you're saying.''

''Don't be too down-hearted.'' Markby didn't want a negative note to creep into proceedings, not as early as this, at any rate. ''Put yourself in the position of the person or persons who buried her. A body isn't the easiest thing to move. Don't forget that ten, twelve or more years ago, many present stretches of motorway didn't exist. Now it's no problem to transport a corpse fast over long distances and dump it anywhere in the country. Then, well, it would have been more awkward. This was an attempt to conceal a death, for whatever reason. Whoever was responsible would have wanted to do it in the quickest and most convenient way.'' Markby gave a brief grin. ''And he didn't have a garden!''

Father Holland pulled a wry face. ''Burying it in a churchyard shows a certain logic, I suppose. Best place for a body, after all!''

''Absolutely! As for her identity—well, if no one comes forward or we can't trace her any other way, there are techniques for reconstructing an image of the face from the skull. We're not stumped yet, James. I feel fairly confident we'll put a name to her soon.''

He wasn't nearly so confident as he sounded but James Holland needed some reassurance just now.

The vicar had been listening closely and one aspect of Markby's speech seemed to have struck him with particular force.

''Strange!'' he murmured. ''To think a face can be rebuilt from nothing but a skull! It's a sort of resurrection of the body, isn't it? Putting flesh on dead bones. Discussing her intimately, calling her by name, as if she were here with us. We're taking her up from the grave and making her walk among us again. Poor girl.''

''If we can identify her,'' Markby said quietly, ''then

obviously that increases the chances of finding—of finding who buried her.''

He had almost said, ''who killed her.'' As yet it was still only a suspicious death—officially. Unofficially they were inclined to agree with the local force. They had a murder victim. They'd have to wait until they could piece together the whole story, if ever they did! But in any case, knowing who she was would be a start. Although, it would be a long and painful road from knowing that to knowing the full sorry tale.

To Holland he said, ''Eventually you'll be able to lay her decently to rest.''

''Rest? Oh, yes, rest . . .'' The vicar spoke absently again. ''I'm accustomed to death, as you must be.'' He glanced at Markby. ''Not, of course, in quite so gruesome a way! I'm spared things like autopsies and mutilated bodies in sacks and all the horrors one reads of. But that skull, gazing up at me from the earth, it had a life of its own, if that's not a nonsense. Do you know what I mean?'' He looked questioningly and in some embarrassment at the other man.

Markby nodded. ''I know what you mean.''

''Afterwards, I found myself muttering bits of Shakespeare to myself. 'Alas! poor Yorick. I knew him, Horatio.' Odd, you know. That must be one of the most famous quotations in the English language and most people get it wrong. They will say 'I knew him well!' Anyway, what I want to say is that, to Hamlet, that skull remained Yorick, the person he'd known. To me, the skull Denny and Gordon uncovered, that was still someone. I felt almost as if it wanted to tell me something. Later, when Inspector Bryce told me it had been established as a young woman, I found myself wondering if she'd been pretty. When it was suggested she might be a murder victim, I began thinking of crimes of passion and it didn't appear so lurid as to be impossible. But I was over-romanticizing, of course. Now that you've told me about the unborn child, it just seems sordid and cruel and selfish. Human wickedness, no more or less.''

The vicar spread out his broad hands. ''What kind of a

man would do such a thing? The killer must still be around, mustn't he? Twelve years isn't so long ago, after all. If he was a young man then, he'll not be more than thirty or so now. Forgive me, I'm wandering. It's been a shock.''

"I understand. And you're not wandering, you're thinking around the problem as we do, looking at it from all angles. Remembering that we're dealing with real people. Somewhere there are probably relatives of the girl who are still alive.'' More briskly, he went on, "I take it the Gresham funeral has been put off indefinitely?''

"Oh, yes. The police have quite taken over the churchyard. Well, you'll know that! One thing I came here to ask you was how much longer . . .'' Father Holland looked embarrassed. "I don't mean to hurry you along, but the activity of the police and all the paraphernalia, the screens and so on, it does attract sightseers. They climb over the other graves and break down shrubs. They are doing quite a bit of damage and obstructing access for relatives who come to tend other graves. There have been complaints.''

"I imagine the police search of the area has messed things up pretty thoroughly,'' Markby said ruefully. "I'm sorry. We do have to comb that churchyard. We'll be as quick as we can but we can't cut corners.''

"I quite understand, Alan!'' The vicar held up his hand. "I don't want to interfere in your job. But I'm worried about mine. I still have to bury Eunice Gresham! There's also some question now as to whether her final wishes can be respected. It might be better to put her elsewhere, even in the new cemetery. We should have decided on that at the outset, I suppose. But if we hadn't been trying to do as she wished, we wouldn't have found—''

He broke off and looked around for his crash helmet. "I really must be going. Oh, there'll be an inquest, I suppose, and I shall have to attend?''

"You'll be required but the coroner will almost certainly adjourn to give us time to identify her and establish circumstances of death. I think we may be given a slot on Wednesday.''

The vicar nodded. "I'm glad you're in charge of this, Alan. It's a great comfort. Although . . .'' Father Holland paused and frowned. "Shouldn't you and Meredith be going on holiday about now? On the canal? I do hope this won't interfere with your plans. Meredith is looking forward to it all so much."

Markby sighed. "Not now all this has blown up. I'll have to break it to Meredith that the trip will have to be put off until later in the year. I don't know how she's going to take it. I know she's very keen."

"She was going to borrow a book from me about inland waterways. She called for it the other day but the Lowes had just—Oh, dear. Well, I'll be seeing you both on Saturday, I expect? I understand we've all been invited to dine with our member of parliament."

"That, too . . ." said Markby glumly.

Father Holland managed his first smile of the entire interview. "Troubles never come singly!" He reached a hand across the desk in farewell. Then, suddenly, he burst out, "Whoever he is, the killer, if he's heard we've found his victim, he'll have had one heck of a shock! Wonder what he'll do?"

Markby said grimly, "With luck, he'll make a mistake!"

Four

The right Honorable Lars Holden, MP, sat at his desk in the cramped office he shared with a fellow member.

To anyone walking by the extravagant Victorian Gothic exterior of the Houses of Parliament the buildings appear suitable in every way for the business of state carried on within. Anyone actually conducting a large part of their working life within those famous portals knows only too well that the Commons, in particular, has long been too small for present-day needs.

There are not seats enough in the Chamber should every MP decide to turn up. Office space is at a premium and those who miss out may find themselves working on a table in the library. Others, like Lars, shared.

At the moment, however, he had the room to himself. His parliamentary colleague was in some African trouble-spot, "observing." Lars was enjoying the unaccustomed privacy. In fact, he was feeling altogether in rather a good mood today. Only a few more days and the Commons would rise for its summer recess. The assorted honorable body would be off on its holidays.

He rubbed his hands briskly together. They were narrow hands with long, slender fingers. His mother had hoped he'd be a musician, as she had been, but since early childhood he'd known exactly what he wanted. He wanted to be in control, at the heart of things. He had wanted to be

here, a member of "the best club in London." And he was
here.

True, he hadn't achieved greatness yet. But political
commentators were agreed he was "one to watch." He'd
held minor posts of one kind and another and the next re-
shuffling of the Cabinet would almost certainly lead to promotion to a more senior position. (Well-informed sources
had it that the prime minister would reshuffle the Cabinet
in the autumn when the House reconvened. Lars could be
excused for sensing that glory was within reach of his fin-
gertips!) Yes, he was on his way.

Smiling happily at all these thoughts, Lars murmured,
"Now, let's see what we've got today!"

Ruth, his secretary, had just put a stack of constituency
mail on the desk. Each letter was opened out flat and she
always put on the top anything she thought might be of
special interest to him. Today she had hesitated by the desk
and indicated that the top-place letter in some way displeased her.

"Probably a crank!" she said. "But the address, it's
quite near to where you live. I thought you might recognize
the name and know who it was."

Lars's good mood was somewhat spoiled as he turned
his gaze on the creased scrap of cheap ruled letter paper.
It appeared to him the sort of thing that, when he'd been
very young, he'd been told never to touch "because you
don't know where it's been!"

This looked as though it had been stuffed in the pocket
of an unsalubrious pair of trousers. But he was a consci-
entious constituency MP and a constituent had written. He
would give it due consideration. Many a career had foun-
dered because the grass roots had been neglected. The loyalty of voters could never be taken for granted. Besides,
Ruth had said something about the address.

Lars smoothed back the thick flaxen hair he'd inherited
from his Nordic mother. Unconsciously, even though he
was alone, he struck an attitude. He was a handsome man,
unmarried and, with so much going for him, inevitably an
eligible bachelor. He had plans to change that status. Those

plans were one of the few avenues in his life where an obstacle had arisen to block the path ahead.

He put any thought of this personal problem firmly out of his mind as he picked up the letter. "Good God!" he exclaimed aloud. "It's that wretched old man! What on earth does he want?"

At once much of his good humor evaporated. He recognized the address all right, as Ruth had thought he would. He could see the dwelling in his mind's eye. See its inhabitant, too, the writer of the letter. The twin mental images caused Lars to grow hot under the collar. He pushed back his chair, jumped up, and went to the window for some air and to give himself a moment to restore the equilibrium of his thoughts.

Behind him the door reopened to admit Ruth carrying his coffee. "All right, Mr. Holden? You look a bit flushed."

She eyed him in the proprietorial, slightly bossy way with which he was familiar. She was in her late forties and had been his secretary since he'd entered parliament. He relied upon her utterly. She was a mine of obscure information and a walking encyclopedia of matters pertaining to parliamentary business and etiquette. Even Margaret Holden spoke of Ruth with respect.

"I'm fine." He knew he didn't sound altogether assured and saw doubt on her face as she turned away.

"Ruth?" He was accustomed to make use of her as a sounding board for difficult bits in speeches and she paused by the door, expecting the usual "How does this sound?"

But he said thoughtfully, "It must be a nuisance, don't you think, for a parent to find he doesn't actually like his child?"

Few things shocked or surprised her. She raised her eyebrows beneath her cropped mousy-brown hair and replied calmly, "Very much so, I should think. Rather unnatural, too."

"What? Not to like one's child? I'm not talking of drunks and perverts who abuse their own kids. I'm talking of perfectly decent, responsible, well-meaning persons who—well, I'm talking of my father. He's dead now, been gone some eleven or twelve years. I'm sorry to say I don't miss him. We never saw eye to eye. He never played football with me or took me on country rambles or taught me to ride a bike or any of those things.''

''Perhaps he was too busy,'' said sensible Ruth. ''And all those things, do all fathers do them? It always seems to me that it's the mothers who find time for that sort of thing.''

Lars considered this. ''Perhaps. My mother taught me to play the piano, not ride a bike. She would have assumed I could teach myself to master a bike and I did. But at least she talked to me. My father and I never talked, either when I was a child or later as I grew older. Hardly an unnecessary word, not even to shout or criticise. At the end of his life, when he was ill, he seemed to withdraw even more. Perhaps just because he was sick. He certainly didn't seem to place any special value on the little time left for us to spend together.''

Lars saw that Ruth pursed her mouth in disapproving fashion. He hastened to redress the balance.

''To be fair, he was always generous about money and I don't think he ever objected to anything I wanted to do. When I had some sort of success, say passing an exam, he'd say, 'Well done, well done!' Then he'd hand over a tenner and walk off. Occasionally he'd struggle to find something else to say and he'd manage, 'Paper give you much trouble?' I always told him it hadn't, even if every question had been hell, because he wouldn't have known what to say. He behaved in every way as a decent man trying to do the decent thing in the face of his own inclination. I mean, he didn't like me, Ruth, but he was too much of a gentleman to admit it!''

She gave him an old-fashioned look. ''I'm sure that's not so, Mr. Holden! He must have been very proud of you. I know your mother is.''

''Oh, she is!'' Lars said shortly. ''But he wasn't. It may sound stupid or vain, but I think he was a bit resentful of me.'' He shrugged. ''I took up so much of Mother's time, perhaps. We weren't a happy family. We didn't quarrel. But we seldom joked, either. There was no teasing. We were always terribly polite to one another. That can't be natural, can it?''

''Now what's brought this on?'' Ruth asked him severely. ''You're not sickening for something, are you? There's a bug going round. You don't feel a bit fluey?''

He ignored her. ''When my father died he left the family property in trust for the use of my mother in her lifetime and thereafter outright to me. You can interpret that however you like. I take it to mean he didn't believe I would look after my mother. What did he think? That I'd put her out on the street?'' Lars's voice rose, aggrieved.

''He might have thought she'd remarry,'' Ruth said reasonably. ''He wanted to make sure the property remained intact for you eventually. I thought The Old Farm was lovely, that time I went there. I do like those old historic places, especially the brick and timber ones like yours.''

''It's a Grade II listed. It dates from Tudor times,'' Lars said absently. ''Did anyone show you the traces of the hidden Catholic chapel in that tiny room off the back stairs?''

''Yes, so romantic!'' She shivered pleasurably. Her favored reading matter tended to be thick sagas of royal plot and misdeed. ''But that's what I meant. The house is so special. I'm sure all your late father wanted was to make sure it didn't go out of the family.'' Ruth indicated his desk. ''Drink up before it gets cold.''

''But the house isn't all!'' Lars ignored her gesture toward his cooling cup of coffee. ''You see, in addition there are two small former laborers' cottages on land adjacent to the main building. You probably didn't notice those. When Father died we sold the woodland and some grazing areas, but kept the cottages. One's leased to a retired army man. He's a loyal volunteer party worker. Excellent chap, always ready to do a bit of canvassing, push leaflets through doors, sit all day telling the number of voters on election days.

''The other—'' Lars's voice and expression grew agitated. ''The other is lived in by a dreadful old man called Bullen. He's written to me. Lord knows why! It's that letter.'' Lars pointed at his desk. ''He's nothing but trouble. He doesn't pay any rent, you know. He just sits in that cottage, year after year, never going out except to the pub up the road. That's what all his money goes on, drink!''

"Lucky him!" said Ruth. "Sounds like the ideal retirement!"

"It's ridiculous! I don't suppose he even gives me his vote. I've told my mother again and again that there's not the slightest reason why we, that is I, should subsidise Bullen! All she replies is that he's a 'poor old man who has only got his pension and can't last much longer.' ''

Lars's expression grew more and more wrathful. "He's pickled in alcohol and likely to go on till he's a hundred! He's as old as the hills already and quite disgusting. God knows why Mother is so sentimental about the old reprobate! She's normally such a level-headed woman. I'd even call her sharp, wouldn't you?" He stared fiercely at Ruth.

Ruth had work to do. "Your mother is very sensible and I'm sure she has your best interests at heart. As for this old man, I dare say your mother means to be kind. If you want to drink that coffee cold, that's up to you, but I'm far too busy to have time to make any more!''

She marched out. Lars sighed. No doubt Ruth was right and his mother was both sensible and kind-hearted. But Lars knew she was also obstinate and, lately, in the matter of Bullen, he'd begun to suspect her of an unworthy wiliness.

Lars put his hands on the windowsill, gripping so tightly his knuckles shone white through the skin. But this wouldn't do. He'd better get it over with. Lars glanced back at the table. He was surprised the bibulous old scoundrel was *compos mentis* enough to set pen to paper. Lars trailed back to his desk and sat down again. He seized Bullen's letter. So, what did he want?

"Dear Sir, Mr. Holden," it began with belt-and-braces prudence.

I thought as you should now (sic) what they have done. There is a bit in the local rag and I have cut it out for you. It will be all right, but they ought not to have done it. It is Denny Lowe's fault. They ought never to have given him my job.

Yours fathfully (sic)
N. Bullen.

Lars read it twice but it made no more sense the second time than the first. It did conjure up the writer as a wizened and malevolent wraith in the corner of the room. Lars fancied he could even catch a whiff of whiskey. That or sulfur. He'd always thought there was something devilish about Bullen.

"He's gone potty!" he said briefly aloud to himself. Rambling letters. What next? Demands that he'd be given back his churchyard job? More likely, that Lars install a new bathroom or central heating or some such thing in the cottage. To make Bullen more comfortable and encourage him to stay? Hah!

"I have cut it out." There must be an accompanying newspaper cutting. Had Ruth failed to see it in the envelope? She usually slit them right open. He hunted around and was about to go and ask her about it when he saw the square of newsprint lying on the carpet under the desk. The draft from the open window must have wafted it from the pile of letters. He stooped and scrabbled for it.

"MYSTERY OF UNKNOWN REMAINS" the headline ran.

Council workmen have made a grisly discovery in the churchyard of All Saints, Bamford. On opening the grave of Walter Gresham (mayor of Bamford 1936–37 and 1940–41) in readiness for the burial of his daughter, Eunice, the skeleton of an unidentified young woman was discovered not far below the surface. It is thought the unauthorized burial took place during the incumbency of the late Reverend Maurice Appleton. A police spokeswoman said, "We are treating this as a murder inquiry." Father James Holland, vicar of All Saints told our reporter, "This is a very distressing affair. Many people in Bamford will remember Miss Eunice Gresham who died recently aged eighty eight. She was for many years a tireless worker in voluntary causes and a local councillor. Older town residents will also remember the Reverend Appleton, a popular parish priest, keen gardener, and frequent judge at local flower shows."

The report had its priorities right. It was the local associations which interested its readers, not the shocking discovery as such.

Lars drummed his fingers on the desk. He had the unpleasant sensation of feeling both hot and cold at the same time, sweat trickling down his body while he repressed a shiver. Perhaps he had picked up the "bug" Ruth had spoken of. He did feel a bit as if he'd got a spot of 'flu. He passed a hand over his forehead.

The old man was up to something. There was a clear underlying threat in that brief phrase, "It will be all right." Why shouldn't it be? Was Bullen intending to cause trouble? Blackmail, was that what the old blighter was up to? It would hardly be in his interests. Bullen was living very comfortably under the wing of the Holden estate. He wasn't foolish enough to rock that particular boat.

Nevertheless, Lars felt uneasy, even alarmed. A man in the public eye, as any politician was, especially an ambitious young hopeful like Lars himself, was always vulnerable to scandal. Notoriety sometimes resulted from trivialities, forgotten incidents of years before, youthful misdemeanours or the errors of subordinates. The press whipped these things up. You could never be too careful. It was a golden rule. The very sight of the letter and clipping, in themselves fragile, mundane objects, suggested danger. Bullen's ghost in the corner of the room was replaced by a shadowy and faceless thing which made Lars feel very afraid. He returned to the window.

A keen breeze from the river played on his sweating brow. After a single violent shudder which shook his frame the unwarranted chill left him. His body's thermostat was working properly again. He managed a little laugh. He was crazy to allow himself to be upset by a semi-literate note from someone like that. He'd been working too hard, was tired, needed the approaching holiday. He must not, in any circumstances, lose his grip on things as he'd seen others do. It must not happen to him. It would not happen to him.

The Thames, running past the joint Houses, was busy with traffic today. A sightseeing launch passed by. A man with a loud-hailer was pointing at the façade, calling attention to the familiar tower of Big Ben. Coming up fast on the launch a police powerboat clove the dark oily water into twin foaming crests as it sped about some urgent business. At the sight of it Lars frowned.

He turned back to the desk and reread the letter and clipping. A wave of anger sweeping over him, he crushed them both in his hand. But as he was about to toss them into the wastepaper basket some instinct made him hesitate. He smoothed them out again, folded them and tucked them in his breast pocket. He was going down to his constituency at the weekend. He'd go and see Bullen and make it quite clear that whatever little plot he was hatching, it was null and void from the outset.

"He's picked the wrong man!" said Lars grimly. "He needn't think he can try his tricks with me!"

The desk phone rang shrilly, making him start. He reached for it.

"Miss Pritchard is on the line, Mr. Holden," came Ruth's voice. "Shall I put her through?"

"Of course!" Instinctively Lars's free hand went to his hair again.

A different female voice echoed in his ear. "Darling!" said Lars. "Yes, of course," he added after a moment. "Are you sure?" he asked next, his voice less confident. Finally he said, "This weekend? Well, if you think so, Angie. Yes, you're right, of course, my dear. I agree, you know that." By now his voice had become quite edgy. "But unfortunately she's arranged a dinner par—"

The voice at the other end of the line burst into energetic argument. He moved the receiver a little from his ear and capitulated. "Whatever you think best."

He put down the phone and looked at the window. The sun, feeble enough today as it had been, had now gone in entirely. Vanished, just like his good mood.

But he reassured himself that he'd sort out the present

little problem, just as he'd always done others in the past. He was a man whose star was in the ascendant. Nothing must change that. Nothing.

"Multiple non-accidental injuries inflicted by a large-bladed knife or machete." Markby looked up from the report. "Dr. Fuller seems sure."

"The bones are chipped and scored in several places," Louise Bryce said. "Heavy blows delivered with considerable force."

"Could the killer have tried to dismember the body, found it too difficult, abandoned the task and just buried her as she was?"

"Dr. Fuller thinks more a random set of blows. A frenzied attack."

He looked sour. "No chance of finding the weapon after so long!"

"We're searching the churchyard. Round the sides nothing's been disturbed in years. Grass is two feet high and the brambles have covered a lot of ground. We're cutting them down and if anything was thrown in there, even twelve years ago, it's still there."

He indicated a second set of stapled sheets. "What's that?"

"It's from forensics." Bryce flipped through the sheets. "They've had the remnants of fabric under the microscope, together with plastic buttons, probably from a summer dress, and the remains of sandals. The man-made soles have survived better than the leather uppers. A small size fitting. Mass-manufacture, chain-store type. Mixed in with that and the surviving traces of human tissue and the soil samples, they found an unusual number of insects, or bits of insects. They passed it over to the bug experts. I've got a list a mile long here!"

Bryce consulted it rapidly. "They include woodlice, fragments of earwigs and wasps and the eggs of *Calliphora vomitoria*." She paused. "That's common blow-fly, apparently. Bluebottles, I've always called them. They're surprised at the number of the blow-fly eggs. The body must have been crawling with horrible things buzzing away.

Their conclusion is that it lay around for several hours un-
buried and unprotected, only the cloth used as a shroud
thrown over it. Plenty of time for every creepie-crawlie in
the neighborhood to investigate it.''

Fresh rain spots spattered the windowpane. Markby
glanced at it. Even Meredith would admit it was no weather
for an outdoor activities holiday. Unless you were a fish-
erman, of course. He wasn't himself, but was vaguely
aware that the fishermen, or the fish, quite liked this sort
of weather. Fish liked flies. Flies had been unusually plen-
tiful around this corpse.

"Woodlice, wasps and earwigs! You a gardener, Lou?"

She shook her head and grimaced. "I live in a flat. I've
got a couple of pots of geraniums on a balcony. What's on
your mind?"

"I'm thinking," he murmured, "of somewhere like a
potting shed."

Perhaps the idea of fish had lodged in his subconscious,
because he stopped on the way home and bought fried cod
and chips for his supper. He liked the sound and smell of
fish and chip shops, the hiss of the fryer and the clatter of
the utensils, the acrid scent of the vinegar, all rather more
than he liked the actual product. But tonight he was hungry.

He unwrapped the package in his kitchen. It was still
warm but not as hot as it had been. He scraped it onto a
plate, resolutely ignoring the amount of grease left behind
in the wrapping paper, and put it in the oven to warm up
again. While he did that, he cut himself some bread to
butter. He liked bread and butter with fish and chips.

But subconsciousness was still working away. Markby
paused in mid-slicing to gesture in the air with the bread-
knife, making stabbing motions. A large knife. A frenzied
attack. A crazed killer? Generally he didn't believe in madness as a reason for murder. But when it was, the killer
was usually apprehended quickly. The killings often took
place in a public area or accompanied by noisy disturbance.
There was frequently a history of violent mental illness.

But burying a body in a churchyard in a manner so secret

it had lain undisturbed for years until unearthed by chance, no, that wasn't madness. That was cunning.

So if not madness, what? Hatred? Anger?

"Passion!" Markby said aloud.

That got him thinking about Meredith again. Guilt swept over him. He still hadn't talked to her about the holiday. To delay any further was inexcusable. On the other hand, just telephoning and announcing baldly down the line that he was going to be unable to take time off was both impolite and unfair. He ought at least to call around and tell her in person. He'd wait till after the inquest because, who knew, there was just a remote chance the matter might get cleared up quite suddenly. Cases sometimes were, against all expectations. Satisfy the coroner and he could go on holiday with clear conscience.

Beneath the drizzle, a line of figures picked stolidly through the jungle of undergrowth around the perimeter of the old churchyard. Denny and Gordon Lowe, both of them totally indifferent to the weather whatever it might be, sat outside their hut and watched.

As seats they used a couple of wheelbarrows in which they reclined with their booted feet dangling over the ends. They looked not unlike a couple of sacking and straw Guy Fawkes, such as children wheel about the streets around Bonfire Night, begging pennies. They smoked squashed hand-rolled cigarettes and from time to time made a muttered comment to one another.

"What they doing over in that corner?" Gordon asked. "Gresham grave is over here. What are they looking for?"

"Beats me," said his brother.

"They've been taking away the bloody earth in sacks!" said Gordon.

"Found some buttons, so I heard. I told 'em, they could've been in the earth years. Needn't belong with those bones at all."

"Reckon they can tell?" Gordon asked in a tone of curiosity mixed with disbelief. "Like, reckon they can tell where them buttons came from and how old they are?"

Denny spat over the side of his wheelbarrow. "They

want to see some of the things I've dug up in my time!''

Gordon nodded slow agreement.

One of the stooped searchers, glancing toward them, muttered to his colleague alongside him, "Look at those two, like a couple of crows! They fair give me the creeps!''

"This whole job's giving me nightmares!'' said his colleague dourly. "I don't know what I'm going to find here next! Yah!'' He jerked his hand away and jumped back.

"What is it?'' The other stopped work and peered.

The one who had cried out was examining his hand with disgust. "Bloody dog shit!'' he said.

On Wednesday morning an inquest was opened and adjourned on the remains of a young woman and her unborn baby discovered in the churchyard of All Saints, Bamford. The coroner was satisfied that the burial was unauthorized and gave the police time to investigate it. The proceedings were over in minutes.

It rained again that day. The tiny room in which inquests were held was stuffy and smelled of damp raincoats and Jeyes Fluid from the toilets down the hall. Two middle-aged women and a youngish man, who'd been seated at the back of the room, hastened out immediately. Few people had attended. Those who had were mostly from the press.

Markby fended off the reporter from the *Bamford Gazette*, a personable young woman with short dark hair, and—less easily—a sharp-faced young man from a national tabloid newspaper.

"Readers like this sort of thing,'' said this gentleman. "Got any gruesome details, Super?''

Markby, who disliked being hailed as "Super'' and being pumped for voyeuristic titbits, snarled, "No!''

One didn't dislodge the gentlemen of the national press that easily.

"Go on, something! How about missing persons? You must have some suspicions about identity! Any beautiful local girls gone missing in strange circumstances? Any unsolved sex crimes?''

"Not in Bamford,'' said Markby coolly. "I understand from Inspector Dawes of the local force that the off-license down the road was broken into last night, if you want a crime story. Oh, and they've installed a speed camera on the main road with remarkable results.''

"Thanks!" said the hack sarcastically.

Father Holland, who had been lurking mistrustfully in the background, came up as the reporter made off in search of more promising quarry. "Wretched fellow! He came to my vicarage! I told him to mind his own business!"

"Your business is his business, that's what he'd tell you," Markby said glumly. "Still, we might need the press. Doesn't do to upset them."

"Glad this is over . . ." They had left the inquest room and were proceeding down the corridor. Father Holland looked and sounded his relief. "But only just beginning for you, really."

They passed the reporter. He'd located Denzil Lowe and was attempting to get a spadeful by spadeful description of the disinterment.

"We dig up a lot of bones," Denny was saying casually. "Not a lot of new ones, of course. Lot of old ones. Sometimes a fox has tunnelled his way in there and chewed 'em up a bit. 'Course, you find handles off coffins and rotted wood."

"But this time I understand there was no coffin?"

Markby, passing by, said loudly, "This matter is still before the court, Denny! There may be a trial eventually. Mind what you say!"

"You heard the superintendent!" said Denny sourly to the reporter. "I can't tell you nothing more!"

"Then I'll have my fiver back!" snapped the hack.

"He'll be lucky!" Markby murmured to Father Holland, who chuckled.

Five

Meredith had also attended the inquest, although she wasn't quite sure why. She wasn't a witness but felt as though she was. She had a purely practical reason, too, for wanting to talk to Alan. Today at the latest they had to decide about the holiday. That seemed a trivial, even selfish, matter compared with what had been discussed here. But trivial matters have to be settled also. She'd already taken the precaution of ringing up the boat owner and warning him there might be a problem. Today she'd have to ring and either confirm or cancel.

She saw Alan cornered by what appeared to be a pressman. The vicar was also hovering in his vicinity. The smell of lavatory cleaner was getting stronger. She decided to wait outside in the fresh air.

She wasn't the only person waiting about on the steps. Sheltering under the eaves of the building and fiddling with a showy gold wristwatch, was a young man. Meredith, huddled into her own corner against the cool breeze, studied him for want of anything better to do.

She thought he was probably in his early thirties, trying to look confident but only managing to look nervous. He lacked the lean and hungry look of a pressman. He was sharp-suited and sported a short haircut, his general appearance tending to overweight and prosperous. He looked

51

so out of place and was clearly so ill at ease that she wondered what on earth he wanted here.

At that moment, he looked up and caught her gaze. He started toward her.

"Are you an official of the court?"

He blurted the words and waited hopefully for an affirmative reply. Meredith thought crossly that years of being "an official" turned one into such a being even when off-duty. She looked like someone who knew what was going on, even when she didn't.

She said, "No, I'm sorry."

"Oh." He looked as if he didn't quite believe her. "Nothing to do with the police?"

She was beginning to be curious. "No. But I'm waiting to speak to Superintendent Markby."

"Is he the chap in charge?" When she nodded, he went on, "Perhaps he's the one I ought to talk to."

"What about?" It wasn't her business but he'd started this conversation. Besides, instinct told her he wanted to tell someone.

"These bones." He gave a diffident grin. "I—er—I might know the identity of the—the girl."

"Then you certainly ought to talk to him, Mr.—?"

"French," he said. "Simon French."

"Meredith Mitchell." They shook hands. "Alan—the superintendent—won't be long."

To prove her correct, Markby emerged at that moment. He bid farewell of James Holland and came toward her. The vicar made for his motorcycle, saluting the group with a wave as he hastened past.

"Alan, this is Simon French!" Meredith urged her protégé forward.

Markby raised his eyebrows. "Didn't I see you inside, at the back of the court?" He added more sharply, "Are you a newspaperman?"

The young man looked startled. "Me? No! I'm in the restaurant business."

Markby caught Meredith's eye. What's he want? his expression asked.

"To talk about the skeleton," she said in answer to his

unspoken question. "I'll go on back to my place. Perhaps you could call around later, Alan?"

French seemed loath to have her leave. Looking toward her as if she'd confirm his words, he hurried on with, "I understand you're in charge of this—this business—Superintendent! It's rather difficult to explain. I saw the news on television, regional program, about the skeleton being found. I heard there was going to be an inquest and I came along, hoping to learn a bit more. But the coroner adjourned. It was a waste of time turning up, really." A touch of grievance entered his voice.

"We're all pushed for time!" Markby's tone suggested he suspected French to be one of those freaks who collected macabre murder cases.

French took the hint. "It's possible I've some information for you. I waited till the inquest in case you'd already got it all sorted out and the—the remains identified. But you haven't so I thought I'd better tell you what I've been thinking. I could be quite wrong." With a change of tone he added, "And look, it's been worrying me and I want to get it off my chest so I can forget all about it!"

"Mr. French," said Markby, with a gesture toward the building they had just left. "Perhaps we could go back inside and you can tell me all about it."

"See you later then," said Meredith to their retreating backs.

Markby took Simon French back to the now deserted courtroom and sat him down. The fellow could still be a crank. Would-be informants came in all shapes and sizes. There were the liars, the seekers of a moment of glory who actually hadn't a clue. Sometimes you got the nutters. Also the genuinely mistaken, and the pathetic parents, achingly wishful of some trace of a lost loved child, even after many years. French didn't look like a nutter and he wasn't old enough to be a parent of the dead girl. He could even prove—dare one hope it?—the bearer of genuine information.

French wriggled about uncomfortably on his wooden chair. "I know this is going to sound odd. I could be haring up the wrong path. I just wondered if those bones, if they could be Kimberley Oates.''

This was getting serious. Cautiously, Markby interrupted him with, ''Why don't you tell me about yourself first, Mr. French?''

French looked startled. ''Me? Oh, well, I suppose you do want . . . I've got identification.'' He began to search through his wallet and brought out a miscellany of driver's license, credit cards, check book, even a library ticket.

Markby stopped him hastily. ''No, I mean—just who you are, what you do. You're a Bamford man?'' He sounded his doubt.

But French surprised him. ''Yes, I went to school here. I left the town when I was in my early twenties. I didn't come back here until a year ago to take up a new job.'' His voice gained pride. ''I'm manager of The Old Coaching Inn. It's just outside town on the Westerfield road. Perhaps you know it?''

Markby nodded. ''I have to admit I've not visited it since it was done up. It used to be a tumbledown sort of place.''

''It's been completely renovated!'' French seized the opportunity to promote his new baby. ''I hope you give us the honor of your custom! We do a very good carvery and our Sunday lunch—'' He caught Markby's eye and reddened. ''Sorry, this isn't the time . . . But there is a connection. I've always been in the restaurant business. I did a course in hotel management at the local Technical College on leaving school. But my first job was for Partytime Caterers, a Bamford firm. I was nineteen, a trainee barman. I—that's where I knew Kimberley.''

Markby's spirits were rising. The man was genuine. He still might be mistaken, but he wasn't deranged.

French hastened on. ''She was a waitress with Partytime. She was younger than I was. She'd have been sixteen or seventeen, tops, when I first knew her. We worked together for about a year.'' He fell silent.

''What makes you think it might be Kimberley?''

''Because she disappeared about twelve years ago and she was pregnant at the time. Because it seemed really strange, even back then. I remember thinking—'' French broke off again. "It's very difficult to explain this. Believe me, I don't want to give you a load of duff information! But on the other hand, I've always thought it was a funny business."

The door had been left ajar. Markby got up and went to close it, shutting out the smell of disinfectant and the murmur of voices.

"All right, Mr. French. Just tell it the easiest way you can. Don't worry if it sounds jumbled or extraordinary. We'll sort it out."

"Fine." French cleared his throat again. "We used to go out and about on different catering engagements. Sometimes clubs and office parties, sometimes private houses, weddings, all sorts. A lot of it was evening work. Well, one evening, Kim didn't turn up as she should and Mr. Shaw, our boss at the time, was pretty mad because it left us short-handed. He rang her home and whoever answered didn't know anything about it. So Shaw said, she'd better have a good explanation or he'd give her the sack! But she never turned up again. No one ever heard from her or saw her after that. I heard that the police made inquiries because the relative she lived with reported her missing."

"You're sure about this? The police were involved?" Markby asked sharply. Mentally he crossed his fingers. Please the Lord the file had survived!

"Yes, they came and talked to Shaw. In the end, everyone decided that she'd run away from home and that was that."

"Everyone but you, it seems?" Markby asked gently.

Simon flushed. "Yes, I mean, I wasn't sure. It seemed odd."

"How did you know she was pregnant?" Markby asked suddenly.

Alarm crossed his visitor's plump face. "Hey! Look, it wasn't mine! I don't know whose it was! She didn't say! The only reason I know about it is, one evening at work— we were at the Golf Club. I remember that, Captain's Dinner, they called it. We were the caterers. Kim turned up all right that time, but she went missing for a bit and I went to look for her. She was being sick in the loo. She came out looking pretty awful. I asked her if she was all right to carry on working. She said she was, and asked me not to mention it to anyone, because old Shaw would get to hear of it.''

French was relaxing, the words spilling out of him now. ''I asked her if she was ill. Because, you know, handling food you can't be too careful. If she was ill, she ought to have stayed home. But she laughed and said, 'Don't be daft! I'm only pregnant!' ''

French gave a twisted smile. ''I wasn't that surprised. She was on the tubby side normally, but she'd got quite a bit fatter lately and her face had that bloated look, you know?''

''Did you ask her about the father of the child?''

''I assumed it was some boyfriend. I asked her what she meant to do about it and if he, the boyfriend, would stand by her. She said, I remember it quite well, 'Oh, I'll be all right! I'll be looked after. I'll make sure of that!' ''

Markby raised his eyebrows. ''Did she, indeed? How was her general manner? And how long was this before she disappeared?''

French considered both questions. ''About two weeks. She wasn't worried! She even sounded sort of—triumphant. I didn't talk to her about it again. I knew she'd have to tell Shaw soon. But that was her problem, not mine. But the day she went missing, I'd met her in town that morning. Not met on purpose, just in the street by chance. She'd borrowed a fiver off me the week before. She said, 'Oh, Simon! I'll give you back that five pounds tonight at work!' We chatted for a few minutes. I don't know what about, nothing much. Then she said she'd see me at work that evening—it was another dinner dance of some kind—and she wouldn't forget to bring along the fiver. But, of course, she never turned up at all, as I told you.''

French made a gesture of contempt. ''Look, she wasn't going to have done a runner just because she owed me five quid, was she? She definitely thought she was going to see me that evening. She'd intended to come in to work. Then there was her condition. It wasn't the time to choose to go running away, was it? And she wasn't upset!''

"She might have joined her boyfriend, the baby's father, somewhere?" Markby suggested.

His visitor gave a malicious smirk. "She might. I doubt it."

"I see." Markby eyed him. "Then obviously you know something more. Or you suspect something."

French leaned forward earnestly. "Let me explain about Kimberley. I used to chat to her at work the way you'd talk to any colleague. But we weren't friendly outside of work. We had nothing in common. To her it was just a job. I wanted a career. I mean, I didn't intend to spend my life working for Partytime! It was just a stop-gap job, getting a bit of experience. I wanted to get away to London as soon as I could. She was—well, she was all right as a waitress. But she had no style. She wasn't ever going to be anything else. She lacked professional ambition." The last words would have sounded stilted if French hadn't spoken them with such reverence.

So Mr. French, at the tender age of nineteen, had already had an eye to the main chance, Markby surmised wryly. And the main chance wasn't around his native small town. He hadn't intended getting involved with a local girl. He had his sights on the big city. On the other hand, if he had got involved with a local girl whom he came to feel was a handicap, he might have been desperate to get rid of her . . .

"And you did go to London?"

"Yes, as I said. I worked at two or three places in the West End and after that on a cruise ship for a while. I tried to get in as much varied experience as I could—for my cv. If you go for a decent job, you've got to show you've done it all." The visitor looked pleased with himself, an expression which sat easily on his plump features.

Under Mr. French's *aegis*, The Old Coaching Inn was likely to soar up the list of desirable eateries, thought Markby. He recalled it as a rambling, dusty building which had sold Ploughman's Lunches, dry sandwiches and flat, warm beer. No longer, it seemed. French wouldn't be satisfied until the place got itself a favorable report on the *Sunday Telegraph*'s Food and Wine page!

"But there is something you know about her?" Markby prompted in a kindly tone.

"She was attractive," Simon said grudgingly and frowned. "She had a good enough brain but her ideas were limited. She used to read a lot of romantic fiction in the mini-bus on the way to venues. I think she had ideas about meeting someone rich who'd sweep her off her feet—"

French grimaced. "She thought she might meet someone like that through working for Partytime. She was ticked off a couple of times for flirting with guests at the private parties the firm organised. You can't have that, not in quality catering. It's the one thing you have to make sure the staff understand. I mean, sometimes if a girl's pretty, a male guest will make a pass at a waitress. They have to be told how to say no without offending the customer. Same for the women guests. Some of them, especially the, you know, the won't-see-forty-again ones, they'll slip a young barman a few quid and let him know there's a bedroom upstairs empty."

"Indeed?" Markby was intrigued. He wondered if anyone had ever tried to turn Mr. French into toyboy of the moment. If so, the lady had probably got nowhere. Not with prim, sensible Mr. French!

"And Kimberley, she understood the rule about no hanky-panky with the paying guests?"

"Of course she did!" French sounded shocked. "But she still—I told you, she had dreamy ideas. On one occasion I even told her, I remember, that she was daft. I mean, people who can afford to hire professional caterers to put on their parties, and Partytime didn't come cheap—" Simon shrugged. "They wouldn't bother seriously with someone like her."

Oh, he must have been a tough and sanctimonious little blighter, our Simon! thought Markby. Lecturing Kimberley on keeping her place, indeed! "And what did Kimberley say, when you told her that?" he asked. He really wanted to know.

"I can't remember!" said Simon stiffly. As Markby suppressed a chortle, French went on, "But after she disappeared, I did wonder if the baby's father might have been someone she'd met at one of the catering engagements. Especially when I remembered what she'd said about being "looked after." That was a funny way to put it. It sounded as if she thought she was going to get some money from somewhere."

"You thought she might be contemplating blackmail?"

French looked horrified and then embarrassed. The mix of emotions lent him a comical expression. But he said, "I don't know about that. It does happen, doesn't it? Look, I've told you all I know."

He made to rise but Markby hadn't finished with him. "When inquiries were being made about her disappearance, did you mention your doubts to anyone?"

"No one asked me," French said simply. "They talked to Shaw, but not to me. Anyway, I thought if Kim was in some sort of trouble, I'd better keep quiet. I didn't want to make it worse for her. Look—I didn't think she was dead!"

"Until you saw the news item about the skeleton?"

French said miserably. "Until then. I bloody wish I hadn't waited to talk to you now!"

"I'm very pleased you did! Thank you very much, Mr. French!" Markby sounded enthusiastic, as indeed he was. French brightened and assumed a faintly smug expression which Markby suspected was habitual.

They'd check French's story, of course, but he had a gut feeling the man had told them what they wanted to know. Whether he'd told them all he knew was another matter. Markby suppressed the desire to wipe the self-satisfied look from that florid cherubic countenance.

"Perhaps you'd be good enough to give all this in a written statement for our file? Go to this place," he scribbled on a sheet of notepaper, "and ask for either Inspector Bryce or Sergeant Prescott."

French looked alarmed. "Look, I only felt I ought to tell you. I don't want to get involved in anything—"

Markby held up his hand soothingly. "You did quite right. But obviously we have to get it written down. After that, you're pretty well off the hook! Unless you remember something else. I wish other people came forward as quickly as you have, Mr. French!"

French looked relieved. "Sure thing!" he said breezily, thereby setting the seal on Markby's dislike of him.

Meredith had stopped off to pick up some shopping. When she got home, Alan had made it ahead of her. She saw his car parked outside her terraced cottage and Alan himself, sitting on the low brick wall.

She was surprised, but her first instinct was to recall how much it had cost to have that wall built. "It's three yards long and a yard high!" she'd pointed out to the builder. "Not the Great Wall of China! It can't cost that much!"

"It's the labor," he'd replied reproachfully. "And the price of bricks has gone up, not to mention sand—"

"All right!" She'd given in but the memory still rankled.

She pushed it out of her mind. A small smile touched her lips. Alan looked uncomfortable on that wall. He sat with his arms folded, his long legs stretched in front of him across the pavement, his head inclined forward so that his fair hair fell over his face. He was clearly lost in his thoughts, and whatever those thoughts were, they worried him.

An elderly woman had just emerged from a door at the far end of the row of dwellings. Moving stiffly, she dragged a wicker shopping trolley behind her as she approached Alan from the other direction. Even from this distance Meredith could see that the woman was directing looks of deepest mistrust toward the waiting man.

"Hullo!" Meredith greeted him. "Why didn't you wait in the car? Or, come to that, where's your key?"

"At my house."

The elderly woman had drawn level with them. "Excuse me, young man!" she said loudly to Markby. "You're obstructing the pavement!"

"Sorry!" he apologized, scrambling to his feet.

"Hullo, Mrs. Etheridge, how are you today?" Meredith asked.

"Not so bad, thank you!" said the woman brusquely. She looked disapprovingly at Markby and hauled the shopping trolley onward.

"Etheridge?" Markby seemed momentarily distracted. "I've heard that name somewhere."

"She lives in the cottage at the other end of the terrace. She suffers from arthritis. I feel sorry for her although she isn't the friendliest person, rather prim. She probably disapproves of my having gentlemen callers! Especially if they hang about outside! Wasn't that wall damp?"

"Didn't notice . . ." He followed her into the house.

"Do you want a cup of tea or a glass of wine?"

"A cup of tea. I've got to go back to the office."

"Does that mean Simon French has come up with some information?" She was unable to suppress the eagerness in her voice.

He hunched his shoulders. "We'll have to check it out. I've just called by Bamford station. According to French, this may relate to a missing persons case they handled twelve years back. A girl called Kimberley Oates."

While she was brewing up, he told her French's story, adding, "Smart Alec! Too sharp and will cut himself, as my old grandma used to say."

"You didn't like him, obviously. A suspect?"

"Murderers have been known to be lured by the publicity into coming forward under some pretext. It's as if they feel it's their show and they want to be involved. French might think he can play cat and mouse games with us. On the other hand, my feeling is that he's genuine as far as his information goes. I'm prepared to believe he wasn't emotionally involved with the girl. I don't see French emotional about anything but his own career prospects!"

Alan was clearly anxious to move onto another subject. "But that's not what I'm here about. Meredith—" He caught her inquiring look. "About this new case, or rather, about this holiday . . ."

"You don't want to leave the case," she said wryly. "You can't take the time off. Alan, I can see that for myself! You're obviously up to your ears in work on it. Anyway, things are starting to move, aren't they? If French is right and that is the body of Kimberley Oates. You're already in the middle of it and you can't walk off the case now. It's too late."

He looked miserable. "I don't like to let you down. I know you're set on this canal trip. I was looking forward to it, of course! If you really can't bear to cancel, naturally I'll try and give the case to someone else, but everyone's busy and it might look as if I was trying to pass the buck."

She took pity on him. He was making her feel guilty. "I'll be honest. I was having second thoughts about it. The weather's been so rotten. As soon as I knew about this business of the Gresham grave, I had a feeling it would mean you couldn't take the time off. It's all right, really. I rang the boat owner yesterday and warned him we might have to cry off. I'll ring him tonight. He did say that any cancellations were usually snapped up. It should be all right."

He didn't look convinced. "We can go later."

"Leave it. Wait and see." There were few words more final, she thought as she spoke them.

When he'd left, the reality of the rest of this week and the next two was borne in on her. She was on leave. She had nothing to do and now, no holiday. So how on earth was she to spend so much free time? Wasted free time! She was sorry now she'd been so nice about the cancellation of the trip. Yes, she'd been less than enthusiastic, but hang it all, she'd lost her share of the deposit and she'd taken precious leave, three whole weeks of it, on the understanding they were going on holiday together and now—

"Police work!" snarled Meredith to herself. Depression settled. That was the way of it, always. She picked up the phone and dialled the boat company.

By early evening she needed someone to talk to and clearly Alan was out of the picture. One other person understood the situation. Meredith got out her car and drove the short distance to the vicarage. She'd had enough of that wretched bicycle, and now she wouldn't be going on the canal trip, the bike could go straight back to its owner.

Cloud cover meant the evening was darker than it ought to have been at the time of year. Light beamed from the vicarage kitchen where James Holland was preparing his supper. He wore, not his cassock, but baggy corduroy trousers and a sweater obviously hand-knitted by someone with a problem. The cable-stitch design was sprinkled with mistakes where the cable twisted in the wrong direction or just forgot itself altogether and went straight up.

"Hullo, Meredith!" he waved a sharp-looking knife in greeting. "Join me in my humble meal?"

"Haven't come to cadge a dinner, James. Only to talk to someone. Is it inconvenient?"

"Of course not. Is it about the hoo-hah in the churchyard? It's on my mind, too." He indicated a chair with the knife. "Park yourself there. Do stay and eat. A bit of company would be nice." Eagerly he added, "I'm no cook but I've got this!"

He delved into the fridge and emerged with a magnificent hand-raised pie. "Chicken and ham. The speciality of a grateful parishioner who presented it to me. I get presents occasionally. Like this sweater." He tugged at it. "I saw you looking at it. The knitter's eyesight isn't good so it represents a particular achievement for her. I have to wear it."

He began to chop up a cos lettuce. Meredith watched for a few minutes. "Can't I do something to help?"

"Open that bottle of wine over there. And then tell me your troubles."

"Trivial ignoble ones." She grimaced wryly. "Alan's told me the holiday is off. I did expect that. But it means I'm at a loose end. You haven't got any jobs I can do? Anything reasonable. I'm not very good with kids."

"A volunteer!" The vicar practically purred. "My dear girl! Of course I've got any number of things you can do. In fact, so much of my time is being taken up with this Gresham grave affair that all my little routine visits have quite fallen by the wayside. I'm getting in the urgent ones, but it's the regulars, like Daisy Merrill."

Wondering if she ought to ask, Meredith did. "Who is she?"

"Miss Merrill? She's a dear old soul. She's out at Westerfield in the nursing home there, The Cedars. I try to call and see her once a week because she has no one else. She's such a bright old lady and loves to talk. You couldn't, I suppose . . ." He let his voice trail away.

"Would she want to see me?"

"Oh, she'll see anyone!" Father Holland assured her, perhaps not entirely tactfully.

He added tomatoes to his salad bowl and took a large jar of chutney from a cupboard. "Do you mind if we eat here? I don't use the dining room. We'll talk about The Problem in the Churchyard afterwards."

"Alan thinks they might have a name for her," Meredith said a little later.

James Holland topped up her glass. "Quick work!"

"Someone came in. It looks as if she might be local. If she is, her killer might still be around, don't you think?"

"Not if he's got any sense," said the vicar. "He probably cleared off as soon as he could."

"But someone, quite a lot of people, should know her."

"Ah, but will they come forward? The instinct to keep one's head down is very strong. Still, let's hope Alan gets to the bottom of it soon. It worries me. I'll be glad to get the police and the sightseers out of the churchyard!"

It was dark when she left the vicarage, having promised to visit Miss Merrill. She hoped she didn't get stopped driving home since they'd finished the bottle of wine between them. Meredith stepped out of the gate into the street and took the car keys from her pocket.

A scrape of a footstep caught her ear. She looked up.

Two figures emerged from the dusk into the outer ring of lamplight. They stood silent, side by side, watching her. They were extraordinarily alike, wearing workmen's clothing and woolly hats. Their faces were closed yet bright-eyed, like some sort of wild animal's. They observed her in every detail and gave nothing in return. Their whole aspect was incredibly sinister.

My God! she thought. I'm about to be mugged! She opened her mouth to say she had no money on her but one of them spoke before she could.

"Evening, miss!"

The country voice was reassuring. Suddenly she guessed their identity.

"Denny and Gordon!" she exclaimed. "The grave-diggers, right?"

"That's us, miss."

"What are you doing out here at this time of night?" She looked from one to the other and the second, slightly shorter one, answered this time, as if she'd appealed directly to him.

"We just had a look to see if it's all safe and tidy, back at the churchyard. Round the Gresham plot where everyone is so busy."

"And is it?"

"Oh, aye. We were just going to tell the vicar."

They edged past her and into the gateway to the vicarage. "Goodnight, then, miss."

"Goodnight," she replied. She didn't envy the vicar his strange visitors.

Regional crime squad HQ was ablaze with lights, a beacon amid the surrounding darkness. Otherwise the building was quiet. The buzz and clatter of daytime had given way to the echoing sound of footsteps and occasional voices in empty corridors and offices.

Markby's door opened and he looked up to see Louise Bryce, flushed and triumphant.

"Got it! Bamford have just sent it over!" She brandished a dog-eared file. "Twelve years ago, almost to the day!"

"Splendid! Let's have it!" He reached out his hand.

She beamed, her round cheeks dimpling, as she handed it over.

She was a stocky, freckled, young woman with curling ginger hair cut in a fringe and normally a good-natured set to her mouth which even her chosen career hadn't yet managed to eradicate. Without any unkind intent, Markby thought Bryce looked rather like Miss Bun, the baker's daughter, in the Happy Families card game. He didn't, on that account, underestimate her intelligence or her persistence.

"Kimberley Oates," he read aloud from the front of the file.

"Yes, sir. She was reported missing by her grandmother, Mrs. Joan Oates. I'll get onto local dentists first thing in the morning to check their records. It's starting to look as if your Mr. French is right."

"He's not 'mine'!" said Markby. "He's just a good citizen who came forward."

Bryce cast him a curious look but said nothing.

Markby opened the file. A clutch of glossy photographs lay on the top. He picked up the first one and, despite himself, couldn't avoid giving a little exclamation of surprise.

The bones took on flesh and life. A professional portrait showed a plump, pretty teenager, smiling broadly. The gap between her front teeth was clearly visible and rather endearing. French had called her attractive and Father Holland had wondered whether the dead girl had been pretty. Here was the answer. She'd been very pretty. Too pretty for her own good, perhaps.

He picked up the other photos. One was a summer snapshot of the same girl, perhaps a year or so younger, standing in the back garden of a modest dwelling, holding a kitten. The other was quite different and very much a posed picture.

It showed a table splendidly set for a cold buffet. There was a whole poached salmon with beautifully arranged sliced cucumber "scales," a glazed ham studded with cloves and all kinds of salad. To one side stood two girls, one of them Kimberley, and a young man, recognizable as a younger, slimmer, fresher-faced Simon French. All three were smiling self-consciously as if they'd just been told to do so. Simon wore a waistcoat and bow tie. The girls wore black skirts, white blouses and black ribbon bows at their collars.

"Ah! The bar staff!" Markby murmured.

"She worked for Partytime Caterers, as French told us, sir. The firm's still in business but I don't know if it's under the same management. It's on the trading estate along the Burford road."

Markby studied the picture again. The location appeared

to be a private house. Behind the table was a wide brick chimney breast with an oak mantel dotted with framed photos. On the wall hung some sort of certificate and just the corner of a painting could be made out at the upper edge of the photo. French had mentioned that the firm catered for private parties.

"I'll get onto them tomorrow to see if anyone else there still remembers her." She fidgeted. "Shall I leave the file?"

"What? Oh, yes, I'll read it and return it to you. You go and do whatever you have to do."

When she'd left he spread out the file so that the ceiling light beamed its white glare directly on the typed sheets. To his annoyance, flyspots had speckled the overhead neon tube, casting a sprinkling of dark shadow marks over the pages as if presaging something rotten at the core of the subject. He began to read, absorbing the details of someone else's tragedy.

It was a not unfamiliar tale. A sixteen-year-old, Susan Oates, had given birth to a baby but had been unable to identify for sure the father. The baby girl hadn't been put up for adoption because Susan had wanted to keep her. She hadn't, however, wanted the hard work or the restrictions on her own life which would have resulted from looking after the child. All that fell to her widowed mother, Joan.

A year later, Susan Oates, having tired of the baby completely, took herself off. Her mother was left with the child on her hands. At first Susan sent birthday and Christmas cards accompanied by cheap gifts and little messages. Then the gifts had stopped and only the cards came. Then the little messages in the cards stopped and they were merely signed. Eventually, all correspondence ceased.

The baby, named Kimberley, grew up cared for by her grandmother. She left school at sixteen and got a job with Partytime Caterers as a waitress. When not waitressing, she helped out in general duties. She'd been popular with fellow workers and the management was satisfied with her work, although she'd been warned about flirting with clients. She had lacked, the manager had said, "a professional attitude.'' It was obvious where Mr. French had received his initial training in attitudes to the job!

The lectures on attitude clearly hadn't impressed Kimberley. But then, she'd been very young. One day in late July Kimberley had not been required to go into work until the evening when the firm was responsible for arrangements regarding a dinner dance. In the earlier part of the day, according to Mrs. Joan Oates, Kimberley had ''dressed up'' and gone out. Her grandmother thought she had probably gone shopping or to meet friends. She didn't return. Later, the manager of Partytime rang Mrs. Oates to ask where Kimberley was. She was needed. She hadn't appeared for work. They were left short-handed and he was extremely cross. Mrs. Oates became worried. Kimberley didn't come home all night. The next day Joan Oates informed the police.

Kimberley was never seen again. Mrs. Oates had admitted that there had been a number of quarrels between herself and her granddaughter. Kimberley had been ''difficult'' over the last few weeks. Significantly, there was no mention of any pregnancy. Kimberley probably hadn't told her grandmother of her condition, but at four months it was beginning to show, even on a plump girl like Kimberley. She was having to face up to confession time. Possibly she hadn't been able to do so, and had simply left home. She had packed no bags, however. Markby pressed his lips together thoughtfully. Quite often, runaways didn't. They decided, whilst out of the house, simply never to go back.

Asked about boyfriends, Mrs. Oates had said Kimberley had ''lots of friends.'' Joan Oates had the impression, however, that there'd been someone special lately, but Kimberley hadn't confided in her. On reflection, Joan thought Kimberley had seemed secretive. Unwillingly she admitted that Kimberley had stayed out all night before and Joan had been very angry about it. She'd feared Kimberley would turn out a chip off the maternal old block. But she'd never failed to turn up for work. ''She needed the money,'' Joan Oates had said simply.

Joan had told the police one other thing which they'd at first thought might be a lead. Joan had kept all her defaulting daughter's birthday and Christmas cards with their brief, loveless messages, together with their envelopes, in a box. One Sunday morning, she'd found Kimberley sorting through them and making notes on a scrap of paper. She was gathering any information about her mother she could from the scant amount to hand.

Mrs. Oates thought Kimberley may have had some idea of tracing her mother. She'd been alarmed and distressed by the incident and tried to dissuade Kimberley from the idea. She knew her daughter Susan and had a shrewd idea what might happen if Kimberley were successful.

In the event, the police traced Susan Oates. She turned out to be living in Wales and now to be married to a man named Tempest by whom she had two young children. Contacted by the police she was both frightened and furious. Although the police had approached Mrs. Tempest with as much discretion as possible, neighbors had reported their visit to Mr. Tempest, who'd immediately wanted to know what was going on. He had not known that his wife had an illegitimate child elsewhere and took the news badly. Susan claimed she'd seen nothing of her daughter nor did she wish to. Her husband "wouldn't have it." Tempest apparently lived up to his name. The last time she was interviewed, Susan Tempest née Oates was observed to have a black eye.

Kimberley had been just eighteen at the time of her disappearance and therefore of age. Had they been seeking a minor, the police would have pursued matters further. But with no evidence that any crime had been committed, the police report concluded that a young woman had simply chosen to leave home after repeated family rows. Possibly she'd gone to live with a boyfriend. Such things happened every day. She was classed as missing but everyone knew this was a technicality. It was not an offense to disappear. Dozens did so and often for excellent reasons. It was noted that her mother had done the same. The matter was unofficially considered closed although in the absence of Kimberley the file had been left open as a formality.

Markby closed the folder and sat with it in his hands for some time, staring toward the window and the night sky.

*   *   *

An early-morning trawl around the town's dental practices struck paydirt at the third attempt. Kimberley Oates's dental chart had survived and was matched perfectly to the skull's teeth.

"You're lucky!" said the dental nurse involved. "Mr. Gupta's been reminding me to destroy those old files. We don't usually keep them more than five or six years."

So, after all, what had promised to be a long, complex search for the skeleton's identity had been unexpectedly simple, thanks to Simon French and a dental nurse too busy to weed outdated records. Markby told himself that he really must try and rid himself of his absurd prejudice against French. They owed him nothing but gratitude.

They were sure now that Kimberley had not left home voluntarily. She had been murdered. "And someone," Markby said grimly, "ought to have suspected that at the time. Someone missed something."

He sought out Louise Bryce, whom he found snatching a cup of coffee from a drinks dispenser.

She looked puffy-eyed from lack of sleep and set down the plastic cup at his approach with an air of resignation. "I'll go along and see if Mrs. Joan Oates is still at that same address, sir." She nodded toward the Oates file in his hand. "She's not technically the next of kin." Bryce's full lips twisted wryly. "But the girl lived with her and morally speaking, as you might say, Joan is more entitled to be called next of kin than Susan is! We'll get onto the Welsh force to try and trace the mother. I doubt she'll be very pleased to hear from us again!"

Twelve years had passed but probably Joan Oates still hoped her granddaughter was alive. After all, Susan had left home and survived. Poor Mrs. Oates. Twelve years of wondering, blaming herself, no doubt, for having failed first her daughter and then her granddaughter. But it was the police who had failed Joan Oates. Failed to establish the truth behind Kimberley's disappearance and avoid so many years of uncertainty and heartbreak.

"I'll go and see Mrs. Oates myself," Markby announced. He tapped the file. "There's a photograph in here obviously taken on some professional occasion. We'll get hold of our friend Mr. French again and ask him if he can put a name to the other girl in it. We might be able to trace her. Oh, and there's a framed certificate of some sort on the wall behind the table. Get the lab to blow it up and see if they can make out what it is. It's probably nothing to do with this, but we'll have to chase down every little thing. We haven't got much to go on.''

He flipped open the folder and stared down at it morosely. Then he pushed aside the photo of the two waitresses and barman, and slid out the portrait photo of Kimberley. He studied it, frowning. ''What do you make of this one, Lou? This other picture, not the Partytime one. To me it looks as if she's wearing a school uniform.''

Bryce took the photograph. ''It's one of those school photo session jobs, sir. You know, the photographer takes portraits of all the students. He knows nearly every family will buy one. My mother's got one of me at home, just about identical to this one, taken in my last year.''

Markby handed it to her. ''Release it to the media, all of them but especially local outlets, press, TV, the lot. If every student was photographed, one of the others may still be around and the picture may jolt a memory. Ask for it to be put out as a matter of urgency. And don't neglect the nationals. People move away from home these days and may end up anywhere! We really do have to run down anyone who ever knew that girl!''

A twelve-year-old case. Memories dulled by the passage of years. Witnesses scattered to the four winds. Simon French's information had been an unexpected break but they'd be foolish to expect another. Both Markby and Bryce knew the investigation was going to be uphill, all the way.

His glance fell on the plastic cup of cooling coffee Bryce had abandoned. It resembled nothing so much as liquid mud.

''Oh, and Lou!'' he said. ''Go over to the canteen and get yourself a proper breakfast, for goodness sake!''

Six

It was a short road, really only a back lane. It skirted the town center, running behind a public house, a motor spares warehouse and a Chinese takeaway restaurant. Historically it was one of the oldest thoroughfares in the town, a medieval alley, and signs of this could still be seen in the ancient foundations of the cottages which lined one side. Rear access to the commercial premises mentioned above took up the other.

Too narrow for most modern traffic, the lane was left to pedestrians and cyclists. Grass sprouted in the cracks in its surface. Dogs sunned themselves without danger, sprawled across its narrow strip of pavement, or even in the middle of the thoroughfare itself. Cats prowled happily around the refuse bins of the Chinese restaurant and the public house. The rumble of traffic from the main road was muted, swallowed by the jumble of ancient bricks and stone walls, resulting in a self-contained little islet of peace in the middle of the surrounding bustle.

Alan Markby had parked his car at the bottom end of it. He walked slowly along it on foot, taking mental note of traces of the past, such as ancient arches now bricked up, and the disused pump which had once supplied all the water for the dwellers in the lane. At the same time he was examining the cottage doors. He stopped halfway down and checked that he had found the right one. It was a little difficult to tell. There were few house numbers to be seen. Number one was at the end where he'd started and Markby had counted his way along to where he thought he now was. One or two cottages had names like Rose or Laurel, even though neither of these shrubs was in evidence. The postman presumably knew where everyone lived.

He took stock of the cottage which ought to be number seven. It was gray stone with a low roof and tiny windows set in thick walls. Incongruously, it also sported a dish aerial fixed to the front wall. It had no front garden proper, but it was set back a few feet from the lane by a chainlink fence and a strip of untidy grass. A large black cat relaxed on the grass and watched the superintendent with amber eyes, summing him up as he summed up the dwelling. Neither Markby nor the cat looked particularly impressed.

The little dwelling needed considerable investment in time and money to bring it up to a decent standard, all things more fundamental than tacking a dish aerial on the front. Basically it looked sound but nothing had been done for years. The sight of it made Markby feel a little apprehensive.

He'd come to break the sad news to Mrs. Joan Oates and, if she were in a fit state, ask her if she had any idea what Kimberley might have been doing, all those years ago, that had led to her death. But it was borne in on him as he contemplated the house just how long it had been since, as the harbinger of bad news, he'd knocked on the doors of complete strangers. For too long now, others had been left to do this difficult task, whilst he'd sat at a desk. In his eagerness to regain the human contact aspect of his work, he'd overlooked this fact. He ought perhaps to have let someone else do it, someone who still had the knack. Since this was an elderly woman maybe he should have given the task to Louise Bryce. However, he was here and had to get on with it. He hoped he got it right.

Markby walked briskly up to the front door, which was painted lilac. The cat lowered its head and flattened its ears as he passed, and began to lash its tail. It was a long tail with a kink at the end of it denoting some Siamese ancestry. Markby, who knew little about cats although he liked them and admired their intelligence and agility, thought the crooked tail denoted some past injury. "Hullo, puss!" he said as he rang the bell. "Been in the wars?"

The amber eyes closed slowly and reopened, filled with feline scorn.

He was disconcerted when the door was opened by a brisk young Asian woman in jeans and a jade silk shirt. Complicated silver filigree earrings swung at her earlobes against a waterfall of jet-black hair and contrasted oddly with steel-rimmed spectacles. He had disturbed her at study. She held open, and pressed jacket-side outward against her chest, a volume entitled, "Principles and Application of the Law of Torts."

"Are you the builder?" she asked fiercely.

Markby apologized for not being the builder. He didn't need to ask whether she was Joan Oates. Obviously, she wasn't. What's more, as it turned out, she'd never heard of Mrs. Oates or anyone of that name. She and her husband, the pair of them fledgling solicitors, had bought the cottage two years before from some people called Hamilton.

"You could try next door," she said. "Mr. and Mrs. Archibald. They've lived here for years." She shut the door firmly in his face.

Markby retreated, still apologizing, past the cat, which looked smug, or so it seemed to him. Inwardly he was cursing. Twelve years was a long time. People move house. Especially if a particular dwelling holds sad memories. Even a beginner should have thought to check the electoral register before setting out! He proceeded up the short pathway to the door of the next cottage, hoping the neighbor would know where Joan Oates had gone. The thought of returning to base to admit failure to his junior colleagues wasn't to be entertained.

This time a press on the bellpush called forth musical chimes. At first he thought he was going to be out of luck here too. It was some while before anyone answered. He began to fear he'd have to check every cottage in the lane. Then, as he was about to turn away, he heard shuffling footsteps approach. Next came a wheezing sound as if someone were operating a small pair of bellows. The door clicked and swung open, releasing a blast of fetid air into his face.

A large woman with an unnaturally purplish complexion stood before him, quite filling the tiny doorway. Her gray hair was permed into unflattering tight curls. She wore a cotton sweater and a baggy floral skirt with drooping hem. Swollen white legs terminated in broad feet bulging out of flat sandals. Her shapeless bosom heaved beneath the cotton top and her lungs seemed to be creaking as the air was dragged in and forced out. "Emphysema!" Markby thought with some sympathy.

"Yes?" She almost gasped the word and he hoped she wasn't going to have a turn of some sort.

He showed his identification and explained that he had called next door, hoping to find Mrs. Oates, but had learned she'd moved away. "You wouldn't happen to have her address?"

"No, dear . . ." Mrs. Archibald croaked. She put out her hand against the doorjamb. "No one's got that!" She gave a laugh which turned into a cough and another wheeze. "Dead and gone . . ." she gasped.

"What?" Another thing he hadn't thought of! Twelve years was a *very* long time! "Are you sure?"

"Course I am, dear! She died, let's see, nearly five years ago. Just faded away. She was never the same after the girl went missing."

"Kimberley?" Markby seized on her words as a drowning man at the proverbial straw. "You knew Kimberley?"

Mrs. Archibald chuckled hoarsely. "Oh, yes! Little madam! Like mother like daughter, I say!"

"Mrs. Archibald," Markby asked with his most charming smile, "I'm sorry to trouble you. Could I come in and talk to you about Kimberley?"

She eyed him. "All right. This way." Perhaps she didn't receive many visitors. She seemed happy enough to talk to him.

She led him into a small, cluttered sitting room where she indicated a chintz-covered armchair and subsided into its twin. "I'm not too good on my feet," she explained.

He took a look around him as he sat down. The room

was spotlessly clean but filled in every nook and cranny with bric-a-brac. A line of china animals marched across the mantelshelf. A flamenco dancer doll posed coquettishly above the television set. A dozen or more horse brasses were tacked along the blackened oak beam which ran across the ceiling.

Nor was moral guidance lacking. On the wall a piece of polished wood bore the poker-work legend, "Neither a borrower nor a lender be!" Alongside it, a framed sampler, exquisitely worked in tiny cross-stitch, read:

> *From all the enemies of truth*
> *Do thou, O God, preserve my youth,*
> *And keep me through this Vale of Tears*
> *From youthful sins and youthful snares.*

The woman was observing him closely. "My husband's grandma worked that when she were ten year old. Catch a ten-year-old doing embroidery like that now!"

The stitcher had probably ended up blind as a bat at thirty-five through eye-strain was Markby's belief. "This is a nice old place," he said politely.

"Been in my husband's family nigh on a hundred years," she told him proudly. "Archibald, the butcher's."

Markby, who tended to buy his few groceries from a local supermarket and didn't go in for roast joints, wasn't familiar with the shop and looked blank.

"Family butcher in the High Street," she explained. "The business is nigh a hundred years old as well. Been here since the Flood, have Archibalds."

He thought he recalled it now. He had an image of a butcher's shop with a window full of trays of meat, and a pink plastic pig in the middle of it, grinning at passers-by.

"So you'll have known Mrs. Oates well," he said. These old local families, they all knew one another and all the gossip. Perhaps his luck was going to pick up.

"Joan Oates? I knew her forty years. She had no luck. She was left a widow when she wasn't more than twenty-eight or nine. She had a little girl, pretty little thing, Susie. Turned out bad."

"Bad?"

"Loose knicker-elastic," said Mrs. Archibald coarsely.

Markby, to his astonishment, felt himself blush. "I see."

"She had a kid—I'm talking of Susan now. She had the kid when she was about sixteen or so. I told Joan at the time, you get that baby adopted. There's people wanting babies. It'll have a good home. But no, that Susan, she said she wanted to keep the kid. But you could tell from the way she talked about it, it was like a kitten or a puppy to her. She had no sense of responsibility. The baby was a plaything. Kimberley, she called the little thing. She got tired of it and off she went. Left Joan holding the baby, as you might say!" Mrs. Archibald wheezed again, coughed and snorted.

He supposed she had intended to laugh. His original sympathy for the woman had faded and he was beginning to dislike her. He wished he *had* left this job to Louise Bryce. In the stuffy room he was beginning to perspire uncomfortably. He hoped it didn't show.

"What about Kimberley, the baby?"

"Pretty, like her mum." Mrs. Archibald made it sound like a fault. She paused to reflect. "Though she didn't favor Susan so she must have favored her father, whoever he was! She grew up just like her mum, though! Little tart."

A long-case clock in the corner chimed, making Markby start. Mrs. Archibald produced a handkerchief from her skirt pocket and mopped her face. "I can't be doing with warm weather."

Until he'd entered this house, he hadn't found the day particularly warm. It had stopped raining but it was still dull. But now his initial discomfort increased. How airless was the little room, its windows tightly shut, a stale odor permeating everything.

"Did you know any of Kimberley's boyfriends?" he asked doggedly.

Mrs. Archibald sat back in the armchair resting her broad hands on the chintz arms and stared at him. Her eyes were slightly protuberant.

"Secretive, she was. Never told Joan anything. Poor Joan, she used to worry something terrible about that girl.

Thought she was turning out just like Susan had been. I wasn't surprised when she went off. A man, you can be sure.''

"But you wouldn't know which man?"

Again Mrs. Archibald stared at him, breathing heavily. Her massive bosom rose and fell and the faint creak of clogged lungs with it. She must be very ill.

"Could've been anyone, like her mum. She wasn't choosy. And look at that job Kimberley had. She used to go around the big parties and dinner-dances and that with her waitressing. Could've been someone she met at one of those. Anyone at all. Tramps, they were, the pair of them, Susan and Kimberley. It wasn't Joan's fault. She was a respectable woman. She tried hard to bring those girls up decent. But they're all the same, modern girls. No shame. No morals. No respect for their elders. The world's gone to the dogs.''

She squinted, her pop-eyes disappearing into folds of puffy flesh. "Why are you so interested all of a sudden in Kimberley? Must be ten, twelve years ago that she disappeared.''

"Just checking on something," said Markby. He stood up and almost cracked his head on the oak beam. "Thank you, Mrs. Archibald.'' He saw she was struggling to haul herself to her feet and added, "Don't get up! I'll let myself out.''

When he got outside, he found that he was forcing back nausea. The little cluttered sitting room had been claustrophobic but also, in some other way he couldn't quite finger, highly unpleasant.

More than a hundred years of respectable tradesfolk, hardworking, thrifty, devout, and censorious. Narrow lives and narrow minds, he thought, setting off down the lane. Mrs. Archibald's opinion was that the world had changed for the worse. Markby thought that it had probably changed for the better.

Sergeant Prescott had been given the task of contacting Simon French again, with the photograph. To save himself a wasted journey, he took the precaution of telephoning the restaurant first, something his superintendent would have appreciated.

"I wonder if I might come out and see you, Mr. French?"

"What for?" demanded French's voice, instantly suspicious. "I came in and told you all I knew."

"Yes, we're much obliged. It's just that there's something I'd like you to take a look at. It'll only take a few minutes."

"You can't come here!" French objected. "I mean, you're very welcome as a customer, sergeant. In fact, I hope you'll try us! I mean, I'd rather you didn't call professionally. Frankly, that sort of thing causes gossip. Some of my staff are very young. They get silly ideas. They'll make stupid jokes. It'll undermine my authority."

Prescott meditated several answers but confined himself to, "Then could you come here, sir?"

"All right," said French sulkily.

He arrived half an hour later and sat looking martyred as he was shown the photograph of the three Partytime staff, including his younger more innocent self. It was explained what was required of him.

"You are at the moment just about our only lead, Mr. French," said Prescott with a wooden politeness that would have rung false to anyone less self-absorbed than his visitor.

French, mollified and flattered, perked up. "Well, that's Kimberley all right!" He pointed at the plump girl in the picture.

"What about the other girl? Do you remember anything about her? Her name would be helpful."

"I've got a memory for names!" French said smugly. "I reckon I've got what they call total recall!" He tapped the picture. "The other girl was called Jennifer. A foreign surname. Something Polish. Let's see, Jennifer Jurko—no, Jurawicz, pretty sure of it. Jurawicz. She always had to spell it out for people. She was a nice girl." French nodded. "She only worked with us for a short time. She got herself a more permanent, daytime job. I heard, I think I'm right in saying this, that she got married. But I couldn't swear to it."

They let him go. He bolted out of the office and was minutes later seen scorching the surface of the car park as he drove off in a new Porsche.

From the window Prescott observed wistfully, "Let's hope that new speed camera they've got out at Bamford does its stuff. Then perhaps they'll get him for speeding if nothing else!"

Louise Bryce said, "Just pray he doesn't pile himself up on the motorway. He's one of our few leads! Start looking for Jennifer Jurawicz. We ought to be able to find her! How many Polish families could there have been at that time in a town the size of Bamford? French says he thinks she got married. If so, she may have got married at the Catholic church. Ask the priest to check his register. Or the Catholic primary school. She may have been a pupil there. They could still have an address for the family. Is there a Polish club or association? She has to be traceable."

With that, Bryce departed on another line of inquiry, one which took her to Kimberley's former employers.

Bryce had earlier phoned the offices of Partytime Caterers to let them know she was on her way. No one there had offered to save police time by coming over to the incident room. In fact, Bryce had been obliged to make an appointment if she wanted to see anyone at all, after a brief exchange with the director's secretary.

In a shocked voice this person had informed Bryce it was absolutely necessary. "Mrs. Stapleford has a full diary!"

"So've I!" snapped Bryce down the line, but made the appointment.

Partytime was housed in a single-storey prefabricated building on the outskirts of town, positioned between a busy main road and the sports ground of a preparatory school. The school kept itself to itself behind high walls and trees. Not so Partytime which was clearly visible to anyone driving past and had cut down all the shielding trees between it and the road, with or without permission. The firm's name was newly painted on a bright sign by the entry, decorated with a sketchily drawn chef's hat and party-streamers. Pains were being taken to indicate a thriving business was being carried on here. Several cars stood in the car park together with a smart van painted with the company logo. When Bryce got inside the place, there was, besides a pervading odor of curry, an air of brisk efficiency and signs of extensive recent modernization.

This was probably due to the new director, Pauline Stapleford, a lady of indeterminate years and close-cropped, dyed, auburn hair. She had the sort of totally straight, flat-front-and-rear figure which passes for elegant in women of a certain age. Smartly dressed in a tailored, pinstripe suit, beneath it she wore, inadvisedly, a scoop-neck sweater revealing deep "salt-cellars" disguised by a gold-link choker. On scarlet-tipped fingers glittered knuckle-duster rings.

She greeted Bryce with, "Well, Inspector! I can't give you more than ten minutes at the most. I have an appointment with a valued client!"

Bryce gritted her teeth and forced a smile. She could have pointed out that murder investigations carry a certain precedence, but it wouldn't have washed with Mrs. Stapleford. She explained her purpose.

Mrs. Stapleford greeted it with a snort of derision. "Twelve years ago! Look, dear, how much space do you think we've got here to keep old order forms and bills?"

"You might have kept them for tax reference purposes!" Bryce said, growing acerbic. It was the only way to deal with Pauline, she decided.

The director gave a hoot of mirthless laughter. "Seven years, dear, is the recommended time limit on keeping old statements and bills. If we kept twelve years' worth, we'd be up to our bloody necks in bits of paper! Anyway, the firm's changed hands since that time."

"You do have books, though?" persisted Bryce.

"Books?" Pauline gazed at her as if Bryce had suggested ancient artefacts. "Everything's on the computer, dear!"

"I'm actually interested in staff records," Bryce pointed out.

Pauline was growing impatient, glancing at her watch. "Accounts Department has the details of permanent staff

engaged on food preparation. If you want bar staff and
waiters, you have to understand that in this line of work
we use a lot of stand-by personnel. We train them properly,
mind! But they come and go. No one's been with us more
than two or three years. I had a clear out when I took over.''

"I bet you did!" Bryce muttered.

Pauline overheard but took it as a compliment. "That's
right! New brooms sweep clean. I knew what kind of image
I wanted for us and it wasn't a lot of old dears in frilly
pinnies staggering round with the canapés. Bright, sharp,
young! That's what I wanted and that's what I've got. I've
turned this firm right around. It was running at a loss when
I came, now it's in profit. Not many businesses can say that
after such a long period of nationwide recession, can
they?''

It was true. She had a point. Bryce gave Mrs. Stapleford
grudging recognition of her business acumen. "So nobody
here is likely to remember this girl, Kimberley Oates?'' She
brought out the studio portrait of the girl. After Pauline had
given that a dismissive glance, Bryce tried the Partytime
photo of the three youngsters by the buffet table.

That took Pauline's interest and she studied it closely.
"Look at that buffet! That's the sort of thing they were
offering when I took over! Talk about traditional! People
don't go for that now. Well, older people perhaps. And
weddings don't change much. But younger people want
exciting food! We do any kind of evening you want, Ca-
ribbean, Mexican, Greek—you name it.'' She peered at the
picture again and added, "Tsk! You've got to make a real
work of art of the buffet table, not just plonk it all down!
We had a table centerpiece made of coconuts and palm
fronds at the Hawaiian evening we did last week. All real.
Everyone admired it. I don't go for plastic plants. Looks
cheap.''

"I meant you to look at the three people!" Bryce said,
exasperated.

"Wouldn't get away with those untidy hairstyles in any
business I ran!'' said Pauline. "Never seen any of 'em. But
then, I wouldn't. When was this taken, ten, fifteen years
ago?''

"Is there anyone here I could talk to, anyone at all who might have been here twelve years ago. A janitor? A night watchman?"

Pauline handed back the photos. "Night watchman? We use a security firm. They patrol with dogs. Young blokes, ex-army mostly. Some of 'em ex-coppers! I'm sorry I haven't time to offer you coffee, Inspector," She glanced meaningfully at her watch again. "But I can't afford to run late. You can't keep a client waiting. Time's money and being late is lôst orders!"

"It's all right," said Bryce, gathering herself and her photographs together. "Thanks for your help."

Seven

Louise Bryce wasn't the only one having a frustrating morning.

"My view," said Mr. Truelove, "is that we bury the old girl and get it over with!"

Father Holland eyed the solicitor with some disfavor. "The police haven't finished with the Gresham plot."

"I don't know about you," said Mr. Truelove, "but as far as I'm concerned, we can forget about the Gresham plot! We tried to follow Miss Gresham's wishes, but we couldn't, there! I mean, we can hardly bury her in her parents' grave now, can we? Not now someone has found a murder victim in it! Desecration or something, must be. You should know, you're the vicar."

Father Holland sighed and looked around the law office. Metal filing cabinets and a shelf of thick reference books lined the walls. Each and every book held the answers to dozens of questions of law. You looked it up and there it was. Questions of morality, however, conflicts of duty and loyalty: where did you look for answers to those? In your Bible, or your prayer book if you were religious. In your heart, others would say. Your instincts will tell you if something is right. Father Holland's bearded face set in a scowl of frustration.

Mr. Truelove, rocking his chair behind his untidy desk, folded his hands and asked impatiently, "Well?"

84

"What? Oh, yes, well . . . I agree, I suppose. In fact, several parishioners have mentioned it to me. They don't think it quite right that Miss Gresham should be buried in that plot now. There is space in the new cemetery. It will increase the cost of the funeral.''

"Estate can cover it." Truelove glanced down at a hand-written letter lying in front of him. "I've heard from the principal beneficiary, a godson who lives in New Zealand. He won't be coming to the funeral and, as far as I can see, no one is going to be upset if we don't put her with her parents. Who's to know, frankly?''

"Quite. It's just, she wanted it that way," Father Holland protested.

To his own ears the protest sounded naïve. Did Mr. Truelove believe in any form of life after death? Probably not. To argue the case on behalf of someone who'd ceased to exist would be a waste of time. Besides, what the solicitor was saying made excellent sense. It was unrealistic to suppose Eunice Gresham could now be laid to rest with her progenitors. But the dying old lady had held Father Holland's hand in her bird-like grip and asked him especially to see her wish was carried out. Every instinct, his heart if you liked, told him he had to try.

"Anyone can express that sort of wish in a will," the solicitor told him. "But, in the end, how you're buried is up to your heirs. I mean, they've got to make the arrangements. I know old Macpherson when he was here was a great one for fancy wills with pages of codicils and specific bequests. I always tell clients to keep it simple. If you go leaving a diamond ring to someone without specifying which diamond ring, there's hell to pay. Chances are, when that's been decided, no one can find the damn thing and it causes endless trouble. Of course we try to carry all wishes out. We tried to bury the old lady as she wanted. But we couldn't and we have to make other arrangements. When can you do it?''

"Do it? You mean, hold a funeral service?" Father Holland was unable to disguise his annoyance.

"Yes. Let's see.'' Truelove twisted in his chair and studied the calendar behind him. "This coming Monday all right? I'm free."

"I don't know!" Father Holland snapped. He pulled out a diary and riffled through the pages. Unwillingly he said, "Yes, Monday would be possible but it's rather short notice for people who might want to attend."

"No, it isn't," said the practical Mr. Truelove. "She'd have been underground by now if Bill and Ben hadn't dug up a skeleton."

"Denny and Gordon!" snarled Father Holland, refusing to join in the joke.

"Monday it is, then. I'll make a note of it. Tell you what," the solicitor offered generously. "I'll phone round a few people who might be interested in attending, tell 'em of the new arrangements, how's that?"

"Thank you!" snapped Father Holland, his black beard bristling.

"All in a day's line of work," said Mr. Truelove. "Much the same for you, too, I dare say. You'll arrange for the what'stheirnames, the Lowes, to dig out another grave, will you? In the new cemetery. Only make sure they don't give us a repeat performance and dig up another set of bones! Tell 'em to try and find a nice, empty bit of ground."

Father Holland growled. "You're in touch with the funeral directors! You ask them to pass on your messages to Denny and Gordon!"

He stomped out.

On Saturday morning Meredith set out on her own quest. Less a quest, perhaps, than the keeping of a promise.

She'd had time to regret volunteering unspecified help to James Holland. It had been the impulse of a moment and now she was landed with visiting an extremely old lady who, ten to one, wouldn't know who she was, or why she'd come.

But having said she'd do it, she couldn't wriggle out of it. That same evening, at the Holdens', she'd be seeing James Holland and he'd expect some sort of report. Conditioning came into it, too. Several years of having had people rely on her, often when they had no one else to turn to, had made her duty-conscious. She and James probably shared that nagging sense of obligation. She wondered, wryly, if she would have made a good clergy wife. But no, she hadn't enough patience nor, frankly, would several episodes in her past private life have stood up to the necessary scrutiny.

Meredith set out for The Cedars Nursing Home, hoping this would chalk up a few plus points in the heavenly balance sheet, against the many minus ones St. Peter had already recorded under her name.

In fact her reluctance lay less in the visit that lay ahead of her than in one that lay in the past. Westerfield was the first place to which she'd come in the area. Here she'd met Alan. A host of memories, many of them painful, were stirred at the sight of its road sign. The meeting with Alan had turned out as neither of them would have predicted. But so had other things. It was impossible to suppress a twinge of sadness.

But time went by and life moved on. She couldn't avoid the village. She'd come to live in the vicinity of the place and she had driven through it a number of times. She'd always had the urge to put her foot down on the accelerator as soon as she got near it. But not today. Today she was headed there as her goal.

The place hadn't changed much, other than it had acquired a new housing estate on the outskirts. Brick boxes of houses, Meredith thought them, crammed together with little squares of lawn in front of each one and communal parking areas instead of proper garages. It hadn't improved the village. She passed the turning to the former rectory, averting her eyes. But not before she'd spotted a new notice indicating that the house was now a business center run by some commercial firm she'd never heard of. *Sic transit gloria mundi.*

The Cedars was another old house which had been extensively converted and extended to turn it into a private nursing home. Built in the days when land was cheap, it was surrounded by well-kept lawns. In the middle of one grew the tree that had given the place its name.

Meredith got out of her car and leaned against it, arms

folded, to survey the scene. As such places went it looked pleasant enough. It also looked expensive. This was no state-run-on-a-budget place. This was intended for people who either had the money, or whose families could afford to pay for it, to spend their declining years in reasonable comfort.

It still filled her with a sense of reluctance to enter its portals. We all fancy we'll end up differently, she thought. We don't imagine ourselves in institutions, no matter how swanky or well-appointed. Say what you like, once you get inside one of these places, you don't come out again.

The hallway matched the exterior of the house. It was very neat and highly polished. Vases of flowers were strategically placed. An overweening impression of gentility pervaded the place. It was trying hard to pretend it wasn't a nursing home at all, but a sort of residential hotel for the elderly. New arrivals, and their families, probably appreciated the well-meant deception.

A faint odor of boiled vegetables spoiled things a little. A television set could be heard from a day-room, turned up to full volume. These twin intrusions ripped aside the veil of pretence. This was an old people's home, however disguised.

The day matron was a short, stocky woman with a red face and blunt features. In keeping with general policy here, she didn't wear uniform, but a print dress. Her stiff gray hair was brushed straight back and stuck out behind like a wire brush. Meredith thought she looked as if she'd been standing out in a Force 9 gale. The impression was heightened when the lady spoke.

"Hullo, there!" she boomed.

Meredith explained who she was and why she'd come.

"We know about you!" bawled Matron happily. "The padre gave us a bell. Daisy will be chuffed. She likes to see a new face! She's on the veranda."

They passed the day-room on their way. A monstrous television screen was beaming out a totally inappropriate children's program. Three old ladies sat in front of it. Two were talking and ignoring the screen. One had fallen asleep. On the floor by her chair stood a suitcase for no apparent reason. Meredith wondered, in view of the racket from the television set, how either conversation or sleep could be possible.

"They like it on," said Matron in a hoarse whisper. "It makes them feel something's happening. Boredom, you know, is a problem. We get people in to give talks and show films. The padre says you do that sort of thing very well. Couldn't come over and give us a little show, could you?"

"I'll think about it," Meredith said, trying to disguise her alarm.

"Just something short and simple. They tend to fall asleep in the middle of it anyway."

The veranda was enclosed in glass and on the sunny side of the house. A number of elderly persons were dozing in chairs, bearing out Matron's words. One was awake and demanding loudly who had taken her teeth. Meredith began to feel apprehensive again.

"We'll find them in a minute!" Matron assured the owner of the missing dentures as she steered Meredith past.

Daisy Merrill, Meredith was relieved to find, was a sprightly birdlike figure sitting bolt upright in a wicker chair. A colorful crocheted blanket lay over her knees and spectacles were propped on the end of her nose. She appeared to have been reading the newspaper. All the signs were that she still had her wits about her.

"My visitor!" she said, laying aside the newspaper. "How nice of you to come, my dear. James Holland rang us up and told us all about you."

This was a promising beginning. But Meredith was beginning to wonder just what James had told them all. "He's sorry he couldn't come himself. How are you, Miss Merrill?"

"Call me Daisy. Everyone does. I'm very well, thank you. Tell James, I quite understand how busy he must be. It's this horrible murder, isn't it? I've been reading about it."

Daisy rustled the sheets of her newspaper until she found the article she wanted. "It's in here. In the national press, just fancy. They've printed a photograph of the girl."

Perhaps Miss Merrill was one of those people whose interest was in gossip, preferably lurid news. Possibly, if one lived at The Cedars, tales of mayhem and misdeed had an inevitable attraction. Meredith said cautiously, "Yes, it's attracted a lot of interest."

"Not a bad picture," said Miss Merrill with an air of judgment.

Meredith thought the picture looked rather fuzzy and poorly reproduced all round.

"Very good, really," said Miss Merrill in direct contrast. Even more unexpectedly, she added, "Good likeness, I mean."

Meredith felt a twinge of something in the pit of her stomach. "Likeness? How do you know?"

Daisy Merrill folded the paper so that the photo of Kimberley remained on the top. She didn't answer Meredith's question directly.

Instead, she said hesitantly, "I'm rather glad you're here today, because I want to ask someone's advice. I could ask Matron but she's always so busy. Besides, I want an independent view. You look sensible. I'm sure you'll be able to say something practical."

"Ask away, but I don't know if I can help." Meredith settled herself in a chair and tried not to sound too eager. It would be too easy to frighten Daisy off confidences. "What's it about?"

Daisy pushed the newspaper toward her again. "It's the girl, you see." Her wrinkled finger prodded the smudged picture. "I keep wondering if I ought to ask Matron to telephone the police. But I'm afraid I'd just be wasting their time. Only, it does say, in the paper here, they want to talk to anyone who knew her."

"You knew her?" Meredith sat up with a jerk. "Are you sure? I mean, sorry, of course you are. But how?"

"In the first place, because I brought her into the world!"

Daisy's eyes twinkled as she saw the surprise on her visitor's face. "I was a midwife. Didn't James tell you? Obviously not. But then, why should he? I worked most of my professional life in Bamford and round about. I brought a generation into the world, not just little Kimberley.''

"And you kept in touch?'' Presumably Daisy had, since she'd recognized the photo of the teenaged Kimberley.

Daisy's wrinkled hands rested lightly on the newspaper sheet. Her faded eyes looked past Meredith and out, through the windows of the veranda, across the gardens, but seeing things and people that were not out there.

"Delivering so many mothers, one doesn't recall them all. But the Oates family was unusual in several ways. To begin with, the baby's mother, Susan, was so very young. She was only sixteen and the family doctor wanted her to have the baby in hospital. It really wasn't a suitable case for a home birth. But Susan disliked any kind of authority. She was a willful sort of girl and wouldn't listen to any advice. She just said she wouldn't go into hospital and wanted to have her baby at home. So she did.''

"It was a trouble-free birth?'' Meredith asked.

"Oh, yes. If we'd anticipated any problems, we'd have insisted on her going into hospital, but no. Very young mothers often deliver easily. The baby was a little girl, a beautiful child.'' Daisy sighed. "And of course, Susan announced she would keep her.''

The newspaper rustled and slid to the floor. Meredith picked it up and refolded it. Daisy turned to her. "Please don't mistake me! Many single mothers make excellent parents and manage very well. But I could see that Susan wouldn't! She was mature in body but very immature in mind. She had no sense of responsibility and, as I already mentioned, she wouldn't be told anything. Advice went in one ear and out of the other! I saw straight away that the burden of rearing the child would inevitably fall on Susan's own mother, Joan Oates. She was a widow, not young and not robust. It was very unfair.''

Daisy's voice had become grim. "I had quite an argument with a social worker about it. She was for Susan keeping the child. She told me, if you please, that I knew nothing about it and had no business to try and part a young mother from her baby!

"I told the social worker, 'That girl is little more than a

child herself! She has no younger siblings and no idea of
what caring for a baby means. She's accustomed to spend
all her money on herself, music cassettes and the clothes
youngsters like! Self-denial and self-discipline are equally
foreign to her. In time she'll meet other young men. She'll
make relationships which take no account of her having a
child and when she finds the baby is in the way, she'll
abandon it.' And I was right. I was ignored, needless to
say. Susan kept the child and, as I foresaw, in due course
she abandoned it!''

The old lady's voice softened. ''I used to see Joan Oates
around the town, with little Kimberley in her pushchair.
We'd stop and chat and Joan would ask me things about
the baby, minor ailments that worried her and such. Joan
Oates raised the child as best she could. Kimberley was
always clean and well-fed and Joan gave her affection and
a comfortable home. But little Kimberley realized, quite
early on, that she'd been abandoned by her mother and no
one knew her father. It was bound to affect her. She became
very unruly as she grew older. Joan had a terrible time.

''Yet Kimberley was always lovable, with such an endearing little grin. She had a gap in her teeth, here . . .''
Daisy tapped the front of her own dentures. ''And there
was no malice in her. Whenever she saw me in town, she'd
stop and call out, 'Hullo, Nurse Merrill!'. Always cheerful.
She was a bright little thing too, but did badly at school
because of misbehavior. She was, I believe, expelled eventually as being a disruptive influence and for bringing can-
nabis into the school. Poor Joan Oates told me about it,
quite distraught. She said Kimberley was hanging about
town with all the worst elements.''

Daisy shook her head. ''To think the poor girl met such
a dreadful end! But her whole life was so sad. Joan told
me how she used to fantasize.''

''Tell lies?''

Daisy gave her a reproachful look. ''One should always
be careful before accusing a child of lying. They do, of
course! But often it's imagination running riot. They believe the story, although in another way they know it's not
true. Children who've been abandoned, like poor little Kim-

berley, often fantasize about their background, invent rich parents who've died in airplane accidents, that sort of thing. It's quite normal.''

''And this is what Kimberley did?''

''I don't recall exactly everything she told people. It would get back to Joan eventually and Joan had always to deny it. Nothing about an airplane, anyway. I was just using that as an example.'' Daisy's eyes grew absent as her memory wrestled with the past. ''It was a long time ago.''

''If you could try and remember some of Kimberley's fantasies?'' Meredith begged. ''There might have been a grain of truth in some of them.''

''I should think that extremely unlikely!'' Daisy gave a little chuckle. ''Let's see. She claimed her mother was an actress and always on tour. That showed originality, didn't it? But mostly she talked about her absent father. Yes, that was it. A rich father, needless to say, who couldn't own her because of some taradiddle. He was entirely invented, I need hardly tell you! She was due to inherit a fortune one day, that was another story. Also entirely invented. Her father lived in a fine house and she used to visit him! Poor little thing! Such a pathetic tale! Oh, and one day, he would come and claim her and take her away with him. That is a favorite fantasy with unhappy children. He never would, of course. He never would. Perhaps he didn't even know she existed. I dare say he was only someone her mother met in a public house one evening!''

The old lady sat up straight. ''I do recall this—just before she ran away, no, she didn't run away, did she? We know that now. Just before she disappeared, then, I met Kimberley in the town. She was anxious to stop and chat. She asked me if I knew anything about her mother. I got the impression she was keen to find her. I couldn't tell her anything and I rather hoped she wouldn't pursue the matter. But of course, when I heard Joan had reported her missing, I assumed Kimberley had gone in search of Susan. I was very sorry. I just hoped she didn't find Susan. She'd have got no welcome there!''

Daisy sighed. ''Kimberley had a sweet nature. Susan, her mother, was just a trollop! A deceitful, conniving little madam with a vicious streak! Harsh words, perhaps, but true.''

There was a pause while Daisy dwelt on this for a moment. Then she said, ''She worked as a waitress.''

''That was Kimberley,'' Meredith said. ''Who worked as a waitress, not Susan.''

''I know it was Kimberley,'' said the old lady. ''That's what I said.'' She frowned. ''Didn't I?''

''Daisy,'' Meredith said, ''I'm sure the police would love to hear about all this. I've a friend who's a policeman. May I tell him?''

''Of course you can, my dear!'' Daisy wagged a crooked finger at her. ''But warn him, I really can't tell him anything of any real use in a murder inquiry! But I do hope they find out what happened to Kimberley.

''Now then,'' she reached out to a nearby push-button bell. ''That's more than enough on such a sad subject. I'll ask them to bring us some tea and you can tell me all about yourself! James Holland told us you were a great traveler! So let me hear all your adventures!''

Eight

"I was at Westerfield this afternoon," Meredith said as they drove down the narrow road on Saturday evening.

It was blessedly mild. The damp countryside had mellowed in the soft light of a sun low in the sky. So much recent water had promoted growth. The hedges were thick with leaf. They had sheltered the verges from chemical spraying and the reward was wayside banks of wild grasses and plants.

Probably, Meredith reflected silently, now the holiday was cancelled the weather would change for the better. That was life for you.

"What took you out there?" Markby slowed as they passed a horse and rider. The rider raised a hand in acknowledgement.

Was it concentration on this traffic maneuver that made Alan's voice sound terse? Or just her imagination? There was always a certain awkwardness between them when Westerfield was mentioned. She took a surreptitious glance sideways at him. He was staring, very commendably, at the road ahead.

She had an impulse to shout, "I wasn't digging up old memories!" Instead she told him about Daisy Merrill and her connection with the Oates family. Alan gave a snort which sounded sarcastic.

"That bears out the original report of Kimberley's disappearance. Like mother, like daughter! Only Kimberley put it about with a little more charm. The main thing to emerge from Daisy's tale, from our point of view, is that Kimberley appears to have been an inventive liar!''

"Fantasy, so Daisy says. There's a difference. She's very clear about that!''

"Daisy may call it what she wishes! As a copper, I call it an untruth. What it means is that anything we learn Kimberley told a third party may be fantasy, as you call it. That's all we need, really. The deceased was a congenital liar!''

Meredith felt aggrieved that her discovery of Daisy Merrill hadn't been better received. "At least I found someone you could interview! Suppose I hadn't gone to see her? She might not have asked Matron to phone you. Or Matron might have talked her out of it! You should see Matron. She's a sort of female Captain Cuttle!''

"We appreciate it. All right, I'm grateful!'' He glanced at her. "I am, really. It does all help. And it's encouraging that you found Daisy so soon. With Simon French that makes two people who've volunteered knowledge of Kimberley. She's obviously still remembered.''

"Do you think there might have been anything in her tales of a rich father? After all, Susan might have told Joan Oates in confidence who Kimberley's father was.''

"She might have done, but I doubt it. It seems to me that Joan Oates was the old-fashioned sort. If she'd known who the father of her grandchild was, she'd have wanted him named. So that he didn't get away with it, that sort of attitude! He may have been married, of course. But still, when Kimberley disappeared I'm sure Joan Oates would have told the police the father's name if she'd known it. She did suggest Kimberley might be trying to find her mother. But not her father. That suggests to me no one knew for sure who the father was, not even Susan.''

They rounded a bend in the road and a clump of trees appeared ahead of them. "We must be nearly there," Meredith said.

"Two minutes. The house is tucked away, but there's a clearly marked entrance. This used to be all woodland on this side of the road. It was cleared some time ago. Those trees are all that's left.''

''You've been to the Holdens' house before, obviously.''

Markby mumbled something she didn't catch. More clearly, he added, ''A few times. A couple of years back they held a fund-raising fête in the grounds. You know the sort of thing. Tombola, potted-plant stall, homemade cakes, teas, guess how many beans in a jar, mini dog-show. The local police mounted a road safety stand and a Neighbourhood Watch exhibition. The St. John's Ambulance demonstrated first aid. The Air Training Corps' band played. It was very well attended. Margaret Holden organized it. She roped me in to present some of the prizes and draw the winning raffle ticket. She runs that kind of thing well. I believe they raised quite a large sum of money.''

''She seems a capable woman. That's helpful for Lars, I suppose. Is that what we call him, Lars?''

''What else? He'll greet you as Meredith and be full of bonhomie. He's a politician. You're a voter. Don't, whatever you do, let him draw you into a discussion on the future prospects for Bamford.''

Meredith grinned at him. She pushed back a lock of rebellious brown hair. What to wear had been the subject of much agonized decision-making. It wasn't every evening one dined with one's MP. She'd settled for black crêpe silk pants and tunic top, black tights and black high heels. The ensemble had struck her as a little funereal when she'd put it all on and stared critically into the mirror, so she'd added a string of chunky turquoise-colored beads. It would have to do.

''You sound as if you don't like our MP very much!'' she said.

Markby slowed at another bend in the winding single-track lane and was a moment before answering. ''I've got nothing against the fellow. He's not a bad sort, maybe even better than most! Ambitious, naturally. But aren't they all? No, it's—'' He paused again. ''Why don't you wait until you meet him?''

They were passing a pair of cottages. One was well kept, the windows sparkling in the evening sun, the garden immaculate, an equally highly polished, well-maintained car parked at the side.

The other garden was overgrown with weeds and the dwelling appeared abandoned despite grimy curtains at the unwashed panes.

Markby slowed again and turned into a gate. Meredith hadn't noticed that they were so near to the house. It was set well back from the road and disguised by a high stone wall and the trees she'd spotted from afar. Now she gave a gasp of surprise and pleasure.

The Old Farm was well named. It was a large building with an uneven roof and walls that bulged so that the whole thing seemed about to lurch to one side. Its timber frame hadn't a right-angle in it. Its windows were all at different levels and in a variety of styles. And yet it seemed so solid and immovable in the shadows cast by the setting sun that it looked good for another four hundred years or so. Nearby what had obviously been a barn or stables had been converted into garaging.

"I'd expected it to be built in stone as so many of the other old buildings around here are," she said.

Markby, too, had been sitting behind the wheel staring thoughtfully at the old house. "James is here already," he said. "We aren't late, are we?" He pointed toward a motorcycle by the front door.

Oscar greeted them. He had heard the car and was waiting, tail wagging in greeting at one end while his booming bark warned off potential intruders at the other. However, a sniff at Meredith's hand seemed to tell him he'd met this one before and Markby was recognized as a welcome old friend. The visitors' credentials checked, Oscar bounced cheerfully ahead of them into the main reception area.

That was a better description than to call it a room. It was formed out of an entry hall together with the well of a staircase and a large recessed area to one side. It was comfortably furnished. Its uneven oak-plank floor creaked gently beneath their feet and was waxed to a mellow sheen. Wool rugs of geometric pattern in tawny oranges, black and white were scattered across it. They suggested a Scandinavian origin.

James Holland was seated by the large open fireplace and rose to his feet as they entered. A smart, military-looking man did the same. A middle-aged woman in a lilac floral-patterned silk suit, presumably his wife, smiled nervously.

Margaret Holden had come forward to greet them in competent welcome. She, too, had chosen to wear black and with her fair hair presented a striking image. Yet Meredith thought that she looked somehow strained. She wondered whether Mrs. Holden had had some bad news during the day. Her smiles and cheerful words carried the hint of effort. Meredith regretted her own choice of black. Two of them in somber hue gave the scene a look of a wake, or, at the very best, a parents' evening at a school run by nuns.

"You already know James!" Margaret said briskly. "But not Major and Mrs. Walcott. Ned and Evelyne are tireless workers in the cause!" She smiled brightly.

Ned and Evelyne murmured deprecatingly. Hands were shaken. Ned informed them that he and Evelyne had walked over. It was such a pleasant evening after all the rain they'd had lately. They lived in one of the cottages "on the roadside, before you get to the gates." Meredith felt there was no need to ask which one.

James Holland, crammed into a suit obviously bought when he was a few pounds lighter, muttered to her, "Thanks for going along to see Daisy. She enjoyed your visit immensely. Matron hopes you'll go back again. Give them all a little talk."

"Don't promise anything on my behalf, James. I might, but I need time to psyche myself up to it!"

"I hope," their hostess said, when they'd been supplied with drinks, "that Lars isn't going to be late." For a second the air of competence slipped and she sounded fretful. "He promised me he'd be here at lunchtime. Then at the last minute, he phoned to say something had happened to delay him, but he'd be here by seven without fail." She glanced at her gold wristwatch. "It's seven-fifteen!" she murmured, more to herself than to them.

There was a moment's embarrassment. That Margaret Holden, beneath her sophisticated manner was uneasy, even tense, was obvious. The Walcotts exchanged glances, a marital semaphore which hinted that they knew the reason.

Ned cleared his throat and began to expound on the virtues of the local golf-course. After a while, finding he wasn't among *aficionados* of the game, he faltered. Father Holland took up the conversational challenge, albeit in slightly disconcerting fashion.

"We're burying Eunice on Monday!" he said suddenly. "Forgot to tell you, Margaret."

"Oh? The police have finished with the—the site in the old churchyard then?" Margaret glanced at Markby.

"No, putting her in the new cemetery. Pity. Solicitor thought it best."

"I shall certainly attend!" she said firmly. "And so will Lars!" To the others she added, "She was so interested in Lars's career!" A slight frown crossed her forehead. "It's not a private funeral, is it? It will be all right to come along?"

"Certainly!" said the vicar. "No family to attend. Won't be many there."

"I shall be there," Markby said. "In the circumstances."

"Investigating officer!" said Major Walcott wisely, nodding.

Evelyne squeaked. "Oh, yes, the skeleton! Are you—?"

"Evelyne!" intoned her husband. "He can't talk about it."

"Oh, no, sorry, of course not!" She blushed deeply and cast Markby a confused look.

"As it happens," Markby said, "I knew Miss Gresham years ago. I'd like to pay my last respects." He smiled at her and she became even more confused.

Oscar, who had been wandering around in a desultory manner, now attracted attention by a low bark. He was standing at the far end of the hall, ears pricked. A car engine coughed and fell silent. Oscar immediately became very excited, squeaking and running around in circles, his claws rattling on the polished floorboards.

"It's Lars!" Margaret couldn't disguise her relief. "Oscar knows the sound of his car. It's Lars, Oscar!" she added to the dog, which increased his excitement to fever pitch. He began to whine and yelp.

There was a sound of voices and the front door opened. Bodies filled the entry. A young, solidly built, fair-haired man came in with something of a rush.

"Good evening, everyone! So sorry to be late! Traffic, you know!" He bestowed a peck on his mother's cheek. "Sorry, Ma! Hullo, Oscar, yes, yes, old chap, I've seen you!" He stooped and patted the dog. Then he turned to usher forward a leggy, slightly horsy brunette who had been standing behind him.

"May I introduce you all to Angie, my fiancée? Angela Pritchard!" He beamed.

Margaret Holden said quietly, "I hadn't realized—how nice to see you again, Angela!"

"She's come down for a few days, Ma!" said Lars so defiantly that Markby's eyebrows rose and the Walcotts engaged in another exchange of the semaphore.

Angela Pritchard said loudly and confidently, "Hullo, everybody!"

She moved forward, Lars at her side. Holden began to introduce the others to her and, in the case of Meredith, to introduce himself as well. He exuded a fussy competence and appeared rather red in the face. Angie Pritchard, cool as a cucumber, shook hands and smiled in the gracious way associated with the wives of dignitaries. There was, thought Meredith with some amusement, a touch of the ambassador's lady about her. Together she and Lars had made quite an entrance.

Yet what was happening wasn't amusing. For Lars and Angela, by their joint maneuver, had contrived to leave Margaret Holden alone on the edge of the throng with nothing to do.

She stood there for a moment, Oscar at her side, then muttered abruptly, "I'll go and tell Doris to set another place!" She moved rapidly to a door at the back of the hall. Oscar, after a tiny hesitation, seemed to make a decision on his loyalties and trotted smartly after her. Perhaps he thought it best to ally himself with whoever had charge of the kitchen.

It was a curious, somehow symbolic moment. Father Holland had noticed it, too. He murmured, "Oh dear!" but so that only Meredith heard him. She met his eye. "The queen is dead!" he whispered. "Long live the queen!"

The dining room at The Old Farm was long and narrow. A stone fireplace at the far end looked down the room toward the door by which they'd entered. The table ran parallel with the long walls. An antique and exceptionally solid piece, it was notched and scored, black with age and polish. It suggested origins in a refectory or wooden ship of the line.

The initial unease in the atmosphere had faded. It was an excellent dinner and Lars, now in full swing, was an excellent host. Meredith, studying him more closely, thought that he was a good-looking young man in a rather heavily built way. He might possibly have been an athlete when in his teens but muscle was now just beginning to turn to fat. He'd have to watch that, she thought.

Perhaps his fiancée would insist he went on a diet. Angie Pritchard presented a more intriguing source of study. No beauty when examined feature by feature, she nevertheless managed to exude an air of glamor. It was a question of style and confidence, Meredith decided, to say nothing of being expensively well-dressed. The excellent cut and condition of the brunette hair certainly owed much to the hand of one of the more fashionable hairdressers. She'd chosen to wear bright royal blue.

"Thank goodness," Meredith thought, "that Angie hasn't worn black too!"

She noticed that Angie was being exceptionally attentive to Major Walcott. The good major wasn't insensible to Miss Pritchard's charms. He'd grown quite loquacious.

Father Holland was talking energetically to Margaret Holden. Alan had not contributed much to any conversation. He seemed instead to be interested in the wall above the fireplace. Eventually Lars noticed his preoccupation.

"Interested in that painting, Alan? I think my father picked that up in a second-hand shop somewhere, didn't he, Ma?"

"In Bournemouth," said Margaret Holden tonelessly. "In the early years of our marriage."

"It's quite a nice Victorian seascape. Unknown artist. We had a chap from Sotheby's look at it once. No great value but still fetch a reasonable sale-room price," Lars went on.

"Your father liked it for what it was," his mother said a trifle coldly. "Not for its value."

"Quite. Well, I like it too!" Lars was unfazed.

"And the certificate there, just by it?" Markby asked casually.

"What? Oh, good lord! That's one of my childhood achievements. A piano exam."

"It's your Grade Seven!" Margaret's voice was sharper. "Lars was a very promising pianist. But of course, there wasn't the time to practice, not once he became interested in politics as a student."

"My mother's very musical," said Lars.

"Do you play, Miss Pritchard?" Evelyne Walcott asked ingenuously.

"Afraid not. I'm very fond of the opera."

"Oh, the opera? How lovely. But a pity you don't play," murmured Evelyne, "if you like music."

Meredith warmed to Mrs. Walcott. It never did to underestimate those dowdy little women. They could turn the tables neatly if they wished and Evelyne had done just that. Uppity Angie Pritchard had been impeccably put down.

It was impossible, Meredith thought, not to feel that battlelines were being drawn up here and alliances decided. It was all rather like the board game "Diplomacy." The players weren't passing notes to one another but the messages were there. Evelyne Walcott, like Oscar, was loyal to Margaret Holden. Major Walcott was being wooed successfully by Angie. When the Walcotts got home that night, however, Evelyne might reverse that.

Angie was casting her net further than the Walcotts. When Meredith emerged from the bedroom set aside for the ladies as a cloakroom, later that evening, she found Angela Pritchard at the top of the stairs. She guessed Lars's fiancée was lying in wait for her.

"Everything all right, Meredith?"

"Fine, thanks. Lovely old house."

"Yes, isn't it?" Angie smiled on her. "Seen round it?"

"No—but perhaps we ought—" Clearly Meredith was about to be offered a guided tour. But Angie, even if she was Lars's fiancée, wasn't yet mistress of The Old Farm. It wasn't for her to display Margaret Holden's home to an outsider.

Angie cut short any suggestion that they should return downstairs and rejoin the others. "Let me at least show you the secret chapel!"

That sounded too tempting to be refused. Meredith allowed Angie to lead her along the corridor and around a corner. Here they stopped, facing the wooden doors of some kind of cupboard. To the left a narrow staircase ran down to regions unseen. Once upon a time, housemaids had toiled up and down these "back stairs." Angie pulled the cupboard doors open. A row of winter clothes, shrouded in plastic for the summer months, hung before them. There was a faint odor of ancient mothballs.

Angie grinned at Meredith conspiratorially and pushed the clothes aside. Behind them was another door in the back of the cupboard.

It led into a further room, windowless and very small, but equipped with a ceiling light which Angie switched on.

This must be one of the oldest parts of the building. The ceiling was curved in the surviving remnants of ribbed vaulting which must be concealed by a false flat ceiling elsewhere on this floor. Traces of faded paint showed that the ceiling had been decorated in pictorial style. Meredith could just make out foliage and the outlines of a pair of figures. Installing the electric light had wrecked part of the ribbing in an act of unforgivable iconoclasm.

"Adam and Eve!" Angie pointed up at the faded figures. "In the garden of Eden, but about to be expelled. Over there you can just see the arm of the avenging angel carrying the flaming sword. The angel's body's been scraped off or flaked away. This was all under whitewash but Lars's father uncovered it. He was interested in history. In Tudor times the house belonged to a family true to the Old Religion. They stayed so right through to Stuart times, including during the Commonwealth when Roundheads came and occupied the place but never found this little chapel. The family died out in Georgian times and the house has changed hands frequently since then.''

''It's fascinating . . .'' Meredith said slowly. It was also sad. What stories these old walls could tell! And what a turbulent family history had been lost! Why had the expulsion from Eden been chosen as decoration for the ceiling? Surely with symbolic relevance to the political situation of the early seventeenth century.

The tiny room wasn't empty. An ancient sofa stood by one wall. There was just enough room for it. There was also an old-fashioned hat and coat stand, more pictures, dusty and stacked against a wall, and a box containing bric-a-brac.

Meredith pulled her attention back to the present. ''Thank you for showing it to me, Angie!'' She meant it. ''But we really ought to go back now. They must all be wondering where we are!''

Angie had achieved her purpose. ''Of course!'' she said cheerfully.

''I see what you mean about Lars Holden,'' Meredith remarked as they drove away from The Old Farm. The evening had continued until late. It was now nearly one in the morning. ''And why you were keen not to prejudice any judgment I might make.''

''So, what judgment did you make?''

She bit her lip. ''He came across as a pleasant sort of man. But he oughtn't to have treated his mother like that. I didn't like that at all.''

The headlights cut through the solid black of a country night, briefly illuminating verges, hedges, roadside trees. Alan Markby, thoughtful at the wheel, murmured, ''No, I didn't like it, either.''

After a moment he added, ''But I can see how it's happened. Margaret Holden is a strong-minded person and she isn't one to step aside meekly and let another woman usurp what she clearly sees as her place. Lars's career has been her whole life. It's not just a question of gaining a daughter-in-law. It's more like being sacked and seeing the office junior promoted in your place. I dare say her attitude has made it difficult for her son and Miss Pritchard. But he shouldn't have humiliated Margaret in front of her guests, and he shouldn't have let Angie Pritchard do it.''

''Margaret has forced him to choose between them and he was telling the world he's chosen Angie, is that what you mean?'' Meredith wriggled in her seat. She was beginning to doze. She pushed sleep away.

''Something like that.''

''Out of the frying pan and into the fire, then! Angie strikes me as being the same sort of dominant female his mother is. Perhaps he likes having these strong women organize him. Yet I wouldn't have thought he was a weak man.'' Meredith frowned in the darkness.

''It doesn't have to be weakness. It could be a kind of laziness. 'If she's so keen, let her get on with it!' That kind of thing.''

''Angie showed me the secret room while we were upstairs after dinner. Have you seen it?''

''I've heard about it, but no, never seen it. Is it really hidden? How big is it?''

''About the size of an old-fashioned walk-in broom cupboard. Not much more. They seem to use it as a lumber-room. It's hidden away all right. The entrance is through another cupboard which forms a sort of false front.''

''Hm. Kimberley Oates was in that house on at least one occasion, you know.''

That snapped Meredith into immediate wakefulness. She sat bolt upright and was tugged back by her seatbelt. ''What! How do you know?''

''Let's say I'm ninety percent certain. I'll know for sure, I hope, on Monday morning. I recognized the lay-out of the dining room from a publicity photo put out by Partytime Caterers. It shows Kimberley, Simon French and another girl.''

''Caterers? They must have held a number of large parties in that house over the years. So Margaret called in a firm of caterers from time to time. It doesn't have to be significant.''

"I realize that. But Partytime is the only channel through which I can learn about Kimberley's movements in the last months of her life. I have to run down any sighting. We're still looking for her mother. She's moved from her previous Welsh address. But she's unlikely to be any help. The last time she was contacted, twelve years ago when Kimberley disappeared, her sole concern was to avoid scandal and any threat to her marriage. We don't know how she'll take the news that her daughter is dead. Perhaps even with relief."

"She sounds a pretty lousy mother."

"She was only sixteen when Kimberley was born and, reading between the lines of what Daisy told you—supposing Daisy to be correct—Susan was something of a spoiled brat. Still, it was awkward for her when Kimberley went missing and the police turned up on her doorstep in Wales to ask if she'd seen her. Her husband at that time— he may still be—hadn't known his wife had a baby from a previous relationship. She was afraid for her marriage. When people are motivated by fear they often behave in a way which looks, to others, bad."

And sometimes out of character to the extent that they lose their heads entirely, he thought.

After a moment Meredith said, "If you really are going to that Gresham funeral on Monday, I'll come with you."

He glanced sideways at her. "Fine. I'll collect you at your house a little before eleven."

They were entering the outskirts of Bamford. The first posts of street lights formed a guard of honor and Alan dipped his headlights. On this side of town a new light-industrial estate had sprung up. Its arrival had been greeted with mixed feelings in the town. It brought much-needed employment, but its modern, utilitarian workshops, warehouses and offices struck a jarring note in the landscape and had meant the loss of fields and ancient woodland. Lars Holden, Meredith remembered, had been much involved in setting up this development. Jobs were votes.

Perhaps Alan's memory had also been jolted by the sight of the gaunt sheds and blocks with their empty windows and eerie, fluorescent security lighting flickering on abandoned desks and worktops.

Moodily, he observed, "Lars Holden is full of good intentions. But, as the saying goes, the way to hell is paved with those!"

Meredith leaned her head against the seat rest. She was recalling the woodland Alan mentioned as sold off by the Holdens. Perhaps Lars had got more than votes out of the development scheme. Ten years ago land values had been sky-high in this part of the world. Who had owned this land where the industrial units now stood?

"He's not altogether what he first seems, is he?" she said slowly. "I mean, he comes over on first impression as a bluff, open sort of chap. Actually, he's more complex than that. Politics must call for a certain deviousness. I wonder if Angie realizes it."

They turned into Station Road where Meredith's modest terraced cottage stood.

Alan said suddenly, "I wonder what Margaret will do about this business of a rival. She isn't the sort of woman to do nothing." He switched off the engine. "Watch your back, Angie Pritchard!"

"Her problem, not ours!" Meredith said firmly.

They didn't get so much time together that they could waste it worrying about Lars and his formidable womenfolk.

"I like this outfit," he said later, of the black crêpe.

Meredith, stepping out of it, paused. "I think it makes me look like a nun."

"Believe me, I've never been turned on by the sight of a nun. But you in that, yes. And the black stockings."

"I thought Angie looked very glamorous."

"The grim Pritchard? Not a chance . . ."

Some time later, Meredith said into the darkness, "This case, it's one of those special ones, isn't it, the ones you feel deeply about."

The bed creaked and moved as Alan sat up. He reached over to the bedside table to pick up his watch and squint at the illuminated dial. She could see the outline of his head and shoulders, etched dark against the window blind. He dropped the watch but remained sitting up. The duvet moved as he crooked his knees and rested his arms on them.

"I suppose it is. It's a Bamford murder. It happened twelve years ago. I'd just arrived here then, so it happened on my patch while I was in overall charge. Having said that, I didn't have anything to do directly with the inquiry at the time. I'm not saying that the people who handled it didn't do a good job or that I'd have done any better. They did everything they could. They quizzed the grandmother about the girl's habits and ran to earth the mother who'd abandoned the kid when she was a baby. They found nothing to suggest a crime had been committed. Teenage runaways aren't rare. The girl had been quarrelling with her grandmother and we now know she was pregnant."

He scowled. "But it wasn't an ordinary runaway case. It was a murder and there must have been something which was missed, some clue, so small or apparently so ordinary that no one saw it. It oughtn't to have happened. Now I'm being given a chance to put things right. Second chances don't come along too often in police work."

They don't come along too often in any walk of life, Meredith thought. She had been presented with an unexpected second chance. A chance of a relationship which was something more than superficial. Alan also. They were both almost painfully aware of it, almost afraid to believe such good luck had come their way.

She didn't want anything to upset the apple cart now, but it seemed the police work always hovered, threatening to disrupt things. She wondered if he knew how much she resented it. How ashamed she was that she did so, because it was important, both as a job and to him personally. But she did resent it. Margaret Holden saw Angie Pritchard as a rival. Meredith too had a rival. The name changed with the case under investigation, but the unseen presence of a victim was always there, taking first call on Alan's attention. Just now the rival was called Kimberley Oates.

Meredith reached out in the dark and ran the tip of her finger down his spine. The bare skin felt damp to the touch. Duvets were always too warm in the summer. He turned toward her, propped on his elbow, and said, "It's your annual leave which this has wrecked. I'm well aware of it. I'm sorry.''

"Told you, can't be helped. Doesn't matter.''

He stooped over her and kissed her. "Well, thanks, anyway.''

"Some things matter more,'' she said, putting her arms around him.

Denny and Gordon Lowe had been enjoying their Saturday night in their usual fashion, which was to eat their supper around six-thirty. Later, around eight-ish, they'd go to the nearby pub and sit there drinking silently until ten.

Gordon was the cook and housekeeper in their spartan household. In reality the Lowes were not poor. They were bachelors and both in long-term employment, quite a bit of it cash-in-hand and unknown to the tax authorities. They lived in a cottage which their father had bought at the close of the last war for a hundred pounds.

However, Gordon's ideas on home management came from his mother and by descent from her mother and very likely her mother before that. They hadn't changed as they'd been passed on from one generationto another. They remained those of the impoverished rural working class. Add to that an inherited reluctance to spend any money, even if they had it, for fear of falling on hard times later on, and the pattern of the Lowes' lifestyle was set. Tight-fistedness was seen as a virtue.

Thus they went shopping for the week's supplies late on a Saturday when fresh produce was often reduced in price. That way, they bought a large joint of meat for around two-thirds of the price. They also bought a sack of potatoes, cabbages and carrots, all cheap. Other purchases were bacon and sausages, the strongest cheese they could find, and a large economy-sized tub of margarine. Perishables were stored in their elderly throbbing refrigerator, except for the meat.

That was stored in an ancient meat-safe, a metal cupboard with a perforated door which was nailed to the larder door in the draft from the window, and always surrounded by curious bluebottles. Meat put in a fridge, they reckoned, lost its flavor. Say what you like, their joint of beef always had plenty of flavor, and frequently quite a high smell as well.

On Sundays, Gordon produced the roast joint with roast potatoes and boiled cabbage and carrots. They never bothered with afters except at Christmas when they bought a pre-cooked Christmas pudding. In this they deviated from their mother's pattern in that she had been a dab hand at boiled suet puddings tied up in a cloth to be turned out, sliced, and doused with syrup or jam and Bird's custard.

On Mondays and Tuesdays the Lowes ate the remains of the Sunday joint, forced through the clumsy old hand-operated metal mincer bolted to the kitchen table, or just hacked cold into slices, with the left-over vegetables fried up in bacon grease. By Wednesday, this Sunday fare was all gone and they existed for the rest of the week on some combination of the bacon, sausages and cheese, with plenty of thick-cut bread.

A modern nutritionist would have deemed their diet shockingly high in fat and low in fresh vegetables. It was virtually non-existent in fruit except when a neighbor gave them a bag of "fallers." But Denny and Gordon had survived well enough on it all their lives. They put it down to an outdoor life spent in physical hard work digging graves, together with a little jobbing gardening on the side.

Their supper tonight consisted of sausages and fried potato. They sat side by side to eat before their television. They were watching a game show. The hysterical contestants were winning luxury prizes which were totally irrelevant to the Lowes' way of life: holidays in Las Vegas, powerful cars, cases of champagne, gigantic stuffed toys too big for any child to play with, dishwashers and microwave ovens. The Lowes watched all these consumer items pass across the screen, exulted over by the game-show host in his midnight-blue jacket, his blond pneumatic assistant at his side. Each tinsel-bedecked display was greeted with squeals and shrieks by the unseen audience and in total silence by the Lowes.

After a while Gordon asked, not taking his eyes from the

screen, "Reckon the police will get to the bottom of it, then?"

"Couldn't say." Denny picked up the bottle of tomato ketchup and upended it over his plate.

"Reckon I knows," said Gordon, putting a forkful of potato into his mouth.

The winning contestant on the screen burst into tears of joy over a trip for the whole family to EuroDisney. The studio audience roared approval.

"So do I," said Denny.

The tomato ketchup was slow to come out of the bottle. Denny grunted and struck the bottom smartly with the heel of his hand. Red sauce shot out in a thick mass and smothered his sausages in gore. Undeterred he began to mop up the scarlet mess with a hunk of bread.

"Reckon it's true, then? What they used to say?"

"Oh, aye." Denny's sharp little stoat's eyes gleamed and his mouth, smeared round with scarlet, twisted into an unlovely grin.

Nine

Louise Bryce and Sergeant Prescott were engaged in one of those desultory, early Monday, exchanges of conversation which inaugurate the new week in almost any office in the world. To their considerable alarm, Superintendent Markby burst through the door on one side of the room. They had just time to notice he was wearing a dark suit and a black tie before he bore down on them.

"Good morning! Everyone got time to stand about chatting today, have they? Have we traced either Susan Oates Tempest or Jennifer Jurawicz? If not, why not?"

"I called around to the presbytery," said Prescott hurriedly. "Father Dooley is checking their marriage register."

"So give him a call and ask him to hurry it along! Did you get that photo blown up by the lab?" he demanded of Bryce. "The Partytime one."

"Yessir!" Bryce, startled, began to shuffle the papers on her desk.

"Bring it into my office!" Markby swept past them and disappeared out of the door on the further side, down the corridor and into his own private sanctum.

"Blimey!" mumbled Prescott. "He's on the warpath this morning, isn't he?"

"You just get on the blower to the Welsh police!" Bryce told him severely. "And find out if they've got a lead on Susan Tempest. Or she may be calling herself Susan Oates again, remember, if her marriage has broken up. Tell 'em to get a move on!''

"Yes, ma'am!" said Prescott meekly.

Bryce put the two versions of the photographic enlargement sent across from the laboratory on Markby's desk, side by side. One was a general enlargement. The other was a more detailed print showing the framed certificate on the wall which Markby had noticed when he first saw the picture.

The superintendent searched irritably through the top drawer of his desk. "A magnifying glass! There must be one in here somewhere! Even Sherlock Holmes had a magnifying glass! I suppose I've got a computer I hardly use and nothing so simple and useful as—ah, here it is!''

He pored over the second of the two enlarged photos as Bryce waited patiently. Markby straightened up and handed her the magnifying glass. "Take a look. Tell me what you see."

She stooped over the photograph. "Royal Schools of Music . . ." she read. "Grade—Seven? I can't quite make out. Awarded to Larry? No, Luke? It's smudged. Surname Hollen.''

"Lars!" Markby said dourly. "Lars Holden.''

She looked up. "I recognize that name. Can't remember from where.''

"He's your MP!" Markby told her.

Bryce set down the magnifying glass. "Oh!" she said, investing the word with a wealth of meaning.

"Exactly. No need for me to tell you any interviews with the Holden family will have to be conducted with kid gloves on." He sat back, put both hands flat on the desk, and sighed. "In fact, I'll do it myself when the time comes. That's no criticism of your ability and tactics, by the way. I'm sure Lars would very much prefer to talk to someone in his own age range rather than an old-timer like me.''

Bryce, who knew Markby to be forty-three, suppressed a smile.

"But I already know the Holden family socially," he went on. "They might take it more kindly from me. Inasmuch as they'll accept being questioned by the police in this matter at all!''

''If they hired the Partytime caterers twelve years ago, it doesn't have to mean a thing!'' she pointed out, repeating Meredith's objection. ''Those sort of people throw large parties and often bring in temporary staff.''

''I accept that. But MPs are sensitive when it comes to publicity of any sort. Questioned by coppers investigating a murder—the murder, incidentally, of a young and pregnant woman—the Lars Holden Protection Society will spring into action! Everyone, from his constituency chairman and his political agent to his mother! Possibly, in the worst scenario, his parliamentary colleagues and the Cabinet will want to have a say! Oh, and his fiancée, whom I had the honor of meeting on Saturday evening and who would be a formidable opponent if we upset her!''

His fingers beat a rapid tattoo on the desk. ''So I'll do it and if anything goes wrong, it lands in my lap!''

''When do you think you might be able—?'' Bryce ventured.

He glanced at his wristwatch. ''I'm going to a funeral this morning.''

''Wondered about the black tie!'' Her impish grin won the struggle with professional gravitas.

He grimaced. ''Eunice Gresham's funeral service. She was the old lady who should have been buried in her parents' grave, had the Lowe brothers not turned up the remains of Kimberley Oates! She's being interred in the new cemetery now. The point is, Mrs. Holden will be there, Lars's mother. Possibly Lars himself. I might be able to arrange to call on Margaret. As for Lars, it would be better to meet him privately. I'll play it by ear.'' He grinned unexpectedly and tapped the photograph. ''Royal Schools of Music,'' he explained. ''Play it by ear!''

''Yes, sir,'' said Bryce dutifully. ''I do get it.''

''Oh? Well, you can't expect brilliant humor on a Monday!''

''How old is he exactly, Lars Holden?'' she demanded suddenly. ''From his election campaign pictures, quite young. He wouldn't have been much more than a student twelve years ago when this picture was taken.''

"By my calculation," Markby squinted into middle-distance, "Lars would have been no more than nineteen at the time, if that. Which opens up an interesting line of investigation, Lou. Kimberley, according to Simon French anyway, was apt to flirt with the customers in the hopes, French says, that some wealthy man would fall for her charms and take her away from all that.''

"He's quite good-looking, Holden," said Bryce. "He probably had no trouble getting girls. But you're right, sir. They won't like being asked about it, not one bit!''

"You really didn't have to come," Markby murmured.

The service in the church had been brief but quite well attended. Better attended, Markby thought, than it would have been without the notoriety surrounding the Gresham plot, still invisible behind police screens in the churchyard.

Miss Gresham's coffin had traveled by hearse the short distance from the church to the allotted space in the new cemetery alongside the old churchyard. It had been unloaded and borne by the pallbearers to the fresh grave and lowered in. Father Holland had spoken a brief oration and the final prayers. Truelove, the solicitor, had thrown in a handful of soil on behalf of all present and it was over. The weather had at least been kind.

Most of the onlookers had dispersed almost at once. To Father Holland's obvious disapproval, Truelove had disappeared with almost indecent haste. Perhaps, thought Markby charitably, he had an appointment. Now he and Meredith were walking toward the gate. Ahead of them, the vicar walked with Margaret Holden, deep in conversation.

Lars and Angie Pritchard, who had stood self-consciously prominent throughout, edged their way toward Markby and Meredith. Angie wore the sort of smart black and white suit and large black hat seen at memorial services in the city of London. The skirt stopped well above her knees and set off her shapely legs in black stockings. During the graveside ceremony, Markby had noticed the pallbearers' gaze wandering toward Angie more than once.

"We came separately to Mother, in my car," Lars said

awkwardly. "Mother had—she gave a lift to someone else. Look, Alan, this is an odd moment to choose to talk business, but I wonder, Angie and I wondered, if you're not busy and haven't to go back to your office straight away, we could all have a spot of lunch together? I mean, Angie and myself and you and Meredith. A pub lunch, possibly."

"Fine! Meredith?" Markby looked at her inquiringly.

"Fine by me!" she said promptly. Whatever Lars had to say, she had no intention of missing it.

"I know the very place," Markby said cheerily, "The Old Coaching Inn. You know it, perhaps."

Lars frowned. "Run-down place, as I recall."

"Under new management!" Markby assured him. "Been renovated. I'm anxious to see it! I understand they have an excellent carvery."

"Oh. Right." Lars gave a nervous grin. "We'll see you there." He glanced at his wristwatch. "Say at about one-fifteen? Okay?"

It was just after twelve. Meredith wondered, as Angie and Lars made their way hand in hand between the graves, what plans would be hatched in the intervening hour.

"Old Coaching Inn? Didn't you say that Simon French was manager there? Alan, you're up to something."

"No, no," he denied blandly. "But don't mention French to Lars or Angie. I rather want to spring him on them."

"I'm glad I came today!" she said promptly. "Anyway, I feel involved in this funeral. After all, I was at the vicarage the morning the grave-diggers found—found Kimberley's remains."

Markby's attention was taken by something in her voice. He said firmly, "Involved in the funeral, if you like, in the investigation, no!"

"I led you to Daisy Merrill!"

"By chance! And it's enough. I appreciate your help but one of these fine days you'll get yourself into a spot you can't get out of! Be told, will you?"

"It's my holiday!" she retorted. "Since I'm not now spending it on the canal, I suppose I can spend it any other way I wish?"

"Not interfering in police business, you can't!"

"I don't interfere," she told him with some economy of truth. "I'm only taking an interest in your work. I thought I might as well do that, since it seems to dominate your life!"

"I thought we'd sorted that one out?" He added, knowing he sounded pettish, "What about your blasted job?"

"*I* leave it behind me when I get on the train to come home!" There was a moment's silence. She said, "Sorry, I didn't mean to gripe. Funerals are sad occasions and lead to glum thoughts."

"I'm sorry too. About the holiday, about it all. Yes, it's a sad occasion. I remember Eunice Gresham. A sprightly old lady with a wicked sense of humor, as I recall. I'd have come along today, anyway, even if it wasn't connected with our investigation."

"Is it? I know Kimberley was buried in the Gresham grave. That was pot luck, surely?"

"It might be. I wouldn't wish to assume that. Why the Gresham grave? Why bury Kimberley in that one particularly? The old churchyard has some really ancient graves in it, eighteenth-century some of them. Why not choose a grave which was so old no one would ever be likely to reopen it? Or even visit it? Why pick a grave which was used in 1962 and likely still to have the occasional grieving relative visit it?"

"I hadn't thought of it that way," she admitted.

He gave her a wry grin. "Besides, it's always interesting, you know, to see who turns up at funerals. They sometimes bring very odd birds down from the trees!"

As if in direct relation to his last words, they passed a group of yew trees. A whiff of cigarette smoke floated past Meredith's nostrils. She looked across. Two unkempt, woolly-hatted figures stood in the shadows, leaning on spades. One was smoking. Their attitude recalled the carved soldiers on the war memorial, helmeted heads bent in respect and weapons resting on the ground.

"Denny and Gordon," said Markby quietly. "Waiting for us all to be out of the way before they go and fill in the grave."

"The resurrection men!" Meredith said, remembering how the news of their discovery had struck her.

Alan Markby said grimly, "In the bad old days, the Lowes might well have had that profession! A peculiar pair, Denny and his brother. Not that they've ever been in any trouble. Unlike old Bullen. He used to be grave-digger here." He sighed. "I wish I could talk to him. But I haven't seen him around for years and he probably wouldn't remember anything. But he would have been in charge of the churchyard at the time of Kimberley's unauthorized burial. We'll have to try and track him down if he's alive, which I doubt. He must be long gone."

They had reached the gate. Lars and Angie had already driven off. Margaret Holden was standing by her car, keys in hand.

"Rather a better turn-out than I expected," she said as they joined her. "Poor Eunice," she added, unlocking the door. "So sad she couldn't be buried with her parents as she wished."

Oscar, who had been imprisoned in the car, jumped out and made for the nearest tree.

Father Holland looked unhappy. "I ought perhaps to have delayed today's proceedings and decided if, after all, we couldn't have laid her to rest in the Gresham plot. But Truelove was keen to have the funeral held. It seemed an unnecessary hurry to me, but you know how it is. It's true it didn't seem suitable to bury her in what has become a desecrated grave. But it worries me."

"You did quite right, James!" Margaret Holden said with such conviction that the vicar brightened.

She called Oscar, who was investigating a promising hole beneath the tree roots, and returned him to the car. As she was about to climb into the driving seat, Markby stooped over the door and asked quietly, "I'd like to come out and have a word with you, Margaret. Official. When would be a good time?"

She glanced up at him. "Any time," she said with a touch of bitterness. "I really have nothing to do now." Her gaze slid to the mirror in which Angie was reflected, about to swing her long black-clad legs into Lars's car.

Markby looked thoughtful as he watched her drive away.

Father Holland slapped his broad hands together. "So that's that! I'll—"

He broke off. An unexpected sound had filled the air, that of quarrelling voices. It came from behind them, from the spot they'd just left. As one, all three of them turned and hurried back the way they'd come. As Miss Greshman's last resting place came into view, a weird and wonderful sight met their astonished eyes.

Three, not two, figures armed with spades worked feverishly around the open ditch. Denny and Gordon, one either side, shovelled earth with fierce efficiency, all the time giving vent to the most unsuitable language.

The third figure, tiny, wizened, but active, leapt in and out between the other two, snatching up small spadefuls of soil and tossing it wildly in the general direction of the grave. More often than not he missed, and the earth showered the Lowes, who swore vigorously each time it happened. Undeterred, the little man strove to shovel away as Denny and Gordon tried to ward him off with their elbows and from time to time brandished a spade at him threateningly. The gnome-like figure retorted with a shrill tirade of abuse and darted around them, out-maneuvering them.

"You let me be! It's to be done proper! You don't know how! I knew Miss Greshman best part of sixty year! I want to see her buried proper!"

"Get out of the way, you daft old bugger!" yelled Denny, swinging his spade and narrowly failing to decapitate the intruder.

"Don't you call me names, Denzil Lowe! You took my job, you did! No better than thieves, like your dad! I remember your dad! He was a rogue! And you take after him! You got no business here! You clear off, and you, Gordon! Pair of ammytoors, both of you!"

"Get—out—of—my—way!" howled Denny.

Father Holland bore down on the unruly group, cassock and surplice flapping.

"Stop this at once!" he roared. "What on earth do you think you're doing?"

The three shovellers froze in mid-attitude. Denny recovered first and rested his implement.

"The silly old bugger turned up out of the blue, Reverend! Never saw him. He must've been in them bushes, waiting."

" 'Tis my job!" shrilled the wizened figure.

The vicar's jaw dropped. He stood as if unable to believe his eyes and unable to speak.

Markby moved forward and, at the sight of him, the Lowes fell back warily. Not so their adversary who, gripping the shaft of his spade in his blue-veined knotty old hands, stood defiantly before the superintendent. His thin, yellowish-gray hair flew in a tangled halo around his distorted features and his unshaven chin wobbled with anger.

"Don't you come interfering neither!" he squawked.

"Well, well, what a surprise," Markby said, a smile breaking over his face. "Nat Bullen! We all thought you were dead!"

"Well, I'm not dead!" snapped Bullen.

After some further argument, the former grave-digger had been persuaded to leave the Lowe brothers in peace to fill in the grave, and to accompany the vicar, Alan Markby and Meredith back to the vicarage. They all sat around the table in the kitchen. Mrs. Harmer, radiating disapproval, placed a tray with mugs of coffee before them.

"Haven't you got anything a bit stronger?" Bullen inquired hopefully. "The damp weather gets into my old bones something terrible. A drop of whiskey does 'em good. Or brandy."

"You think yourself lucky I've let you in my kitchen at all, Nat Bullen!" retorted Mrs. Harmer. "And you needn't think you're going to start your drinking in here! I know all about you!"

Bullen's wizened features twisted into a sneer directed at the housekeeper's back. "Old misery, she is, always was! Her husband, he used to go visiting with the barmaid of The George."

Mrs. Harmer whirled round, her face red with fury, and advanced on Bullen. "He never did! You lying old soak!"

Father Holland thought it time to intervene. "Now I'm sure that's not true, Nat. It's all right, Mrs. Harmer. Perhaps you'd better leave us. We know it's only Nat's joke."

She stalked out.

" 'Tis true!" said Bullen unrepentantly. "And one time they was disturbed by another of her fancy men come calling. Joe Harmer went running out the house with his trousers around his ankles!" Bullen cackled. "She were a right goer, that barmaid!" He pulled one of the mugs toward him and blew noisily on the steam. "Got no biscuits, then?"

Meredith got up and fetched the vicar's chocolate digestives. Bullen rummaged in the tin, getting his fingers onto nearly every biscuit in it, and eventually took two.

"Where have you been these last ten years or so, Nat?" Markby asked.

"Nowhere," said Bullen simply. He slurped coffee. Meredith grimaced and caught the vicar's eye. Father Holland shrugged resignedly.

"I've been here," Bullen went on. "That is, I've been in my cottage. I lives just outside of town. Mrs. Holden, she's my landlady. She's a nice lady, she is. Very good to me is Mrs. Holden. I don't go anywhere. Mobile grocery van comes around and I buy my porridge and tea and such from that. The landlord of the pub down the road lets me have a bottle of whiskey off him. If I needs anything special, like a prescription got from the chemist, Mrs. Holden she fetches it out for me. She's a real lady, one of the old sort, the best." Bullen slurped again. "Not like him!"

"Who?" asked Meredith tersely, unable to stand much more of the slurping.

"Her son, young feller, pollytician." Bullen looked up, squinting villainously. "He wants to get me out of my cottage. But I'm not going and he can't make me!" He suddenly appeared quite evil, reminding Meredith of some sort of malicious sprite.

"Nat," Markby put his clasped hands on the table and leaned forward slightly. "You know what was found in the old Gresham plot?"

Bullen was smacking his lips together disapprovingly.

He drew the sugar bowl toward him and added another spoonful to his mug. He began to stir, sending coffee splattering around and causing Father Holland to roll his eyes toward the ceiling, perhaps seeking heavenly intervention.

" 'Course I do. See it in the paper. That's what comes of letting Denny and Gordon Lowe have my job.'' Bullen's small faded eyes with their yellowed whites turned on the vicar. "You done that. You give me the boot. You didn't have no right.''

"You'd reached retirement age, Nat,'' said the vicar soothingly. "And digging graves is hard work. As you say yourself, your old bones wouldn't have stood for much more of it.''

"Hard work never killed no one!'' retorted Bullen. "It's only since I stopped the digging that my bones seized up. Comes of having nothing to do! I seen some of the digging done by them Lowes. Call that a proper job? They can't do no neat corners. Earth is all falling in. Sides isn't smooth. There's an art to a good grave, there is. I was a craftsman. Them Lowes, they're amytoors.''

"How did you come here today, Nat?'' Markby asked. "Catch the bus?''

The old man shook his head. "No. I asked Mrs. Holden and she brought me in. I asked him, first off, but he wouldn't let me get in his fancy car. They all started arguing about it and then Mrs. Holden said they'd be late for the funeral, and she'd get out her car and bring me. I had to sit in the back with her little dog. But I don't mind dogs. Though that sausage dog of hers is a noisy blighter. Smart though, that dog is. Smarter than some people, naming no names!'' Bullen tapped the side of his nose in a disagreeable gesture.

"I told Mrs. Holden I'd make my own way home. I should've been allowed to finish filling that grave. Them Lowes, they got no right. I know'd Eunice Gresham since she were a girl. I wanted to see her buried right.'' Bullen drained the last of his coffee and set down his mug. "Everyone got the right to be buried proper. The thought of them Lowes having my job makes my blood boil. And it's all your fault!'' he repeated vehemently to Father Holland.

"As you like," said the vicar. "But I think the super-intendent here wants to ask you a few questions."

Bullen turned to Markby and raised his sparse eyebrows. "Oh, super-in-tend-ent is it, now? Last I heard, you was a chief inspector over at the town station!"

"I got promoted, Nat." Markby repressed a smile.

"Not surprised," said Bullen.

Meredith, unseen by the ex-grave-digger, pulled a face at Alan and mouthed, "An admirer!"

She was wrong, as Bullen almost immediately revealed. "You're a Markby. Local nobs, they was. Gentry. Surprised they ain't made you chief constable!"

"I'm working on it, Nat!" Markby told him seriously.

Bullen shot him a sharp glance, suspecting he was being mocked. "What do you want to know, then? How to dig a grave? Go and ask them Lowes if you all think they know so much about it."

"I want to know about the Gresham plot, Nat."

"Old churchyard," said Bullen. He paused. "They was still burying people in that in my time. They stopped soon after. I suppose that was your doing, too, Mr. Holland?"

"No, Nat," said the persecuted vicar patiently. "The old churchyard was full. The town had grown considerably. The parish council and the diocese together decided to open up the new cemetery. We were lucky to get the land adjacent."

"I remember it. Chicken farm it was before. Could smell them chickens a mile off." Bullen sat back and surveyed them all, obviously revelling in the fact that all three were waiting on his words.

"I never dug the original plot for Walter Gresham," he said. "That was before my time. I opened it up for his wife when she died. But I didn't go finding no skeletons in it. Well, I found a bit of Walter's but I covered it over before anyone saw. I dug well down, you see, because it was a three-decker."

"And you never touched it again, Nat?"

At Markby's question, Nat Bullen suddenly became shifty. "Depends!" he mumbled.

There was a silence. "Go on," Markby prompted.

"Can't recall," said Bullen. He looked up, staring Markby straight in the face. "Long time ago. Forgot."

Meredith caught Father Holland's eye and made a time-honored mime with one hand, imitating a glass being downed.

"Nat," said Father Holland, "perhaps I could just find a small glass of brandy."

Bullen brightened. "That's the ticket!"

A few minutes later, nursing his glass of brandy, he said, "Now I don't remember when, mind you! But what happened was this. We had a lot of rain. Much like this summer it was. And Miss Gresham, she come to me one day and she said, 'Nat, my parents' grave has sunk right down. Earth's subsided,' that was her word for it. 'Can't you do something, Nat?' "

Bullen paused to sip his brandy. He rolled it appreciatively around his mouth and swallowed. A paroxym of coughing followed. When calm was restored he said, "Good drop of stuff, Vicar!"

"The Gresham plot, Nat!" Markby urged.

"I'm telling you, ain't I? Bit of patience, that's what you need. You learn patience digging graves. Got to take your time and get 'em true. Them Lowes, they got no patience. That's their trouble. Where was I?" Bullen paused aggravatingly.

Old ham! thought Meredith, grinning to herself. He's enjoying himself thoroughly.

"Well, I took a look and sure enough, it'd sunk right down. So I fetched a couple of barrows of soil and tipped it on the top, built the grave up again in a hummock." Bullen made the shape with his hands. "It gradually settled down again."

Markby muttered under his breath and sat back. He gestured with a sweep of one palm at Meredith and Father Holland.

"This could be the reason the killer chose to bury his victim in the Gresham plot! There was a heap of fresh earth on it and so no one noticed any sign that he'd disturbed it. He just scraped the soil aside, dug out a shallow trench for Kimberley, and piled back the earth as Bullen had left it.

Are you absolutely sure you can't remember the year this happened, Nat?''

''No,'' said Bullen. He had finished his brandy and suddenly seemed to have regained his fit of the sulks. He huddled in his chair. ''Can't remember no more. I want to go home.''

''I'll get out the youth club mini-bus and run you home, Nat.'' Father Holland stood up. ''You won't want to go on the back of my motorbike, eh?''

Bullen looked up. ''Yes, I should! I had a motorbike when I was a lad. Norton, it was. Ain't you got a spare crash helmet?''

''I don't know about this,'' said Markby doubtfully a little later.

Father Holland's Yamaha was disappearing down the road. The vicar in his leathers was obscured by the small but triumphant figure of Bullen, perched behind him wearing a large crash helmet, and clinging on for dear life.

''He must be eighty-five at the very least.''

''James is only taking it slowly. Well, as slowly as a bike like that goes! Bullen was clearly as pleased as punch!'' She glanced at Alan. ''He did help you.''

''In a manner of speaking. It's conjecture. We don't— or rather, he doesn't—know when exactly he piled the fresh earth on the' plot. But it would explain very nicely how someone could bury Kimberley in it and no one be any the wiser.''

The motorcycle had disappeared. ''But I really don't think I should have let the only witness of any kind I've got so far ride off on the pillion of James's bike. I hope he doesn't fall off!''

Ten

The events involving Bullen meant that they were a few minutes late arriving at The Old Coaching Inn. But as they drove into the large, newly surfaced car park, they saw Lars and Angie, just getting out of their car.

"Ah, there you are!" said Lars, sounding relieved. "I was afraid we'd have kept you waiting. We had to go home first. I wanted a word with my mother. All well at the vicarage?"

Meredith wondered why Lars should assume they'd spent the intervening time at the vicarage, even though they had. She also began to ask herself whether, as Lars must have known Bullen was likely to make an unwelcome appearance at some point, he and Angie had hurried away before he did. She felt strongly, and thought Alan probably did also, that Lars was "up to something."

Angie had left her hat behind at the house. The breeze blew fresh across the open space and tossed her glossy mane of hair around her face. She scraped it aside and suggested with some acerbity that they all go inside.

The outer stone fabric of the inn had been preserved. Inside, some ancient rough-hewn beams were all that had been left of the original building. It had been entirely transformed and not, perhaps, in the happiest way. The owners had decided to take a bygone way of life as their theme. As a result old yokes, flails, horse-collars and any number of smaller agricultural mementoes were tacked to the walls. All had been treated with a variety of preservatives which had successfully destroyed any appearance of their being genuine, which was a pity, as they probably were. Amongst them a profusion of poor quality sporting prints and market handbills completed a bewildering display which puzzled the eye and disoriented the senses.

As the four of them entered, Simon French chanced to emerge from a door behind the bar. Seeing Markby with a party, and clearly not on official business this time, he bore down on them with a bright smile.

"Hullo, there, Superintendent! Take up my invitation? Table for four, is it?"

He was ushering them to a corner table beneath more pictures of blacksmiths' forges and gentlemen in gaiters shooting at ducks. Beside it stood the empty hearth, its oak mantel laden with assorted old china plates of the kind picked up for a few pence on charity stalls. Meredith wondered just what effect it was all meant to produce. An old inn? An old farmhouse? A tarted-up second-hand shop masquerading as an antiques showroom? It was as if the place wanted to pretend it wasn't a restaurant at all.

"How about a drink?" French signalled to waiter. "Courtesy of the management, of course! I'll send over the menu."

He hastened over to the bar. A young man appeared to take their drinks order and hand around enormous menu cards hidden inside heavy, mock leather book-covers. French had remained by the bar but was signalling surreptitiously to Markby to join him. Markby ordered his drink, murmured an excuse, and got up to join French.

"I say, Mr. Markby," whispered French excitedly, "isn't that Lars Holden, the MP, with you?"

Markby stifled an exclamation of annoyance. He had been hoping that French would recognize Lars, even after twelve years, as a former client of Partytime. Even better, would remember being in The Old Farm and the photo with Kimberley and the other girl being taken. French had boasted of his power of total recall of faces and names, so why not? But, as Bryce had already mentioned, Lars's name and face were well enough known from election leaflets, hoardings and the local press. French had easily identified Lars, but alas, only as his parliamentary representative. The association could color anything French might claim to recall.

He confirmed that the MP was indeed sitting at the table. French almost crowed with glee and descended on the party again.

"Mr. Holden? May I say how honored we are to have your company today? I'm sure—"

Lars rose to the tribute with consummate ease and grace. He shook French warmly by the hand. He congratulated him on the transformation wrought in the restaurant. A spasm of mutual admiration ensued, which finished with French begging them to express any wish they had regarding details of their meal, and Lars confident of another vote secured.

Markby had rejoined them and, as he sat down, exchanged a glance of stifled disgust with Meredith, who grinned.

French departed. Lars resumed his seat and declared, "Just the sort of energetic young businessman we need!"

"I thought," Markby said mildly, "you might have recognized him."

Lars frowned. "I meet a lot of people, Alan. I've addressed several meetings of the local Chamber of Commerce. I don't think . . ."

Angie stirred on her chair and lifted her gin and tonic to her lips. Her eyes, fixed on Markby, were watchful.

"He used, some time ago, to be employed by a local firm of caterers, Partytime. I think they provided some sort of buffet party at your home some years back. French was a trainee barman then."

An awkward silence fell. "I don't remember him," Lars said at last. "But I—" He looked toward his fiancée for guidance.

"Why don't you show Alan the letter?" Angie put down her gin. "Lars has something he'd like to discuss informally, Alan. It's all a storm in a teacup. But in Lars's situation gossip can be exaggerated into scandal. Not that there is anything scandalous, or in the slightest way wrong, but you know how it is."

"Letter?" Markby turned his gaze on Lars, who reddened.

"I ought to explain something first, Alan. It's about, well, you've been out to the house and you've met my mother. She—she likes to run things in her way."

Angie said coolly, "That old woman, the one we buried this morning, she understood Margaret. She gave her a brooch, a horrid thing, an eagle's talon in a silver clasp. She could have given Margaret any piece of jewelry but she chose that because it symbolized Margaret's attitude so well. She grasps what she wants and doesn't let go."

"Oh, come on, Angie!" Lars protested feebly. "Mother's not as bad as that!"

Angie twitched an eyebrow and shrugged.

Lars, looking even more harassed, hurried on. "The thing is, Mother has control of our family property and she allows an old fellow called Bullen to live rent-free in one of the cottages."

Beneath the table Markby's foot pushed against Meredith's. She scowled at him. She wasn't so stupid as to go blurting out anything.

"The former grave-digger, is that right?" Markby asked innocently. "He showed up in the cemetery after you left."

Lars groaned. "I was afraid of that. I told him to stay away from the funeral service itself. He'd hardly add a note of dignity! He insisted on coming along this morning. He turned up at the house early, togged up in what I suppose is his best suit, and carrying what looked for all the world like a small spade wrapped up in newspaper. He's clearly completely mad. I refused to have him in my car. He smelled to high heaven of whiskey and mothballs. If mother wanted to take him in her car, fine. He could ride in the back with Oscar. Mother has a soft spot for him, don't ask me why!"

"I know why," Angie said silkily.

Lars cast her an uneasy look. "I don't know, Angie . . . I admit, it's odd, but would she really—"

"Really, what?" demanded Markby, showing signs of impatience.

Angie spoke. "It's simple, Alan. Lars and I want to get married. When we do, we'll need a home in the constituency. Of course, Lars has one, The Old Farm. The problem is, Margaret won't move out and we can't make her. It's because of the terms of Lars's father's will. I need hardly add that the idea of sharing a roof with Margaret just isn't feasible."

That was true enough. Margaret Holden regarded the house as her home and had been running it for something like thirty-five years. Meredith said aloud, "Two women into one kitchen don't go!"

"Exactly!" Angie beamed on her. "I wouldn't be able to change a lightbulb without Margaret breathing down my neck! As for redecorating—! But please don't think I'm unaware of Margaret's position. She's used to her own place and of course she should have one. But not The Old Farm. Ideally, the old man Bullen should go into a retirement home. We would completely renovate the cottage and Margaret could move in there, as a sort of dower house. She'd have Ned and Evelyne next door, which they would love. She'd be near friends and near to us. She could use the gardens and still have a role to play, if much reduced. Oh, it would be perfect! But she won't do it!"

Angie clasped her hands and struck them on the table top, making all the drinks rock dangerously. "Of course, if Bullen could be made to move out, Margaret's case for staying on in The Old Farm would be weakened. She knows that. She's determined that cottage will not become vacant. That's why she charges Bullen no rent! So long as he lives there rent-free, naturally he won't move out!"

The waiter returned for their order. There was a necessary break in the conversation for which Lars appeared grateful. He had become redder in the face and was sweating slightly.

Ordering took time. Both men chose the soup and Angie the melon. Meredith passed on a starter in order to be able to enjoy something sweet and sticky afterwards without feelings of guilt. Then more time was taken to discuss the various main-course dishes. Markby settled for the carvery and went off to indicate his choice from the hot table. Meredith and Angie decided on the chicken Provençal and Lars, after some mumbling about diet, asked for a medium-rare steak, a baked potato and a salad without dressing.

As the waiter left the table, Markby returned to his seat and asked, "What's all this about a letter?"

"Oh, this." Lars put his hand in his pocket and produced a crumpled scrap of paper. "Bullen sent it to the House of Commons. He's crackers, but it's the sort of crackers that has a weird competence. I didn't know what he was on about when I first read it and nearly threw it away. Later, I found out about, well, this murder investigation of yours and the name of the dead—of the person. The letter seemed sort of sinister. I've asked Bullen what on earth he meant by it, but the old rogue just gives me sly looks and taps the side of his nose. I think," said Lars honestly, "I could cheerfully strangle Bullen."

"Please don't!" Markby begged. He read the letter twice then folded it. "May I keep this?"

"All right," Lars said unwillingly. "But you won't let anyone else see it, will you? Other than Meredith, I mean. I'd like her opinion."

"Only as necessary. Do you look upon this as a threatening letter? To send such a thing is an offense under the law. Are you making a complaint against Bullen? What, in fact, do you want me to do about it?"

"I don't know!" Lars's voice rose and he looked around furtively to see if anyone had noticed. "See here, Alan!" he hissed, leaning across the table. "It's a question of gossip! I can't afford gossip!"

"Lars!" Markby said crisply. "Do you believe Bullen is trying to blackmail you?"

"No!" Lars yelped. "How could he? I've done nothing—he knows nothing—"

"Lars!" said Angie firmly. "You'll have to tell Alan about the girl."

The meal was very good, as it happened. French appeared at the start of the main course to inquire whether everything

was all right and engage in a further exchange of pleasant-
ries with Lars. Urged on by the manager, the waiter popped
up at regular intervals wanting to know if they needed more
breadrolls, wine, anything else? They could, thought Meredith, have asked for the kitchen sink and it would have
been hauled in on wheels for their inspection.

Between interruptions of this sort, and those necessary
for eating, Lars's tale emerged.

"I do remember the ruddy girl, Alan. Just about, mind
you! It was my eighteenth birthday party. Mother got in
these caterers. One of the waitresses was very pretty."

Lars gave his fiancée a hunted look but Angie had assumed the famed expression of the sphinx. "Well, she
seemed—interested in me. I'd had a couple of drinks. You
know how it goes . . ." Lars managed to sound both plead-
ing and truculent.

"Where?" asked Markby expressionlessly.

"Where?" Lars looked momentarily bewildered.

"I assume you're going to tell me you and the waitress
slipped out of the party for a few minutes and—"

"And had it off!" said Lars coarsely. "Well, you're
right! I was eighteen, for goodness sake, and she was, oh,
about seventeen or so! We were young! It was a party!"

"Where?" Markby repeated his original question. "In a
bedroom? Wasn't it risky? Another guest might have come
in, or even your mother?"

"No," said Meredith, who had been watching Lars
closely. "I can guess where. In the hidden room, the secret
chapel, am I right?"

Lars gave her a look almost of gratitude. "Yes. I offered
to show her the secret room and when we got in there, well,
it just happened." He put down his knife and fork and sat
up straight. "See here, she was quite willing! There was
no question of force!"

"And then what?" Markby asked him.

"Then nothing. We went back to the party. She went
home with the other catering staff in their mini-bus."

"Did you see her again?"

Lars looked down. "I did bump into her, as bad luck
would have it, during the following week in the middle of

town. I took her for a cup of coffee. I found out her name.
I suppose she'd told me what it was before, at the party,
but I'd forgotten it. So she told me again. Kimberley. She
didn't seem cross that I'd forgotten it. She just seemed very
pleased we'd met up again. She kept hinting she wanted
me to take her out. I didn't want to! I mean, stone cold
sober and in the middle of the day I didn't even fancy her
any more! But she kept hinting. And she—well, she reminded me of what we'd done at the party.''

"She more or less blackmailed you into offering her a
date, is that it? What did you say, that she'd turn up at the
house and talk to your mother?''

"She didn't say it outright. But the threat was there. I
know now I should have told her to forget it, that I wasn't
interested and that Mother would chuck her out if she went
to the house. But I was young and embarrassed about my
family knowing.''

Lars sighed. "I took her to the pictures. I can't remember
what the film was. Something deadly boring. She hung on
to my hand like grim death throughout and nibbled my ear
when the lights went out.''

A muffled sound came from Meredith, who had put her
napkin to her mouth.

"It was bloody embarrassing!'' said Lars, aggrieved.

"And did you see her again, after that?''

"A couple of times. I always took her away from Bamford because I didn't want anyone who knew me to spot
us! Then, thank God, the new term started and I went back
to school to finish my "A'' levels. After that I went on to
university. I never saw Kimberley again, Alan, and that's
the truth, I swear it!''

Meredith caught an urgent glance from Alan. She was
getting to be quite a mind-reader, she thought. Alan was
asking her what a young girl, fancying herself "in love,''
would have done.

"Did she write to you, Lars, while you were at college?''
Meredith asked.

"Couple of times,'' Lars said gloomily. "I didn't answer. Reading the damn letters made me crawl with embarrassment. I burned them straight away. Honestly, you

wouldn't believe the sort of things—the words—she put down on paper! She was sex-mad!''

''And she didn't appear during the vacation when you went home?''

''I didn't really go home that first vac,'' Lars explained. ''Only for a couple of days to collect my gear. I went back-packing around Europe. When I did go home again—the vac after that—she wasn't around. I didn't go looking for her!''

No one said anything. The answer hung in the air. Lars had not gone looking for Kimberley, but after twelve long years Kimberley had found him.

In the awkward silence, the dessert trolley was wheeled up to them. They all turned their attention to its contents with suspicious eagerness, although neither Lars nor Angie seemed hungry any longer.

Angie said, as one carrying out an unpleasant but necessary duty, ''I'll have the fruit salad, please, no cream!''

''Just the cheese board,'' said Lars in deepest gloom.

''I'm going to have the chocolate gâteau!'' said Meredith cheerfully. ''With cream!'' What the heck. Once in a blue moon didn't hurt and she'd forgone the starter.

''I'll join you,'' said Alan Markby, himself cheering visibly.

After a few minutes spent concentrating on these various delights, Markby asked, ''Well, it seems fairly straightforward, Lars. If it's as you say, you shouldn't have anything to worry about.''

Lars, a piece of Brie speared on his knife, looked like a man who had just heard he'd been reprieved from a death sentence. ''That's very decent of you, Alan!''

''I told you Alan would sort it out!'' said Angie complacently.

Markby frowned slightly. ''I don't know about that. Only if Lars is telling me the truth, all of it, and I do need to know all of it, Lars!''

''Oh, I have, I have!'' Lars told him fervently. ''And you do!''

''You don't recall anything she might have told you during these dates you had with her, she didn't mention any problems at home, any plans to leave, to seek out her mother, perhaps?''

''No, she just talked about sex all the time! I didn't know anything about her family!''

''Then there's just one last question and it's important you tell me the truth, Lars! Did Bullen at any time during this period see you with Kimberley around the town? Did he have any reason to suspect you were dating her? Because, you see, going by this letter he sent you the other day, he obviously thinks you have some personal interest in the discovery of her remains.''

Lars looked deeply uncomfortable again. ''To be frank, Alan, yes. I tried to take her out of town, but there were a couple of occasions when I met up with her and we spent an hour or so together in Bamford. He—he came on us one day, by accident. We—we were fooling about in the bushes.''

Markby raised an eyebrow. ''Oh? Where?''

Lars swallowed and blurted out, ''In the undergrowth at the back of the old churchyard!''

''What do you make of it?'' Alan asked Meredith as he drove her home.

''Methinks the politician doth protest too much. Look, he was eighteen and at eighteen all of us have over-active hormones! Kimberley didn't talk about sex all by herself! And it takes two to fool about in bushes! He had a hyper-active sexual liaison with a local good-time girl when he was in his teens. Now it's come back to haunt the poor man! He's in a complete panic. Angie knows it. She means to see he makes all the right moves. She got him to spill the beans to us today in a pre-emptive bid. She smells tabloid scandal. She's blocking up the leaks. She's a shrewd lady.''

''He's not telling me everything!'' Alan said doggedly. ''Neither he nor Angie. There's something else on their minds. They're trying to be clever. They're going to have to tell me in the end and, in the meantime, they're messing me around! I don't like it. Incidentally, you're missing a very significant point in Lars's story. It concerns Bullen and the letter.''

"Hang on!" she said. "Let me think." After a moment, she said, "Got it! When Bullen wrote that letter to Lars at the House of Commons, the remains had been discovered, but they hadn't yet been identified! So how did Bullen know they were those of Kimberley?"

They drew up before Meredith's cottage. Markby switched off the engine and turned to face her. "Ever tried to dig a large hole? Dig a small hole, come to that? I have, many times. Ask any gardener. Digging holes isn't the easiest! Believe me, to bury a body takes a certain knack.''

"There was soft earth on the grave, or so you think. The earth Bullen had tipped there with his wheelbarrow.''

"Possibly. If Bullen can't remember when he did it, I can't prove it. But certainly to scrape a shallow grave in soft earth would be easier than digging out solidified soil. But it still means that someone had to know about it. Someone had seen the fresh soil and remembered it." He heaved a sigh. "I'll let you out. I can't stop. I've got to get back to work!"

Meredith, her hand on the doorcatch, asked, "Alan? No one is mentioning the unborn child. Do you think Lars was the father of the baby Kimberley was carrying when she died?''

"Now isn't that the 64,000-dollar question!" Markby muttered. "And while you're puzzling over it, think over this as well. We've heard Angie's theory. But what other reasons could there be why Margaret Holden doesn't charge Bullen any rent?''

Eleven

Meredith watched him drive away.

"I'll give you a call sometime to let you know what's going on. I don't know when—or when I'll see you!" He'd grimaced.

"Sure, don't worry about it," she'd told him, feeling a lot less charitable than she'd sounded.

She turned to go indoors. At that moment her ear caught the rumble of wheels. Looking up, she saw Mrs. Etheridge toiling down the street again, the shopping trolley lumbering behind her. The woman presented a dispiriting picture of respectability in a faded print dress. Her hat of glazed straw resembled a squashed bird's nest. It was obvious that she was having more trouble than usual today. Meredith went to meet her.

"Why don't you let me take that indoors for you? You look all in," she said sympathetically.

Mrs. Etheridge hesitated. "It's this damp weather. It makes the joints play up. All right. Thank you."

Meredith pulled the trolley to the door and after Mrs. Etheridge had unlocked it and advised her to mind the step, the hall carpet and the walls, dragged it inside and along to the kitchen at the rear of the little house.

There Mrs. Etheridge subsided onto a wooden chair and offered, "Would you like a cup of tea? It's very kind of you to help."

"I'll make it!" Meredith said. It wasn't often that Mrs. Etheridge offered tea and gratitude and it was a mark of how exhausted the poor woman felt today.

When the tea had brewed and they sat at the table, Mrs. Etheridge observed, "You're dressed very smart today, dear."

Meredith realized that she still wore the dark skirt and jacket she'd worn to Eunice Gresham's funeral. She hadn't had time to come home and change before meeting Lars and Angie for lunch. She explained about the funeral service to Mrs. Etheridge.

The woman nodded. "I heard it was today. Well attended, I dare say. She was well known, Miss Gresham. I used to go regular to that church but I haven't been inside it for, oh, ten years or more. Not since the new vicar came, the one who roars around the town on a motorbike, if you please!" She gave a snort.

"Father Holland. I don't think you should let the motorbike put you off."

"Motorbikes," said Mrs. Etheridge crisply, "aren't for men of God! Not to my way of thinking. You wouldn't have known Father Appleton who was here before. He was a lovely old gentleman. I was a member of the PCC in his day."

"The parochial church council? I hadn't realized that."

"I left after Holland took up the living. It wasn't the same. Mind you, during the last year or so of Mr. Appleton's time, he was very sick. It was difficult to get anything done."

Meredith said suddenly, "You'll remember the old grave-digger, then, Bullen?"

That brought an immediate reaction. A flush mantled Mrs. Etheridge's thin cheeks and her eyes sparkled. "Dreadful old sinner! An alcoholic!"

"He turned up at the Gresham burial."

"Nat Bullen, still alive?" Mrs. Etheridge gazed at her incredulously. "Well, that's something I wouldn't have expected! He used to be drunk all day long. I'd have thought the drink would have carried him off by now!" She sipped at her tea. "I tried to raise the matter at the PCC meetings because it was getting the church a bad name. But no one supported me. They did get rid of him later on, after they closed the old churchyard. Not before time!''

Mrs. Etheridge was feeling a little better and had recovered enough to remember the squashed straw hat. She unpinned it, set it on the table, and gazed at it thoughtfully.

"Even early in the morning he was drunk, you know. I do remember one occasion particular. A friend of mine had been in hospital and she needed a bit of help getting up and dressed in the morning. So for a week or so, I cycled over there and got her out of bed, washed and dressed. Made her a bit of breakfast and washed it up, and then cycled back here to see to my own place. That was before the joints started to trouble me like they do now and I could still ride the old bike. Haven't been able to for years now. Who'd have thought it? I used to be so active. There, that's age for you.

"Anyhow, I was riding over there early one morning. It was summertime and daylight although it was only about six o'clock. I was going by the churchyard and Nat Bullen came stumbling out of the gate in a terrible state. His eyes were rolling and he was muttering to himself. Probably had the DTs.

"Certainly when he saw me he let out a squawk like he'd seen a ghost! He turned and started on back into the churchyard again. I called out after him. Told him he was a disgrace and to get on home and get himself sobered up before anyone else saw him. I got a stream of abuse in return. Dreadful language. He shook his fist at me!'' Her cup rattled in the saucer as her emotion transmitted itself down her thin arm. "He looked terrible, though, and sort of furtive with it, like he'd been up to no good. What was he doing there that time of the morning, I ask you?''

"You don't remember exactly when this was?'' Meredith asked carefully.

"No, about the time Father Appleton retired. But all manner of odd things went on then. Matters having generally got lax, you see.''

"What sort of odd things?'' Meredith hoped the woman didn't think she was being unduly curious.

But Mrs. Etheridge had few visitors and was willing to talk. "There was that matter of the candle and the flowers. There, now. I promised Father Appleton I wouldn't tell anyone. But it was twelve years ago and he's dead and gone so it can't do any harm now. But I often think of it. It's my belief someone had held a Black Mass!"

"I'll put the kettle on again!" Meredith offered as Mrs. Etheridge was growing a little hoarse with the unwonted long speech. "Then you can tell me all about it."

Mrs. Etheridge told her. "Cosmos flowers they were. I remember distinctly. The bishop should have been informed. The altar should've been reconsecrated. But there, Father Appleton wasn't bothered and Derek Archibald didn't want it made public, frightened for his butchery business! People sacrificing chickens and so on. Such wicked things! But then, I'm a vegetarian, have been for years. So we both of us promised, Derek and I, not to say a word and nor have I till today. I don't know about Derek Archibald. He's another who likes a pint on the quiet and may have gone gossiping in the pub before now."

She eased herself up out of the chair. "There, I feel much better. I can put those groceries away myself, don't you bother."

Meredith recognized she was dismissed. But she wouldn't go empty-handed, metaphorically at least. Alan, she felt sure, would be very interested in Bullen's early-morning behavior and in the tale of the candle and the cosmos flowers.

Mrs. Etheridge's mind was still running on the matter because she said suddenly, as Meredith went out of the door, "I mind when it was! Both things happened that same week. The week I saw the candle burning in the church of an evening was the week I met Bullen drunk in the early morning. I tried to raise both matters at the PCC. But Derek Archibald wouldn't let me start a discussion on Bullen because it was going on late and they all wanted to get off home. We were going over to the church anyway, with Father Appleton, to check on that candle."

Meredith went home and rang Markby's office number

but was told he wasn't back yet. She wondered where he'd gone.

Alan Markby hadn't, in fact, driven straight back to his office. Instead he drove out into the country, along the road which led to The Old Farm, but pulled up some two hundred yards short of the pair of wayside cottages. He had no wish to be spotted by the Walcotts.

He walked the short distance and turned into the gate which led to the untidy dwelling of Nat Bullen. Country people were not much given to using the front door and Markby made his way to the back.

There he found Bullen sitting on a wooden bench outside the open kitchen door, gazing mistrustfully at a patch of earth which had been cleared amid surrounding weeds and planted with cabbages. Bullen had changed out of his funeral suit and wore ancient flannels and a singularly loud red, blue and green checked shirt which looked as though it might have come from a jumble sale. It was too large and he'd rolled up the sleeves from which his thin but wiry arms protruded. His scraggy neck stuck up from the collar like a plucked fowl's.

"How are you feeling now, Nat?" Markby asked him, seating himself on the wooden trestle by the old man.

"Well you might ask," mumbled Bullen. He spat to one side—not Markby's side, the superintendent was relieved to note. "You ought to have a bad conscience. Stopping me doing the right thing by Eunice Gresham!"

"Not your job any longer, Nat."

Bullen scowled. After a while he said, "See them cabbages? There's a blasted rabbit gets in my garden and nibbles at 'em! I set snares for the bugger but I an't caught him yet. I will, though, and then he'll be rabbit stew!"

"Talking of bad consciences," Markby went on affably, "there must be a few people around here who've got things on their minds."

Bullen rolled a yellowed eyeball at him but only grunted.

"I've just been lunching with Mr. Holden."

Bullen muttered, "I suppose you've got plenty of time for that sort of thing now you're a superintendent!"

"As I was driving home I started thinking to myself," Markby went on serenely. "Just letting my imagination roam, as you might say. It was your saying how tricky a job it is to dig a grave properly that set me off."

"You don't want to take any notice of what I said!" Bullen told him immediately. "Not that I take it back, mind! But what I said was meant for those Lowes, not for you."

"I started thinking, only my fancy, how about if Nat had buried that girl? He knew about the fresh soil on the Gresham grave. He'd make a neat tidy job of putting her in there. Of course, I don't think you'd have had anything to do with killing her!"

"Thanks very much, I'm sure!"

"But you might have buried her for some reason which seemed good to you at the time. Perhaps you found her body in the churchyard. Or perhaps you thought you knew who might have killed her? I was just speculating, of course."

"You can go speceylating what you like," said Bullen. "I can't stop no one thinking. Please yourself. Makes no difference to me what you think. But I reckon you ought to watch that imagination of yours. People who start imagining things, finish up imagining they're the king of England or a hatstand. Besides, police has to prove what they say. And proving is another kettle of fish altogether."

Lars was right, thought Markby, amused. The old man might be crazy, but it was craziness of a competent kind.

"I can prove you wrote to Mr. Holden at the House of Commons, because he's given me your letter. Why did you do that, Nat?"

"Thought he ought to know."

"Why? What interest could he have in it?"

Bullen turned faded but crafty eyes on him. "He's my MP, ain't he? I got the right to contact my MP, I have. He's my constitoo-en-cy member. You want to ask Major Walcott as lives next door. He'll tell you. He's always running around putting leaflets through folks' doors and the like."

"And you're running around me, Nat! Come on, a

straight answer. Why did you write to Lars Holden about the discovery of unauthorized remains in the Gresham grave? Nobody knew then the skeleton was that girl's—or nobody admits to knowing!''

"They give my job to them Lowes," Bullen said aggressively. "What do they know about digging a good straight grave? They go digging bones up! I wouldn't have dug no one up what ought to be resting in peace! Serve you all right for giving my job to the Lowes. That's why I wrote to Mr. Holden. To tell him they shouldn't have give my job to Denny and Gordon. I knew their dad. He were a poacher. And they poached my job! Runs in the blood, does thieving!''

It was true that, in his letter to Lars, Bullen had referred to Denny Lowe having been given his job—unjustly, in his view. Taken line by line, there was nothing in it to suggest Bullen knew the identity of the victim. Produced in court as supporting evidence of a conspiracy of any kind, any competent lawyer would dismiss the letter in seconds.

Aware that Bullen knew this, Markby went on, "Burying her without a word to anyone was wrong, whatever the reason. It was against the law. But after all this time I doubt anyone would get into serious trouble for it. Not if that was all the person did.''

"Take things for granted, don't you?" said Bullen sarcastically. "Thought you'd have known better, important chap like you.''

Markby conceded temporary defeat.

"All right, Nat. But you think it over. Perhaps there's something you haven't told me and you might decide you'd like to tell me. If so, call me and I'll come out here. All right?''

"New wire fencing, chicken wire, might keep that rabbit out," said Bullen. "If I was to sink it in the soil about a foot, otherwise he'd just dig under it.''

Markby sighed and felt for his wallet. "Twenty quid, Nat, for new chicken wire! And think about it! If the person owns up now, it's likely he won't get into serious trouble. Carry on refusing to cooperate and things won't be so easy for him. What's more, if that person knows something, and is keeping it to himself, he could be in danger! I'm not the only one with an interest in police inquiries. There's very likely a murderer out there somewhere. He's got a very keen interest in stopping us making progress. Remember that!''

Bullen's hand shot out and gripped the two ten pound notes. "I told you all you need to know!" he said.

Bryce was waiting for him when he got back to his office.

''We've traced her! Susan Tempest! Or rather, the North Wales force has. We've got an address. A local man has already visited her and spoken to her briefly about her daughter's remains being found. She's been warned to expect a visit from one of us.''

"I'll go!" Markby said crisply. "I shall be interested to meet Susan Tempest formerly Oates!"

"And a Miss Mitchell rang. I left a note on your desk. She asked for you to ring back, she has something to tell you.''

"Right!" Markby muttered.

Since he'd seen her a few hours earlier and she knew he was up to his eyes in work, the message meant she had learned something which might have relevance to all this.

Coming so soon after his words in the churchyard, his first reaction was one of exasperation. He knew that Meredith liked to sleuth privately. He had repeatedly explained, both patiently as today, and on occasion much less patiently, that this was both unwise and in some instances improper. Chiefly it was the danger that worried him. Murderers kill. This apparently obvious notion sometimes seemed to elude her.

However, in his heart, he knew he couldn't stop her. It was a fact that she often turned up odd facts which the police hadn't for some reason or other managed to glean. She had the knack of chatting to people and getting them to unburden themselves of gossip and ancient history of all kinds. This too, though helpful, was dangerous.

''You use other informants,'' she'd pointed out once, when he'd been especially angry over something she'd done.

"If you mean petty crooks who act as our ears and eyes in the underworld when they think there might be something in it for them, yes! But you wouldn't compare yourself with them, I suppose? And I'd like to point out that any underworld grass knows the danger he runs and at the first sign of things turning sour, he dives for cover!"

"I will be careful," she had promised meekly. Too meekly.

Markby sighed aloud at the memory but it was with some curiosity that he rang her back.

"All right, what's it all about? I wasn't here when you called because I'd driven over for a word with Bullen. What's going on? Have you been up to mischief? Can't I leave you for five minutes? Does everything I say go in one ear and out of the other?"

She ignored his reproaches to zero in on the one point that interested her. "Bullen? Why? What did he tell you?"

"I got no information out of him. And I don't agree with Lars that he's crazy. Bullen, in my opinion, has all his senses! I've invested twenty pounds in some chicken wire to go around his cabbage patch and got him to think over what he's told us already and anything he may not have told us. Or so I hope. But you haven't told me why you rang. I hope and pray you're not meddling!"

"I'm doing no such thing!" she said indignantly. "And if you're going to be like that about it, I'll keep my nuggets of information to myself!"

"Speak on!" Markby growled. "Let's hear it! Who've you been gossiping with?"

"Mrs. Etheridge. She's the old lady with the shopping trolley who nearly ran it over your feet, the other day, while you were sitting on my wall, remember? I've got a little story to tell you about Bullen. Two stories, actually. The other one is about strange goings-on in All Saints' church twelve years ago. I got both tales from her."

He was hooked and knew it. Markby capitulated. "You don't fancy a drive up to North Wales tomorrow, do you? When I got back just now, I was told Susan Tempest, Kimberley's mother, has been traced to an address there. I thought I'd go and have a word with her myself. You could tell me your two stories on the way. We could get some lunch by the seaside, with a bit of luck!''

"Sounds fine!" she told him.

Markby set down the phone. The trip to North Wales to interview Susan Tempest probably wouldn't yield anything but he was interested to meet her. If nothing else, it would help him understand Kimberley, and he needed to understand the dead girl. At the moment she remained elusive. People remembered her, but could say nothing of any deep significance about her except that she would appear to have been sexually rapacious. She had to have been more than one of the local amateur tarts.

A tap at the door announced Louise Bryce. "Sorry to disturb you, sir, but thought you'd like to know. We've traced the other one now. Jennifer Jurawicz.''

"You have?'' Things were certainly starting to move at last!

"She's married now to a man named Fitzgerald. She lives with him in the Nottingham area." Bryce dimpled. "You'll never guess, sir!''

"Go on, then, tell me!" he invited.

"Her husband is a police officer!''

Markby's eyebrows shot up. "Is he? Then at least she'll cooperate! You'd better get up to Nottingham tomorrow and talk to her. I've arranged to go over to North Wales.'' He paused. "Married to a copper, eh?''

"Thought you'd like it,'' said Bryce.

Twelve

Meredith was awoken during the night by the sound of the wind. It rattled at the window frame and sent the curtains billowing into the room through the open transom. She got out of bed and closed it.

Outside, a tree which stood just by the house bowed its branches before the rising gale in alarming fashion. A plastic bag bowled along the pavement. If this worsened, the drive to Wales was going to be a battle against nature.

Alan collected her at eight sharp. He had allowed plenty of time for the drive, with a coffee break halfway, but it was looking as if it would certainly be lunchtime before they got there.

"She lives in Rhos-on-Sea," he said. "She knows Kimberley's remains have been found. She'd read it in the newspaper before the North Wales police got to visit her. That was inevitable with the delay in tracing her."

"She didn't come forward, then, when she read of it?"

"No." A gust of wind across the motorway caused the car to shudder and rain speckled the windscreen. "They had to ferret her out. It seems her attitude hasn't changed in twelve years. She still wants nothing to do with Kimberley, alive or dead."

"She sounds quite heartless."

"We'll see. She's a widow now. At least we don't have

to deal with Tempest, who sounded an awkward sort last time.''

''What happened to him?'' Meredith asked, mildly curious.

''Industrial accident. I gather the firm which employed him paid her generous compensation in an out-of-court settlement. She'd probably have got more if she'd gone to court, but would have had to wait for it, and the firm would've contested it. Lawyers cost money and it suited both sides to settle. She sold up and bought herself a new home on the coast on the proceeds. That's all I know.''

Some time later, in a noisy motorway service area cafeteria, he asked over the coffee, ''What was all that about Bullen?''

She told him as she unwrapped a croissant from its cellophane shroud, adding the story of the candle and cosmos flowers in the church.

''Archibald,'' Markby murmured. ''That's a coincidence, or perhaps not! I interviewed a Mrs. Archibald.''

''The one Mrs. Etheridge talked of, Derek Archibald, is or was a butcher in the town.''

''Then it's the same one. Archibald's the butchers, that's what she told me. She appeared inordinately proud of the fact that the shop had been nearly a century trading in the town. And guess what?'' Markby said grimly. ''The Archibalds live next door to the cottage inhabited by the late Joan Oates and her granddaughter Kimberley!''

Meredith shuddered, partly because she had just bitten into the croissant. It was soft and doughy instead of crisp and flaky. ''Odd coincidence,'' she said indistinctly. ''This is like eating a wad of Kleenex tissues.''

''So Archibald would have known Joan Oates and Kimberley.'' Alan was mumbling. ''Come to that, your Mrs. Etheridge would probably have known of her. Ask her. Etheridge!'' He snapped his fingers and Meredith looked up, startled.

''Keep that going and stamp your feet at the same time and you'll get a job as a flamenco dancer!'' she advised him. ''I wish I'd had a Danish pastry.''

''I know where I've heard the name Etheridge! James

Holland mentioned it to me when he came over to regional HQ. She fell out with him over something and quit the church.''

''Didn't care for dear old Father Appleton being replaced by a motorcyclist. Before that, so she tells me, she was an active member of the PCC.'' Meredith washed down the remains of the croissant with copious amounts of coffee. ''Alan, do you think they'd stumbled on a Black Mass? It sounds very sinister, a black-shrouded candle on the altar.''

He looked doubtful. ''But no other signs of it or anything else? No pentacles or reversed crucifixes or whatnot?'' He pulled a face. ''And from all we've learned, Kimberley hardly qualified for the role of sacrificial virgin!'' He fell silent, then murmured, ''Black cloth, candles, flowers . . . What does that suggest to you?''

''Having just been to Eunice Gresham's funeral, a burial service of some sort.''

''Or a requiem mass.''

Meredith put her elbows on the plastic table. ''For Kimberley?''

Markby uttered a muffled curse. ''I just wish I could find out more about what was going on around that church twelve years ago!''

''So ask Mrs. Etheridge and Derek Archibald! They were both members of the PCC!''

''I will, tomorrow. I hope Derek Archibald is less sanctimonious than his wife. She's one of these 'the world has gone to rack and ruin!' philosophers!''

''Derek was on the church council so he's probably just as bad.''

Markby groaned. ''Right now we'd better get on our way and talk to Susan Tempest! She'll probably turn out holier-than-thou, too!''

''With her record?''

''Those are the ones,'' he told her. ''The more they have to hide, the more respectable the front they put up!''

''Cynic!'' Meredith accused him.

''Copper!'' he replied simply.

*   *   *

They drove on into Wales, climbing past stone-walled hill-side fields of grazing sheep. They had quitted the motorway and soon negotiated a twisting road through trees. A shallow stream splashing over rocks to one hand and, rising above them in the distance, the bare mountain tops, together with the occasional ruined wall, reminded travelers of the wild history of this ancient land. Both Meredith and Alan had fallen silent. Alan, probably, was thinking of the forthcoming interview. Meredith was prey to a jumble of old memories.

As the road approached the North Wales coastline, the sun came out. But the wind was not appeased. At Rhos-on-Sea the promenade was under siege from the ocean. The waves, whipped into a frenzy, lashed the seawall and sent pebbles and sand showering across the road. Beaches and promenade were deserted, despite the sunshine. Holiday-makers huddled within cafés and shelters or had taken themselves elsewhere for the day.

Susan Tempest's name seemed more than suitable for the scene. But her home suggested, in contrast, an oasis of tranquillity. It was a large bungalow, white-walled and set back from the road in a neat garden. It had mullioned windows and a glass stormporch encased the front door. Within it, safe from the elements, hanging baskets of lobelia and geranium could be seen on either side of the front door. It looked comfortable and utterly respectable.

Markby drew up at the curb. "I'll be about an hour. Why don't you drive onto Llandudno and take a look round. Keep an eye open for a decent restaurant."

She watched him walk up the path and try the door of the glass porch. It opened. Markby entered and rang the front doorbell. She ought to drive on now, but made the excuse to herself that she'd wait until she'd seen the door answered, in case no one was home. The truth was she was as curious to see Susan Tempest as he was.

The door opened. Meredith could just glimpse a female form, dumpy and disappointingly ordinary. Markby stepped inside and the door closed.

Meredith was about to drive off when she heard the sound of a motorcycle. Surprised that anyone should have chosen to venture out on such a day on a motorbike, she looked into the windscreen mirror and saw, coasting up behind her, a leather-clad figure in a helmet, faceless behind the smoked-glass visor.

The figure stopped, got off its steed, hesitated, then came toward the car. It took off its helmet and stooped down by the door, revealing a youth of about nineteen with long brown hair and a tendency to acne.

Meredith rolled down the window and they stared at one another appraisingly.

"Don't think I'm being fresh or anything," said the youth. "But can I ask what you're doing parked outside our house?"

"Mr. Tempest?" Meredith asked.

"I'm Glyn Tempest. Mr. Tempest was my dad. He's dead. You're not anything to do with the police, are you? Because some supercopper is supposed to be visiting my mum today."

"Yes—I mean, I'm not a policewoman, but Superintendent Markby has just gone in."

He wetted his lips as the wind tugged at his long hair. "I came over to lend a hand," he said. "Mum, she's had enough, what with Dad being killed a few years back and now this! It's not her fault! I mean, it was all in the past."

"I'm sure Superintendent Markby will be very tactful."

"He better bloody had be!" said Glyn truculently. "I'll make sure he is!" He set off up the pathway to the bungalow, helmet under his arm, and opened the front door for himself.

As he disappeared inside, Meredith wondered if she ought to wait now in case Alan needed support. But he could probably handle Glyn Tempest, who, despite his truculence, was a slightly built young man.

"Mum can't help you. I don't know why you had to come bothering her!"

Markby cast Glyn Tempest an irritated glance. He hadn't come all this way to talk to a spotty youth in motorcyclist's leathers.

Mrs. Tempest said soothingly, "It's all right, Glyn. Why

don't you go out to the kitchen and make us all a cup of coffee?''

Glyn glowered at Markby but got up and shambled out. He could be heard distantly rattling cups.

''He feels he has to look after me since Jack died.'' Mrs. Tempest smiled nervously at her visitor.

''I haven't come with the intention of distressing you,'' Markby said. ''I only wanted a word. We have to build up a dossier, if you like, on Kimberley. We want to know where she was, what she did, whom she saw during her last days. Did she contact anyone? Did she write or phone? Did anyone contact her? Can anyone give us a name, someone we don't yet know of, but could go and ask. We have to get to know Kimberley. It's proving difficult.''

''It's Mum you'd have wanted to see.'' She looked away, at the window and the distant prospect of the sea. ''She brought up Kimberley. I can't tell you anything about her. I didn't know her, not after she was a year old. I suppose you think I was a bad mother.''

''It's not for me to think anything of the sort,'' he pointed out mildly.

She turned her head back and faced him defiantly. ''I didn't mean to abandon her. When I first came here to Wales I thought I could make a new life, a new home for us both. When I was all set up, I'd send for Kim to join me. I kept in touch, sent letters and presents. I really meant it. But I was very young. I had no idea how difficult it would be. I knew Kim was all right. I knew Mum would look after her well. I started to realize that, on my own, I couldn't cope with a baby, and keep a full-time job, and save up for a decent place to live. I kept putting it off, the sending for her, I mean.''

The door swung open and Glyn tramped in bearing a tray with three mugs of coffee with the spoons sticking out of them. He set it down gracelessly.

''You should have used the good cups,'' reproved his mother. ''What will the superintendent think?''

''He won't mind!'' said Glyn.

''Indeed I don't. I prefer coffee in a mug.'' Markby availed himself of a strong-looking brew. Glyn had retired to a chair and slumped there, glaring and stirring his coffee noisily.

"Anyway," his mother went on. "Then I met Jack. He had a good job and I knew if I married him we'd be able to take out a mortgage and buy our own place. That wasn't why I married him. I loved him. He was very handsome—" Her eyes drifted to a nearby photograph. "He was a good husband and a good father to Glyn and Julie. But he was a strong sort of personality, if you understand me. He believed a man should be master in his own house. He didn't like people arguing with him. He liked being in charge and he had very fixed ideas about right and wrong. He wasn't the sort of man I could tell about—about my already having a baby. So I didn't tell him.

"We got married. I started to be scared that Mum would find me and turn up on the doorstep with Kim in her arms. So I—gradually I stopped writing. I know I never put an address but I still was afraid that somehow she'd trace me. All the time the fear haunted me. The police did come one day, years later, to say Kim had run away. They asked, had I seen her? It all came out. Jack was furious. But we had the children by then and somehow we patched it up. I admit, I was terrified she'd find her way to Wales and me. Jack had finally said, 'All right, we won't talk about it any more.' But if she'd actually appeared, flesh and blood standing there, I don't know what Jack would have done." She glanced at her son. "Sorry, Glyn, but you remember how your dad was."

The wind rattled the window. The lace curtains moved in response.

Markby was visited by a mental image of Kimberley, discovered by her grandmother sorting through old Christmas and birthday cards, seeking a clue as to the whereabouts of her missing mother. It wasn't for him to judge. Indeed, it was impossible to know what to decide about it. Susan had reasoned it out to her own satisfaction. She'd persuaded herself of everything she'd told him, that it had been just like that. Her youth, in memory, had been sanitized, expurgated, rendered acceptable. He wondered how, when obliged to admit to Jack that she had a child already, she'd explained the circumstances surrounding the infant's conception. Some glib tale or other which Tempest had accepted. She would hardly have described herself as the headstrong tearaway remembered by Mrs. Archibald or Daisy Merrill.

He felt a burst of irritation because there was more than a whiff of hypocrisy here. This room, the whole bungalow, had a remorseless, outdated, gentility about it. Everything was polished and hoovered and dusted to within an inch of its life. If there'd been any blemishes, they'd been eradicated, in just as thorough a job as Susan had done on her own background.

Markby looked toward the large studio portrait of the late Jack glowering handsomely from a sidetable. A dark-haired, thick-browed, lantern-jawed thug. Women often found that type attractive. Glyn didn't resemble him particularly. Perhaps he rode around on the motorbike, dressed up like Darth Vadar, to compensate.

In his leathers, the lad looked out of place in the neat room. Markby wondered about his sister. Her name was Julie, Mrs. Tempest had told him. She was a nurse. He asked, "Did you ever phone your mother?"

She shook her head miserably. "No, I was afraid to. I know how bad it looks."

"It's not her fault!" Glyn said loudly.

Markby ignored him. "You have no other relatives or anyone you can think of, a family friend perhaps, whom Kimberley might have been in touch with?"

"No. I didn't forget Kim!" Defiance returned. She looked almost spirited. "But thinking about her made me feel so guilty I blocked it all out. It was easier that way. Mum, too! I still loved her and missed her. I wanted to know how she was. Glyn and Julie never knew their grandma nor she them! I knew it was all wrong and I was sorry, but what could I do? I was hurt, too!"

"When your husband died, you didn't try to get in touch?" He felt cruel but he was here to ask questions. He wished the youth would go away. She might tell him things without Glyn's presence which she'd not mention before the boy. But, on the other hand, he felt she drew some strength from the young man's brooding figure. She didn't resent Markby being here nearly so much as she'd have done, had she been trapped, alone with him.

"I didn't." Her voice was almost inaudible. "I didn't even dare go back when Mum died, not even to her funeral. I just wrote to the solicitor to give her stuff to the Salvation Army!" She cleared her throat and tried again. "I didn't contact her when Jack died because by then it was too late. There would be too many explanations, like why I'd left her. I'd have to tell Glyn and Julie about it all. That they'd had a grandmother they'd never seen and—and a—that I had another child. They'd look at me and wonder what sort of person I was. What sort of mother. They'd wonder if I'd ever have left them—"

Glyn broke in, "No, we wouldn't! We love you, Mum! We'd have understood, Julie and me!"

She looked gratefully at him and when she turned back to Markby it was with renewed assurance. "I am truly sorry, Superintendent, for everything that's happened. I hope you find whoever—whoever killed Kim. I'm sorry she was murdered. That hardly seems a strong enough way to put it, but what else can I say? I can't undo it. I can't make it different to how it was. I'm sorry. I'm really sorry. But I can't change anything. We never can, can we?"

"No," Markby said ruefully. "We never can."

"If I have to be quite honest with you, then I have to say that if bringing Kim here to Wales all those years ago would have meant I'd lost any chance of happiness with Jack, then I would have resented it. It wouldn't have been the poor little mite's fault but I couldn't have helped blaming her. I'm only human. I was very young when I had her. I was younger than my daughter Julie is now. I was younger than Glyn here! I was only a child myself! I should have put up Kim for adoption, perhaps. But I thought Mum could manage and at least Kim was with her own grandma. She was with her own family. I knew where she was. If I'd let her go to strangers, I'd not have known what had happened to her."

The flaw in her reasoning struck her and she added with a sigh, "But I didn't know what had happened to her, anyway, did I? But you know what I mean. At the back of my mind I felt Kim must be all right because she was with my mother. As time went by, and I didn't go home, I thought it was nice for Mum, too. I thought well, at least Mum has got Kim! She's got someone with her. I thought they were probably quite happy together. I did think, I honestly believed, that everything had turned out for the best. If I'd got in touch, it would've rocked the boat. Upset everyone, disturbed all the arrangements which had worked themselves out.''

Markby reflected that it did not seem to occur to her, or she had suppressed the thought, that Joan Oates might have preferred to have been spared the work and worry of a young child. And that at an age when Joan might have expected to start taking things easier after bringing up one difficult child.

Susan was growing aggressive. ''I wasn't to know, was I, that she'd be murdered? It was a dreadful shock to see it in the papers, about the—bones being found in that grave. At first it was just a report, something which had happened in Bamford. But it gave me a funny feeling because they said the bones might have been there about twelve years and that's the time Kim disappeared and the police came to see me. Then the police came here. They'd traced me from the last place we'd lived, before Jack died. They said it was Kim. I felt numb. It's not the sort of thing you expect to happen!''

Her eyes flashed defiance at him and her pudgy little hands were clasped tightly in her lap. A old-fashioned mahogany-cased clock on the sideboard chimed the hour.

''No,'' Markby said, rising to his feet. ''You weren't to know. Thank you for making time to see me. Thanks for the coffee, Glyn.''

'' 'S all right!'' said Glyn.

Meredith had driven on along the coast through Penrhyn Bay, under the shadow of the hill called the Little Orme, and on to Llandudno. She hadn't visited the seaside town in years. She remembered it from childhood holidays. The memories came racing back, of the amusement arcade

where she'd spent so many happy afternoons trying to
scoop the penny-falls, the pier, the Punch and Judy show.
She parked the car on the promenade at Craig-y-Don and
got out.

The wind struck her face bringing a tang of salty sea air.
The waves roared and rumbled as they rushed at the beach.
She trudged along the promenade with head down and
hands in pockets. The ice cream sellers were doing poor
business today.

She found the park and the bowling green, deserted by
its sternfaced *aficionados* in today's inclement weather, and
the miniature golf links. She had won small triumphs on
the miniature golf. But she'd been rebuffed by the regulars
on the bowling green, intolerant both of child observers and
inexperienced young players on the hallowed lawn. It all
seemed long ago and misty in memory. It must have rained
then or been blustery occasionally as today, but not in recall. In her mind the sun shone down on her childish form.
It brought to mind her parents, too. Her mother in a navy
frock with white piping trim and white sandals and her
father in his short-sleeved "sports shirts." She almost forgot Alan, and had to hasten back to the car, to drive as
quickly as possible back to Rhos.

She made it just in time. Glyn's motorbike had been
moved from the roadside into the drive at the side of the
bungalow. But Markby had survived Glyn's appearance. As
she drew up, the door of the bungalow opened and he came
out. A woman came with him and they stood together in
the glass porch talking for a few moments.

Meredith was able to see her clearly now. She was ma-
tronly and in her late forties, neatly dressed in a crisp white
blouse and blue cotton skirt. She twisted her hands together
nervously as she talked, but as Markby finally left, shook
hands with him and, seeing Meredith waiting in the car,
gave her a wave of acknowledgment.

Meredith automatically raised a hand to respond. So that
was Susan. No floozy, no hard-hearted monster. Just a
frightened little woman who had clawed her way to respectability and was terrified of losing it. The animosity,
which Meredith had harbored toward the errant mother who

had abandoned Kimberley, evaporated now she'd seen for herself. If Joan Oates could look down on her wayward daughter, standing between the hanging baskets at the door of her pristine bungalow, she'd be well satisfied. Susan had, despite an inauspicious beginning, made good.

But it had all come too late for Kimberley.

"What happened?" she asked impatiently when they were seated a little later in a small Italian restaurant in a side road.

"Not very much. The boy turned up right at the beginning. But you know that. He said he'd spoken to you. I wasn't best pleased but it turned out for the best. She felt happier with him there giving moral support. She was frank enough, as far as it went."

Markby frowned. "But she was telling lies, even so. Unconscious lies, perhaps. Or even conscious ones. I wish I knew. Over the years she's rehashed the story in her mind and now she believes the version she told me. She didn't intend to abandon Kimberley but events prevented her fetching her to Wales and so on.

"It was feasible. Some of it was probably true. Some of it adjusted a little. It's obvious that she's been an excellent mother to the boy and his sister and they think the world of her. On the other hand, I've dealt with enough child cruelty cases in my time to know that often the neglected child has been singled out for some reason and other children in the family are well cared for.

"All I can say is that she is probably unable now to tell the truth. The fear hasn't gone away but she's done her best to live down an unpromising start to her life and been fairly successful. She was sorry that Kimberley had been murdered."

"Sorry!" Meredith goggled at him. "Is that the best she could do?"

"She knew it was inadequate. She admitted it. But as she said, what else could she say? She hadn't seen Kimberley since she was a baby. When Kimberley disappeared she had been afraid the girl would turn up on the doorstep. She feels ashamed of that now, but at the time, as she points out, she had a new marriage, other children and a husband who had known nothing of her past.

"It was a shock to read in the papers about the bones, and to learn that Kim, as she calls her, was dead. She couldn't tell me anything. Perhaps I oughtn't to have wasted my time coming. On the other hand, one always learns something. Even when people lie."

Desperation, that was what had motivated Susan Tempest.

Desperation could lead to desperate measures. Even to kill? He pushed this highly unpalatable thought to the back of his mind where he knew it would linger. He said, "I hope Bryce is getting on better with Jennifer Fitzgerald."

"Who on earth is she?" Meredith paused with a forkful of spaghetti in mid-air.

"Jennifer Jurawicz, the other waitress in the photo. Thinking it over, I have high hopes of that interview. I wish I'd decided to take that one instead of this one. But Jennifer's still young, and might talk more easily to a younger woman, so I sent Louise Bryce. Girls chatter together, don't they? Swap tales of boyfriends and so on?"

"You're suddenly very knowledgeable," Meredith told him. "You think Kimberley might have confided passionate secrets to Jennifer?"

"Let's hope she did!" Alan said fervently.

"Yes, I remember Kim Oates!" said Jennifer Fitzgerald. "I rather liked her. We got on well."

Bryce relaxed. It was a long way from Bamford to Nottingham. She didn't know how the super was getting on, driving up to North Wales, but the blustery weather had made Bryce's own journey hazardous enough.

Jennifer lived in a bright new house on a bright new housing estate. All the furniture was new. The carpet and curtains were new and still smelled of the stores where they'd been purchased. The sink unit in the fitted kitchen where tea had been made shone like polished silver. Bryce had duly admired it all.

"We bought all new when we bought the house!" Jennifer told her, smiling radiantly. "We had all old stuff anyway, when we got married, what people gave us. So we chucked it all out. Nice, isn't it?'' She gazed complacently around her little kingdom.

She was a pretty woman in jeans, sweatshirt and trainers. Her long hair was tied back with a scarf and pink plastic hoop earrings dangled at her earlobes. There was a Slavic cast to her countenance and a whiteness of skin which suggested the Baltic coast. But otherwise she was no different to any of the other young women on this estate.

''You work? I mean, you have a job?'' Bryce asked her.

''I used to be a receptionist, down at the health center, before the twins were born. But after that, I couldn't do both, could I?'' She cocked her head, listening. ''They seem to have gone off all right.''

The interview had been delayed for some fifteen minutes while Jennifer settled down two plump infants, as alike as peas in a pod, for their nap.

''Tell me about Kimberley,'' Bryce suggested.

''Like another cup of tea, Inspector? Let's see. Well, she was the outgoing sort. Loved the job because it meant going to all those parties. I know we weren't guests, but we were part of it, if you see what I mean. At sixteen, seventeen, it was all the same to us.''

Bryce was mindful of Markby's final warning words. ''Be careful how you mention Lars Holden. You can't just drop an MP's name casually into the conversation and expect it to land without a resounding clatter!''

''There's been a suggestion,'' Bryce said carefully, ''that Kimberley occasionally flirted with the customers, even though it was strictly forbidden by the company.''

Jennifer wriggled on her mock-leather sofa and pulled a little moue of worldly wisdom. ''Well, we were all very young, you know! It didn't mean anything.''

''She never spoke to you of boyfriends, or of one in particular?''

Jennifer grew thoughtful. ''Now it's funny you should ask that. I was trying to remember, before you came, everything Kim ever said to me. But it was a long time ago and a lot's happened since then, to me, anyway!'' She giggled.

''We couldn't believe it when the doctor told me it would be twins!''

''I'm sure you were surprised and delighted. About Kimberley—'' Bryce prompted.

''Sorry, you want to know about Kim. She was a bit of a daydreamer in some ways. We all are at that age, aren't we? She didn't have much of a home life. She lived with her grandma. They didn't get on too well. Generation gap, I suppose. The grandma was inclined to be a bit strict. What Kim wanted was a flat of her own. She told me she'd got a new boyfriend. He had money and he'd set her up in her own place. That's what she said. I didn't really believe it, to tell you the truth. She read a lot of books and magazines. I think she made it up. Where would she meet someone rich in Bamford, I ask you!'' Jennifer trilled laughter again.

''At one of the parties arranged by the firm?'' Bryce suggested.

''Oh, there, well, yes. She might have met someone there.'' Jennifer sounded doubtful and bit her lip.

''You can't remember any particular occasion when, say, Kimberley disappeared for a while during the evening?''

Jennifer gave her an old-fashioned look. ''I know what you're talking about. I don't say it never happened. But she couldn't go missing for long or she'd have been in trouble. A quick kiss and cuddle, in a cloakroom, perhaps. I'm sure nothing more. Although—''

Jennifer's jaunty assurance faltered. ''When I said, she'd have been in trouble, I meant she'd have got the sack. Not the other kind of trouble. But now you mention it, I did think—'' Jennifer's embarrassment grew. ''I wasn't at all sure. But the last few weeks before she disappeared, left or whatever, she did seem to me to be putting on weight. She was never slim, you understand. But her waist had got much bigger. We wore straight black skirts for work and you could see hers didn't button up and her tummy was bulging out in front. I did wonder if she could've been, you know, pregnant. I didn't like to ask. I did say, I remember, 'You're putting it on, Kim. You'd better stop pinching the cakes!' That was a bit of a joke. If there was something really delicious in the food line at a party, we'd sneak a bit of it. She said she was going to go on a diet.''

Bryce nodded but didn't say anything. Jennifer had noticed Kim's growing waistline and others, presumably, must have done so too. But only Simon French, it appeared, had been party to Kimberley's secret.

"And she *was* pregnant, wasn't she?'' Jennifer said now. "I read in the paper that they found bones of an unborn baby with her. So I was right. But you know how it is. At the time I didn't want to be unfair and we were all young. I didn't know much about it, how long it took for a pregnancy to show and so on. I know now! Especially with twins! I was like a house! Anyway, it wasn't long after that Kim went away. I don't know where. I remember there was a terrible fuss when she didn't turn up for work.''

Jennifer clasped her hands on her knees and looked down. "It gave me a terrible shock to hear she'd been murdered and they'd found her bones in that grave. I couldn't eat anything that evening and we'd gone out with some friends to a restaurant. I just sat there and Paul brought me home early. It was such a shame. We'd got the babysitter in and everything. But I couldn't face food, not thinking about poor Kim. I hope she didn't—didn't suffer, you know? I hope, when he killed her, whoever it was, it was quick.''

"There was nothing else? You can't remember anything, even a little thing, or anything you're not sure of? Don't be afraid to mention it. We'll check it out!'' Bryce urged.

Jennifer looked up and brushed back a stray lock of hair. "Yes. Just at the end, before she disappeared, she had money. I mean, she had some money more than she'd have got from her wages. That's why, when she disappeared, I thought she'd left and gone to find herself somewhere new to live. Because she had the money. I know I didn't believe her when she said she had a rich boyfriend, but maybe it was true at that. She must have got the money from somewhere. Her grandma didn't have any.''

"How much money?'' Bryce leaned forward eagerly.

"She didn't say. She didn't tell me. I saw it—I saw her putting a roll of banknotes in her bag. We were putting on our coats ready to go home one evening. I came into the cloakroom and she was in there on her own. She looked up and gave a sort of gasp, then said, 'Oh, it's only you, Jen!'

"I said, 'What have you done, won the Pools?' She just laughed. She said it was a present, for her to buy herself something. I said, 'pretty good present!' because I reckon it must have been, oh, at least a couple of hundred pounds."

"Jennifer!" Bryce urged. "Try and think where you were when this happened. Was it in a private house? Or a club or where?"

"It was after a dinner dance we'd done, the caterers had done, I mean. It was, let's see, something political. Not in a private house, in a hall. One of these political local associations, couldn't tell you now which political party."

Jennifer gave Bryce a hunted look. "I suppose she could've pinched it. But no one reported any money missing. I don't think Kim would've done that. She wasn't a thief. Any light-fingered behavior and she'd have got the sack outright! I'll tell you what I did think. It's awful, I shouldn't have. But I did wonder, sometimes, if Kim—I know she's dead and one oughtn't to speak ill of the dead. It's not fair. They can't defend themselves."

"Jennifer!" Bryce said firmly, "This is no time to be squeamish. Kim *is* dead and we want to know who, how and why!"

"Yes, I know that." Jennifer looked abashed. "Paul said, I should tell you everything, even the not-so-nice things. The truth is I sometimes wondered if Kim, just on the side, was on the game."

"We've all been wondering that!" said Bryce with a sigh.

There was, after all, a limit to the number of men they could hope to track down.

Thirteen

"A pay-off!" Bryce said. "For sure."

It was the following morning. The wind had abated but the rain returned in a fine drizzle. Markby sat in the gray light by the window and sifted through the neatly typed pages of Bryce's report.

"It certainly looks like it. And she received this money at a function for which Partytime catered. A function given by one of the local political associations."

"It keeps coming back to Lars Holden," Bryce murmured.

"I know!" Markby snapped, then apologized. "Sorry. I realize I'm going to have to speak to him again. More to the point, I'm going to have to speak to Margaret Holden as a matter of urgency. Fortunately, I have warned her I'll be calling."

He steepled his fingers. "If the girl was being paid not to make a fuss, paid large sums of money, then remember Lars was only eighteen at the time. He wouldn't have been able to lay his hands on several hundred pounds, not without questions being asked. It's far more likely someone else, someone interested in Lars's future, paid. It could have been either his mother or his father who is now dead, or both of them, jointly. If his father was trying to get the girl out of Lars's life without his wife's knowledge, we'll never be able to establish it. If Margaret doesn't know about Lars and the girl, it's going to come as a dreadful shock.''

"Holden may have told his mother or Angela Pritchard may have told her. They may have wanted to forewarn her, just as they took the trouble to tell you before you found out any other way. Then, having told you, they might have calculated that you'd call on her!'' Bryce pointed out.

"I'll do it this morning. There's no point in wasting time!'' Markby said glumly.

"Kimberley also spoke to Jennifer of having a rich boyfriend. That sounds like Lars. It is a wealthy family, sir. As Jennifer said, where would she meet someone rich in Bamford? Only at one of the parties Partytime was hired to cater for.''

Markby drummed his fingers on the desk. "Didn't Jennifer also say, Kimberley spoke of this rich boyfriend setting her up in a flat? Lars couldn't have offered her that. So there could be someone else. Or, on the other hand, Kimberley could have been fantasizing again, as everyone likes to call it!

"Let me talk to Margaret Holden,'' he got up and reached for the phone. "At the risk of repeating myself, this is a matter for kid gloves. We cannot investigate an MP without risking a hornets' nest of journalists descending on us. And if we're wrong, remember, we could have ruined his career for nothing! Mud sticks.''

Meredith lowered her umbrella and shook it before folding it as she peered into the shop window. Cuts of meat, all kinds, were spread out on trays, each divided from its neighbor by a line of dark green plastic "foliage.'' The range of colors and shapes in the meat itself presented a striking composition of geometric shapes and contrasts. Coral pink to burgundy red, with all shades in between, trimmed of unsightly fat and gristle, none of it now hinted at the horror of slaughter or dismemberment. It was neat and very clean. No one could reasonably object to any of it. A pink plastic pig presided over it, standing on his hind trotters and leering at prospective customers.

She glanced up at the legend above the window. "Archibald. Family Butcher. Est. 1897.'' That was a family firm, all right. Getting on for a hundred years selling meat from the same shop. A record of some sort.

She pushed open the door. As usual in such old-fashioned stores, modern refrigerated cabinets and cold-stores hadn't eliminated the lingering odor of blood. The counter ran the length of the shop from front to back. Butchers' tools, medieval in appearance, hung on hooks on the wall, gleaming knives, choppers, saws, all the para-phernalia of the amputation theater.

Opposite the door by which she'd entered was another door leading into a passageway which in turn terminated in a back door. As she looked, someone, a stocky figure of a man, came out of a door in the passageway and opened the door at the far end. A cold draft invaded the shop and she glimpsed an untidy backyard and a wooden outbuilding of some kind with a felt roof.

"Can I help you?" inquired a young man in a straw boater and a striped apron.

"Yes, please. Could I have half a dozen of the lamb chops? The ones in the window."

He moved to the window display and leaned over. "These? The ones on offer today?"

"Those." He was too young to be Derek Archibald. As he weighed up the chops, she asked for a pound of beef sausages as well, building up good will.

"Our own? We make them on the premises. We make plain, tomato-flavored and herb. Herb ones are nice. We sell a lot of them."

"Herb then, please." He began to wrap up her purchases. "Does Mr. Archibald still work in the shop?"

"Derek? Yeah. He's out back I expect."

"Oh, you've got a coldstore out there? I saw there's a building at the rear of the yard. Will he be busy there all morning?"

The young man laughed. "No, that's not our coldstore. That's down there . . ." He indicated the passageway. "Out back, that's Derek's old shed. Don't ask me what he's got in there. He keeps it all locked up! He won't be long. Did you want him special?"

"I would actually like to have a word with him, if it's possible."

"Should think so. Hang on a bit and he'll be back." The gust of fresh air blew around her ankles again. "Here he is now. Young lady wants a word with you, Derek."

The stocky figure she'd noticed go out into the yard had come back into the shop and stood appraising her. He wasn't tall, but broad. His flat, red face seemed too big for the features, or they too small for it. Small eyes, almost lost in puffy folds, a squashed button of a nose, small mouth. He looked, there was no denying it, uncannily like the plastic pig in his window. He also wore a straw boater and a navy and white striped apron over his white coat.

"What can I do for you, then, m'dear?" he asked. It was a heavy, slow, country voice. Its owner wasn't one to hurry his judgment.

"My name's Meredith Mitchell. I live near to Mrs. Etheridge. I believe you know her." No response. "It's about something which happened in Bamford a long time ago, twelve years actually. I was talking to Mrs. Etheridge recently and she told me of it. She mentioned you."

If Archibald drew the conclusion from this speech that Mrs. Etheridge had recommended Meredith to speak to Derek, so be it. Meredith consoled herself that she hadn't actually lied.

"Janet Etheridge, eh?" Archibald raised his eyebrows and the tiny eyes widened a fraction. "I haven't seen her in a while. How's she doing these days, then?"

"Not so well. She has arthritis."

"Sorry to hear it. Can't say I'm surprised, though, all that rabbit food she's been eating for years. She wants to tuck into a bit of steak and kidney pudding and a pork chop from time to time!"

The young man in the boater caught Meredith's eye, grinned, and winked at her.

"What's Janet been telling you, then?" Derek Archibald asked.

"It's about something that happened when she and you were both on the parochial council of All Saints' church. Before the Reverend Appleton died. About some flowers and a candle found burning on the altar one evening.''

Archibald pursed his small mouth till it almost disappeared but said nothing.

Meredith plunged on. ''I'm interested in the occult. I mean, I'm not into witchcraft, don't think that! But I thought I could get material for an article for one of the county magazines. Survival of ancient practices, pagan religions, that sort of thing.''

''Nothing like that around Bamford,'' said Archibald, ''You ever hear of anything like that, Gary?''

Gary shook his boatered head and said regretfully that they hadn't any devil-worshippers around Bamford that he'd heard of. ''They're all too bloomin' respectable!'' he opined. ''Catch any of this lot—'' he nodded toward the busy street visible through the window ''—dancing around naked and holding orgies!''

''I didn't mean orgies,'' Meredith protested. ''I was thinking of rituals. Mrs. Etheridge said the candle was wrapped in a piece of black cloth.''

''It was.'' Archibald seemed to make a sudden decision to tell her. ''Though I'm surprised she's brought up that story after all these years. It wasn't anything but kids mucking about in the church. Could've started a fire, of course. But it didn't. It had burned out by the time we saw it. There were some flowers, I recall. Just scattered about on the altar. Old vicar, that's Mr. Appleton, he didn't think it was so serious. I reckon he was right. Not devil-worship, anyroad!'' He chuckled.

''You've never told me, Derek!'' said Gary, aggrieved.

His employer turned his piggy gaze on him. ''What for? What's it to you?''

''Well, I'd have been interested.''

''What's interesting about it? Kids larking about? I'd practically forgot, anyway.'' He turned back to Meredith. ''There's nothing for you to write about. You don't want to go making anything of it. It wasn't no satanic nonsense. As for writing to magazines or newspapers, you don't want to do that. We'd have all kind of loonies coming here to look at the church. Take my advice, forget about it!''

The bell above the door jingled and two more customers

came in. "Excuse me, then!" said Archibald meaningfully. "Half-day closing today and we're always busy."

"Oh, thank you. How much, Gary?"

Gary did a sum on a scrap of wrapping paper with a pencil kept for that purpose behind his ear. Meredith paid and as he handed her her change, Gary whispered, "Here, if you learn anything, you know, about what you were asking, let me know! It'd be a real gas to nip along and see some satanic rites. And if anyone wanted animal guts or a skull, that sort of thing, I could get it for them, no problem!"

Meredith promised to pass the information to any satanists she happened to stumble upon. As she went out, Derek Archibald, busy with the other customers, paid no attention to her departure.

She walked home thoughtfully.

Oscar remembered him. As Markby entered the dachshund began to jump up and down and give little yelps of welcome.

"Hullo, old chap!" He stooped to scratch Oscar's ears. "Thanks for making time to see me, Margaret."

They were in the wide reception area of The Old Farm. A fire had been lit in the stone hearth and crackled hospitably. Oscar's wicker basket was strategically placed to one side of it. Newly arranged flowers stood on a table. It looked, he thought, like something out of the Ideal Home exhibition. Or something out of a stage set. That idea struck him with something of a shock. How much reality was he seeing? How much carefully set-out deception?

"Sit down, Alan, won't you? It's a dreadful day and still summer! One can hardly believe it."

She motioned him to a seat. She was dressed in a tan skirt and cream silk shirt, with a gold chain by way of jewelry. He thought she looked tired.

Oscar, seeing everyone was settling down, scrambled back into his basket. He began to burrow his way under an old blanket, turning around and around until he'd got his bed just so, and nothing could be seen of him but a bump under the covering.

"He's getting old," said his owner. "He likes to be warm. I don't know how he stands so much heat." She smiled sadly. "I shall be sorry when I don't have Oscar for company any longer. He's been a loyal friend."

"He's pretty fit, isn't he? He looks very well."

"Oh, he's fit enough, but he's thirteen, you know. That's old in dog years. Over seventy, in human terms."

An elderly woman came in with a tray of coffee and biscuits.

Margaret said, "Thank you, Doris."

When she had gone and Margaret had handed Markby his coffee and offered him a biscuit, she said, "So, what can I do for you, Alan?"

Markby bit into a biscuit. It was homemade. "I'm sorry to bother you, Margaret. I don't want to upset you or anyone else, but I'm investigating the death of this girl, Kimberley Oates. You must have read of it."

She nodded. Her air of tiredness increased. There were dark shadows under her eyes and she exuded an air of deep sadness.

"She worked for a firm called Partytime. They're caterers. You employed them once, for Lars's eighteenth birthday, I understand."

She nodded again. "I remember. I was quite satisfied with them."

"Kimberley was a waitress that night."

She shifted on her chair and put down her coffee undrunk.

"I know what you're going to say, Alan. Lars has spoken to me. He told me that you and Meredith, he and Angie, discussed it over lunch. I know he had a—a little romantic friendship with this girl. It wasn't important."

"I don't suppose it was. I've told Lars that if he tells me everything and none of it is relevant, nothing will get out—to the press, I mean."

"Thank you." She inclined her head.

Markby couldn't help but feel it was all rather like dealing with royalty. He hardened his heart. He mustn't allow her to dictate the tone of the interview. This was a police matter, like it or not.

"The girl was pregnant when she died, about four months."

She turned her head aside and gazed into the flames. "Have you spoken to Lars about that?"

"No, not yet. Margaret, did Kimberley come to see you?"

There was a silence. She sighed. "Yes, she came here. A common, cheap sort of girl. Very young, and pretty, I suppose. She said she was carrying Lars's baby. I thought, at first, she wanted money. Then I wasn't sure. I think—ridiculous though it might seem—she thought Lars might marry her!"

Margaret turned wide surprised eyes on him. "He was eighteen! Just about to go up to university! It was completely out of the question. Anyway, he was such a bright boy, so special. He was already interested in politics. We could all see he would make a brilliant career. And here was this girl, she couldn't even speak correct English! Her vocabulary was that of a ten-year-old but for the swear-words! I couldn't believe my ears. The worst of it was that she seemed to have no idea she was using foul language. As if that was how everyone spoke. Perhaps people she knew did speak like that. As for it being Lars's child, how could we be sure of that?"

"Your husband was alive then? He was present at this interview?"

"Yes. He was here. He was very angry. Lars and Richard, my husband, they didn't communicate well. I don't mean that they got along badly. Only that they didn't seem to have any natural rapport. I don't know why. Richard had been brought up in a very traditional English way. He was sent off to school at seven and I don't think he saw much of his parents after that. His father was in the army and his mother very much taken up with charity work. I'm afraid that Lars got the impression his father didn't care. That wasn't true. Richard cared very much but he had difficulty showing it.

"At the time I'm talking of, when that girl came here, Richard was a sick man. It was the beginning of his last illness. He couldn't cope. I told him to leave it to me. I told the girl she was wasting her time. If she tried to take Lars to court, any kind of paternity suit, I'd find everyone else who had ever slept with her, and bring them into court to testify she was nothing but the local tart! I wouldn't pay her one penny. It's a mistake to pay blackmailers, Alan. They come back, time and time again!''

Margaret's voice had grown fierce. Kimberley had met her match, thought Markby. She must have realized she would get nothing here. But she had fared better somewhere else.

"Someone paid her, Margaret. Or so it looks. She was seen with a large sum of money."

"We didn't!" Margaret turned on him. "Not one penny, Alan, I swear! Nothing!" She calmed herself with a visible effort. "She didn't come back."

"Did Lars go on seeing her?"

"I don't know." Margaret made a weary gesture of one hand. "Lars was an innocent. I know he was eighteen but he'd lived a very privileged life. He'd never had to cope with any problem. His father and I had always taken care of everything. We wanted him to be able to concentrate on his studies. I'm sure, when he first met Kimberley, he didn't realize what sort of danger he was in. She was a trouble-maker. She had little grip on reality. The idea that Lars might marry her, for example! So foolish!"

"She was also very young," Markby said gently.

"I'm sorry she's dead," Margaret told him with dignity. "I'm sorry for the way she died, or I suppose she died, murdered. But I can't help it. I can't say anything else."

Her words were an echo of those spoken the day before by Kimberley's mother. Sorry—but can't do anything about it. Poor Kimberley, in everyone's way. If one person, at any stage, had held out a helping hand . . . not a hand filled with money, but a hand of love. But no one had.

Love had surely been what Kimberley sought. All those transient affairs. It was an old story.

But it remained a fact that someone had paid her a considerable sum of money. Who?

*   *   *

Markby drove slowly away from the house. It had begun to tip it down. He switched on the windscreen wipers and just in time. At the bottom of the drive, a figure had moved out from under the dripping trees and held up a hand, flagging him down. Markby braked hurriedly.

It was Lars, well protected against the rain by a Barbour and cap, with his trousers tucked into green gumboots. He probably, thought Markby as Lars stooped down to speak through the window, wore that outfit when visiting his farming constituents.

"Alan? I'd like a word." Lars's face was close, wet with rain and furrowed with worry.

Markby leaned across and opened the passenger door. Lars walked around and got in. He pulled the door to, took off his cap, ran a hand over his hair and then sat, staring at the rain-speckled windscreen.

"English summer weather!" he said. "Marvellous."

"Want me to drive somewhere? Might be a pub open. It's twelve." Markby reached a hand toward the ignition key.

"If you like. There's one just up the road, Drover's Arms."

It took only minutes to reach the pub in question. It looked a sad, abandoned place in the rain, only one other car in its car park. Inside it smelled of damp clothing, dust and the lees of barrels. They took their pints to a gloomy corner and sat down on the grubby seats.

"You've been to see Mother," Lars said.

"I had a few questions for her."

"You needn't have worried her. I told you all I knew."

"No, Lars, not all."

Lars sipped his pint and pulled a face. "Awful beer in this place. But at least Nat Bullen isn't sitting in a corner, drinking away his pension money! He comes here. Mother can't help you. She doesn't know anything."

"She knows Kimberley claimed you were the father of her baby."

Lars put down his glass. "Got a cigarette, Alan?"

"Sorry, don't smoke. Gave up twenty years ago."

"I don't normally, but I fancy a smoke now. Hang on. I'll be back."

He got up and made his way to a cigarette machine on the wall. After a few moments, he was back. He tore open the packet and lit up.

Inhaling deeply, Lars watched the smoke curl up to the blackened beams. "She's never said to me—neither she nor my father ever said a word about it. But I realized they knew. I could tell. Had she—had Kimberley been to see them?"

"Yes. You accept it was your child, then?"

"I don't know. I suppose it was. We never used contraceptives. We were young and stupid."

"You might not have been the only man in her life."

"I realize that—now. But it still could have been mine, why not? Did—did my parents pay her?" He sounded utterly miserable.

"Margaret says not. Did you?"

Lars looked surprised. "No! What with? I didn't have any money. Only my allowance and that didn't take me far."

"Someone paid her. She was seen with a large sum of money shortly before she disappeared. A couple of hundred, perhaps." Markby hesitated. "Her firm, Partytime, had catered for a dinner-dance given by one of the local political associations. It was at the close of that she was seen with the money."

"Anyone goes to those dinner-dances. They're fundraising affairs. Invitations go out to everyone, every local businessman, every party supporter, everyone who ever showed any interest whatsoever in the party. Political parties of any shade are chronically short of money. They don't care who donates it, Alan. Just so long as it keeps coming in."

"I went to see her mother yesterday," Markby said conversationally. "She lives in Wales. She's got other children, boy and a girl. I met the boy. She rejected Kimberley when she was a baby, after first showing interest. I don't suppose Kimberley had much faith in anyone. She thought she had to maneuver and blackmail people because that's the only way she'd get them to do anything for her. My theory, anyway." He lifted his pint. "Cheers!"

"Don't make me feel worse than I already do!" Lars said grimly. "I can't help it. It was a long time ago. I was young, inexperienced and emotionally thick." He looked full at Markby. "Get me out of this, Alan! I don't care what I have to do, but keep my name clear!"

"I'm a police officer. Don't be thick, now."

"But I didn't do anything! I didn't kill her!" Lars's voice rose in an anguished wail.

"Then, believe me, you've nothing to worry about!"

Lars stubbed the cigarette out half-smoked. "But it all revolves around me, doesn't it? However this ends up, I'm going to get the blame."

"Lars will get dragged into it. Someone will make out it's all his fault. And it isn't."

The tone was bitter. Meredith surveyed the speaker. Opening the door that afternoon and finding Angie Pritchard on the step had been a surprise, to put it mildly.

"I've got to talk to someone, Meredith, or I'll go quite mad. I can't talk to Margaret. I can't talk to Lars. If I talk to Alan, he'll probably write it down and make me sign it, or something! So I've come to talk to you."

So here they were, sitting in Meredith's tiny living room over a bottle of wine. Offering Angie tea hadn't seemed adequate. The visitor had abandoned summer clothing for an autumnal light wool suit. Very sensible, in view of the weather. The suit was oatmeal in color with a long skirt and jacket. It looked very expensive. Angie herself looked tense. It struck Meredith that there was, just at this moment, a distinct resemblance between Angie and her prospective mother-in-law. Lars Holden, one way and another, caused the women in his life endless worry.

"The girl was pregnant, you see." Angie, characteristically, came straight to the point. "I know we didn't mention that the other day at lunch, but an unborn child's bones were found with hers, weren't they?"

"Lars's child?" Meredith ventured.

Angie swept back a long swathe of brunette hair. "Who

the heck knows? Lars is naïve in many ways. He's the sort of person who'd believe the girl if she said it was his. He's fundamentally decent. Too decent for his own damn good! He'd never have turned around and said to her, 'Prove it!' He'd have wanted to help.''

''What could he have done? He was only a schoolboy, wasn't he? Hadn't yet gone up to university?'' Meredith poured them both another glass of wine.

Angie picked up hers and surveyed the claret depths moodily. ''He couldn't have done a thing. But I know that kind of girl. She wouldn't have bothered him, because she'd have known he had no money. She'd have gone to his family. Neither of his parents ever owned up, but I am absolutely sure they paid the girl off!''

Angie's eyes burned with emotion and fury. ''So stupid! One should never pay! It's an admission! But they did, I'm sure of it. When we spoke to Margaret about Lars's affair with the girl, she expressed no surprise at all. Just sat there with a stone face, listening, and nodding her head regally from time to time.''

''They may have paid her. But that's not the problem, is it? Someone killed her.'' Meredith tried shock tactics.

''I know! How else do you get rid of a blackmailer?''

Meredith was beginning to see how Angie's mind was working. It was alarming stuff but it had better be brought out into the open. ''Do you think Margaret . . . ?''

Angie leaned forward. ''Look, I'm not saying Margaret's a murderess, not in the ordinary way of it. But she's absolutely devoted to Lars, always has been. She had a miserable marriage. Lars's father was a real cold fish. All the— the passion in her went into her feelings for Lars. She was—is—unhinged where he's concerned. She'd do anything, really anything, to protect him! She's Scandinavian, you know. They're prone to gloom and dwelling on things. It's all those long dark nights which lead to alcoholism and suicide! They go berserk and chop up their relatives with axes. Happens all the time.''

''She's lived in England for years!'' Meredith protested at this sweeping denunciation of Nordic life. ''Anyway, they're not all gloomy and suicidal.''

"She'd do it!" Angie declared. She tossed down her wine. "Take it from me, Meredith, Margaret could have done it. I wouldn't be at all surprised if she did!"

Meredith, moved to even stronger protest, argued, "Listen, Angie! You're talking about your future mother-in-law here! It's Lars's mother, for pity's sake! How would he feel if he knew what you were saying about her? Even if—and it's the remotest of possibilities—even if Margaret did flip and attack the girl, it would be manslaughter not murder."

"Exactly!" Angie said firmly. "No court would find her guilty of murder and any decent lawyer would get her a suspended sentence. Perhaps she could volunteer for a course of psychiatric treatment. There are luxury clinics, more like hotels than hospitals. Perhaps Switzerland. Or we could even send her back to Sweden. They have excellent clinics in Sweden."

"Angie!" Meredith was temporarily bereft of speech. "All that would hardly help Lars!"

"It would clear the air. I'm a realist, I'm practical, Meredith! There is no way Lars's name is going to be kept out of this. Of course I wish it could be, but you know as well as I do, that sooner or later, some bright journalist will sniff it all out. How brutally do you want me to spell it out? Better that Margaret gets a suspended sentence for something which happened when she was temporarily out of her mind. Also while Lars was still a boy and for which he can't remotely be held responsible . . . than people start saying Lars killed the little tart!"

Meredith picked up the bottle. She didn't know about Angie but she certainly needed another drink.

"You think I'm a cold-blooded bitch!" Angie said.

"I think you're taking things to extremes and leaping to conclusions."

"I'm not leaping anywhere! I've worked it out. If I could rely on Lars doing all the right things, I wouldn't have to worry. But I told you, he's got a conscience."

"Glad to hear it. It always seems to me a political life doesn't leave much room for conscience!" Meredith said unkindly.

Angie straightened a fold of the wool jacket. "Lars is

different. People recognize that. That's why he'll go far. People trust him. He could go right to the top. This is off the record, of course! Just between us!''

Angie Pritchard had learned the basic rules, all right. Don't talk to journalists and even be wary of talking to friends.

"Thank God," Meredith said suddenly, "that it's not me. I always thought being connected with a copper was bad enough. I don't think I could cope with being married to a politician.''

"You were in the consular service, weren't you? Is it so very different?" Angie seemed surprised.

"Consular service isn't political. It's British nationals in car crashes or getting into local jails, lost passports and tourists who get beaten up, any and everything, I suppose.''

"If you can deal with that," said Angie, "you could deal with life as a political wife. It's dealing with emergencies, just the same. Being ready for anything. This is an emergency. I'm dealing with it. I'm not saying it's easy! That's why I'm here!''

Meredith eyed her. "So, what do you want me to do? You haven't come here just to talk.''

"Surprisingly enough, yes. Well, mostly." Angie sighed. "I'm not made of cast-iron! And Margaret just looks at me. You know the expression, if looks could kill? Believe me, it was tailor-made for Margaret. If I was superstitious, I'd worry about the Evil Eye!''

"Is Lars superstitious?" Meredith asked suddenly.

The question caught Angie unawares. She stared at Meredith and fiddled with a gold chain bracelet while she thought of an answer.

"He doesn't mind walking under ladders or crossing knives." Angie frowned. "He does sometimes talk as if he believed in Fate.''

"How about religious, then?"

"Oh, well, he was brought up in the Anglican church, got confirmed and everything. He doesn't attend now unless it's a remembrance ceremony or a major church festival. He's got a lot of respect for the church.''

"He's never fooled around with the occult? Not even as a youngster?"

"Good grief, no!" Angie stared at her, appalled. "Why?" Her gaze sharpened.

"Not sure. Someone may have done." She told Angie about the candle and the cosmos flowers.

"Someone crazy," said Angie firmly. "And all those years ago, whoever it was, is probably not around any more." She gripped her wine glass. "And it's the last thing I need! Witchcraft! Sacrificial virgins—Oh, my God!" The wine glass tilted and a red stain appeared on the pale wool jacket. "You don't think that girl was killed as part of some ghastly ritual?"

"I don't think it's more unlikely than that Margaret Holden killed her."

"Rubbish!" said Angie, but sounded distinctly uneasy.

As for Alan Markby, the conversation with Margaret and subsequently with Lars had left him feeling dispirited. Perhaps it was an aftermath of the long drive to Wales and back the previous day, or the talk with Susan Tempest there, or the sheer misery of the weather.

More than any of it, it was the frustration. Not that the many frustrations of police investigative work were unknown to him. This time was much as other times, but for the high profile enjoyed by a couple of the persons involved.

Margaret declared neither she nor her husband had paid Kimberley. Lars, presumably, could not have done so. So who did? And what, Markby muttered to himself as he drove back to his office, had happened to the money, the actual cash?

Jennifer Fitzgerald had described it as a roll of notes. At least a couple of hundred pounds in her estimation. She could be wrong about the exact amount, but a roll of notes remained a roll of notes. Shortly after this, Kimberley had disappeared. She hadn't had time to spend so much money. The report into her disappearance made no mention of her grandmother having found any money in Kimberley's room. So what had the girl done with it? It must have been more money than she'd ever had in her hands in her life. Even frittered away on records or magazines or clothes, she couldn't have got rid of it all in such a short time.

The little puzzle niggled at Markby's mind. He felt a need to do something to take his mind off it for a while. If he went straight back to his office, he'd only sit there and dwell on it. There must be something else he could do.

It was at this point that he remembered Meredith's two tales, of the candle and the cosmos, and of Bullen's curious early morning antics at about the same time.

He could make a shrewd guess as to what Bullen had been doing. But he couldn't fathom out the candle and cosmos flowers, not just at the moment. Mrs. Etheridge could safely be left to Prescott to interview at a convenient moment. Derek Archibald he'd rather like to talk to himself. Derek must have known the dead girl. That, in itself, made him of interest. He might also have his own theory about the candle business. Mrs. Etheridge was inclined to believe in satanic rites. Markby was not.

He turned onto the main Bamford road and found himself eventually in the town's shopping area. He drew up before the butcher's. But he had forgotten it was Wednesday. Archibald's, a family firm, still observed half-day closing, unlike the supermarkets. The blinds were drawn down and the door locked. Markby considered whether to go to the Archibald home. But he was loath to venture a second time into that claustrophobic den. Better to talk to Derek in his shop tomorrow.

He got back in the car and drove slowly through the town. It was quiet with that closing-day torpor. Bamford still had enough of its individual small shops remaining to make that a factor. The two supermarkets were bright with neon and goods and shoppers, but elsewhere little was happening.

The shops, connecting in his mind with food, reminded him that he'd missed out on lunch and it was now late afternoon. He'd had nothing since a mid-day pint with Lars Holden. His stomach confirmed this with a plaintive growl.

There was a sandwich bar up ahead. A new place or at least he didn't remember it. That was open. There was also a convenient space at the curb. He drew in, got out and went to see what could be bought to stave off the hunger pangs.

It was a neat little place. Behind a glass counter the fillings for the sandwiches lay in plastic trays. Some of them, sliced ham, prawns, even tuna mixed with mayonnaise and sweetcorn, he could recognize. Some of the mixtures were beyond identification.

There were two tiny tables and some fragile chairs. One could, if so desired, eat one's sandwich on the premises. Markby chose bacon and salad with brown bread. To drink was a straight choice between coffee and a soft drink. He chose black coffee to sharpen up his tired brain.

From his seat by the window, he watched the world go by as he munched his sandwich and sipped the strong brew. The few people strolling past looked ordinary. But no doubt some of them harbored dark secrets. Not criminal secrets necessarily, but little sins of commission or omission, episodes of all too human failing. A Susan Tempest in other guise, perhaps. Or a Jack Tempest, that good husband and father, who—as far as Markby could tell—had been a tyrant of the worst order under the domestic roof.

The girl at the counter said apologetically, "We're closing now."

Markby looked at his watch, startled. More time had slipped by than he'd expected. People passing by now were clearly home-going office workers. He bid the girl goodbye and set off back to his own office.

For some reason, perhaps recent habit, he chose to drive past the churchyard. He really didn't need to come this way. They'd finished with the Gresham grave. The screens had been removed. But voyeuristic interest hadn't yet dwindled. As he drew level, Markby slowed and peered into the trees that stood between the churchyard and road, to see if any ghoulish visitors trampled around the graves just now.

There was a figure, but not a visitor. At least, not one who'd found what he'd expected.

Markby braked and the car stopped with a judder. He threw open the door and jumped out.

Through the trees a disheveled form could be seen stumbling toward the road. Both arms were held on high in a kind of supplication. The face was white, the mouth open in horror, the eyes staring. It was one of the Lowes. Markby wasn't sure yet which one.

He ran through the gate and plunged over the intervening graves to head the grotesque figure off.

It was Gordon, the younger one. Markby could see that now and yelled, "Gordon! What's happened?"

Gordon wheeled toward him and let out an animal cry of pain and distress. He sank down and buried his head in his arms as if he couldn't bear to see Markby's face as the superintendent stooped over him and shook at his shoulder.

"Gordon! For God's sake—what's wrong with you, man?"

Gordon's huddled body was convulsed by a great sob. He raised his face from his arms. Neither of the Lowes could ever have been described as beautiful to behold and now Gordon's face seemed hardly human. His mouth worked, spittle dribbling from the corner, his stubby, yellowed teeth chattering.

"The—the hut . . ." he whispered.

Markby stood up and turned to go toward the all-purpose groundsman's shed and store. But Gordon lurched to his feet and caught at his sleeve.

"Don't, Mr. Markby! Don't go, sir! It's—it's in there . . ."

"What is, Gordon?"

"I seen it . . . I seen him . . ." Gordon gave another inarticulate cry.

There was no sense to be had from the man. He'd had a terrible shock of some kind and was scared out of his wits.

Markby shook himself free of the clinging hand and set off with determination toward the shed. He could see the door swinging open, an abandoned wheelbarrow by the side of it. He was vaguely aware that Gordon was stumbling along behind him, moaning and muttering. Markby braced himself.

He'd reached the shed. He said, "Wait there, Gordon!"

in as calm a voice as he could, and went inside, into the dark interior, temporarily blinded.

He bumped into it with sufficient force for it to send him staggering back. Rough woollen cloth scraped his face and the smell of earth and of stale nicotine filled his nostrils. The hut was small and a good deal of the space taken up with tools and junk. In stumbling back he scraped the back of his calf painfully on some metal implement. He stood for a split second in a haze of discomfort and horror until gradually awareness of his surroundings forced itself on him.

Above his head tree branches scraped at the roof with trailing twig fingers and water dripped down to ooze through cracks. Inside a faint creak came from an overhead crossbeam as the thing that had almost sent Markby sprawling was set in motion by the collision. He could see it clearly now and there was no mistaking it.

Hanging from the beam, the body of Denny Lowe turned slowly, first to left and then to right, in the breeze from the open door.

Fourteen

Lars stood before the open cupboard doors at the end of the corridor. He had pushed the array of plastic-shrouded clothing to either side and he was looking through it at the concealed door to the old secret chapel.

He was thinking that it had been years since he'd been in there. He couldn't remember the last time. To be honest, ever since that fateful night of his eighteenth birthday when he'd taken the waitress there, he'd had an aversion for the place.

To think that her name hadn't even registered at the time in the alcoholic haze and he'd had to ask again what it was the next time they'd met! She hadn't seemed to mind the lapse. But she was having sweet revenge now she was dead and had returned to haunt him.

But the haunting had begun almost at once, long before she disappeared from his life. In the cold sober aftermath of the party the sex act had seemed sacrilege in such a setting. He'd developed adolescent guilt about it. How could he have done it, brought her here of all places? Here under his parents' roof? And why, oh why, had the unease persisted until the present day?

"I should have thrown that off by now," Lars murmured to himself. He stepped forward resolutely and opened the doors, passing through the curtain of bagged-up clothing and into the chapel. He switched on the electric light and the door closed softly behind him as he confronted his phobia, determined to lay it to rest.

The tiny room smelled fusty. That was not surprising because there was no window. He looked up at the painted ceiling and the swinging naked lightbulb. It illuminated the figures of Adam and Eve, their painted features long since flaked away. Now they seemed to take on the faces of himself when young and of the girl, with her funny gap-toothed grin. The rest of her face was hazy in memory. He could only recall a around chin and dark curly hair. But the grin, both comic and endearing, he could remember that very well. Too well. His gaze traveled down reluctantly to the battered old sofa. On there. They'd made love on that disgusting old thing.

First they'd sat on it and smoked a couple of joints. That was something he hadn't told either Markby or Angie and never would!

The details of the love-making that followed were equally hazy. Just a lot of panting and sweating and feeling nauseous because of all the booze slopping about inside him. To say nothing of the lightheadedness from the joint. But he'd remembered that, drunk as he'd been, he'd been afraid of the tell-tale stains. She'd had a cloth of some sort, tucked in the waistband of her pinafore, and they'd put that down to protect the velvet surface. When he'd seen her again, in town, he'd asked her what she'd done with the soiled cloth and she'd said simply she'd put it in the dustbin outside the kitchen door, just like any other piece of rubbish.

Seeing the appalled look on his face, she'd added, "Don't worry, I pushed it down inside a cornflakes box already in there. No one would've seen it!"

It was probably at that point that he'd realized she'd done this sort of thing many times before at other parties with other men. It was at that moment, too, that simple loss of interest in her had begun to turn to active distaste. She was what his mother would have called a slut and her ways were sluttish. She disgusted him.

Slowly Lars seated himself on the sofa. "God!" he whispered. "This is an awful mess!" He sank his head into his hands.

He didn't know how long he sat like that. He was suddenly aware of movement, of the doors opening and someone coming in to join him. Hands gripped his shoulders. Lars looked up fearfully, more than half expecting to see that face with the gap-toothed smile. Words rose to his lips, asking why she persecuted him like this when there was nothing more now he could do for her. Before he could speak them, he recognized his mother bending over him.

He whispered, "Ma? What do you want?"

"Don't break down now!" she said in a fierce low voice. "You mustn't let this destroy everything we've achieved! That girl was nothing and what happened to her nothing!"

Her pale eyes glittered and her face was deathly pale. With her colorless eyelashes and blond hair she presented a strange sight, almost like a carved marble head. He thought she looked terrifying, like a Valkyrie come to escort him to some icy-halled Valhalla, whether he wanted to go or not.

Lars said in a thick voice, "It's all right, Mother. I'm not going to let it destroy me."

Her grip relaxed but she still kept her hands on his shoulders. "Whatever happens, Lars, we can arrange matters. We can put it right, you and I. Believe me! There's always a way to put things right!"

Lars straightened up and the movement dislodged her hands. She took them from his shoulders and stood waiting. He said, "It's odd. Things you do unthinkingly, stupid things and so ordinary, the sort of things countless other people do and think no more of. Those same things can return years later to make your life a misery. Who would ever have thought that girl, of all girls? How could I ever have known?" He gazed up at his mother, bewildered.

"Everything we ever do stays with us always," she said grimly. "We can never walk away from what we've done. As the years go by we talk of it less. But we don't forget. You just have to believe it was worth it."

"Kimberley wasn't worth it!" Lars said with an awkward smile. But the awkwardness came from the fact that he knew she wasn't talking about the same thing as he was. The smile faded as a new dread came on him. "What did you do, Ma?'' His mouth and chin trembled.

The pale marble eyes fixed him. ''Does it matter?''

''Of course it matters!'' Emotion flooded his voice. ''For
God's sake, Ma! Angie says—''

''Oh, Angie?'' Sarcasm dripped from the words. ''And
Angie knows all about it, does she? Oh Lars, at least learn
by your mistakes! Don't just do it all again!''

''You can't compare Angie with Kimberley!'' he said
angrily.

''Can't I?'' She gave a short hard laugh. ''Oh, but I can!
What did that little waitress want from you, Lars? She saw
a rich young man with prospects, who would take her away
from her dreary little life and make her wealthy and secure,
able to have whatever she wanted and mix with people she
could only gaze at from afar! Doesn't Angie want much
the same? She sees a young politician with a bright future.
She sees herself eventually as the wife of a minister and
even, who knows, wife of the prime minister, one day! It's
all possible.''

The combative instinct, honed by exchanges with heck-
lers on the hustings, came to his aid. Lars leapt to his feet
and faced her. ''That is incredibly insulting, both to Angie
and to me! I love Angie and she loves me!''

To his horror, increasing his terror, the marble face before him contorted into a mask of passionate hatred.

''Love, love!'' Margaret Holden's voice rose and
cracked. ''What do you know about love? What does that
bimbo know? I'll tell you about love! It suffers, oh, it suffers, Lars! It hurts, real pain—here!'' She struck her breast.
''It tears you apart, and it possesses you entirely just like
a demon! It can make you do anything! Remember this—
when your Angie has left, just as when Kimberley left, I'll
still be here for you! I'll never desert you, Lars!''

He whispered, appalled, ''Oh God . . .''

But she turned and walked out, leaving him in the secret
chamber, alone and more frightened than he'd ever been in
his entire life.

The television screen was showing a magician. He wore a
shiny black suit with glittering jacket and trousers, a pink

shirt and a bow tie. His assistant wore a kind of one-piece bathing costume with spangles and fishnet tights. An old-fashioned sort of showgirl outfit, Meredith decided, looking at it critically. You'd have thought they'd have come up with something more modern, snappier, by now. Showgirls wore that kind of thing at the Hippodrome in Victorian times. Thicker tights, probably flesh-colored, and button boots, that was the only difference.

The magician was making things disappear. He invited the studio audience—although it was supposedly taking place in some nightspot, so presumably the audience had paid to be there—to part with small items which he wrapped in a silk handkerchief. He then begged them to watch his hand closely.

"Don't!" Meredith advised the audience from her sofa. It stood to reason, when a man you knew was out to deceive you begged you to watch his right hand, you ought to be watching his left. The audience knew that too, but they'd still watch the right. That was what was so very irritating about magicians. They were blatantly in the business of deception, of cheating. They knew it, you knew it, but everyone went along with it. There had, she thought, to be something fundamentally wrong with that. Was it the skill which they were invited to admire? Or was it just the magician demonstrating that he would always be quicker, slicker, smarter than they were?

She got up and switched off the set. She had tried to phone Alan on and off all day since Angie had left. At first the switchboard had said he was out. Then it said he was unavailable and would she like to leave a message? She tried his home but he wasn't there.

She knew the signs. Clearly some new development had taken place. Possibly something to do with Kimberley's case, or it could be something entirely new. That was policework for you, as well she knew. The working day was elastic. It stretched out or contracted according to last-minute dramas or sheer lack of time to make up necessary reports which involved finishing them late. Someone was always on leave or off sick. There always seemed to be some reason why Alan had to go himself or do it himself or type it himself.

She looked at her watch. It was nearly ten. She picked up the phone and made one last attempt at contact, calling his home number.

To her surprise he picked it up almost at once. He must have been standing nearby.

"Hullo?" He sounded weary.

She realized he'd probably only set foot indoors minutes before. Meredith felt guilty, sorry she'd disturbed him. She said so.

"Don't be daft," he retorted, sounding brighter. "I thought you were Louise Bryce calling me back in again."

"Has something new happened? They told me at your place you were unavailable."

"Mmn . . ." he mumbled. It sounded as though he were eating, probably a hastily assembled sandwich. "Denny Lowe's dead."

"Denny? You mean one of the grave-digger brothers?" The image flashed before her mind of those two strange, woolly-hatted figures emerging from the gloom at James Holland's gate. "What happened to him?" Her heart sank. "Not murder?"

"Don't know yet. Have to wait for a post-mortem report. It might be a suicide." His voice had grown clearer. He'd swallowed the bread. "Do you want to come over here? I've had a couple of whiskies and I don't think I should get back in the car."

By the time she reached his Victorian villa he had brewed up tea in a large earthenware pot and was wandering around his untidy kitchen in search of cups which matched the saucers. He was doing this with the inefficient determination of the tipsy. The smell of whiskey hung in the air. He'd had more than a couple, she guessed. Crockery clashed ominously as he rummaged in cupboards.

"Use mugs, for goodness' sake! I'm not your maiden aunt!" she told him.

They sat at the kitchen table to drink the tea. Alan tended to live in his kitchen. It was a large room, formed from knocking together the former scullery and a breakfast room. There were two more rooms on the ground floor, but he hardly went in to either of them, so that both had the shrouded, moth-balled, slightly damp air of a house abandoned by its owners for lengthy duration.

"I ought to sell this place," he said now, à propos of nothing at all. "Get a flat." The quest for matching china abandoned, gloom was now setting in. The tea, however, seemed to have sobered him up a bit.

"You'd hate a flat."

"I know I would. But I still ought to do it."

They sipped more tea and she waited for him to tell her. He set the mug down at last and explained about Denny's body in the groundsman's hut in the old churchyard. As he talked, his voice grew clearer and presumably so did his head.

"He was hanging from the crossbeam, so it could be a suicide. He was a morose sort of man. On the other hand, if it's murder, someone has tried to make it look like suicide. Post mortem will sort that out."

"What does the other one—Gordon, isn't it? What does he say? Was his brother depressed?"

"Gordon's making no sense at all, poor chap. We won't be able to interview him until tomorrow. I took him across to the vicarage and left him with James Holland. All I could get out of him was that he, Gordon, is the cook and gets an evening meal for the pair of them, around six. Tonight, Denny went out about an hour beforehand, leaving Gordon shaping up to the stove. Gordon expected him back in time to eat as per usual. He didn't come. Eventually Gordon went to look for him, and found him, basically. It was difficult getting that much out of him." Alan rubbed his hand over his mouth.

"Why on earth should anyone want to kill Denny? Most people respect grave-diggers even if they go in awe of them. Grave-diggers are a necessary sort of people. On the other hand, it must be a depressing job. There's the business of digging up Kimberley's bones. That might have got him down."

He pulled a disbelieving face. "Didn't strike me as that.

He seemed to take it in his stride. Gordon was more upset by it. If it had been Gordon hanging from the crossbeam, I'd have thought he'd been brooding on the business, and tipped over the edge. But not Denny. It's the wrong brother, if you see what I mean. Still, wc'll scc.''

"You've got enough on your mind, I know, but I have been trying to ring you. Angie Pritchard came to see me.'' Briefly, she summarized Angie's tale. "She's an awfully tough lady. But there's a grain of reason in it. If it does get out about Lars and the girl, someone will start a whisper that he killed her all those years ago, and now a cover-up is in progress. But while I agree with her that Margaret would do almost anything to protect Lars, I just can't believe that she'd kill.''

"Almost isn't the same as absolutely, you're right. But given the right motivation, who can say they wouldn't kill? To protect their children, wouldn't most women kill to do that?''

"Lars wasn't a child.''

"He was eighteen or nineteen and as far as his mother was concerned, you bet he was still a child! Parent-child isn't a relationship that changes. He's still her child now.'' He was shaking his head, dissatisfied. "What I'd like to know is, who paid Kimberley a large sum of money shortly before she disappeared?''

Alan scratched his head, giving his hair a disheveled look which matched the lines tiredness had etched on his face.

"I believe Margaret when she says she didn't pay up but chucked the girl out of the house. And what happened to it? To the money, I mean, the actual cash-in-the-hand banknotes? Kimberley hadn't time to spend it. It may seem a trivial point, but I don't like loose ends like that. If Joan Oates had found it, she'd have told the police when they inquired into the girl's disappearance. It would certainly have been in the police report because it would have indicated that it wasn't a simple runaway from home. Runaways take their money with them. It would, you see, have made all the difference. If the police had found that money then, they'd have been more suspicious about the girl's sudden departure and the fact that she'd left it behind.''

''And they'd have wanted to find out where she got such an amount of cash. From whom and why,'' Meredith murmured.

''Oh yes,'' Markby said softly. ''That too. So, you see, the absence of the money starts to take on definite undertones. Did someone, fearing police inquiry, try to recover it when she disappeared? Had she given it to someone for safe-keeping and, when she vanished, did that person simply hang on to it? I just wish I knew.''

He put down his teamug. ''But I've had enough of it for tonight. Can we go to bed?''

''Thought you'd never ask.''

It had stopped raining by the following morning. Having phoned in to say he would be a little late, he ordered Prescott to go and interview Mrs. Etheridge. Denny's death didn't mean investigation into Kimberley's was suspended. For himself, however, the new case took temporary precedence.

His head was clear this morning with only the faintest ache. Breakfast with Meredith had sent him forth with a positive attitude to the day. He fantasized briefly as he drove to the churchyard, imagining Meredith always there at breakfast-time. One day, perhaps. One day he'd talk her into something more permanent than their present arrangement.

He parked and walked across the damp grass to the hut. An officer was already there, protecting it from sightseers and talking to James Holland.

They greeted Markby as he came up. ''I simply can't take this in,'' the vicar said frankly. ''Why? Denny didn't strike me as a manic depressive. Basically I'd have said he was an old-fashioned sort of countryman with a robust attitude to life and death. I should have realized it wasn't like that. I feel responsible to some extent.''

Clearly Father Holland was under the impression the question of suicide had been settled. Though he was sorry that the vicar labored under a burden of guilt, Markby decided to leave him with that for the moment. No point in complicating things. It might, after all, prove suicide. In his own heart, he was sure it wasn't. But that was policeman's instinct, honed over many years. He had to await the post-mortem report before he knew.

He exchanged a word with the uniformed man and went into the hut. Viewed in the morning light, it was like all such huts. There was a lawnmower in one corner, an ancient model no one would be likely to steal, and stored here in perfect safety. It was on that he'd scraped his calf so badly last night. It was still sore this morning.

Other tools—spades, shears, hoes, a mattock . . . you name it, he thought, surveying them all. They'd get it all fingerprinted. He looked up at the beam again. They'd cut Denny down and the remaining length of rope had been removed from the wooden bar as evidence.

Markby put his head out of the door to where the uniformed man and the vicar still stood. "Gordon recognize that rope?"

"Couldn't say." Father Holland frowned. "But there's usually rope there in case it's needed. The coffin ropes, you know, for lowering the casket into the grave. They might break or something. It's never happened to my knowledge but one has to be prepared."

Markby returned to the hut and looked around again. No other rope was to be seen. It seemed likely, then, that Denny had hanged himself or been strung up by A. N. Other by means of the appropriately named "coffin rope."

Spiders' webs festooned the corners of the hut. A blue-bottle was caught in one and buzzed feebly, observed by the predator from a corner. As Markby watched it, the spider began to move in fits and starts, but purposefully, across the web toward the prey. He looked away. *Calliphora vomitoria*. The name stirred in his memory. Flies. Insects. A body kept somewhere for a while before burial. Possibly in a hut. If only Bullen would talk. But as long as suspicion attached to any member of the Holden family, the old man would keep his silence. That didn't mean that a Holden was responsible, only that Bullen, in his tortured way, thought so.

Markby did not believe that Bullen had done anything but bury the girl. Probably he'd found the body in the churchyard. It would be very useful for the police to have confirmation of that. Tracing Kimberley's last movements could lead to her killer. But Bullen was not—had never been—of a cooperative disposition. Markby could only hope to win his confidence slowly. Very slowly.

As for Denny's death, he couldn't see how that could be connected with the inquiries into Kimberley's. But two bodies in one churchyard, that was to say, two bodies which oughtn't to be there, was stretching coincidence. He went outside again.

"Where's Gordon now? At home?"

Father Holland nodded. "I kept him with me for an hour or so last night. He'd calmed down a bit and he wanted to go home. He kept muttering about his kitchen and having left the food on the table for their supper. He was all at sixes and sevens but he seemed to know what he wanted to do. I let him go. I haven't seen him today yet. I was just on my way over there."

"I'll walk there with you, then," Markby offered. "I'll have a word with him while things are quiet."

It took about a quarter of an hour to reach the back lane where the Lowes' ramshackle cottage stood. The road surface was stony and pitted with pot-holes forming treacherous water traps. They were on the extreme edge of town here and fields stretched beyond. There were only four dwellings in the entire lane, each surrounded by an unkempt garden and a pile of litter: tin baths, dismembered cars, old fridges.

At the first one they passed, a dog of mixed breed, tethered by a length of rope to a post, emerged from a crate provided for his shelter and barked at them. An unseen voice enjoined him with curses to silence.

"Not a Neighborhood Watch area!" Markby observed.

Father Holland, hastening ahead of him, rightly dismissed this leaden attempt at humor.

"The Lowes' cottage is at the end. I can't see anyone. But the curtains in the front are open. That's a good sign. Gordon must be up and about."

Markby looked up at the tiny dormer windows, blind

eyes beneath eyebrows formed by the shaggy thatch. The little house had a deserted air about it. He felt a premonition of all not being well.

They tried the front door and the back to no avail. Both were locked and although they hammered and called, no one came. They peered through the unwashed windows but could see little.

Father Holland, growing more distressed by the minute, pushed open the rusty letterbox and shouted into it, "Gordon! Gordon, it's me, the vicar! Open up! Are you there, Gordon!"

No reply. The vicar turned haggard features to Markby. "He's done something stupid! I should have thought of this! The Lowes were very close. You saw what a state poor Gordon was in last night. I should have kept him with me at the vicarage! I should never have let him go home all on his own! It was too much! Alan, we've got to get into this cottage! Minutes could be vital!"

They had moved around to the back of the building again. A large ancient wooden barrel by the door served as a rainwater tank, catching the overflow from the gutter. Recent rains must have filled it to overflowing and a wooden lid had been pushed across it to prevent yet more water getting in. Markby slid the lid aside and peered in. Barrels had contained bodies before now.

This one contained only rainwater. He dabbled his fingers in it. It felt silky soft, unlike the hard, chlorinated stuff which came out of the taps, hygienic perhaps, but wellnigh undrinkable in his view.

He pushed the lid back again. "He could have gone out."

"It's early!" the vicar protested.

Markby consulted his watch. "It's nine-thirty. I doubt that's early for the Lowes. They'd be in the habit of getting up at six or even earlier in summer, I'll be bound."

A woman had come out of the cottage next door, ostensibly to pin washing to a clothesline. She could be seen across the weed-infested garden, watching them with slatternly curiosity. Markby called out to her.

"We're looking for Gordon Lowe! Have you seen him this morning?"

"Gordon?" She looked blank. "No, not seen nothing of him." She turned and trudged back to her own home.

"We are wasting precious time!" Holland almost shouted in frustration. "I'll never forgive myself if I let Gordon—didn't prevent him doing as Denny did!"

"We don't know yet what Denny did!" Markby said sharply. "Don't start blaming yourself. But I'm inclined to agree. We need to get into the house."

He looked around. Potato sacking was stacked in a moldering heap by the back door. The Lowes must have bought their spuds by the hundredweight. He fetched a strip of the rough weave and wrapped it around his right arm. A half-brick lying handily nearby served to smash the kitchen windowpane. Markby reached in his swathed arm and undid the catch.

"Careful, Alan!" Father Holland gasped automatically as Markby scrambled through, adding in the same breath, "Can you see anything of Gordon?"

Markby looked around. There was no sign of the food that the vicar had spoken of Gordon having prepared. All mugs and dishes had been neatly washed up and stacked on the draining board. He went to the back door. It was locked fast and there was no key on the inside.

Father Holland's black-bearded features were pressed to the broken window. "What's there? Can you open the door? Do I have to climb through as well?"

It was unlikely the vicar would be able to maneuver his considerable bulk through the tiny window. "You'll have to go around the front!" Markby called.

The front door was a Yale lock and he was able to open it from inside, albeit with difficulty. Damp had swollen the wooden frame and it was stuck fast through disuse. As soon as it was dragged open a shower of dirt and dead insects was dislodged with it.

Father Holland burst through. "Gordon!" he bellowed.

"Not down here. Try upstairs."

They pounded up the narrow stair. In both tiny bedrooms the beds were neatly made. There was no sign that anyone had been there the previous night. The bathroom was a primitive place. Markby ran a finger around the cracked washbowl. Bone dry.

"Well," he said, turning to the vicar, who stood in the bathroom doorway. "He came back here last night because he cleaned up the kitchen, got rid of the food, washed up. He then left by the back door, locking it and taking the key with him. We don't know when but I'd say also last night. He's not been here this morning. The point is, where did he go?"

Father Holland let out a moan of distress. "He's got no family! He's dangling somewhere from a tree! Poor Gordon!"

"Don't let your imagination run away with you, James! Either he'll turn up of his own accord or we'll find him, I promise. I don't want harm to come to him any more than you do."

They left the cottage, but not before Father Holland had scribbled a note to Gordon on a leaf torn from Markby's notebook, and left it on the kitchen table. "In case he comes back. I've told him to get in touch with me at once."

"Good idea. I'll get hold of the local police station and tell them to start a search and then I'll go to HQ and see how many men we can spare there. You go back to the vicarage. If Gordon gets in touch with anyone, it's likely to be you. If you have to go out, try and arrange for someone to stay by the phone. One of the uniformed men in the churchyard if necessary. I'll leave word. And don't worry, James. It's most likely he's just wandering around in a daze. We'll find him."

He certainly hoped so.

Fifteen

Meredith returned to her own home after an early breakfast with Alan, and gazed disconsolately around her.

"Side-lined again, Mitchell!" she said aloud. "Second fiddle to policework!" She had no idea when she'd be seeing Alan again. He clearly had more than enough to occupy him. But in truth, that wasn't what worried her.

Angie Pritchard worried her. She couldn't get the conversation with Lars's fiancée out of her head. Clearly, Angie had settled on Margaret Holden as Kimberley's killer. No matter how many excuses Angie might produce for Margaret by way of exaggerated mother-love or mental instability, the basic charge remained the same.

Perhaps she was right. Perhaps Margaret had done it. But Meredith didn't think so and an obstinate instinct made her determined not to let Angie get away with planting the idea in everyone's head.

She, Meredith, had been obliged to pass on Angie's theory to Alan, and she'd been relieved that he'd received it with some skepticism. But he must know it was a possibility. He wouldn't have discounted Margaret, or Lars, come to that.

"So it's up to me," Meredith muttered, "to prove Angie wrong."

In addition to which, she had no intention of playing second fiddle to anything or anyone.

But if the Holden household were discounted, who else could possibly cast light on all this? Meredith sat down and listed everyone whose name had come into the matter, even by passing reference. Then she crossed out Margaret and Lars. She was left with Bullen, Simon French, Jennifer Fitzgerald née Jurawicz, Derek Archibald, Mrs. Etheridge and the late Reverend Appleton.

The last named was dead. Jennifer's address in Nottingham she didn't have. She could, however, tackle the other four. People were often nervous of talking to the police. They feared being asked to sign statements. A chat over a cup of coffee with a neighbor was a different matter.

Meredith went along the road to call on Janet Etheridge.

She found that lady polishing the brass letterbox and knocker on her front door.

"Feeling better today, Mrs. Etheridge?" Meredith asked.

Janet, polishing cloth and tin of Duraglit in hand, paused. "Much better today. I have my good days and my bad ones. When I have a good day, I like to get on and do a few odd jobs, although what with one thing and another, I'm late starting this morning."

Perhaps this was a hint that she didn't want to stop and talk. If so, Meredith ignored it. "I was talking to Mr. Archibald yesterday. That is to say, I was in his shop. I told him I'd seen you and you'd told me about the candle and flowers."

"Really?" Janet Etheridge gave her a disapproving look, probably because of the implied admission by Meredith that she ate meat. Perhaps she also felt Meredith had broken a confidence. "I should have thought Derek would be ready to retire by now."

"He seems very active and not that old. He asked after you, by the way."

Mrs. Etheridge mellowed. "Did he? Well, I used to see Derek often in the days when we were both PCC members." She put a hand to her hair, waved in regimented furrows. "Had the police been to see him, did he say?"

"No, he didn't say!" Meredith was surprised. "I don't think so."

"One's been to see me this morning. That's why I'm so late. You don't usually see me out here at nearly eleven! You only just missed him. A young police sergeant, nice young man. Very polite. Somehow or other he'd heard about that business with the candle on the altar and the flowers, too. Word does seem to be getting around!" Her sharp eyes rested thoughtfully on Meredith again.

Meredith tried to look innocent. "Had he? What did he say?"

"Not much. He wrote down what I told him. I did think afterwards he might have heard about it from Derek Archibald, though why Derek should want to bring it all up now, beats me. No one can do anything about it now!" She pursed her lips. "He probably came to see me as I was the one who found it. If it hadn't been for me, no one would have been any the wiser!" She looked well pleased at this observation but then added tartly, "Not that anything was done at the time!"

"Mr. Archibald told me what he thought about the incident."

Mrs. Etheridge gave way before Meredith's determination. Perhaps finding herself the subject of some attention was not displeasing. "Would you like a cup of coffee, dear?"

When they were seated in her neat little sitting room with the coffee, Mrs. Etheridge—who had removed her pinafore and, for some reason, changed her shoes—offered a plate of dry biscuits and asked, "So what did Derek have to say? I suppose he'll go on working in that shop until the end. They've no children. He'll sell up the business on retiring, I dare say, and it will lose the name of Archibald."

"That would be sad after so long, but a buyer might keep the name on." Meredith nobly bit into one of the dry biscuits. It formed a pasty substance in her mouth which stuck to her teeth.

"It wouldn't be the same!" said Mrs. Etheridge firmly.

"Mmn." Meredith tried to scrape the cement of the biscuit mix from her teeth with her tongue. "He thought the business of the candle was probably children playing around in the church.''

"Derek may think as he wishes!'' her hostess retorted. "I think differently! I told that young police sergeant earlier. There are things going on.''

She left this cryptic sentence hanging in the air. Meredith had succeeded in dislodging a lump of biscuit and swallowing it. She washed it down with the weak coffee brew.

"Mr. Archibald seemed very sure.''

Meredith had read the expression "curled his lip'' but had never seen anyone actually do it until now. Mrs. Etheridge curled her thin lip. "Derek Archibald has not always conducted himself as a member of the church should! He used to go straight from Evensong to the public house. I often saw him go in with my own eyes. And once—''

Mrs. Etheridge reddened and fell silent.

"Yes?'' Meredith prompted.

The woman appeared undecided. She wanted to tell Meredith but the matter was obviously embarrassing. Surely she wasn't going to say Derek had once made improper advances?

"That evening,'' Mrs. Etheridge said carefully. "The evening we found—that is to say, I found—the candle burning on the altar, the three of us went back to the church to investigate, after the meeting at the vicarage. Derek and I with Father Appleton. We searched the building. I was really very alarmed and it was getting late. I had walked over to the vicarage but I really didn't fancy walking back alone. I asked Derek to give me a lift home as I knew he had his car.''

Meredith blinked. What on earth was coming?

Mrs. Etheridge appeared suddenly coy. She fiddled with the crocheted lace edge of a tablecloth on the little Pembroke table which carried the coffee tray. "Derek unlocked the passenger side door for me and told me to get in. Then he went and had a last word with the vicar. They were talking for quite a long time. Derek used to bring his PCC notes and papers in one of those thin flat cases. Not like an old-fashioned briefcase with sides that bulge. A rigid case with little locks.''

"I know the kind," Meredith assured her. "An attaché case."

"Is that what they call them? I don't know why Derek had to have one. Just to make himself look important, I dare say." Mrs. Etheridge fidgeted with the tablecloth again. "He'd put it on the driver's seat. He was such a long time talking to the vicar that I leaned across the seat to see what he was doing. The case was knocked to the floor. He hadn't locked it. The top opened and everything fell out."

"Ah?" It might have happened that way. She might just have snooped. But obviously Janet had found something unexpected.

"I picked it all up and tidied the papers together to slip them back in again. And—" she grew redder still—"I was quite shocked. Amongst all the papers there was—a magazine."

"A parish magazine?"

Mrs. Etheridge cast her a withering look and said with some acerbity, "No, dear! One of *those* magazines! For men. A certain sort of man."

"A girlie magazine?" Meredith exclaimed.

"Ridiculous name! This one was entitled—" Mrs. Etheridge drew a deep breath. "Nudes!" From red she turned pale. "I had never in my entire life seen pictures like it! Women—doing things. Posed in—most odd positions. I—I pushed it all back into the case and shut it. Naturally I didn't tell that young police fellow any of this! But I've never been able to think well of Derek Archibald since."

Meredith saw that discussion of the hapless butcher was closed. She tried another tactic. "About Bullen, the grave-digger. He must be very old. I expect he knows a lot of local stories, local history. I was thinking of having a talk with him sometime."

"He might know the history of the local pubs!" said Mrs. Etheridge grimly. "I doubt he knows anything else. A drunkard. Older now but no wiser, I don't doubt. I advise you not to go talking to Nat Bullen. He is a foul-mouthed and disgusting old man!"

That dealt with Bullen, too. Mrs. Etheridge seemed to have met more than her fair share of reprehensible men in her blameless life. Meredith wondered about the late Mr. Etheridge. There were no photographs of him to be seen.

Mrs. Etheridge was gathering up the empty coffee cups.

Meredith took the hint. "Yes. Thanks for the coffee and—and the talk. I'll remember what you say—about Bullen."

"Depravity," Mrs. Etheridge informed her, "is everywhere!"

Meredith walked on into town and bought a newspaper. On impulse, she continued on her way until she reached the vicarage. In search, possibly, of somewhere free of depravity.

Father Holland had been in his study but shot out of the door as she stepped into the hallway through the ever-unlocked entry and called out to him.

"Oh, Meredith!" He stood dejectedly in the study doorway. Then a flicker of hope crossed his broad bearded face. "Alan send you?"

"No. Are you expecting a message from Alan?"

"Yes—no. I don't know. It's Gordon Lowe. We can't find the poor chap anywhere. Just lost him completely."

Meredith followed him as he went back into the study and sat down in one of the battered armchairs. James Holland sat opposite her, his hands folded loosely on the knees of his cassock. He looked quite miserable.

"Perhaps he's gone to see a friend?" she suggested. "How long has be been missing?"

He told her. "It's my fault. He was distraught last night, having found his brother—hanging. The Lowes are not like other people. They're very close. Were very close," he corrected. "Always lived together. Neither ever married to my knowledge. No other family, either, that I know of. As for friends, I don't think they needed them. They were self-sufficient in their way and quite isolated from the mainstream of life. Denny had been in the army years ago as a national serviceman. They did send him abroad, to Germany, I think. Sometimes Denny used to say jokingly that he'd traveled, but that was the sum of it. Gordon, being the younger by a few years, escaped National Service so he hadn't even done that and never been away from Bamford. It seems an odd sort of life but they both appeared quite happy. Obviously there were currents beneath . . ." His voice trailed away.

"Gordon may be suffering from a mental blackout." Meredith considered the possibilities. "Unable to accept Denny's death. But if he is, someone will find him wandering about."

"I'm hoping he'll come here." Father Holland sighed. "I should have kept him here last night."

"You couldn't lock him up, James!" she pointed out.

He made a gesture of hopelessness. "Alan seems so sure they will find him, find him safe. I wish I could feel the same."

"If Alan's sure, then they will!" she told him firmly.

But Alan Markby was getting less sure by the minute. After informing the local police station, he'd hurried back to headquarters to alert his team. As he hastened toward the operations room, a waiting figure leapt up to intercept him.

Markby, paying little attention, dodged it. But, hearing his name called, was obliged to stop and turn back.

"Major Walcott!" he exclaimed apologetically and shook his hand. "Sorry—I didn't really see who it was. As you see, I'm in a bit of a hurry." He released the major's hand and edged away.

"Don't apologize," the major blurted. "My fault, entirely. The fact is, Markby, I wondered if I could have a word. I do see how busy you all are. Quite a place, this! But I'd appreciate it."

"To be honest, Major, this isn't the moment. There's by way of an emergency. Perhaps someone else—?"

"Oh no!" Major Walcott was adamant. "Has to be you. It's—it's rather personal and a bit delicate." He looked mysterious.

"Oh, I see." That sort of preamble generally meant it was utterly trivial and of no importance to anyone but the person concerned. He tried to detach himself from Walcott with a show of civility. "Well, later on today, then. Perhaps you could call back later, eh?"

With that he left the major standing and carried on into the operations room where Bryce, Prescott and two or three others were gathered.

Prescott was keeping everyone entertained with an impression, apparently of an elderly woman. "Black sabbaths!" he was saying in an arch falsetto, accompanying the words with a coy pat of his hair.

"All right, everyone!" Markby said loudly as they sprang around. "Gordon Lowe is missing, possibly suicidal. We have to find him. Drop everything else."

"I went to see that woman Etheridge, sir." Prescott was red in the face at being caught fooling around and anxious to explain himself. "First thing, just as you said."

"She'll definitely have to wait! She didn't have anything new to tell us, did she?"

"Believes there's a satanic cult going on around somewhere."

"Unlikely!" Markby dismissed Mrs. Etheridge's theory. "Louise, has a preliminary post-mortem report come in yet on Denzil Lowe?"

"Yes sir, just a preliminary, but it's interesting. I was down there first thing this morning, at the morgue." She pulled a face. "There's a circular area of bruising and lacerations on the back of the head. The blood has collected beneath it and there's a suspected hairline fracture. Dr. Fuller says that, in his opinion, the deceased was struck a severe blow, severe enough to knock him unconscious, before he was strung up. He'll carry on with the examination into the fracture to make sure and will you let him know if you'll be coming down there."

It didn't really come as a surprise. "Weapon?" Markby inquired.

"Something heavy-headed like a hammer. One of the tools in the hut? We've found nothing that matches yet. We're still searching the churchyard. We need Gordon Lowe to tell us if anything is missing."

"Check them all! I want everyone on this. I want Gordon Lowe! And I want him alive and well!"

But they didn't find Gordon. They asked at the other cottages in the lane and searched the Lowes' garden and the other gardens and outbuildings. The search was extended to the fields behind. The old churchyard and new cemetery were both combed together with the public park. Anyone who was known ever to have employed the Lowes as jobbing gardeners was asked. The pubs they'd frequented visited. They checked local hospital casualty departments and local doctors' surgeries with particular regard to anyone suffering from amnesia.

They drew a blank. Gordon appeared to have vanished from the face of the earth.

At about one forty-five, Markby, emerging from his office en route to the canteen and a sandwich and coffee, came upon a lonely figure sitting patiently, bolt upright, in the reception area.

"Good Lord! Major? Still here?" Conscience struck him. "Have you been waiting here all morning?"

"Quite all right," Walcott assured him. "I've got nothing else to do. Thought you might have five minutes, although obviously you've got some kind of a flap on."

He could hardly turn the man away now. Markby asked resignedly, hoping wryly it wasn't a donation to party funds which would be requested, "What's it about?"

"It's about some money," said Major Walcott awkwardly. If he'd said it was about pornographic films he would have displayed the same embarrassment.

"Money?" Was he going to be asked for a subscription, after all? Markby gazed blankly at his visitor. "What money?"

"The money I paid to that girl, Kimberley Oates."

There was a silence. Markby said, "The least I can do, Major, is invite you to join me in a pint. There's a pub near here does reasonable sandwiches. It's my lunchtime and I expect you could do with some sustenance. You can tell me all about it there."

Sixteen

It was a small pub. By the time Markby reached it with Major Walcott, it had gone two o'clock and the lunchtime drinkers were straggling away. The kitchen had closed but the usual bar sandwiches were still on offer.

They settled in a corner with a pint apiece and a plate of smoked-salmon sandwiches between them. Major Walcott did not appear to have much appetite. He fiddled with a sandwich while Markby, finding himself hungry, tucked in and waited for Walcott to find his own way of beginning his tale.

"Margaret came to talk to Evelyne," Walcott said abruptly. He cleared his throat. "She told us you'd been to see her. You'd asked about the girl, Kimberley Oates. You appeared to think Margaret had paid the girl some money. The accusation quite upset her."

"I'm sorry," Markby said through a mouthful of smoked salmon. "But we can't worry about being tactless in police work or we'd get nowhere. We try not to distress anyone needlessly."

Walcott hastened to assure him that he wasn't being accused of heartlessness. "I understand! Of course you have to ask these things! Margaret understood that, too. She felt that, in the circumstances, you'd been very kind."

He cleared his throat again. "Margaret's a brave woman. Her life hasn't been easy. All this has given her so much trouble. When she'd left, Evelyne and I talked it over. We decided I should come and have a word with you. To set the record straight. To stop you bothering Margaret again and because these things always come out in the end. This is in confidence, naturally."

"It's a police investigation," Markby reminded him. "Of course we respect confidentiality when we can and we don't publish irrelevant material. But if it's got a bearing on the case, then I can't promise anything."

Walcott nodded. "Understand." He fell silent. "I ought to explain first," he said at last, "that Richard Holden and I were friends all our lives. Well, practically so. We were at school together. After school our careers diverged, but we kept in touch. When I retired from the army, Richard offered us the cottage at a peppercorn rent. In return, I was able, later on, to help his boy with his political career. Oh, only in a very modest way, you understand! Pushing leaflets through letter-boxes and knocking on doors at election time."

"Sterling work!" said Markby, knowing that it was true. Without loyal party workers like the major, little would get done at the grass-roots level.

"Meet some funny people, when you knock on doors." The major was diverted. "Get some abuse. Most people fairly polite. Most bored, to be frank. Hard to whip up any enthusiasm."

"Quite."

The last few lunchtime customers filed out. The publican caught Markby's eye and nodded. He went to close the main door and shoot the bolt across. The pub was, ostensibly, closed for the afternoon. The superintendent, whom the landlord knew well, could stay as long as he liked. The landlord had gone into a back room to eat his own delayed lunch. In the empty bar, Walcott cleared his throat noisily.

"Anyhow, Richard and I were friends, as I told you. I should perhaps describe Richard as I don't think you knew him. He was a reserved person, but that didn't mean he didn't feel deeply. He was devoted to Margaret and to the boy, Lars. I must emphasize that!"

Walcott leaned forward, his pale blue eyes bulging a little. "Devoted to them! But he always had trouble talking to the lad. 'I never know what to say to him, Ned!' he used to say to me. But he was very proud of him, as indeed he could be. Very bright youngster, obviously all set for a brilliant career. Richard was a bright chap, too, but I always felt he'd never really found his niche in life. To my mind, he'd have made an academic."

"What was he?" Markby interrupted to ask. "I mean, what did he do?"

"Do? Oh, at the end just managed the estate. He had several company directorships. He was in the City for much of his life, one of the merchant banks. But he wasn't really cut out for it. He'd had to take up some sort of career because the estate didn't bring in much. He'd have liked to have been just an old-style country gent with an interest in his library. But that sort of lifestyle is long in the past. Poor Richard. It always seemed to me he was an Edwardian born out of his time. He seemed adrift in modern-day life and never truly got to grips with it."

Walcott cleared his throat. "As for Margaret—splendid woman—she took care of everything on the home front and marshalled Richard's private business in a competent way, so he really depended on her. But she was very wrapped up in the boy, Lars. He was her true interest. Mother-love, I suppose. Evelyne and I have no children and I sometimes think I'm glad of it. Parenthood is a damn difficult business.

"I think Richard sometimes felt a little left out of things. Margaret was what I call the Brunhilde type. Magnificent to look at, especially when she was younger, and a very good organizer, but not what you'd call easy to live with. Very high standards. I don't think Richard ever felt he could really relax in his own home. But he was devoted to them!"

"I understand." Markby wasn't quite sure why Walcott was getting so het up about this, but presumably all would become clear in time.

The major took a swig of his beer, girding himself up for the next stage of his confession. "Richard was very ill at the end of the life. Cancer. It had got into him and in those days they couldn't control it as effectively as now.

He had all kinds of treatment and in the end he couldn't have any more. They gave him pills. I blame the pills for most of—of what happened. When a man is dosed up to his eyes in medicines of one kind and another, it has to affect his brain. He starts acting out of character."

Walcott made a weary gesture. "I'm making excuses. No one really understands another man or why anyone acts as he does. I've never had any faith in trick-cyclists. I've thought long and hard before coming to see you today, Markby. I felt—I still feel—as if I'm breaking a confidence, talking of poor Richard like this. But Richard wouldn't have wished any misunderstanding to involve Margaret or the boy. The air has to be cleared. Richard would wish it. I lay awake all last night, thinking about it, and that was my conclusion."

"Quite so, Major." The sandwiches were finished. Markby was still hungry. He wished the landlord hadn't left them. Couldn't be helped. He sipped at the remains of his pint.

The major took another swig at his and wiped his mustache with the back of his hand. "I knew the boy, Lars, was having a fling with the girl. I saw them together. Eighteen is a vulnerable age for a youngster. However, a young fellow has to learn about life at some point and I thought the boy was basically sensible. I wasn't able to say the same of the girl. Seen the type enough times, hanging around barracks. Anywhere in the world, you'll find the same sort of girl. Good-hearted and accommodating, but a street-fighter by instinct. Raise a dickens of a fuss if she thinks she's being treated unfairly."

"A camp follower," said Markby with a smile.

"Exactly!" The major was grateful for Markby's understanding. "In the Iron Duke's day, in the Peninsula, a horde of them followed the troops, suffered every hardship, tough as old boots. They got in the way when the men were trying to advance on the enemy. But they were good for morale. Kept the men happy. A necessary evil they used to call it."

Major Walcott gave a little snort. "Going back to the boy. At that time Evelyne and I had a dog, a spaniel. I used to take it out for a walk last thing every night. It was summertime. I took the dog out one evening into the coppice behind the cottages. It's not there now. The Holden estate used to be larger but when Richard died quite a bit was sold off. Anyhow, at that time, it was private woodland but being Holden property, I could walk the dog in it with Richard's permission.''

Walcott's faded eyes narrowed. He seemed to be looking back down the years into the distant past. ''It wasn't dark, but in the woods it was darker than out in the open. Gloomy. Very quiet. I followed a path with the old dog sniffing her way along ahead of me. Suddenly she stopped, pricked up her ears and gave a little yelp. She'd heard something. I put my hand on her collar and told her to be quiet. I wanted to listen too. There had been trouble with trespassers at one time, getting in and breaking down the saplings.

''I heard voices ahead of us. One of them was female. It was a young voice. I thought some youngsters had got in to fool about. I meant to go and chase them out. I set off with the dog and as I got nearer I could hear some sort of quarrel going on. Then I heard the man's voice. It was Richard.''

Walcott looked confused. ''I ought to have turned and gone back to the house. But I thought perhaps Richard was taking an evening stroll and had found someone there and was telling them to clear off. He could have been having trouble so I thought I ought to go and see if he wanted me to lend a hand. As I got nearer, the voices got louder, and the dog began to growl. I stooped to put a hand on her muzzle to quieten her. As I was like that, crouched down, hidden by the undergrowth, who should come around the bend in the path ahead but Richard and with him—that girl.''

Markby opened his mouth but closed it again. He was beginning to see where this was leading. His heart sank.

Walcott carried on with his story with military determination. ''They hadn't seen me. The girl was sniffling. Richard asked her not to cry. I thought perhaps she'd been to see him about Lars and he'd told her to leave the boy alone.

But then, as I watched, he kissed her. Not a paternal, cheer-up, sort of kiss. The other sort.''

"Passionate?"

"Very."

"So the girl was playing games with both father and son?"

"So it looked to me. She was all over him. He was fooling about with her blouse, got his hand inside it. No mistaking it. Richard must have been out of his mind, but then, as I told you, with all the drugs he was on, I think he was out of his mind a little. I was in a panic. I was afraid they'd see me. But after he'd kissed her they turned off down a side path and I was able to get back to the cottage.

"Evelyne could see, as soon as I came in, how upset I was. I never had secrets from Evelyne. I told her. I felt we should do something, we both felt it. Suppose the boy learned? At his age, it would be more than he could cope with. And Margaret? God forbid! And Richard himself, the public shame if it came out!

"We decided, Evelyne and I, that the one thing likely to influence the girl would be money. We weren't well off, but we had modest savings. We thought we could raise about five hundred—"

Markby couldn't help but exclaim, "Five hundred!" Jennifer had certainly misestimated the amount. There must have been some high denomination bills in the roll.

"Yes, not a great deal, but to a girl like that a tidy sum. I went to the bank the next day and took it out. It was all we had. I'm not telling you this because I mean us to look noble, but so that you'll understand that we didn't make the decision lightly. But we owed Richard a great deal, letting us have the cottage at such modest rent, and he was an old and valued friend. It seemed a small price to pay to protect him and his family from scandal and heartbreak.

"The association had arranged a dinner dance for the following week. I expected the girl to be there, waitressing, and so she was. I took her on one side and spoke to her like a Dutch uncle. Put the fear of God into her, in fact! Painted a picture of what would happen if it all came out and how she'd be finished in the town and her family would suffer. I'd taken the trouble to find out about her and knew she lived with an elderly grandmother, respectable sort of woman. The girl did look frightened by the time I'd finished. Then I gave her the money on the strict understanding she used it to get out of town. Go away and start afresh somewhere. She promised that she would. Shortly after that, she wasn't around any more. So I thought she'd kept her promise."

Major Walcott paused. "That's it."

"Not quite. What about Richard Holden? When the girl vanished from the scene, was he visibly upset?"

Walcott seemed to shrivel a little in his seat. "He—he was ill. He seemed to decline after that. He was in a lot of pain, increasingly doped. He—finished his torment himself."

"Took an overdose?"

"So the inquest reckoned. He was suffering. I hope—I hope it wasn't because the girl had left. But I really don't think so. In any case, it would have been worse if it had all become known. It was money well spent, in my view. I understand Richard taking the overdose. In his situation, I'd very likely have done the same."

"I'll need all this in a statement," Markby said.

"Fair enough. I'm relying on your word, Markby, that only necessary bits of this, if any of it's necessary, will be made public. The bit about the girl and Richard, there's no possible reason why that should ever be made public."

Walcott leaned forward. "The boy and his mother must never know! Neither Margaret nor Lars must ever know of it. It would destroy the pair of them! Margaret's family has been her life!"

He sat back. "But I had to tell you about the money and why I paid it, so that you wouldn't go bothering Margaret about it again."

"She didn't leave," Markby said.

"I didn't know that." Walcott met his gaze squarely. "I thought she had. When her bones were found in that grave, I couldn't credit it. I thought there had to be some mistake."

"No mistake, Major. You have no idea, then, what could have happened to the money, the cash?"

He looked surprised. "Of course not. Thought she'd left and taken it with her."

Oh, what a tangled little loveknot! Markby thought as he got up and went to find the landlord. And oh, what a whole list of reasons for murder!

Meredith too had gone to find some lunch.

She drove to The Old Coaching Inn. It wasn't so busy today. Simon French was in the bar, however, perhaps worrying over the lack of trade. He recognized her.

"Miss Mitchell! The superintendent with you?"

"No, I'm all on my own today. I was passing and I wondered if I could get a light lunch, just something small."

"Of course!" He ushered her to a table. "All the dishes on the starter list can be served with a side-salad. How about the chef's pâté? Or the wonton prawns? Garlic mushrooms?"

Meredith settled for the pâté with brown bread and butter and a side-salad and, because she was driving, a low-alcohol beer. She thought the restaurant looked better today or perhaps she was now used to its cluttered pseudo-historical ambience. The pâté was good, anyway. When she'd finished, she ordered coffee and—weakening—the cheesecake from the sweet trolley.

French drifted back as she'd hoped he would. "Everything all right?"

"Lovely, thank you. This is a quiet day for you, I see. But business is generally good, is it?" She signalled her interest in idle conversation by putting her elbows on the table and gazing up at him above her clasped hands.

French assured her that trade was booming, only today was a little slow. "That's how it goes in this business."

"It must be an interesting career. I understand you've always been in this line."

Fortunately French didn't seem to wonder how she came by this information. He was one of those happy to talk about himself. "I started as a barman, like Mickey over there. Only not in a good restaurant like this! I wasn't so lucky as Mickey. I started out with a firm of caterers, local firm, it was. Mind you, they were good and I got my training with them.''

''Would that be Partytime?'' Meredith asked ingenuously. ''I've seen their offices.''

''That's right. But the firm there now, though it's still called Partytime, is a different outfit.''

French, as always anxious to impress, followed nicely where Meredith had been leading him, ''I knew that girl, Kimberley Oates. The one who's been in the news. She and I worked together.'' He looked smug as if this had been some achievement on his part.

''Did you?'' Meredith affected convincing surprise. ''So that's why you thought you might know the identity of the skeleton! I'm sure the police were very grateful that you came forward. What made you think it was her? What was she like, anyway?''

French pulled out a chair and sat down. ''She was a little tart, you know!'' he said confidentially. ''I'm not surprised about what happened. Of course you don't expect people you know to be murdered, but if ever anyone asked for it, she did!''

''Really?'' Meredith's smile was a little icy but French didn't notice.

''Anyone, just anyone! Know what I mean?'' He actually winked. ''She wasn't fussy.''

Meredith nearly asked, ''What about you?'' but managed to prevent herself. ''I expect she thought some of the parties you attended professionally, well, that they were glamorous affairs. It may have turned her head a little.''

''She wasn't stupid!'' French said unexpectedly. ''I mean, she was shrewd in a way but thick in other ways. She used to lead them on. I used to see her at places, looking over the men there, picking out one who'd be an easy touch. She was the type that older men liked. She had a sort of dairymaid look to her, fresh-faced. They thought she was innocent!'' French gave a nervous giggle.

It didn't occur to French that this speech contradicted his claim that Kimberley had sex with just anyone. She wasn't, he was now saying, all that indiscriminate. She went for a particular sort of man and was adept at seeking him out. That indicated a purpose to her search. But French, Meredith had decided, was also one of those who were sharp enough in some ways and remarkably dense in others.

"Perhaps," she suggested, "she thought one of them would be her passport out of the sort of life she had, would offer her something better."

"Kim Oates?" French stared at her. "Pah! 'Course none of them would've done that! Most of them were married anyway. That's what I mean about her being thick in some ways. She could pick out a man easy, but she couldn't see that he'd forget her as soon as she'd come across. She'd been at it for long enough. You would have thought the message would've got through to her!"

Meredith said crossly. "She was only eighteen when she died! How much experience could she have had?"

French got to his feet and gave her a worldly-wise look. "You don't know what goes on in small towns, Miss Mitchell!"

He left her to go and welcome in a newly arrived party. Which was a pity, thought Meredith, because Mr. French liked to gossip. But his last words were an echo of Mrs. Etheridge's "There are things going on!"

But what things? That was the frustrating part of it. Everyone hinted but no one actually said!

Meredith remembered something Alan had once told her, long ago, on a quite different case. "Somebody always knows," he'd said. But they didn't tell the police, that was the thing. There might be a dozen reasons why. They might not even realize that they knew or the importance of their knowledge. Or it might be misplaced loyalty or even that the knowledge gave them a little secret power which led to silence.

The bill for the pâté, salad, beer, cheesecake and coffee was quite high. Meredith thought ruefully that she might just as well have ordered a main course and been done with it.

* * *

She drove away from The Old Coaching Inn. The early afternoon was mild and sunny. The rain had dried up leaving only a few puddles on the roadside. After following a maze of twisting lanes Meredith finally came out on the road that passed the The Old Farm and the pair of cottages. She stopped outside Bullen's and went in search of the old man.

She found Bullen wrestling with a roll of chicken wire and cursing fluently as it refused to straighten. He was trying to hold one end steady by standing on it with his heavy boots. Oscar was tethered to a rusty wheelbarrow nearby and watching anxiously. He barked loudly and with a touch of hysteria at regular intervals.

"How are you, Mr. Bullen?" she shouted above the general racket. Oscar, seeing her, began to whine and tug at the restraining tether.

"How d'you think?" snapped Bullen. "Got eyes in your head, haven't you? You can see I'm not doing very well!"

"Perhaps I could give you a hand?"

Bullen straightened up and looked her up and down. "All right. You look a strong sort of girl. Only you want to be careful. This stuff whips around and can give you some nasty scratches."

Between them they managed to unroll a length of wire which Bullen snipped free with wirecutters. "Over here!" he ordered.

She followed to where a deep trench had been excavated around a cabbage patch. Stakes had been fixed in it at intervals.

"Now what I want you to do," said Bullen severely, "is hold that stake steady, while I fix the wire to it with these double-ended pins here, these ones, see?" He held one up. His attitude was that of a master craftsman explaining the trade to an apprentice. "You hold the stake steady when I give it a whack with this hammer."

His other knobbly hand held up an ancient hammer, the head of which appeared insecurely fixed to the haft.

"Mr. Bullen," said Meredith nervously. "How about you hold the stake and I use the hammer?"

"I never met a woman could hit a nail in straight," said

Bullen. "They always do it crooked. You don't want to worry I'll hit your kneecap. I'm not blind."

Meredith held the top of the stake and contrived to stand as far away as she could. Bullen, who had swung back his thin arm in readiness, lowered it again and eyed her with disgust.

"What you doing standing over there? How can you hold the stake steady if you're all at an angle yourself? Come up next to it!"

Meredith edged nearer. Bullen swung the hammer. Oscar tensed.

Wham! The stake shuddered but Bullen had struck the pin unerringly. Oscar threw himself to the end of the leash and set up a frenzy of barking.

"Shut that noise, damn dog!" yelled Bullen.

Oscar sat down and put his head on one side.

Bullen gave a chuckle. "He's got a clever old head on his shoulders, that dog. He knows what I say to 'im. He's a smart old feller, is that one."

"What's he doing here?" Meredith asked.

"She's gone into town." Presumably Bullen meant Margaret Holden. "And the major and his missus have both gone off somewhere too. So I'm baby-sitting as you might say. Come along, then. Next bit!"

They repeated the wire and pin routine. As they worked their way around the patch, Meredith grew more relaxed and Oscar also quietened down. Bullen knew what he was about. She was astonished at the strength in those old arms. But Bullen had worked out of doors all his life.

"Wondering how old I am, are you?" he asked suddenly.

"Yes," she told him frankly.

"Well, I'm not telling you. There's younger men not as fit as I am. But they live soft nowadays. I started work fourteen year old. Didn't have any schooling after that. Didn't need any. I could read and write my name. That was enough."

"Always been a grave-digger, Mr. Bullen?"

Nat straightened up with a grunt of effort. "No. First off I did general farm work, then hedging and ditching, then grave-digging. I became grave-digger in 1949. Some people mightn't have liked the job but it suited me fine. I worked on my own, no one staring over my shoulder. Quiet in the churchyard but not lonely. Early in the morning you see any amount of small animals, rabbits, stoats, foxes. Birds, too, all kinds.''

"Bit creepy, though," Meredith observed.

Bullen rolled a yellowed eyeball at her. "The dead folk? They can't do you no harm. Live ones, now, you want to worry about the live ones! But the dead ones? No—not unless, of course, you've done badly by them!" Bullen paused in thought. "Ah!" he said aggravatingly and fell silent.

They had progressed around the cabbage patch by now. Bullen took a last swipe at a pin with his hammer and set it down. "Reckon us could do with a cup of tea."

He untied Oscar and the three of them proceeded to Bullen's kitchen. It wasn't nearly such a disaster area as Meredith had imagined it. Bullen brewed up tea in an enamel teapot and produced milk in a bottle.

"Help yourself." He settled himself down across the table from her. "What do you want, then?"

"You've heard Gordon Lowe is missing?" she asked him.

Oscar had found something on the kitchen floor and was eating it. She wondered what it was. She tried to see.

"Don't worry about the dog," said Bullen. "He's better than a vacuum cleaner, is that dog. I heard about Gordon— and about Denny. Gordon very likely gone off his head with the shock. He'll be wandering about out there in the fields and woods. He'll come back when his senses do."

"Do you think Denny hanged himself?"

Bullen put his head on one side and squinted at her. "Damfool thing to do if he did."

"But do you think he did?" she insisted.

"Might've."

"And you can't think of anywhere Gordon might be?"

"I never had nothing to do with the Lowes," said Bullen. "They pinched my job. I'm sorry about Denny and for Gordon's trouble. But there you are. Folk are strange."

"Did you know the girl who died, Kimberley Oates?"

"Got a load of questions, haven't you?" Bullen sniffed. "Can't see what all the fuss is about. She's dead and gone. It'll be twelve years or more. Why can't they all leave it alone? They'll never find out what happened to her."

From above their heads came a faint creak. Meredith looked up at the ceiling.

Bullen did not appear to have noticed. He said, "That what you came to ask me?"

"More or less."

"Markby send you?"

"No, it was my own idea."

The ceiling creaked again. Meredith looked for Oscar, who might have found his way upstairs. But Oscar had gone outside through the open back door and was engaging in a little gardening of his own. He was scraping energetically with his stubby forepaws at a grassy bank. From time to time he seized a tussock in his mouth and tugged at it.

She turned back to meet Bullen's yellowed and malicious gaze.

"Badgers," said Bullen. "Them little dogs is bred for digging out badgers. Major Walcott told me that. Give 'em a chance and they go digging. It's their nature. Like digging is my nature. That's why me and that little dog we get along so well. We both like digging."

Oscar tore the clump of grass loose at last and shook it vigorously to kill it. Dirt flew in all directions.

"You tell Markby, when you see him, we got the chicken wire fixed up," Bullen said.

There was little point in asking any further. Unlike Simon French, Bullen didn't gossip. Nor, as Markby had already found out, did he believe in answering questions. Not unless it was about the advantages of a grave-digging life.

Oscar, his head and shoulders covered in earth, plodded in. His mud-caked tongue trailed out of his mouth. The tussock, well and truly dead, lay abandoned on the path. He was a happy dog. He made his way to a bowl of water, brushing against Meredith's leg and loosing a shower of dirt. She stooped to pat him as he passed and said, "I'll be getting along then, Mr. Bullen."

"Fair enough," said Bullen.

As she drove away, Meredith peered into the windscreen mirror. She could just see the frontage of Bullen's cottage. It seemed to her that a curtain moved at one of the dusty upper windows. Perhaps the breeze or perhaps Bullen had gone upstairs and watched her drive off. Very likely he wanted to be sure she'd left.

"So we've got another two suspects for our list!" said Bryce. She held up the typed statement Major Walcott had signed. "Walcott, although I know he came forward voluntarily. But they often do, don't they?"

"They do indeed, Lou," Markby agreed. He visualized the major's earnest, slightly protruberant blue eyes as he sought to assure Markby that Richard Holden had been a devoted family man.

"He and his wife had paid over all their savings to Kimberley on the understanding she left town. If they later found she'd reneged on the promise, taken their money and laughed at them, I reckon he'd have been mad enough to kill her. He was twelve years younger then and an ex-soldier."

"Oh, yes . . ." said Markby in a depressed voice.

"And Richard Holden." Bryce screwed up her face. "Tricky one, that. He's dead. But according to Walcott, he killed himself. He might have killed the girl and then himself. That's happened lots of times. He could have persuaded or bribed Bullen to bury the body for him. A local landowner like Holden would have no trouble persuading a tenant to do that for him. We'll never be able to prove it."

"Thank God . . ." Markby murmured. Bryce looked surprised and he added, "Just thinking. If Richard Holden was her lover, why didn't she ask *him* for money?"

"Perhaps she did. Perhaps he'd paid her some small amounts. Perhaps he was the rich boyfriend Jennifer told me about, the one Kimberley hoped would set her up in a flat? On the other hand, perhaps he couldn't pay over much money without his wife getting suspicious. Mrs. Holden's the sort of woman who would notice cash seeping out of a joint account. I reckon he couldn't pay Kimberley more than a few pounds now and again to keep her in junk jewelry and tights.''

''But then she went to Richard and Margaret together and asked them jointly for money, claiming to be carrying Lars's baby.'' Markby scowled at Walcott's statement, lying on the desk.

''Makes sense!'' said Bryce with undimmed enthusiasm. ''She'd already asked Richard. She might even have told him the baby could be his, but he told her it was impossible to pay her a large sum without Margaret knowing. Kimberley was angry. She thought he'd let her down and she wanted revenge. She promptly went to Margaret, told her the baby was her son's, and what about it? All Richard could do was look on helpless. He saw this girl about to wreck his whole family. He was besotted with her but at the same time the threat she posed was more than he could allow. And she was taunting him, too, by saying the baby could be his son's. Perhaps he also got very angry and wanted to hurt her in some way.''

''Love and hate,'' murmured Markby. ''All muddled up together in the mind of a man who was terminally ill and being dosed with any number of drugs.''

He wondered whether Major Walcott had also drawn the conclusion Louise Bryce had. That Richard might have killed the girl. But Richard had been Walcott's friend and he'd respected him deeply. To admit he'd been a murderer was not an idea Walcott was likely to entertain.

''If you ask me,'' Bryce concluded, ''Richard might well be our man. But like I said, we'd have the devil of a job proving it.''

Seventeen

As Meredith drove back to Bamford she reflected that she hadn't achieved very much. French undoubtedly had more gossip to impart but might grow suspicious if she returned a second time alone to his restaurant and led the conversation around to Kimberley.

She really needed to speak to someone else who had known the dead girl. It would be nice to speak to Jennifer, but she couldn't ask Alan for her address and she had no authority or even the most specious excuse for seeking Jennifer out. Kimberley's former colleague was now married to a policeman, so Markby had told her with some amusement. Jennifer's husband would know at once that Meredith had no right to be asking questions.

So it was left to her to find anyone still in Bamford who had known Kimberley. There must be dozens of people. Girls who were at school with Kimberley, for example. But they'd proved curiously unwilling to come forward although several must have seen and recognized the photograph printed in the press. Alan, she knew, was disappointed by that, but not surprised. "People don't want to get involved," he'd said.

So, if not fellow-students, then how about neighbors?

"Neighbor!" Meredith said aloud and swerved. Fortunately there was no oncoming traffic but she did approach uncomfortably near the roadside ditch. Derek Archibald.

She would have tried to speak to Derek again in any case, but perhaps Mrs. Archibald would be more forthcoming? Alan had already interviewed her. He hadn't precisely described Mrs. Archibald but his manner had indicated a certain distaste. Alan was generally fair-minded, with occasional lapses into what Meredith called "copper-thinking," and tolerant. So his attitude on this occasion made Meredith curious.

She would need an excuse to call on the woman. She couldn't mention the case. Mrs. Archibald had already spoken to the police and so would be suspicious of a lay person asking questions. It was time for the Bamford Black Magic circle to get out its broomsticks again.

The persistent rain had returned by the time she got to the outskirts of town. Wings of spray rose to either side as she drove through the puddles like the parting of the Red Sea. Pedestrians hurried by, heads buried in umbrellas. They pressed themselves against the walls to avoid the curb and the inevitable drenching.

Mrs. Archibald was at home. Meredith had trawled the address from the phone book. There was only one Archibald, Derek, twice listed, once the shop number, beneath it a street address. Meredith identified the cottage by much the same process of deduction and exploration as Markby had. Before ringing the doorbell she had taken a moment to stand in contemplation of the next-door dwelling, which had been the home of Kimberley and her grandmother.

She felt a sense not only of curiosity but of melancholy. It was not possible to know if the little house had changed much with the passage of years. Probably not, although it was undergoing change now. Some building work had begun, a loft extension by the look of the scaffolding and tarpaulin covering the roof. The wind had found its way under one corner and caused the tarpaulin to slap noisily against the stone wall.

Beneath the low lintel of that front door Kimberley Oates had walked, up the narrow path and out into the lane, on her way to her final assignation. "Dressed up," in the words of her grandmother, as spoken to the police when she reported the girl's disappearance. A sad touch, but also extremely interesting. For, Meredith reasoned, if Kimberley had taken pains to make herself attractive, she was going to meet a man. Not a man she expected to see that evening—it ruled out Simon French. No, someone she had to meet during the day. Had the lane been empty at the time? Had anyone else met her on the way? The report didn't say. But it wasn't too fanciful to imagine Kimberley exchanging brief greetings as she hurried down the narrow throughfare.

"You look very smart today, dear!" Mrs. Etheridge's words echoed in Meredith's head. Had someone perhaps said much the same thing to Kimberley on that fateful day?

A gust of rain found its way down Meredith's neck as she turned away and hurried up the path to Mrs. Archibald's front door.

"Black Masses?" Mrs. Archibald, wedged in her armchair, gazed at Meredith. She expelled breath in a long painful groan. "Not that I ever heard of! What, here in Bamford?"

Disbelief fought with curiosity on her empurpled face. She didn't believe it—quite. But she plainly wanted to hear about it.

"I did ask your husband about the incident, some years ago now, when he and Mrs. Etheridge found a candle and flowers on the altar one evening. In those days they were both members of the PCC. Perhaps Mr. Archibald still is?"

She shook her head. "No, he gave it all up several years ago. That Father Holland has got his own ideas. Poor Mr. Appleton, he was a different sort of man altogether, an old-fashioned sort of vicar. He was very much missed. Of course, he was ga-ga at the end."

The late Maurice Appleton was thus dismissed. It didn't take great powers to work out that Derek Archibald had much preferred being a member of the PCC under the lax rule of the former vicar, rather than have Father Holland's forceful leadership to follow.

"I expect your husband told you about the candle business at the time?" Meredith prompted.

The gas fire had been lit. It hissed gently and its pale

flames flickered. From time to time, a faint roar came from the chimney behind. The day might be wet and chilly but Meredith privately thought the heating excessive in the tiny room. However, she wasn't elderly and infirm. Mrs. Archibald was obviously both. Her wheezing breath was alarming. Every intake of air seemed a battle. The stuffy atmosphere must make it worse. Why didn't the woman open a window and let in the breeze?

Roar—hiss—wheeze. It was like being incarcerated in the engine room of some old steamship.

Meredith was assailed by guilt. She oughtn't to be here, worrying a sick woman.

But Mrs. Archibald showed no sign of objecting. Visitors were probably few. "Yes, I do recall something. Derek came home late from the meeting and said Janet Etheridge had caused a fuss." Mrs. Archibald snorted. "That was nothing new! She insisted everyone go traipsing over to the church and when they got there, there was nothing to see. Just a burned-out candle and a few wilting flowers. Kids, Derek said. Little devils, the kids around here, I can tell you!"

Mrs. Archibald grew agitated and the creaking of her chest worse. "I've had so much trouble with them! You wouldn't credit how they've behaved outside this house! They know I'm in here and can't get out much, let alone chase them! I was never strong. I was a delicate child. The doctor told my mother I wouldn't live to grow up. I used to have a photo somewhere. In it I look just like one of those."

She pointed to a bone-china figurine of the Dresden type, a shepherdess in pink and green. "Just a little wisp of a thing."

This was hard to imagine in the absence of the photograph referred to. Meredith suspected the word "delicate" was an embroidery on the truth. "Sickly" might have been a better choice. Mrs. Archibald's present appearance was due to her affliction, but her general build suggested she'd been large all her life. A solid pale unhealthy kid was more like it. She was beginning to understand Alan's antipathy toward this woman with her self-pitying and critical attitude.

Mrs. Archibald was still lamenting the unruly nature of modern children. "I'd never have behaved the way they do when I was young! But we were kept in check! Now they just run wild! I wouldn't like to tell you what they get up to!"

The last part was clearly untrue. She was dying to tell Meredith what the local children had done. The conversation had to be conducted on Mrs. Archibald's terms. Meredith said encouragingly, "I know. They can be dreadful. What did they do?"

Mrs. Archibald was pleased to have support. "Stood outside here and shouted things, they did! Filthy things! Things, words, no child should know! And pushed dirty pictures through my letterbox!"

"Dirty pictures?"

"Naked women! Torn out of them nasty magazines. They've got them in the newsagents now. Disgraceful, I call it. They put them up on the top shelf, but the kids still get hold of them!"

According to Mrs. Etheridge, so did Derek Archibald, but his wife presumably didn't know that. Where, Meredith wondered, did Derek keep his stock of pornographic literature? Not here at home. In the shop?

"I was that upset! And so was Derek, him being a member of the church all these years." Her face was by now so discolored it seemed she would have some sort of seizure. "They wrote on my garden wall! They wrote 'Derek Archibald is a dirty old man!' I phoned the police. They came along and said, did I know who did it? I told them, the kids did it! They said, which ones? But I couldn't tell them which ones, so that was that. Nothing was done! They got away with it!"

"Oh, dear," said Meredith feebly, hoping Mrs. Archibald would calm down.

Perhaps Mrs. Archibald realized she was becoming dangerously overwrought. Her bloated fingers, gripping the arms of her chair, relaxed.

"But as to satanic goings-on, that I don't know about.

Derek never said he found anything else in the church after that one time. If you go talking to Janet Etheridge you'll hear all sorts of nonsense. She's one of those people gets ideas in her head and you can't shift them! Vegetarian, she is! There was a terrible row between her and Derek one time. She stood outside his shop handing out leaflets against eating meat. Claiming slaughterhouses were cruel and the meat was bad for your health! I've eaten meat all my life," added Mrs. Archibald, wheezing furiously, "and it never did me any harm!"

"Is there anyone else I could ask?" Meredith paused. "How about your neighbors along this road?"

The woman shook her head. "They're mostly newcomers. There's only Derek and me left from the old days. I wouldn't know whom to send you to. Next door used to be Joan Oates. She didn't own, only rented. She died and some people called Hamilton bought the place. They sold out to a young couple. They've got the roof off, did you see? Putting in a study in the attic, so they said. I wonder they got planning permission. Joan Oates, her granddaughter was the one whose bones they found in the churchyard not long ago."

"Yes, I read about that. So you knew the girl?"

"Young Kimberley? Little madam! Pretty little thing, I suppose, but then, so was her mum, Susan. Poor Joan was left to bring up the kid after Susan left home. Kimberley used to come around here quite often when she was just a little tot. She took a fancy to Derek. He used to take her for walks and buy her sweets. We never had any children, Derek and me. I've always had bad health. Derek made quite a fuss of the kid. I was sorry Kimberley turned out bad, but I wasn't surprised."

It really did seem unwise to keep Mrs. Archibald talking any longer and Meredith had no wish to be responsible for any kind of deterioration in the lady's condition. Besides which a dozen ideas were buzzing in her head and she wanted to get away and sort them out quietly. She thanked Mrs. Archibald for her help and got up to go.

"Nice to meet you, dear," said Mrs. Archibald. "Come again."

*   *   *

Meredith made her way home. The rain was steady now and the afternoon gray. She had to switch on the electric light in her little kitchen to make a cup of tea.

She sat at her kitchen table to drink it and marshal all the new and disturbing ideas which floated around her mind.

Derek Archibald and his wife had no children and probably never led a very exciting sex life. Mrs. Archibald had enjoyed bad health all her life and was of a disapproving turn of mind. Derek bought soft porn magazines. These facts were probably connected. Derek had a locked shed behind his shop which no one ever entered. The assistant, Gary, didn't know what Derek kept in there. Derek's stock of porn? That seemed logical enough.

So far, so good. The rain rattled the window and Meredith glanced up. The cotoneaster that grew against the wall outside was in need of pruning. She kept meaning to ask Alan's advice. A spray with its small dark green leaves swayed before the panes. The movement seemed to be encouraging her. Go on, you've got that far. Keep going.

But going where? It would be all too easy to take a wrong turning. First establish the correctness of the route she'd taken so far.

Meredith got up and hunted through the dresser drawer to find the tattered street plan of Bamford which had accompanied her everywhere when she'd first come to live here.

She spread it on the table. Inevitably, the central crease came right across the High Street, obliterating the spot where Archibald's butcher's shop stood. But it was possible to trace a narrow alley. It ran down the side of the shop, then turned parallel to the High Street, giving a rear entrance to all the shops on that side of the main thoroughfare. Beyond it lay the gardens of the terraced homes in the next parallel street. Meredith folded the plan.

Derek's shed had a felt covering probably tacked on to quite a flimsy wooden roof. To prise up a corner shouldn't be too difficult. It would be as good a way of getting a look inside as any. Much easier than getting through a locked door.

She would have to wait till dark.

By ten-thirty that evening a steady drizzle had set in for the night. Meredith was glad of it. On an evening like this people stayed at home unless obliged to go out and she particularly didn't want to meet anyone who might recognize her.

She'd dressed for her expedition in dark slacks, sweater and navy-blue waterproof jacket, and carried the little flashlight she normally kept in the car. To prise up the slats of the roof she had a long heavy-duty screwdriver. It wouldn't fit into a pocket but she solved that problem by putting the tool into a strong plastic bag and pinning the bag to the inside of her jacket in the manner of a "poacher's pocket."

She grimaced at her reflection. The complete cat burglar. If a police patrol, alerted by a suspicious citizen, stopped her it would be difficult to explain away poacher's pocket and screwdriver. Luckily Alan didn't know what she planned and what he didn't know couldn't worry him—yet.

It was around eleven when she reached the alley to the side of the butcher's shop. On her way she'd seen few people, all of them hurrying home as fast as they could, collars turned up and heads bowed against the inclement weather. No one had taken any notice of her. Most probably hadn't even seen her. It was as well. The screwdriver in the poacher's pocket bumping against her chest was a constant reminder that what she was about to do was probably stupid and certainly illegal. She reassured herself that it was necessary. There was no other way she could get a look into the shed and the desire to do so was overwhelming.

The alley was badly lit. There was a street light on the pavement by the entry which shone part way down. Another, very feeble, little lamp glimmered at the corner where the alley made a forty-five degree turn to the left to run behind the row of shops. Meredith padded down it, the flashlight in her hand sending a narrow comforting beam ahead of her. The air smelled of damp mortar, old brickwork, dustbins and faintly of raw meat from the butcher's premises to her left.

Suddenly a cat shot out from some hidey-hole and scuttled under her feet. It scrabbled up a fence and over it with a deafening racket in the quiet night. Meredith's heart leapt almost out of her chest.

She leaned against the wall and waited until she felt more settled. Sweat trickled down her spine. Her biggest desire now was to get this over with and go home. She turned the corner into the length of alley backing the shops. Beyond the weak beam of the corner lamp it was pitch dark and she didn't know what, or who, might be lurking down there. She looked toward the gardens to her right. They were long and narrow. The old terraced houses to which they belonged were too far away to look down into the alley. In any event all their windows were tightly curtained against the night. No one was looking out.

Meredith flashed the torch beam upwards and it picked out the top of the stone wall and the felt roof of Derek's shed, just visible above it. She switched the torch off and put it back in her pocket.

The wall, built of uneven quarried stone, offered plenty of toe and hand holds and it wasn't difficult to reach the top. Meredith was soon sitting astride the coping stone. She felt along the edge of the shed roof in the darkness and found where the felt was tucked under and tacked down. She gave an experimental tug.

At first she was unlucky and the felt too firmly fixed. She tore a fingernail painfully and had to stop and bite the torn piece off, as children do. The wooden slats beneath the felt were old and dry and easily splintered. A splinter in a finger would be unwelcome, one beneath a nail reminiscent of torture scenes in violent novels. She pressed cautiously against the felt and it ripped away from a doubtlessly rusty nail. To the image of torture was added that of tetanus. When had she last had a booster jab? Years ago.

Suddenly the whole corner of felt came away in her hands, cracking with age. This was rather more than she'd planned. She did not want to make so much damage that

Derek would see it instantly when he next came to the shed. But as she'd hoped, the slats beneath were thin. The screwdriver was easily forced under the end one. She levered it up. With a protesting screech a nail parted from wood. Then part of the slat snapped. Both sounds echoed through the night, making her glance guiltily to the windows of the houses behind. But no curtain twitched. Instead a whiff of stale damp air struck her nostrils from the shed's interior. She experienced a buzz of excitement. She was through the obstacle.

The next set of maneuvers was trickier. She returned the screwdriver to the poacher's pocket and got out the torch. Now she had to hold up the loosened slat and felt cover while, with the other hand, she directed the beam of the flashlight inside the shed. She was forced to press her face against the grimy wet felt and wiggle the flashlight so that it didn't dazzle her and she could see down into the shed.

More fusty air rose up from the depths. Rain trickled down her neck inside the waterproof jacket. At first she could see nothing and then, with an abruptness which seemed akin to a conjuring trick, Meredith found herself looking at a face.

It was a child's face. It stared at her from a large photograph framed behind glass and hanging on the wall. The glass reflected the beam and the face was lost. Meredith wiggled the light again. The face returned.

The child was a little girl of about eight or nine. She wore a sunsuit and was laughing. She had curly hair and a gap between her front teeth. Meredith moved the beam of light along the inner wall. More photographs, some only snapshots pinned up unframed and too small to make out any detail, but all apparently of a child.

Not all showed the subject at the same age. Larger photographs recorded childish contours changing as a young woman emerged like an adult insect from its chrysalis, unsure yet how to use its wings, but about to take flight. Soon awareness of self and burgeoning sexuality began to lend the face an expression which suggested some temerity on the part of the photographer at studying his subject, and even more at the boldness of the intruder on the roof.

And then, to sweep away the last lingering doubt, the flashlight beam picked up a studio portrait of a girl of about sixteen with a round face and bright confident smile displaying the same gappy teeth. A picture Meredith had seen before, when Daisy Merrill had shown it to her, in her newspaper.

Kimberley Oates. Picture after picture of Kimberley Oates! Kimberley as a tot, Kimberley growing up, Kimberley on the threshold of womanhood. The whole shed was a shrine to Kimberley, reflecting a frightening obsession.

Meredith sat up and switched off the torchlight. She felt slightly sick. Words echoed in her head. Mrs. Archibald saying how little Kimberley had taken a fancy to Derek who "used to take her for walks." Walks, no doubt, which only led as far as this shed. Derek had made quite a fuss of the child. Had he, indeed? The nature of this "fuss" didn't bearing thinking about.

And the other children, those who had pushed pictures of naked women through the Archibalds' front door, and chalked 'Derek Archibald is a dirty old man' on the wall. Derek Archibald with his secret stock of soft porn magazines and probably some stronger stuff which was hidden away in this shed. Derek, obsessed with Kimberley at all stages of her life. Obsessed, perhaps, even unto death.

She would have to tell Alan about this. She'd have to own up about tonight's excursion and he'd be furious. But he'd have to know.

Meredith switched on the flashlight again and leaned forward for a last look down into the shed. Her former eagerness was replaced by repugnance but there might be some other evidence in there which she hadn't yet spotted.

A dustbin lid rattled distantly. A cat, perhaps the same one that had earlier startled her. A car horn blared from the main road. She ought not to spend any more time here. She had already lost track of how long she'd taken. Meredith pushed her whole arm through the hole in the roof, trying to see into a far corner. But in doing so her grip on the flashlight was weakened. Her fingers slipped on the rain-wet handle and, without warning, before she could do anything about it, the little torch jumped out of her hand and clattered down into the shed. It landed on the floor, still sending out its beam, uselessly illuminating an empty corner.

"Damn!" she muttered.

She couldn't get it back. Not without ripping off half the roof and ensuring the damage would be visible to Archibald. She'd have to leave it and hope that by morning the battery would have run out and the light be extinguished. It was only a small battery and not new. How much life would it have left running non-stop? Not more than an hour, she comforted herself. Extinct, there was a slight chance Derek might not notice the little torch on the floor.

She sat up and pushed the loosened slat back into place. She couldn't hammer down the nail again, but she pulled the felt over it and hoped that, as this was the rear of the shed, Archibald wouldn't look up here. From inside, with luck, it would look almost the same.

Meredith scrambled back down the wall, scraping her hands on the rough stone blocks. She hurried back down the alley and homeward, scarcely aware of the direction in which her feet took her.

Indoors again she realized she was very wet and very grubby. Her hands were in a specially sorry state, torn nails, scraped skin, ingrained dirt. She stripped off the damp clothing and got into a bath. By the time she got out again and dressed in clean dry clothes, it was one in the morning.

Her instinct was still to pick up the phone there and then, but it would hardly be fair on Alan who wouldn't, in any case, be able to initiate any action until daylight. Stifling her impatience, she made some cocoa and retired to bed.

She slept very little.

Eighteen

The alarm call of the clock radio awoke Alan Markby. It was followed by the day's quota of unencouraging news and the promise of more bad weather. He rolled out of bed and into the shower on auto-pilot and didn't fully waken until he'd reached his kitchen a little later and made a cup of instant coffee.

Mug in hand, he peered disconsolately into the packet of cornflakes. The contents had dwindled unheeded to a few whole flakes and a collection of crumbs. He shook the whole lot outside onto the patio for the birds and shoved two pieces of bread into the toaster. He could boil an egg but it meant time and trouble. He settled for the toast and thick-cut marmalade.

His cleaner came today. He always tried to get out of the place before she turned up, partly because she preferred it that way, and partly because he was ashamed to face her. A house with one man living in it oughtn't to get so untidy but it did. In a token gesture, he rounded up a pile of old newspapers and thrust them into a carrier bag to be taken to the recycling center at some future date—probably when they grew to be so many that they threatened to take over the house. Then he went outside for a quick check on his greenhouse.

That also needed cleaning out and general tidying. It was one of the jobs he'd meant to do during his leave. The leave he wasn't now taking. The tomatoes were doing well in their Gro-bags. The fuchsias were fine. But empty plant pots were heaped higgledy-piggledy in a corner together with half-used bags of compost and watering cans filled with murky water. Bottles and boxes of various chemical aids to better gardening stood dust-laden and out of date on the shelves. Spiders were spinning their webs across the metal frame. If he didn't do something about it, the greenhouse would soon play host to unwelcome guests, whitefly, red spider and others of that ilk. Dirty greenhouses attracted bugs.

"And potting sheds attract insects too!" he said aloud. Sheds like the hut in the churchyard where Denny had met his untimely end. Where, quite possibly, Kimberley Oates' dead body had lain wrapped in a garishly patterned piece of cloth until secretly buried.

Thought of the Lowes, and specifically of Gordon, caused him to hasten back to the house. If he left now, he could stop by the vicarage and collect James Holland. They could make another expedition to the Lowes' cottage together. With luck, Gordon might have come home. Or at the very least, there would be signs that he'd been there. He switched the telephone over to the answering machine and went out.

Which was why, when Meredith tried to phone him about five minutes after this, all she got was his voice inviting her to leave a message. To summarize her discovery in a few words for the benefit of a machine hardly seemed sufficient.

She muttered and slammed down the phone. He'd probably already left for work. She'd ring headquarters later.

Markby wasn't headed for the office. The rain had stopped, although to judge by the puddles it must have kept up most of the night. Now, the sun had come out and the wet bricks and road surfaces glittered as if dusted with spangles. The morning at least promised to be dry. The weather forecast had got it wrong again.

The vicarage garden was wet and smelled fresh and of good earth. A blackbird was at work on the lawn, digging out the worms which the rain had brought to the surface. Father Holland was inspecting his Yamaha in the garage.

"Hullo, Alan!" he greeted Markby. He wiped his hands on an oily rag and added hopefully, "Got any news?"

"Of Gordon? Afraid not. I wondered whether you had."

The vicar shook his head. "Not hide nor hair. I do believe something must have happened to the poor fellow."

"Then we'd probably have found a body by now," Markby consoled him. "That we haven't suggests he's alive and keeps moving. I'd very much like to know why. Had your breakfast? I'm just going out to their cottage again."

"I'll come with you. Mrs. Harmer's here. I'll just let her know, in case Gordon phones." The vicar hurried toward the back door.

They took Markby's car to the lane where the cottage was situated and parked at the end of it. Its unmade surface was littered with water-filled pot-holes this morning. The rubbish outside the inhabitants' doors stood in pools of rainwater and the dog crouched miserably outside his crate kennel, too fed-up to raise more than a token yelp as they walked by.

The Lowes' cottage was still deserted. The window broken by Markby on the earlier visit had been boarded up by the police and showed no sign of having been disturbed again.

"We can enter in civilized fashion today," Markby said, when hammering on the front door had produced no response. "I've got the back-door key."

"Where did you get it?" asked Father Holland as Markby produced the cumbersome Chubb key from his pocket.

"From among Denny's effects. In his pocket. I'm sure Gordon won't mind us using it. Preferable to breaking in again."

The cottage was as they'd seen it last time. No trace showed of any visitor in the meanwhile in any of its rooms. The air smelled stale. Some mail had been delivered through the letterbox. Markby picked it up and riffled through it.

"Football coupon. Some sort of mailshot. Inland Revenue! Good luck to them! Nothing by way of a personal letter, handwritten."

"Who'd write to the Lowes?" the vicar asked simply.

Markby collected the two free newspapers which also lay on the coir mat and put them on the hall table with the other post. "Well, we can safely assume he's not been home."

"So what do we do?" Father Holland subsided onto a rickety chair and sat with his hands on his knees. "He isn't going to come back here. I feel it in my bones."

"That's just the damp!" said Markby robustly.

In truth he was beginning to feel the same way but he still clung to the hope that Gordon was alive. They'd searched thoroughly in the fields and woods behind the cottages and in all the outbuildings for quite some distance around. A body would have turned up. Unless, of course, someone had buried it—as Kimberley's had been buried. Kimberley's remains had taken twelve years to surface. He hoped it wasn't going to be the same tale for the missing Gordon.

He also hoped he wasn't about to fall into the same trap as those inquiring into the original disappearance of Kimberley had done. They'd glibly assumed that the girl must be all right, but had simply moved away. She hadn't.

He was sure Gordon hadn't. He'd left everything behind. Gordon was an old-fashioned countryman and a creature of habit. This was his den, his lair. This is where he'd come eventually if he was alive and well. The longer he stayed away, the more sinister it looked. The other possibility was that he was suffering some form of amnesia. Even so, where was he?

"Right, James," Markby said. "Let's try the next-door neighbor again."

The woman was out in her garden as before. She was pinning up more dingy washing, either because she had faith in the power of the watery sun, or because this enabled her to keep an eye on Markby and the vicar at Gordon's cottage.

Markby walked over to the fence. "Good morning!

We're still looking for Gordon Lowe. Have you seen him?''

She removed the peg gripped between her teeth. ''Gordon? No.''

''You've seen no one? No sign of anyone around the cottage at all?''

''Is Gordon in trouble?'' She sounded suspicious, not of Gordon's activities, but of his interest in them.

''Not with the police. But we believe he's very distressed. We'd like to find him. You know his brother is dead?''

''I heard about Denny.''

''Did it surprise you?'' Markby asked her suddenly.

She seemed taken aback at the question. She frowned. ''Yes, it did. Mind you, they were neither of them what you'd call friendly. I've lived next door to them fifteen years and never done more than exchange a good morning. But I wouldn't have thought Denny would go hanging himself.''

''He hadn't looked more than usually miserable or worried?''

She chewed on the end of the peg thoughtfully. ''Funny you should say that, because it was the other way about. They'd both looked a bit more cheerful than usual. Sort of grinning at each other, like they had a private joke between the two of them.''

''And that was rare?''

''Suppose so.'' She was getting restive under questioning. ''They weren't ones for cracking jokes. Well, they wouldn't, would they? Not in their line of work. Must have been a depressing job, digging graves all day long. Anyway, I've got to get on. Hope you find Gordon.''

Markby walked back to the waiting vicar. ''You heard that? What were Denny and Gordon up to, do you think? Something that amused them. Something they knew, perhaps? A shared secret of some sort?''

''What could they know?'' James Holland looked bewildered. ''They were like children. Totally unsophisticated and uncomplicated. Their lives were the same, day in, day out. Get up, go to work either grave-digging or a bit of jobbing gardening, come home, eat their supper, watch a bit of TV, go down to the pub for a pint, back again and to bed.''

Markby considered this simple routine. ''But somewhere along the line, they may have come across something. They were simple men, James, but they weren't simple in the mental sense. I would have said they were both pretty shrewd.''

Father Holland grunted. ''Denny was. Gordon less so. Oh yes, Denny was all about.''

Markby glanced at his wristwatch. ''I'll drop you off back at the vicarage and then I'd better get on. I want to run out to Bullen's place and check on him.''

Father Holland stared at him in alarm. ''You don't think Bullen's likely to do anything foolish?''

''He's old,'' Markby said obscurely. ''He might do anything.''

But privately he was very worried about the old man indeed. The injuries to Denny's skull indicated murder, not suicide. Gordon's continued absence was beginning to look bad. Someone, somewhere, alarmed at the progress of the police investigations, was stopping up possible leaks.

When he'd dropped Father Holland off, Markby phoned in from his car and told the office he'd be along later. He was going out toward Westerfield.

''Anything happening?'' he asked.

He was told that nothing of import had occurred and the only message was a private one from Miss Mitchell to call her.

Markby glanced at his watch. If things went well, he'd call around to her house before he left the area. At the moment he had something else to attend to. Private matters had to wait.

As he drew up before the pair of cottages, Markby was rewarded with the sight of Bullen, pottering about his cabbage patch toward the rear of the plot. He obviously hadn't come to any harm yet. Markby got out of the car and started toward the gate.

But at that moment the door of the Walcotts' cottage opened and Oscar rushed out. He bounced down the path toward Markby, barking at one end and wagging his tail at the other.

"Hullo, Oscar!" Markby leaned over the gate to greet the dachshund. He looked up. Margaret Holden was just leaving the cottage and talking to Evelyne Walcott in the doorway. The two women waved at him.

Markby waved back. Margaret said a word of farewell to Evelyne and walked toward him.

At the gate, she asked, "Are you coming to see me?"

"I was going to see Bullen, just checking. But he seems to be all right."

"Poor old man," she sighed. "I was just talking about him to Evelyne. He's getting more and more eccentric. He talks to himself. Ned and Evelyne have heard him through the wall."

"Thought these cottages would have had pretty thick walls."

"At the lower level, yes. But the walls grow thinner as the building goes up. Just below the roof they are only a single block thick. They're very old and don't have modern foundations. The base of the walls is thicker for support, I suppose. It's upstairs that they've heard Bullen, chattering away to himself in his bedroom."

"I do that," Markby said with a smile.

She gave a little laugh. "We all talk to ourselves. I too am a culprit! But this is different. It's like an argument he's having in there. His voice gets quite loud, so Ned says."

"Really?" Markby said thoughtfully.

"Why don't you come and have a cup of coffee with us? Lars and Angie are at the house."

Markby glanced again at Bullen's garden, but the old man had disappeared indoors. "All right, but I can't stay long."

It was clear as soon as they walked in that Lars and his fiancée had been having some dispute. Angie was white-faced and tight-lipped. Lars, in contrast, was purple in complexion and looked as if he'd been shouting.

Both put up a fair pretense of being pleased to see the superintendent.

"How's it all going?" Lars asked.

"Found the grave-digger yet?" Angie added.

"It's going as well as can be expected, and no, we've not found Gordon Lowe."

Margaret had gone out to organize the coffee. Lars glanced at the door. "This business is very difficult for Mother to handle."

"Really?" Markby had thought Margaret was handling it well. Lars, on the other hand, looked distinctly frayed and Angie's polished poise was slipping.

"She—she's worried about my career. About the effect adverse publicity could have on it."

"We all are!" snapped Angie.

"You did say, Alan," Lars's eyes fixed him pleadingly. "You did say you'd keep my name out of it."

"I don't think I quite said that," Markby protested. "I said, if you had nothing to do with it, there was no reason why your name should be mentioned."

Angie uncrossed her long legs and stood up. "Isn't that rather naïve?" She went to her handbag lying nearby and rummaged in it for cigarettes.

As she lit one, Lars said nervously, "Mother doesn't like—"

"Too bad!" his ladylove retorted crisply. She glanced around. "Although that's why there's never a damn ashtray about the place!"

Margaret Holden came back at that moment and, overhearing, said quietly, "I'll fetch you an ashtray, Angela. Lars dear, open the window."

"This missing chap, Gordon Lowe, is he important?" Lars asked as he wrestled with the latch. Realizing this could have been phrased more happily, he amended it to, "I meant, is he important to the murder case? Or is it something quite separate. I understand his brother committed suicide. The other one, Gordon, is probably just suffering from amnesia. Shock can do that, can't it?"

"It can. But we don't think Denzil Lowe committed suicide. There are indications which suggest otherwise."

"Another murder?" Lars's voice rose and broke. "Oh hell . . ."

Angie Pritchard said harshly, "Has it got anything at all to do with that kid, Kimberley Oates? Look, Alan, at least come clean!"

Markby studied her for a moment before replying. "Perhaps I could ask that of you, Angie? You went to see Meredith and made a pretty astonishing and very serious accusation."

Lars and Angie both looked at the door though which Margaret Holden had gone to find the ashtray.

"For God's sake, Alan!" Lars hissed. "Not here! Mother might hear us!"

"I know what I said to Meredith!" Angie didn't flinch before Markby's gaze. "But she—Margaret—couldn't have strung up the grave-digger. It would be physically impossible! I recognize that!"

"It would indeed."

She moved toward him, arms folded and cigarette smoldering dangerously above the carpet, threatening to dislodge ash at any moment.

"What I want to know—what Lars wants to know—is, how much more trouble are we in? No one is going to try and stick him with this as well, surely?"

"Look, Angie!" Markby's patience gave out. "No one is trying to stick Lars with anything! Personally I resent the suggestion! It's not the way we—I—work!"

She leaned forward, eyes blazing. "And I resent the way we're all being put through the hoop! Lars didn't kill that wretched girl all those years ago and he certainly didn't kill the grave-digger! So just what are you doing here, Alan?"

From the door, Margaret Holden's cool precise voice spoke. "He's come to have coffee with me, Angela. I invited him. This is, as you know, still my house." She moved forward and placed an ashtray neatly beside Miss Pritchard. "What's more, I intend it shall remain so for the rest of my life."

As he drove away slowly down the main drive a little later, Markby reflected that Tolstoy had written of unhappy families, that each was unhappy in its own way. By any standard, the Holden household rated as unhappy. It had probably always been so, even before the arrival of Angela Pritchard. If all Ned Walcott had said was true, and Markby had no reason to suppose it wasn't, the Holdens managed to thrive on tensions which would have reduced others to nervous wrecks long ago.

He turned into the main road, keeping the same leisurely pace, and drew up again before the cottages. Bullen was back in the garden. Markby got out and went to join him.

"How are you today, Nat?"

"I'm very well," said Bullen crossly. "What do you want? Come to see your chicken wire?"

"You made a good job of that, Nat." Markby indicated the fencing around the cabbage patch.

"Your ladyfriend gave me a hand. I got nothing to tell you."

"I'd still like a word." Markby glanced at the open back door. "Perhaps we could go inside?"

Bullen hesitated but finally agreed with some lack of grace that they could go into the kitchen.

Markby seated himself at the table and placed his folded hands on it. "As a matter of fact, Nat, it's not you I want to speak to."

"Oh?" Bullen fixed his rancorous gaze on him. "Major Walcott is next door if you want him."

"No, I'd rather like to talk to your houseguest." When Bullen said nothing, Markby went on, "I want to speak to Gordon Lowe. He is upstairs, isn't he?" He unfolded his hands to point up at the ceiling. "So be a good chap, Nat. Ask Gordon to come down."

As for Meredith, failure to reach Alan or to have him contact her had become more than she could stand. It was a dry day, after all, so she pulled on a light sweater and set out to walk to the vicarage. James Holland might have news of some sort.

On the way, realizing that it was almost lunchtime, she stopped at a local supermarket and bought a packet of his favorite biscuits. The chocolate digestives in hand, she carried on until she reached the corner of the wall surrounding the old churchyard.

It was very quiet around here, the older part of town, where there were few shops. The houses stood behind high stone walls. The trees of the churchyard blocked out any traffic noise from the town center. Nothing had changed around here very much in the past hundred years or so.

She found herself pushing open the gate to the old churchyard and setting off amongst the ancient graves. It was a pity this old place was full. To her mind, the new churchyard with its well-ordered rows of burial plots was a clinical place in comparison. Nowadays anyone wanting to put up a memorial to a loved one faced a host of petty regulations regarding size, shape and inscription. Fortunately it had not always been so and the old churchyard was rampant with angels, urns and classical columns. Idiosyncratic messages and scraps of mortuary verse conveyed more clearly than anything else could the taste of past generations and their almost tangible awareness of death and the afterlife. The last, Meredith thought sadly, no doubt because they believed in it so firmly. How many really did so today?

The screen had been removed from the Gresham plot and it had been refilled. The fresh earth stood up in a hummock which would gradually settle. The gravestone had been replaced upright but so much rain had softened the already disturbed soil yet further and the stone had tipped forward at a drunken angle and would need resetting. It would have been better to have left it for a while until the soil compacted. It would be a job for Gordon Lowe when he was found.

The sense of not being alone was growing stronger and stronger. She always felt it in old churchyards, but never so much as here, now. The trees rustled and the grass waved gently in response. The cosmos flowers had been beaten down by the rain and rested their magenta or white heads on the ground. Behind her came a snuffling noise such as livestock make. She turned and saw Derek Archibald standing some six feet away, watching her.

The packet of chocolate digestives slipped from her hand and landed amongst the wet grass. She said lamely, ''Hullo, Mr. Archibald.''

Nineteen

"How did you know I was there?" Gordon asked.

They were driving back toward Bamford. Gordon, in the front passenger seat, looked pale. He hadn't shaved for a couple of days and appeared not to have slept much. From time to time he rubbed his nicotine-stained fingers together nervously.

"I didn't, Gordon, until this morning. We looked for you everywhere. I just couldn't understand how we failed to find any trace of you at all. Then I learned the Walcotts had heard old Nat talking in his bedroom, not ordinary mumbling, but loud, argumentative speeches. So I thought to myself that if I were you, and I wanted to hide where no one would think to look for me, I couldn't do better than go to Nat Bullen. Everyone knew he was my lifelong rival and opponent who'd never had a good word for me or my family. No one would look there. The only thing puzzling me now is, how did you persuade Nat to take you in?"

"I went there that same evening, the evening Denny— when I found Denny in the hut. I did go home first but I was afraid. I knew I couldn't stay there. I walked over to Nat's place and tapped on the window. It was late but he opened it up and asked me what I wanted. I told him Denny was dead. I said I wanted to be left alone and for no one to bother me. I asked him if I could stay there a while."

248

Gordon's hand roamed to his pocket as if to seek out his cigarettes. But the seat belt was in the way and his hand fell back onto his lap. "He wasn't too keen at first, though he was decent enough about Denny, spoke very fair. Then I said to him, 'I'll be needing help now with the grave-digging, Nat. Very likely you'll be able to give me a hand sometimes,' and that persuaded him."

Markby gave a little chuckle. Gordon and Denny had shared a practical shrewdness which compensated for little education and no travel. The thing Bullen wanted more than anything was to have his job back and Gordon had played on this unscrupulously. He must know it was unlikely the council, which paid Gordon's wages, would agree to rein-state Bullen, a man well past retirement age, to replace Denzil Lowe.

Gordon swiveled in his seat, straining against the confin-ing belt. They were entering the outskirts of the town and the sight of the familiar buildings seemed to act on him like an electric shock. His eyes were rolling and his body shivered with tension. The scent of fear was on him.

"I'm not going back to my house, I can't go there!"

"Take it easy, Gordon!" Markby slowed. "I won't take you anywhere you don't want to go. How about the vic-arage? You'll feel safe there, won't you? Father Holland will probably let you stay there tonight. If not, I can arrange a safe place for you. You'll be protected, Gordon. But you must tell me what it is you're afraid of. I have to know it all. Otherwise, how can I protect you?"

Gordon was shaking his head. "I can't—he'll find me."

"Who is he?" Exasperated, Markby added more sharply, "You can't hide forever, Gordon! Tell us now and let's get it over with!"

"What are you doing here?" Meredith asked uneasily.

Derek's piggy little eyes gleamed. "I might ask you the same thing! I saw you walking in the town and followed you. Come poking around again, have you?"

"I only—" She looked wildly around. The churchyard was deserted. "I'm interested in the old inscriptions. It's for the article I told you about, the one I'm hoping to write—''

He interrupted her with a snort of disgust. ''I never did believe that load of nonsense! Not when you came first to my shop with your story. That lad Gary might believe it. But you don't fool me that easy! Then you went talking to my wife! So I knew. You were around my shed, back of my shop, last night, weren't you?''

She ought to deny it. It could only be a guess on his part, surely? But as if he could read her mind, Archibald shook his head and took her lost flashlight from his pocket.

Holding it up, he said, ''Found this little gadget on the floor this morning. And a hole up in the roof, as well! I see—'' He turned the flashlight and pointed a stubby finger at one area of it. ''I see someone had scratched M M on it. That'll be that woman who came a few days back, I thought. Mitchell and some other name beginning with M.''

''Oh, damn . . .'' said Meredith. She'd forgotten she'd scratched her initials on the flashlight. She couldn't even remember now why she'd done it.

What could she do now? Only keep the man talking and hope someone else would come into the churchyard.

She said, ''You ought to go to the police, Derek, and tell them everything. They'll find out eventually.''

''Why should they? They wouldn't have done, but for your prying!'' He scowled. ''Didn't find out for the last twelve years, did they?''

Anger swept over her. ''It was a despicable crime! To kill a young girl like that! Did you know she was pregnant? Was that why you did it? Were you afraid people would find out that you'd fathered her child, and all that went before it, the abuse which had gone on since she was a tot? Poor little Kimberley, how old was she when you—''

Archibald's expression had changed. From threatening it had become bewildered and now shocked. With a sinking heart, Meredith realized that she had indeed taken a wrong turning somewhere in her deductions.

She'd got it all wrong. Whatever had happened, it had not been like that at all.

Dimly, as if at the end of a long tunnel, she began to

perceive an outline of the truth. She cursed herself for her clumsy interpretation of the facts. It was never that simple. She ought to know that by now!

Derek had found his voice. "I didn't kill her! What, kill my girl? Kill my own child? My pretty little daughter. Kill my Kimberley?"

Meredith said dully, "It wasn't Kimberley you abused. It was Susan. Susan Oates, her mother. It was Susan whose baby you fathered, and that baby was Kimberley, your daughter!"

Archibald took a step toward her, his face perspiring and twisted in an expression of urgency. "There's been an Archibald the butcher in this town for a hundred years! But my wife and I had no kids! A hundred years that business in my family and no one left to take it over! When I die, that shop will be sold on to just anyone. They'll probably turn it into something else, selling greetings cards or television sets or any kind of modern trash! She told me, Susan did, that the baby she was carrying was mine. I know she had other men friends, but she swore the baby was mine. A mother always knows, don't she? Even if she's been with other men, she knows who the father is?"

It was no time to destroy Derek's belief in this piece of folklore. He'd believed it since Susan first told him of her pregnancy. The knowledge that he had a child, even out of wedlock, had been his solace for years.

Susan had probably hoped to get some money out of him. It might even have been true and Kimberley was his child. At any rate, he'd believed it. So when Susan had run off to Wales, leaving her child behind, she had left Kimberley not only with her grandmother, but next door to her natural father. If Joan Oates had not been able to manage, then Susan trusted that Derek Archibald would have stepped in and made some arrangement. But respectable little Mrs. Tempest had been careful not to tell Markby that. To explain to her children in Wales that the father of her first child was still alive and that he was nowadays an unattractive elderly butcher was not her intention. Moreover, Derek might have arrived on the doorstep in Wales, seeking explanations.

Derek was talking again. "She was a lovely little thing, my Kimberley. I used to take her out, buy her ice creams and the like. Of course, I couldn't say outright she was mine, let anyone know. But I could still make a fuss of her. Joan Oates didn't buy her much in the way of toys and little bits and pieces like that, so I was able to do it. That shed of mine, behind the shop, I used to take her there and she played house in it. It was our little house, hers and mine, our little home together."

"I see," Meredith said, knowing how inadequate it must sound and was.

His broad face reddened. "No, you don't! How could you? She was my little girl! It didn't matter—nothing else mattered! I had her. She was my pride and joy. That's not just idle talk. It's true! She was everything to me!"

He shook his round head and his piggy features crumpled in distress. "As she grew up, Kim changed. Joan Oates didn't keep a close enough eye on her and I couldn't do anything! Those Holdens, they got hold of her! Rich folk. She went to their big house with that catering firm and she met them there. They turned her head! I could see she was carrying a kid. I told her not to worry about it, I'd look after her. But she went to those Holdens. Mr. Richard Holden, the old man, not this young smart-alec politician feller, he paid her. Or he gave the money to that little toady of his, that Major Walcott! Gave him the money to give Kim. Kim came to me and told me she was going away. She had enough money. I couldn't bear the idea. Kim leave me! Take my grandchild away with her? I told her to come to the shed that afternoon, and we'd talk it over. It was a Wednesday, half-closing. No one else would be there."

Derek waved a stubby hand in a gesture of despair. "I would've got some money together. I would've looked after her! I told her that in the shed that afternoon. I told her I'd take care of her and her baby. It would be my grandchild, after all! I said I'd change my will and leave the shop to her and her child. It would be worth a bit, a property like that in the High Street. She could get someone to run it for her. I promised her everything I had, if only she'd think again, if she'd stay. She wouldn't regret it.

"She said she would, or she'd think it over, which came to the same thing. She'd have been bound to see what a good thing it would be for her and her kiddie."

There were tears oozing from the small eyes. The effect should have been pathetic but it was only grotesque and Meredith couldn't quash a feeling of revulsion for the man.

"I left first, not wanting anyone to see us leaving together. I left her behind, in the shed. I never saw her again, alive. When I got back home, my cottage was empty. My wife wasn't so poorly then as now, but still she didn't go out much and I got a sick feeling in my stomach, just knowing something was wrong.

"My wife came in about half an hour or a little more later. She looked strange. She was holding something under her coat. She came out into the kitchen and took it out. It was a knife from the shop. There was blood on it."

Derek's voice sank and was almost inaudible as he recalled the horror of that moment. "I asked her what she'd done. She told me, she'd always known. She'd guessed long since Kimberley was mine. She'd seen Kim leave her house earlier and shortly afterwards I went out, so she guessed something was going on. She'd followed me to the shed and listened outside. She'd heard me beg Kim to stay and tell her I'd change my will. She heard me talking of my grandchild. So she hid and after I left, she went into the shed—and she killed my Kimberley. Stuck her like an animal with a butcher's knife. My little girl . . ."

Tears leaped out of his eyes and trickled down his flat red cheeks. He shook his round head from side to side like a wounded beast. "I ran back to the shed like a crazy man, hoping I'd be in time and save her! I was too late. She lay there, all huddled up with blood all over her. Her arms were all cut about and the back of her dress. It was as if she curled up trying to protect the baby in her womb. Her eyes were open and I thought maybe she was still alive, but she was dead. I called her name and tried to sit her up and wipe off the blood, but it was no good . . . She was dead! Lying dead, murdered, in her little playhouse she'd had as a kiddie! And my wife had done it!"

"I'm sorry . . ." Meredith whispered.

He moved forward a step, shaking his head. "I couldn't let anyone know. So I went back home and got a length of material my wife had bought to make up some curtains. I took it back and wrapped it around my little girl. I knew I had to hide her where no one could find her. The flies was already buzzing around her when I got back to the shed again. You always get the flies around a butcher's. They smell the blood. They could smell hers, even though I'd wiped it off. It was soaked in her dress. I covered her up to keep the flies off her."

Archibald was fumbling inside the breast of his coat. "You're not telling anyone what I told you. You've got to die too. There's no help for it. You oughtn't to have come prying . . ."

From beneath the coat appeared a meat cleaver. The light reflected off the honed steel as he began to move purposefully toward her.

Meredith turned and plunged across the damp earth toward the gate, the road and safety. But he was quicker. She wouldn't have expected he could move so fast. He was just behind her and his breath brushed the nape of her neck. She twisted aside as he lunged out with the cleaver. He missed and swore in frustration.

She wanted to reach the gate but he was so close now he was able to grip her coat. Meredith wrenched herself loose. He struck out again and this time the blade connected with a nearby headstone, sending out a teeth-jangling scrape of metal on stone.

Meredith ducked and doubled back. She plunged along a muddy path beaten between the graves by the police and sightseers until she came back to the Gresham grave. It lay before her, barring the way with its hump of fresh earth.

She leapt wildly over it. But on the far side the muddy ground was slippery and as she landed her foot shot from beneath her.

With a yelp of surprise and dismay, Meredith sprawled full length across the grave. As she scrabbled to regain her feet, the shadow of Derek Archibald fell over her. She looked up in horror to see his arm upraised and the steel blade glittering in a shaft of sunlight.

As the arm descended inexorably toward her, she grabbed it and tried to hold it off. But he was so much stronger. His red sweating face was fixed in a manic snarl. The razor-sharp edge of the cleaver came nearer and nearer. An image flashed through her terrified brain, of Derek in his shop, bringing just such a cleaver down on a hunk of meat and separating bone, gristle, tendons and flesh in one easy blow. If the weapon, wielded by his practiced hand, connected with her, in one blow he'd half decapitate her.

And then, suddenly, something curious began to happen, something which she couldn't at first comprehend.

She was sinking. The more she tried to push Derek away, the more impossible it became because they were both sinking. She saw surprise replace the fury on his face. Then they both realized what was happening.

The soft new earth filling the plot was giving way beneath their combined weight and she and Derek Archibald together were sinking down into the Gresham grave.

Derek realized his danger. He began to try and regain his balance but he was heavy and his feet could gain no purchase. He dropped the cleaver, flailed the air for a moment, then made a grab for the headstone. But the headstone itself was on the move. It crashed forward, striking him on the side of the head.

He collapsed on top of her, the gravestone on top of him. Meredith was trapped, down in the trench, only able to see a glimmer of light beyond the unconscious Derek.

Silence fell in which she was aware only of her own tortured breath. The earth had molded itself to the shape of her body and helped prevent Derek's weight crushing the life out of her. It was as if she lay on a soft mattress. In addition, his bulk was greater than the width of the trench and he'd become wedged. The unturned earth to either side supported him and released a little of the pressure on her chest. It left her with a life-saving space for air. But for how much longer?

Soil and stones trickled down by her ear. The rain-sodden sides were crumbling under the burden. Beneath her the bottom of the grave compacted a little more and she sank another inch. Something cold and clammy was wriggling by her ear. Her searching fingers dug into mud and who knew what nameless mess. "Don't panic!" she told herself.

But a moment's effort told her it was hopeless. She might have been able to claw herself out from beneath Derek. But not from beneath the combined weight and bulk of the inert body of the man and the slab of marble above him, which entombed them both. They were buried here together.

Gordon sat nursing a glass of Father Holland's medicinal brandy. A cigarette smoldered in his fingers. With a hangdog look he said, "Sorry, Vicar, for all the trouble!"

"We were only worried about you, Gordon!" the vicar told him. "Why didn't you come back here to the vicarage?"

"I thought he'd come here looking for me."

"Who, Gordon?"

Gordon's eyes rolled. "Him," he whispered hoarsely.

Father Holland opened his mouth but Markby forestalled him. "Start at the beginning, Gordon. Tell us everything. Take your time but don't leave out anything, all right?"

"Okay," Gordon mumbled. He wiped the back of his hand over his mouth and made a visible effort to pull himself together.

"A job like grave-digging upsets some people. They don't like to think about it. We used to make them nervous. They'd keep out of our way. It didn't worry either Denny or me. We used to go out for a drink of an evening. Regular. If no one ever spoke much to us, we didn't mind that. We'd just sit there and drink our pints. We bothered no one and no one bothered us."

Father Holland already looked restive and Markby threw him a warning glance. A person like Gordon had to be left to tell his tale in his own way.

"After a while, other drinkers got used to us." Gordon raised his eyes and looked anxiously at them both. "They took no notice. It was as if we weren't there, Denny and me. People would talk together in front of us just as if we were a couple of bits of furniture. We'd hear them whisper things. We heard all kinds of gossip. We just sat quiet. It was interesting sometimes," Gordon added naïvely.

Interesting and ultimately deadly! Markby thought.

"That's how we heard about Derek Archibald, the butcher, you know him?"

"Go on, Gordon..." Oh hell, Markby thought, I should've made more of an effort to talk to Archibald!

"We heard about his little habits. People half whispering things and then sniggering to each other. He used to buy them magazines with the naked women in them. He used to go up to London, telling his wife he was going to Smithfield, the big meat market, but he'd go sloping off to Soho and such places. Where they have the fancy tarts and those shows where the girls take off their clothes. You know."

"We know," said the vicar and Markby in unison and Father Holland added quickly, "So I believe!"

"They reckoned he'd interfered with those young girls lived next door to him. First the mother, then the daughter. The older one, Susan she was called, she dropped a little'un and then she ran off and no one ever saw her no more. Derek used to take the little kid about with him, always buying her sweets and toys and such."

Gordon drew on the cigarette and cleared his throat apologetically. "So when we heard, Denny and me, that the bones we dug up belonged to young Kimberley, we reckoned Archibald knew how they got there!"

"He was on the church council at the time!" Father Holland moaned to himself.

"So what did you do, Gordon?" Markby prompted gently.

Gordon's embarrassment increased. "See, Denny and me, we like a joint of meat at the weekend. I can make it last most of the week, minced up and so on. But it's got really expensive, has meat."

Father Holland murmured again, this time, "Oh, no ..."

"So Denny went along to see Derek Archibald and told him what we reckoned. He said Derek wasn't to worry we'd go to the police." Gordon gave Markby a furtive glance. "Sorry, Mr. Markby. But anyway, Denny said, all we wanted was a nice leg of lamb or pork on a Saturday for the Sunday lunch. Derek was a butcher. It wasn't much to ask. He could give it to us easy and never miss it.''

Markby and the vicar exchanged glances. Each knew the other was thinking the same thing. It was asking a great deal too much.

Denny should have asked Archibald for money. Not for meat. Archibald's the Butchers hadn't survived as a family firm for a hundred years in the town by giving away free meat.

''A nice bit of Welsh lamb he promised us,'' Gordon mumbled. ''If Denny would meet him at our hut.'' He sank his head in his hands. ''All right, Gordon,'' Markby said. ''Now, I'll take you down to the local station and you can make a statement there. Tell it all again, just the same way, and sign it, you understand? After that, we'll put you in a hotel room until we can find Archibald.''

Gordon crushed out the cigarette and put down his empty glass. He looked relieved at having got the story off his chest. But something was still worrying him.

''There's something I'd be really obliged if we could do first, Mr. Markby. If the vicar would agree too. I know after all the trouble I caused, I don't have the right to ask . . .''

''Anything, Gordon!'' Father Holland said promptly.

''It's the hut—our hut in the churchyard where we keep our tools. I know I've got to go back into it sooner or later. But when I do, I'll be imagining Denny hanging there. I'm not looking forward to that. Perhaps, on our way to your office, Mr. Markby, we could just stop by the churchyard and I'll look into the hut—with you and the vicar standing by. I'll manage it with you backing me up, as it were. Then it won't be so bad the first time I have to go in there on my own.''

The three of them tramped over the damp grass toward the groundsman's hut in the old churchyard. Father Holland encouraged Gordon as they went along. Markby was silent, his mind on what to do next.

They reached it and opened the door. Gordon peered in uncertainly and then walked inside. They waited. He came out and closed the door.

''It's all right, Mr. Markby.'' He wiped pearls of sweat

from his forehead. "I'll be all right now. I'll come along with you."

"Are you sure, Gordon?" Father Holland asked anxiously.

"Yes—I—what's that?"

There was a silence. Gordon whispered, "I thought I heard a voice. Here, Vicar, could it be Denny, calling to me from the hereafter?"

"If it is," said Markby, "I can hear him too!"

Faintly a voice was crying out in some distress. "It's over there!" the vicar exclaimed.

They hurried toward the sound. "It's coming from the Gresham grave!" Markby exclaimed.

"The stone's fallen in . . ." the vicar panted, holding up the skirts of his cassock and scrambling over intervening hummocks and marble curb stones.

From beneath the flattened gravestone the weak voice cried, "Help! Help me!"

Gordon gave a high-pitched scream. "It's the girl! The one we dug up! Don't touch that stone, Mr. Markby! She'll rise up! It's her spirit crying out to us from the grave!"

"No, it's not!" Markby shouted, leaping forward. "It's Meredith!"

Twenty

Bullen was hoeing his cabbage patch when Markby returned to the cottage. He looked up and greeted the superintendent with, "You got Gordon. Now what do you want?"

"You're a miserable old blighter, Nat. Is that any way to greet a visitor?"

"Pah!" Bullen looked not displeased at the unflattering description. He rested on the hoe. "If you've come to see your bit of fencing, that's all right. Otherwise, you've got better things to do than bother with me. Or are you going up to the house drinking sherry with Mrs. Holden?" He managed to make this sound the last word in dissolute living.

"I've come to see you." Markby contemplated the cabbages. "Rabbit giving any more trouble?"

"No, he can't get in. I still mean to get him one day. I'll put him in a stew with onions and a couple of carrots, the way my old mother did. Rabbit was always a poor man's meat."

"No caterpillars or slugs, then?" The cabbages all looked exceptionally healthy, like a row of fat dark green roses.

"I wash them off with soapy water, what I wash my dishes in. That gets rid of the caterpillars and the little pests. If you want to get rid of the slugs, put down a saucer of

beer. They like a drop of ale, do slugs. They get tiddly an'
lie about drunk and you can pick them up in the morning.'

Somehow they had progressed during this conversation
to the back door and seated themselves on Bullen's wooden
bench. Bullen placed the hoe carefully against the wall. The
sun was trapped here and it was warm and relaxing. Time-
less, too. Country people had sat at their cottage doors like
this since man first built himself a thatched hut. The scene
before them, Markby thought, hadn't changed so very much
either. Give or take a piece of chicken-wire fencing.

Other remnants of former times also lingered, including
a kind of feudal loyalty of which Bullen was probably one
of the last representatives.

In a conversational tone, Markby said, "Lars Holden
didn't kill the girl, Nat."

Bullen didn't reply and remained staring ahead at his
garden.

"I said, Lars didn't kill her. It's no trick. He really
didn't, believe me. We know who did."

Bullen turned to look at him. "What's that you say?"

"None of the Holdens had anything to do with it."

Bullen thought about this. "Who done it then?"

"Mrs. Archibald has been charged, Derek's wife. Family
reasons led her to do it."

Bullen muttered under his breath. "I never did trust that
Derek Archibald! I counted on him to stop them giving me
the sack! He was on the church council, he could have
made sure I kept my job! But he never did!"

"Tell me about it, Nat."

"Oh well," said Bullen, "You might as well know then.
I only did it, mind you, because I thought it was young
Lars! I wouldn't have done it just for Derek Archibald!"
He paused. "Reckon us could do with a drop of some-
thing."

A little later Markby sipped at a generous measure of
whiskey and observed, "This is a very fine malt, Nat!"

"Mrs. Holden gave it to me, last Christmas," Bullen told
him. "A very kind lady and always very generous to me.
I owed her and I pay my debts. That's why I wanted to
help when I thought the boy was in trouble. I knew the lad

...s fooling about with that girl because I caught them a ...uple of times in the bushes at the back of the churchyard. ...didn't say anything. Human nature being what it is, young folk have always done it and always will. I did, when I was young,'' added Bullen and paused to dwell on memories of a misspent youth.

"Archibald?'' Markby prompted.

"Oh, him! Well, he came out here to my cottage one evening, very upset as I could see. He tapped on my kitchen window there.'' Bullen pointed at the window behind them. "Sweating up a lather like a spooked horse. 'Nat!' he says. 'Something dreadful has happened. I've found that girl dead in the churchyard, the one young Lars has been messing around with! I reckon he's killed her!' ''

Bullen shook his head. "It frightened me. I thought what it would do to Mr. and Mrs. Holden, who'd always been so good to me and were decent folk. I asked Derek what he'd done about it already. He said, nothing much, he'd just moved her into my hut so that no one should see her. He said he thought it'd be a pity to ruin the lad's whole life and break his poor mother's heart. It wouldn't bring the girl back again. Besides, Mrs. Holden bought all her meat from his shop and was a good customer, nothing but the best and no quibbling over the price. So he thought we could bury her. Only he needed my help. He couldn't do it alone and anyway I'd see if anyone had been disturbing the earth, so I had to be in on it.''

"I follow that. So you went back to the churchyard with Derek?''

"That's it. The trouble was that people were still about, it being summer. So I said to him that we'd have to wait until dark. Then I took a look at her and she was stiffened already. She was all crooked like he'd put her down, knees stuck up in the air and one arm dropped down by her side. I couldn't straighten them, not unless I'd given them a clout with my shovel and broken them, and Derek nearly threw a fit when I suggested that. Desecrating the body, he reckoned. He wouldn't have it and I can tell you now, straight, I wasn't keen. But she was only a youngster and the stiffness doesn't come on so bad and passes off quicker in the young. You'll know that, being a policeman. So I told him that it would be best to wait till morning, early. Overnight the stiffness might pass off a bit and we could handle her better. So Derek and I agreed to meet at first light.''

Here Bullen fell silent. Markby asked, ''You realized, then, she'd been dead a few hours? Since rigor was so far advanced.''

''Oh yes, I realized that from the stiffness. She must have been dead five or six hours by my reckoning. I did think it was strange I'd not found her myself, earlier, when I was working in the churchyard, if she'd been lying there as long as that. But I thought I could be wrong. I'm no doctor and, anyway, I'd no reason to doubt Derek's word. Though it seems now as if he spun me a pretty yarn or two!''

Bullen paused. ''She was a mess, all cut about. That did give me a shock. The lad must have gone real crazy was what I thought. Her clothes were in shreds and down her arms were great long wounds. Her face was no pretty sight, either, by then. Her jaw had dropped and we couldn't even close her mouth. Her eyes were open wide, staring up at us, and bulging a bit. Derek had wrapped a piece of cloth around her and over her face. He couldn't bear to look at her. He was shaking like a leaf.''

''Muscular spasm,'' Markby murmured. What a dreadful sight for the wretched butcher to see. His pretty child turned to a travesty of herself.

''The next day, at dawn, I was back and so was Derek,'' Bullen continued. ''I suggested to him we put her in the Gresham plot because I'd promised Eunice Gresham, only a day or so before, I'd put fresh earth on it to correct the sinking. So we dug down, and dug up Marie Gresham's arm by mistake which upset Derek, though him being a butcher I'd have thought he was used to bones! Anyhow, we shoved that back down again and we put the girl in on top. She was still a bit awkward to handle but we'd been able to straighten out her arms and legs. Derek was looking pretty green by then. I told him I could finish it alone and he could go home and have his breakfast, though I don't know whether he ate any!'' Bullen gave an unexpected cackle.

"So, he went running off. I fetched a few barrowloads of soil from elsewhere in the churchyard and covered her over, building it up nicely just as I'd do a regular burial. When that settled, no one would be any the wiser. And if anyone wanted to know why there was fresh soil there, why, I was only doing as Eunice Gresham asked me. Then I hurried out of the churchyard—but bless me!"

Bullen's face reddened in rage. "I ran straight into that interfering woman, that Mrs. Etheridge! What was she doing about at that hour of the morning, I ask you? She was always a nuisance and complaining about me. She was one of them wanted to be rid of me. She started on shouting out to me, accusing me of being drunk at that time of day! I'd had enough trouble for one morning already. I gave her back an earful of strong language and she jumped on her bike and went pedalling off for dear life!" Bullen's shrill cackle split the air again.

Then he sobered. "But it worried me, Mr. Markby. I knew it was against the law to bury her like that, with no one knowing. Worse, she'd had no proper burial service read over her and every human being is entitled to that! So a couple of days later, I sneaked into the church in the evening, and I—"

Bullen looked embarrassed. "It sounds daft, but I wanted to do right by her. I made up a little candle and flowers sort of arrangement on the altar and I said a prayer for her. But right in the middle of it all, would you believe it? That woman Etheridge came into the church! Seems like she was following me around and I couldn't get rid of her! She didn't see me. I dodged behind a pillar. She saw the burning candle though. She started clucking to herself like an old hen and went hurrying out. So did I. I thought she'd come back with the vicar. I didn't go back."

Bullen stretched his aged back. "So that's it then. You going to arrest me?"

"No, Nat. I know where to find you. You'll have to come and tell it all again for a statement. There may be a bit of fuss but I doubt you'll be hauled off to jail!"

"In that case," said Bullen, "we've time for another nip of whiskey, I suppose?"

*   *   *

"The problem really is that we're obsessed by sex. It distorts our view of things."

"Do you mean us, you and me, personally?" Alan Markby let the question trail away as he cast a thoughtful eye on the level of the wine in the bottle on the table.

"No! I mean all of us! Look, Kimberley was young, pretty and pregnant when she died. So we all thought aha! A sex-related crime!"

"It seemed a reasonable assumption."

The dessert trolley was being wheeled their way. It was always a moment of truth. Markby tried not to look at its contents. Meredith hadn't seen it yet. She was still expostulating on sex and its way of misleading us all. Too true, he thought with a sigh.

"It was the wrong assumption!" Meredith announced. "Mrs. Archibald had guessed years earlier that Kimberley was probably Derek's child and she'd learned to live with it. What pushed her over the edge into killing was overhearing Derek promise to alter his will and leave the family butchery business to Kim. Not sexual jealousy but covetousness motivated her. Old-fashioned greed."

"These are deep waters, Watson!" Markby picked up his glass and noted with a grimace that a round red stain had appeared on the crisp damask cloth. He consoled himself that The Old Coaching Inn no doubt employed a competent laundry service and had dealt with worse.

The trolley had arrived. There was a moment's guilty havering and then surrender. Meredith had the chocolate mousse ("it's only light!") and Markby the apricot crumble ("with the custard, please, not the cream!")

"We are both going to have to go on a diet," Meredith said. "One person on a diet while the other is eating everything within sight doesn't work."

"I'm not overweight!" he said smugly.

"You think I am?" Panic-stations opposite.

"No! You started talking about diets! I think you're fine just as you are!" Hastily he got back to talking about crime. It was safer.

"It's all a little more complex than you describe. Not

greed, no. Reputation. Mrs. Archibald is obsessed with a highly idiosyncratic view of what's respectable. It was something that struck me when I visited her. I believe it was the fact that altering the will in Kimberley's favor would involve public recognition that she was Derek's daughter that made Mrs. A. pick up that knife. Derek would have made some kind of statement to his lawyers about the relationship. Just in order to protect Kimberley in the event of someone else contesting the will. It was the family scandal becoming public knowledge that Mrs. Archibald couldn't take. She's still in hospital, by the way.''

''You told me she collapsed when you arrived to interview her. How's she doing?''

''Not well. She's a sick woman. Doctors don't give her more than a year if that. It's highly unlikely she'll ever stand trial.''

''What about Derek? And Bullen?''

''Bullen is very old. We've finally managed to establish he's eighty-six. There's no question of his replacing Denny as Gordon's partner in the grave-digging business. Bullen's livid. He sees himself as betrayed yet again. Gordon promised him! He says he's sorry he took Gordon in. He should have left him to his fate! As far as breaking the law goes, it's not up to me. But after so long and in the circumstances, his age and all the rest of it, I can't see proceedings being taken against the old boy.''

''What about Derek?''

''Aside from his activities twelve years ago to conceal a crime committed by his wife, he confesses to murdering Denzil Lowe. It seems he invited Denny to meet him at the hut where he would hand over the first of the joints of meat the Lowes anticipated receiving in perpetuity. He got there first, lay in wait, knocked Denny cold and strung him up. His intent was to silence Denny forever and frighten the wits out of Gordon. He would probably have gone after Gordon later. Gordon realized it and went into hiding.''

''Derek attacked me, too!'' Meredith pointed out, offended.

''I hadn't forgotten he tried to kill you, too! But Derek is also in hospital recovering from injuries received when that gravestone toppled on his head. We have to talk to him. for just a few minutes at a time and piece it all together slowly. We'll get to you!''

Meredith shuddered. ''It was the most frightening episode of my entire life, and I've had a few scary moments since I met you!''

''Thanks a million! May I point out that you get yourself into these scrapes? You were chased around the churchyard by Derek with a meat-axe because you broke into his shed, questioned his wife, and generally made it obvious you were investigating him!''

''Scrapes? Being buried alive with Derek Archibald is a scrape?''

''Learn by a very nasty experience, will you?'' Markby begged. ''Think of me! I nearly had a heart attack when I heard your voice issuing from the grave! So did poor Gordon and James Holland!''

Meredith still mumbled, ''How do you think I felt?'' but more quietly. Then she said, ''It's sad that Derek won't be fit enough to attend his daughter's funeral. He would have wanted that.''

''Let's order coffee. Derek's problems aren't yours. Besides, I have been keeping back a little surprise until this moment.'' Markby produced a glossy brochure by some sleight of hand and placed it before her.

Meredith leaned across to investigate. ''Alan? A cruise in the Greek islands? I thought you wanted a narrowboat holiday on the canal?''

''After all we've been through on this, I think a little luxury is called for!'' He grinned. ''We both deserve it!''

The pathetic remains of Kimberley Oates and her unborn child were cremated in a brief ceremony presided over by Father Holland at the crematorium.

Few people attended the service but there were several tributes of flowers. The Holdens and Angie had sent a dignified selection of carnations. Bullen had made his way to a florist, if not to the crematorium, and sent roses. Various other posies had arrived from people in the town as if Kimerley's story had somehow touched a communal sense of guilt.

They were all dominated by a magnificent display organized by Derek from his hospital bed and which carried a card reading, "Remembering a beloved daughter and grandchild."

Meredith, sharing a pew with Alan, Bryce and Prescott, found the service depressing. But distraction came by way of a couple seated at the very front. The young man, although she could only see his rear view, seemed familiar. There was a young woman with him whom she couldn't identify at all.

The young man, when he turned to leave at the end of the ceremony, was revealed to be Glyn Tempest in an ill-fitting suit and black leather tie. Meredith was surprised and wondered if Susan knew he had come today.

Outside the chapel, she and Alan found themselves beside the Tempests. Glyn greeted them awkwardly and introduced the girl, a beetle-browed young woman, as his sister, Julie.

"Glad you could make it," Markby said, holding out his hand.

Tempest gripped it in a brief, sweaty clasp. "Thanks for all your hard work on this, Mr. Markby. I'm glad you got the killer in the end."

"Mum wasn't up to coming," Julie said with a touch of defiance. "But she was pleased to know that—that Kimberley was being buried properly."

Susan was lucky, Meredith thought. Her surviving children's loyalty to her was both touching and unquestioned.

"Quite so," Markby said noncommittedly.

Julie seemed impelled to explain the presence of herself and her brother. "We felt, Glyn and I, that we ought to come. She was our sister, well, half-sister. It's funny . . ." She paused. "It might have been nice to have known her."

"There are photographs of her on file," Markby offered. "If you'd like copies—"

They interrupted him in startled and appalled unison. "Oh, no!"

Julie Tempest added, "I don't think we want to go as far as that, Mr. Markby! Not now. I mean, it's all too late and—" She struggled for another reason and finished with a simple, "It'd be better not."

Twenty-one

Alan Markby disliked closing a file with unfinished questions still hanging over it. One in particular still bothered him about Kimberley's case. But he had resigned himself to never knowing the answer. It wasn't, perhaps, such an important point, but it niggled.

And then, it was answered. Answered, as things often were, quite unexpectedly and in a way no one had foreseen.

They sat before him, side by side, one wet morning. They were young and very serious. He recognized the girl, her attractive features still somewhat marred by steel-rimmed spectacles and a stern expression. The young man with her was starting to run to excess weight and had a pompous manner. Their name was Das.

"We've met, Mrs. Das," Markby said. "I called at your cottage one morning, looking for Mrs. Oates. Do you remember?"

"Yes, that's why we're here!" she said fiercely. "We knew you were interested in our house."

Mr. Das said, "It is a question of the house extension, you see. We're converting the attic to a study. Of course, it's an old building and listed. But we managed to get planning permission as it's not a question of removing the old beams. Merely of clearing out the space, doing essential repairs to the roof and putting in a floor and power points."

"Quite," said Markby, wondering where all this was

leading. Did they think they had to get his permission?

Mrs. Das chipped in. "We're law students, Superinten-dent."

"Very nice," said Markby. Were they, then, about to bombard him with questions relating to police procedure?

"So we do have some understanding of the law in this matter," said Mr. Das. "But we have come here because we realize that you have been conducting inquiries about the family which once lived in our cottage. We thought, therefore, you should know."

"Know what?" Markby's patience was beginning to wear thin.

"While we were clearing out the attic space, I climbed up into the rafters and I found a tin box."

"Ah!" Markby said. "Old papers? Always very inter-esting. Not a will, was it?"

"No. It contained money." Das put his hand into his pocket and removed a wad of soiled damp-spotted notes. Even at a distance the smell of mildew announced itself.

"It had been there some years. Some of the notes are of outdated design but I understand a bank will still change them. They are not that old. It's not a question of something historical! Perhaps ten to fifteen years old? As for the ques-tion of ownership, the box with the money was certainly in the house at the time we bought it and moved in. No one has come back to claim it. To make sure, we phoned Mrs. Hamilton, from whom we purchased the house, and asked— in a discreet manner, you understand. We didn't mention money. We asked whether, as we were clearing the attic, any of the items we found up there might be of interest to her. She said no. She had never used the attic. Any items there must be from the occupant before her, a Mrs. Oates. Mrs. Oates is dead, I believe."

So that was what poor Kimberley had done with the cash. Naturally enough, she'd hidden it from her grandmother. She'd clambered up into the attic where Joan Oates wouldn't have ventured and tucked it up into the beams to be retrieved later. But she hadn't been able to retrieve it. His question was answered. He imagined Kimberley, scrambling up into the rafters with her tin box of precious money.

The wind rattled the window which was ajar. A gust of cold air ruffled the stack of notes which Das had placed on the desk.

Kimberley's spirit reaching out impotently for the money which was to have bought her a new life, far from Bamford? Or was that only his fancy? Fancy, Markby thought. But knew he wasn't sure.

"So I understand that, in the circumstances, we have clear title to this money. Nevertheless, Superintendent, we have brought it to you. We know you were interested in the cottage and Mrs. Oates. Also because it is quite a sum. Four hundred and ninety-five pounds."

"Five pounds!" Markby murmured. "Kimberley spent five pounds. I wonder on what?"

"I beg your pardon?" Das leaned forward.

"Nothing," Markby told him.

Again the breeze—or something—ruffled the money. At the same time, a little voice in his head seemed to say, "I owed Simon French a fiver!"

"So you did," Markby muttered. Kimberley had promised to repay Simon. She'd taken five pounds from the box before hiding it and had probably had it on her when she died.

"So, Superintendent?" Das said impatiently. He clearly thought the superintendent was a little odd. "I am correct, am I not? The money is ours?"

Major Walcott might have some objection but even if he had, he couldn't uphold it in law. He'd given the money freely to Kimberley, after discussing it with his wife and getting her agreement. Kimberley hadn't asked the Walcotts for it. In any case, whilst all probability suggested it was the same money given by Walcott to the girl, it couldn't now be proved. Not unless Walcott had kept a record of the numbers of the banknotes and it was unlikely he'd done that.

"Mr. and Mrs. Das," Markby said. "Thank you for coming in. You acted quite properly."

They both looked pleased and slightly less pompous. It

was nerves, he realized, that had given them that stiff manner.

"As for the money, I suggest you consult a qualified solicitor. You have some knowledge of the law yourselves, I appreciate that. But it's better to be clear on such a point. Personally, I would imagine you're right regarding your title to the money. It was in the house when you bought the property. Mrs. Hamilton appears to know nothing of it. There is no evidence to suggest it represents the proceeds of a theft or other crime."

They were nodding furiously in unison. "This is what we reasoned, Superintendent," Mrs. Das said.

Moral law might argue differently, but he wasn't concerned with that.

"See a solicitor," Markby said. "It's not a police matter."

But he made a note in the file after they'd left.

Margaret Holden was touring the rambling rooms of The Old Farm, one by one, Oscar trotting at her heels.

As she opened cupboards and made notes in her little pocket notebook, she, too, spoke aloud. But whereas Markby was reduced to talking to himself, Margaret, in company with other dog-owners, had a four-legged listener on hand to receive confidences.

"I'm making an inventory, Oscar, of sorts."

Oscar looked up, ears pricked politely, but clearly bored.

"Because, you know, I think that you and I will be moving house shortly. Yes. I don't want to go, of course, and I don't suppose you do, eh?"

Oscar realized he was being asked a question and contrived to look madly intelligent whilst not having a clue as to the answer. It was a trick perfected by many humans.

"But Lars wants to bring Angie here. He is entitled to do that, I suppose."

Oscar had recognized Lars's name and wagged his tail.

"I told her I wouldn't move out! You should have seen her face, Oscar!" Margaret smiled at the dog and catching the amusement in her voice, he wagged his tail again and gave a little yelp, by way of encouragement. The mood in the house had been somber of late and Oscar had sensed it. He hoped things were going to improve.

"She's such an annoying young woman! But then, if she is what Lars wants, he's a grown man, after all and I suppose I must accept it. Let him dig his own grave—"

She broke off. "I shouldn't have said that. Luckily, I'm not superstitious! But I have to confess, Oscar, that this house is full of ghosts for me now. I shall go, after all. Perhaps to the seaside? You would like the seaside, Oscar. We could walk along the cliffs. I shan't stay here, not close to Lars and his wife, watching her play hostess in my house! Pah!"

She snapped the little notebook shut and made her way out into the corridor. Oscar trotted ahead, hoping that they had finished this tiresome slow walk around the house and were going downstairs, preferably to the kitchen. The word seaside with its sibilants had worried him slightly. It sounded ominous.

But they went to Margaret's bedroom. She sat down in the Lloyd Loom chair by her bedside table and Oscar sat down at her feet, waiting, but with a restless look about him.

"I've lived in this house nearly thirty years, Oscar. It will be hard to move out. I shall have to throw so much away. There won't be much room if I buy a small flat. Personal items will have to go. Not furniture, of course. I shall leave all that for Lars. It belongs in the house. Perhaps I'll take a picture or two. That seascape from the dining room. The one Richard bought. I might take that."

Mention of her late husband turned her memory into another channel. She reached out and picked up the silver-framed photograph on the bedside table and studied it.

"Oh, Richard," she said softly. "If your ghost is listening, then I was sorry to do it to you. But you were in pain, after all. And it was so easy. Just a few pills in a hot drink. But still, I wouldn't have done it, my dear. I wouldn't have done it if you hadn't betrayed me with that girl. Betrayed both Lars and me! How could you? With that girl of all girls? I couldn't forgive that, Richard. And I daren't allow

Lars to find out. So I had to kill you, my dear. I'm sorry. So sorry. But you left me no choice.''

She set down the photograph and got heavily to her feet. ''Come on Oscar, tea-time!''

Oscar knew about tea-time. It meant biscuits. He bounced ahead to the door and set off toward the head of the stairs, his stubby legs moving back and forth at a fast clip.

Over the years he'd been the recipient of many secret thoughts expressed only to him by his mistress. Some of them, such as the one just told him, had been a little startling. But, had Oscar been able to speak, he no doubt would have agreed with the human maxim that it was better to let sleeping dogs lie.

ANN GRANGER

The Meredith and Markby Mysteries

"The author has a good feel for understated humor, a nice ear for dialogue, and a quietly introspective heroine."

London Times Saturday Review

COLD IN THE EARTH	72213-5/$5.50 US
A FINE PLACE FOR DEATH	72573-8/$5.50 US
MURDER AMONG US	72476-6/$5.50 US
SAY IT WITH POISON	71823-5/$5.50 US
A SEASON FOR MURDER	71997-5/$5.50US
WHERE OLD BONES LIE	72477-4/$4.99 US
FLOWERS FOR HIS FUNERAL	72887-7/$5.50 US
CANDLE FOR A CORPSE	73012-X/$5.50 US